Howard Spring was born in Cardiff, where he began his literary career as a newspaper errand boy. He became a reporter on the *Manchester Guardian* and developed a love for the city which would become the setting for several of his novels. It was not long before Spring took over the job of literary critic on the *Evening Standard* from J B Priestley and on moving to Cornwall at the outset of World War II he became literary critic of *Country Life*. His most well-known novel, *Fame is the Spur*, the story of a Labour politician's rise to power, was filmed by the Boulting Brothers and he continued to write until his death in 1965.

GU00459285

Essex County Council

DUNKERLEY'S

A novel by
HOWARD SPRING

HOUSE OF STRATUS

This edition published in 2000 by House of Stratus, an imprint of Stratus Holdings plc, 24c Old Burlington Street, London, W1X 1RL, UK.

www.houseofstratus.com

Typeset, printed and bound by House of Stratus.

A catalogue record for this book is available from the British Library.

ISBN 1-84232-334-2

AUTHOR'S FOREWORD

THIS IS the second volume of a trilogy of novels, and it is encouraging to its author that readers of the first volume, which was called *Hard Facts*, have written from many countries asking with some impatience what has happened to delay the successor.

Well, the war was not, for me, a time when fiction writing was easy. There was much else to occupy and disturb the mind, and, when this book *Dunkerley's* had got some way along its course, these other things became possessive and demanded to be written about and were written about in a book called *And Another Thing* which intervened between the two novels. Only when my mind was cleared of that could I go on and finish *Dunkerley's*.

Now here it is, and I hope that, like its forerunner, it is a piece of work which, while part of a larger whole, may be read with pleasure for its own sake. I have tried to make it so: a self-contained novel. There is no reason why such an attempt should not succeed, for what is any novel but a small part of something more extensive than itself? Let it be as long and detailed as you like, it still must rest as a point between two infinities of experience.

However, if this should fall into the hands of readers who have not read *Hard Facts*, let it be explained that *Hard Facts* was the title of a popular penny journal founded in Manchester in the year 1885 by a jobbing printer named Daniel Dunkerley. Associated with him were his father Sim Dunkerley, who lives on in this present book, and his brother-in-law George Satterfield, who will trouble us no more. Before his death George, like all engaged in this enterprise, became a rich man, and we shall learn here something of the subsequent career of his daughter and heiress.

The editor of *Hard Facts* was Alec Dillworth, a self-educated boy of genius from the Manchester slums, and that book was mainly devoted to his life and his sister Elsie's. Elsie, it seemed, would be a violinist of distinction, but in a moment of passion Alec, seeking to stab a man from whom he thought her to be in danger, stabbed her through the hand.

The drunken besotted father of these two tragic children is a background figure in *Hard Facts*. In this present volume, in which we find Daniel Dunkerley knighted, his affairs operating in London as well as Manchester, with Alec Dillworth editing the monthly magazine called *Dunkerley's*, the father intrudes into the foreground, with consequences which will be here discovered.

H.S.

For Romilly Cavan

CHAPTER ONE

Y OUNG LAURENCE DUNKERLEY couldn't understand why his father treated this old lady with so much deference. She might have been Queen Victoria, and, though she was younger than the Queen, she was not unlike her to look at. Indeed, thought Laurie, watching Miss Jekyll now as she hoisted her heavy body on to the step of the pony-cart, causing it to sag towards her, if she lives she will become the Queen's spit and image. She composed her voluminous black clothes about her with deliberation, directed upon Sir Daniel Dunkerley, from under her black felt hat decorated with cocks' feathers, a friendly but unsmiling face, and raised a chubby hand. "We are ready to depart," her attitude regally announced. "All right, Cox," Sir Daniel said, and the little cart, drawn by a pony as stout, regal and unhurried as Miss Jekyll herself, moved away.

Laurie said to his father: "For a gardener, she rather gives herself airs."

Sir Daniel turned upon his slender slip of a son his eyes of darkest violet blue. They gleamed in the round sunburned face beneath the rather long hair threaded with silver. They were quizzical and ironic. He said: "She gives herself no airs, though undoubtedly she has a splendid air. She is not a gardener — at any rate in your contemptuous sense — but a great artist who happens to use the lie of the earth, and the plants that grow in it, and water and trees and rocks, for her medium. Where is Miss Lewison? Try and entertain her. I must be off to town."

2

So that's that, thought Laurie. One hundred per cent wrong on every point. His father had stepped through the french window which

1

opened upon the terrace. Laurie could hear his voice inside the house shouting "Mike, Mike," and Johnny Carmichael, no doubt, was falling over himself; rushing from his secretarial room with despatch cases full of papers – all the paraphernalia that went with Sir Daniel up to town and came with him down from town. And here was the brougham, the wheels crunching the gravel at the foot of the lovely steps that led down from the terrace. Here and there on the steps were mats of vegetable growth over which his father and Miss Jekyll had pondered last night after dinner. One would have imagined they were as precious as the Crown Jewels. Insignificant florets of pink and blue and yellow grew upon them. Last night, these had seemed to Sir Daniel the most important things in the world. Now he had, as it were, brushed Miss Jekyll off his hands like a little garden earth, and no doubt would soon be pouring another most important thing in the world into Carmichael's attentive ear all the way to town.

Here they came: first Sir Daniel, carrying nothing; then Carmichael, carrying a despatch case in each hand; then Phyfe, the secretary's secretary, carrying a despatch case in each hand and one under each arm. Sir Daniel cast half a glance at *Saxifraga lingulata* and *Daphne cneorum*; and Laurie smiled with faint superiority. He had no imaginative grasp which could comprehend both his father's early life in a blasted Manchester suburb, starved of beauty, and the life of power he now lived.

3

Though he could not imaginatively comprehend what his father's career meant psychologically to his father, he knew, of course, the mere facts of it, and, indeed, could remember some of the outer events. After all, he had spent the first ten years of his own life in Levenshulme, but though the memory of that time was clear it was not potent. Too much had happened too quickly since then. The White House, Didsbury, to which his father had moved soon after the founding of *Hard Facts*, was more operative upon his mind; but he hadn't seen much of the White House because he had almost at once been sent away to a preparatory school, and later to Beckwith. He remembered something of the discussions about the school he was to go to. Beckwith had been chosen because the Reverend Theodore Chrystal, who had been headmaster for about a year at that time, was considered to be what Laurie's father called "a coming man," and Daniel Dunkerley had an uncommon instinct for coming men. Mr Chrystal had changed the whole direction of the school, which had been at first little more than a nest for cheeping parsons, and looked like making it one of the finest of the newer public schools.

So to Beckwith Laurie went, and thence to Oxford, where he was still an undergraduate of Merton; and it was during his first vacation from Oxford that his father had brought him down here into Sussex where an army of workmen seemed to be camped on the ground. It was then that he first met Miss Jekyll, plodding over rough clods in mannish nailed boots, hob-nobbing with a person whom Daniel introduced as Mr Lutyens. Laurie could remember one fragment of that afternoon's conversation. His father had made a suggestion, and Mr Lutyens had swiftly drawn a few lines on the back of an envelope. Then he had said: "I reckon that'll cost you another thousand pounds, Mr Dunkerley." To that Daniel had answered: "When I engage a man, Mr Lutyens, unless he's an accountant, I don't engage him to add up figures. I engage him to give me all he has to give." Mr Lutyens had grinned. "It looks as though we shall get on well together," he said.

Long after everyone else was gone that day, and the winter dusk had closed down on the Sussex landscape, Daniel said to Laurie, as the boy looked about on what seemed to him a scene of unparalleled desolation, chaos almost: "Well, with the greatest living architect, my boy, and the greatest living designer of gardens, and those two loving one another and working hand-in-glove, we ought to see something here soon."

And now one saw Dickons, looking incredibly settled and mature on that tender morning of late June in the year 1895.

4

It seemed as though the heat which, all through yesterday, had poured upon the red brick of the house and the Horsham stone of its roof and the long rectangular slabs that paved the terrace had merely been damped down by the few hours of midsummer darkness, and now, at the touch of the morning sun, was welling up again through the stone. Sitting in flannels and a cheerful blazer on the balustrade of the terrace, Laurie could feel the warmth seeping into his thighs. The air was full of the scent of clove pinks that grew under the front wall and of roses as yellow as butter that clambered about the porch. Laurie could not remember their names. To Sir Daniel they would be Madame Butterfly or something, he thought; but he was content to call them roses, to inhale indolently their ravishing perfume, and to reflect that before him stretched another day, cloudless, windless, everything that was said to his young careless heart by the word Summer.

This half-term affair at Beckwith would ruin the day. It would be a frightful bore to have to change after lunch into a tailcoat and a silk hat, but he had promised old Chrystal to be there. Old Chrystal seemed to Laurie to be very old indeed, though he was in fact but thirty-four. He had got on well enough with old Chrystal, but better with his wife Adela. It had been great fun, being head boy in his last year at Beckwith, because Mrs Chrystal looked upon the head boy as what she called the school's ambassador accredited to the court of the headmaster. That was one of her pretty, fanciful notions, and it meant that the head boy was welcome whenever he cared to drop into the head's house to tea; but all the same, Laurie reflected, lighting a cigarette, and being careful not to throw the match upon the pavement, which would have caused his father to storm, all the same he wouldn't have liked to try any ambassador nonsense with old Chrystal. The head's six foot of sheer physical beauty seemed to him to have a pretty icy heart to which it would not be easy to present the case of Smith Minor. Still, it had been agreeable to take so many teas in Mrs Chrystal's charming drawing room and to lie in a big chair afterwards, listening as she played upon the piano. Once, she said surprisingly: "You know, Laurie, Mr Chrystal used to sit there just like that, years ago, listening to my playing. This was a private house then – before Beckwith was founded. He was a curate at Little Riddings, and used to walk over here to teach me Greek. And do you know," she added with a smile, getting up and closing the piano, "I think he used to be doing no more than you're doing now – and that's just comfortably digesting your tea."

"Oh, really, Mrs Chrystal –" he protested.

"Well, tell me, what was I playing?"

"Oh, one of those polonaise things by Beethoven, surely?"

"Off you go now," she laughed. "I really think Beckwith produces nothing but sturdy barbarians."

Yes; she had been a good sort. He was sorry in his first term at Merton to hear of her sudden death. They said that she had left old Chrystal a pretty packet. With all an undergraduate's contempt for the mealy grub he had himself been a year or two ago, he decided that he would have to make the best of it among the kids at Beckwith. Chrystal liked to see a few of the old boys present.

5

Well, thought Laurie, carefully dropping his cigarette end over the balustrade, where it would be concealed behind a cotoneaster whose horizontal branches cloaked the stonework, orders are orders. I'd better find Miss Lewison. At that moment he heard Miss Lewison's rather sharp high voice, and she stepped from the house on to the terrace. Laurie's cousin, Grace Satterfield, was with her. They were arm-in-arm. They always will be arm-in-arm, he thought. They seemed inseparable. They made him feel rather small. He was twenty, still an undergraduate. Each of the girls was twenty-two, and last autumn they had finished with Cambridge. Grace had been at Newnham and Hesba Lewison at Girton. And so it was Laurie's turn now to feel a mealy grub in the presence of these two women of the world.

Miss Lewison was here at Dickons for two reasons: because she was Grace's friend, and Grace, since her father's death, had lived with Sir Daniel and Lady Dunkerley; and because she was "a coming woman". Sir Daniel had said so, and this was a point on which Sir Daniel was usually right. The greatest thing in the world to Sir Daniel at the moment was *Dunkerley's*, the shilling monthly magazine that was edited by Alec Dillworth. Six numbers had appeared. The first four had shown sales rising slowly – too slowly for Sir Daniel's liking – and in the fifth had appeared the first instalment of *The Happy Go Luckies*, a serial story for children, by Hesba Lewison. The issue was cleared off the bookstalls in twenty-four hours. The issue for this month of June 1895 was twice as numerous as the issue for May; and it was announced that in the August issue Miss Hesba Lewison would be dealt with in the series called "Coming Men and Women."

Laurie, who was not himself either rich (save comparatively, and as a dependent) or celebrated, was intimidated as he saw coming

5

towards him arm-in-arm through the sunshine of the June morning his very rich cousin and her celebrated friend.

6

Miss Lewison had a few sheets of paper in her hand, and she and Grace were laughing at something these contained. Miss Lewison's laugh, like the voice which had announced her coming, was high and abrupt. She, of the two, intimidated Laurie the more. For one thing, he had known Grace too long to be frightened of her, though in the year since she had come down from Cambridge her serene beauty had moved suddenly to perfection like a summer flower, and this – the serenity and assurance of it more than the impact of the beauty itself – made him feel raw and inexperienced. Grace had always been unusually self-possessed, never a chatterer or a giggler, though ready with a sensible and considered answer to anything one might say to her. Now all this had reached its zenith, and she had the appearance of being poised for some great adventure, but capable of the utmost deliberation in choosing the direction of her flight.

Both the girls wore black. Grace's father, George Satterfield, had been dead for nine months, and therefore Grace would continue to wear black for another three months. Then a touch of colour might be allowed to appear in her attire, to show that she was in "half-mourning." She was not one who would in any way outrage a convention. As George Satterfield's only child, she had inherited all his interests in Dunkerley Publications, and in the ten years since these began with *Hard Facts* they had grown to embrace no fewer than a hundred and three papers catering for every imaginable hobby and addiction from fowl-keeping to astronomy. At the moment, Sir Daniel being in a horticultural frame of mind, three new publications were in their birth-pangs, to bring the gospel of floral beauty to the backyard, the middle-class garden, and the seigneurial estate.

Grace was tall and slender. Above her chicory-blue eyes and broad white brow, her fair hair, which had been arranged in a series of plaits, was disposed in a convolution that the morning sun caused to shine like new golden bread. Her clothes, though black, were of a filmy texture that draped itself clingingly to the contour of every movement she made. Clearly, "mourning", she was determined, must have nothing to do with sackcloth; and there were moments when Laurie wondered whether she had deeply, or at all, regretted her father's death. He himself had never prospered with George Satterfield, his mother's brother, and, especially in his most self-conscious public-schoolboy phase, he had thought him what he would then have called a bit of a bounder.

Grace took the sheets of paper from Hesba Lewison's hand. "Look, Laurie," she invited. "What do you think of our little Hesba, aged five?"

Laurie went into the porch and brought out two scarlet cushions which he placed on the balustrade of the terrace. The girls sat one on either side of him, and he considered these pages which were the proofs of the article for *Dunkerley's*, setting out the career of this woman who had now reached the ripe old age of twenty-two. There were photographs of her at various stages of life.

"This is the one," said Grace, whose voice was as cool as her brow. She pointed to the incredible mite pictured there, standing sturdy and scowling, wearing the female counterpart of a seaman's uniform: short skirt, little reefer jacket, straw hat banded with the inscription H.M.S. *Tiger*. The stout legs were hidden in thick black woollen stockings. Under one arm was a telescope, and the background was a "property" cloth painted with date palms and a distant view of the pyramids. Despite this attempt to impart a wide saharan perspective, the child was flanked by a flimsy table with curved slender legs, supporting a potted fern resting upon a large book.

Although everything had been done to distract attention from the person photographed, the person photographed remained nonetheless the dominant thing in this singular composition. The scowl, the stance, the dark impetuosity of the little face, something invincible and Here I Am about the whole figure, riveted attention upon itself and seemed to make an imperative pronouncement of personality. But this was not apparent to Laurie. He saw only the comic and mirthful incongruities of the picture, and said: "Oh, but you mustn't allow 'em to use that, Miss Lewison. It would make you appear ridiculous."

She got up and looked down at him. Standing, she was just able to do so, for she was short. Her black clothes were untidy; they had a rusty look; they made one think that she wore black because it was an easier colour to manage than any other. She was still sturdy and stocky as the child in the picture, with the same dark passionate eyes. Her hair was of lustreless black, harsh like her voice, as she said: "I don't think it makes me look ridiculous at all. Anyway, that's how I was, and that's how it shall appear."

She took a pace or two on the terrace. Her movements, like her laugh and her words, were abrupt, decisive. Laurie felt rather crestfallen. He handed the page back to Grace. Grace said, to soothe the ruffled situation: "What amused us was the book under the pot-plant. Can you make out the lettering on the edge?"

Laurie looked at the picture closely. "Why," he said, "it looks like Hebrew."

Grace said: "It *is* Hebrew. And Hesba says that at that time she was just beginning to learn to read it. At five! The little monster!"

"That's nothing," said Miss Lewison shortly. "John Stuart Mill was learning Greek at three."

Grace got up, and arm-in-arm, fair and dark, tall and squat, the girls went together down the steps that led from the terrace to the drive, and crossed it to the lawn. Laurie listened to the soft indistinguishable words of his cousin, like doves in the summer air, and to the raven rejoinder of Miss Lewison: "Ridiculous, indeed! There's nothing ridiculous about it."

He went indoors to consult the *Dunkerley Encyclopedia* which had appeared in ninepenny parts, weekly. He was not quite certain about John Stuart Mill. He wanted to confirm whether he had something to do with a river called the Floss.

7

Although Laurie had strewn an amplitude of cushions on the floor of the punt, Hesba Lewison sat straight up. She seemed incapable of languorous relaxation. Grace Satterfield had gone back into the house to write letters, and Laurie had invited Miss Lewison, this being her first visit to Dickons, to see the river of which Sir Daniel was so proud.

"Oh, he has a river, too, has he?" she asked, and when Laurie said: "All his very own," she commented with a brief harsh chuckle: "Then we may expect soon to have a weekly paper devoted to rivers."

"Well," said Laurie, "you know he has already caught one or two trout here, and there is *The Amateur Fly-Fisher*."

Above his gay blazer flamed now a cap ringed with red, known as a cricket-cap. She thought it made him look more ingenuous than ever, but she was used to seeing bearded undergraduates of Cambridge wearing this strange piece of dress. And he had the nerve to say that her photograph made her look ridiculous! She had met him last night for the first time, and naturally considered with particular attention a young man who was the only son of Sir Daniel Dunkerley and would, it must be presumed, inherit in due course his father's vast and complicated affairs. He seemed to her completely tongue-tied, intimidated both by her and Miss Jekyll, who had spent the night at Dickons. But he had a kindliness, and his very ingenuousness had a charm. She recognised that his suggestion to her that the photograph should be suppressed arose from concern, however misdirected, for her well-being. But she would not acknowledge this to him.

Laurie strode lithely at her side, his arms plumped out with cushions of red, blue and yellow, and explained that the river hardly perhaps deserved so splendid a name. She would see for herself. It was a stream, but a most pleasant stream, and what commended it to Sir Daniel was that it made a vast loop, amounting almost, but not quite, to a circle, and within the area it defined the estate of Dickons lay. So Dickons was all but an island, and, navigating the waters that encompassed it, one could punt for two miles. "And it's very nice, you know," he said boyishly, "to feel that everything you look at on the left as you're going, and everything you look at on the right as you're coming back, belongs to Father."

"Yes," she agreed gravely, "it must be very nice indeed."

8

Laurie had punted for a mile or so, with no word spoken by either of them. There seemed no need for words. The sun shone, sparkling on the pebbly sallies and eddies of the shallow water. The smell of the wet banks and of mint and thyme filled the air. Wild roses here and there trailed into the water sprays that were jewelled with pale pink blossoms, and willows hunched over the stream their dark torsoes from which the green hair fell to the flood as if for washing. The little dragonflies flashed their wings and added their note to the general hum and drone of June.

9

A gardener's cottage stood near the bank, and here the stream ran ashore in a shallow that was yellow with pebbles looking like washed gold under the sun-silvered water. A little girl, bare-legged, was advanced a foot or two from the shore, and she stood there, with an intent face, screwing a key into the side of a small tin boat. When she had done, she placed the boat carefully on the water; the sides of the pigmy craft quivered with a minute vibration, and the boat proudly propelled itself to a standstill within the circle of a yard.

Hesba Lewison suddenly clapped her hands with delight and cried: "Stop! Let me get out! Let me do that!"

Laurie was surprised. It was the first time since he had met her that she had broken out into what might be called pure joy; and the reason for it puzzled him by its disproportion. He rammed down his pole, pushed Hesba's end of the punt towards the bank, and then went forward to help her ashore. But she needed no help. With a joyous and eager leap she cleared the short distance to the bank, and as she turned to the child her face, he thought, was more attractive than he had seen it yet. There was no scowl now. The dark eyes were alight with laughter and affection and even into the sallow of her skin a little colour washed from the manifest excitement of her spirit.

Laurie stood beside her on the bank, wondering what so strange and pleasurable a disturbance could mean in one whom he had always thought of in rather austere terms: as "a coming woman," a person who looked like having a career in letters, a scholar to whose depth and amplitude Grace was willing at any time to bear witness.

The child was at home with Miss Lewison, and she with the child, who made a dabble of wet fingers on Hesba's skirt as she clutched her with one hand and with the other held out for her inspection the boat that dribbled diamonds of water from its tinny beam. "You do it like this," the child explained, proud in recondite knowledge as she clutched and wound the screw; and Hesba laughed gaily: "You can't teach me anything about these, young woman." She wound the boat's mechanism, set it upon the water, and watched its brief fussy manoeuvre with an enchanted smile.

9

And now, when they had embarked again, she did lie at full length on the cushions, looking up at the clear blue of the sky, or at the green enlacement of leaves and branches, with a relaxation which suggested to Laurie that this encounter had filled her mind with soothing thoughts. The shadow of the smile which she had shared with the child remained on her face, and Laurie did not feel so much afraid of her.

"Did you notice the name under that photograph?" she presently asked, and added: "It was 'Hughes, Llanfairfechan.' It was taken the first year I went to live there. I sold dozens of little tin boats, just like that one. I used to love them. We went there – my father and I – from Manchester."

"But, Miss Lewison," Laurie cried, "if you lived in Manchester till you were five, you and I must have lived there at the same time." This seemed to him a most interesting and agreeable thought. He had, at least, some common footing with this remarkable creature, this "coming woman".

"We lived in Cheetham Hill," she said. "I expect you've guessed from my name that I'm a Jewess. Really, you know, my name is Hephzibah Lewissohn; but I thought that wouldn't look so good on the title-page of a book."

Bit by bit, to the sound of the drag of the punt's prow through the gentle slap of the stream, which ran against them, he pieced together her simple story. He could see the thin little bearded man who had been her father – "He made mackintoshes in a very small way," she said – and the small Cheetham Hill house, crowded into a region even more repulsive than Levenshulme as he faintly remembered it. The old man – but really he could not have been so old when Hesba was five – was an intense devotee of his religion. He was, she said, "a profound student" of Hebrew, a great friend of their rabbi; and all life seemed to have been passed between the house and the synagogue. She had never – literally never, she said – seen a field till she was five. It was then that the doctor told her father he must leave Manchester if he hoped to live. He was in an advanced condition of tuberculosis of the lungs.

So they went to Llanfairfechan, in North Wales; and this was the sharp dramatic cleavage in Hesba's life. Having never seen a field, she now saw nothing that could be called a street. She lived under the shadow of the mountains, at the edge of the sea. There was no synagogue; there was no friendly rabbi; and the old man's feelings turned inward upon the preoccupations of a scholar.

"Yes, it is true," Hesba said. "At five, I began to learn Hebrew. He was my teacher."

It was a life that could be pictured as not without attractions. There was a little money, but not enough. So they took a shop which opened in the summer time, when there were visitors, and frankly shut down in October.

"Have you ever seen those things," Hesba asked with animation, "that they import from Japan: strips of thin glass hanging on threads? You put them in a windowplace, and when there's a bit of breeze they tinkle deliciously. Our shop was like that. It was the smallest imaginable shop and it was hung all over the front with things that rustled and tinkled whenever there was a bit of a breeze. Oh, it was a lovely little shop! We sold postcards and canvas shoes, spades and painted tin buckets, tin ships for the rock pools – all sorts of stuff like that. Whenever the wind blew everything clattered. And there was sand on the pavement and sand in the shop. It used to come in on children's toes. Oh, it was a fine little shop indeed, I assure you!" She smiled at the reminiscence. "I suppose," she said, "it was Mr Gladstone who helped us to a living. You see, he used to take holidays at Penmaenmawr, just next door, and so all the Manchester Liberals began to discover North Wales."

There she was then, this dark little denizen of Cheetham Hill, five years old, transplanted to the fairyland that she was now recreating in *The Happy Go Luckies*. Across the water, whose blue was the grey-blue of slate, not a blue that was intense and burning, there was Puffin Island to which sometimes she sailed in a dinghy belonging to a friendly boy. Her father had gone, too. "Oh, we just shut down the shop. Believe me, we did what we liked about that shop. We were never slaves to commerce. Oh, indeed not." It was beautiful on the island, where not a soul lived, and the turf was bitten down by rabbits to the smooth sinuous contour of the rocks. They made a fire and boiled a kettle and ate their lunch as they looked towards the mainland towering up so suddenly out of the water. The little stone-boats were steaming in towards Penmaenmawr. Had not Mr Gladstone said that North Wales lived by exporting itself?

On one side the island fell to the sea in a cliff which she recalled as fearful and abrupt. She told how a party of children had been taken to this island for some annual picnic occasion. There were twenty of them, and when they were re-embarking and the roll was called there were nineteen. No one ever knew what became of the lost one, and Hesba never went to the island again. Her young mind recoiled from the thought of the sheer cliff and the sudden fall, down through the crying, wheeling gulls to the slate grey sea. "Can you imagine it," she asked now, her face clouded by the memory of that old woe, "the little lonely one who liked to live apart, so happy for a while to be by himself with the blue sky and that lovely turf, and then suddenly face to face with the chasm, and no one there to help, and his foot slipping? It is like that with the lonely ones. However," she said, her face brightening, "I can't put that in the story, can I? No. There were seals on the island, and he will have to be given happy miraculous days in a cave, with the seals for company, till he is found none the worse. There is no reason to tell children the truth. And most people are children all the time. They don't know anything about life, do they?"

Certainly, *you* don't. That, thought Laurie, looking down at her lying in rather a lumpy heap on the cushions, was what she was saying; and it was true enough that life for him had had no loneliness, no chasm glimpsed suddenly as it plunged down to the certainty of disaster. He said nothing, but brought the punt to a standstill, rocking gently on the water. This was the point where the all but complete circle of the river ended. Across a field that was now a shining floor of buttercups stretched wide open under the June sunshine you could see the comely western end of Dickons and the crystal glitter of the conservatories that housed the named and numbered precious blooms that Sir Daniel had gathered from the ends of the earth. Through a gate in the farther hedge they watched a reaping machine come, drawn by a big white horse that wore a straw hat decorated with poppies. Laurie leaned upon his pole, holding the punt steady, till the clattering machine had made a half-circuit of the field. It went by them, within a few yards, and they could hear the swish of the falling swathe, hardly so much a swish as a long sigh, as the grass and flowers all laid themselves down one way upon their last bed. The fragrance of the severed stems rose upon the air, and soon all that shining gold would be snipped from its rootage in the earth and given over to the desiccation of the sun. The flowers must die in order that the field might be born again; and so, of course, must the flowers in the conservatories die. But they would die as pampered as they had lived;

13

while here a vast anonymous sacrifice was being offered up. Laurie had a vague feeling that all this had something to do with what Miss Lewison had been saying; but he was rather puzzled, as though she were a bit beyond him; and this, in turn, made him feel nervous with her once more. He switched the punt round and began poling back the way they had come.

10

She was silent for a while, trailing in the water her fingers that were already round and stout. Her look was abstracted, and he felt that her whole being was turned away from him. Suddenly she said: "Do you know a man named Baudelaire?"

Laurie searched his memory, and truthfully said: "No. I've never known any one of that name."

"No, no," she laughed. "I didn't expect you had met him. He was dead before you were born. I mean, did you ever read his stuff? He was a poet."

Laurie felt a fool again, felt again abashed in the presence of the "coming woman".

"One of his poems," said Hesba, "begins: *Pascal avait son gouffre, avec lui se mouvant*. D'you know what that means?"

Laurie didn't. Beckwith and Merton had not made him acquainted with the French tongue as Hesba Lewison ripplingly spoke it. "No," he said, rather shamefaced. "You must translate. But I expect," he added hopefully, "I'd be able to puzzle it out if I saw it in print."

"It means," she said, "that Pascal was haunted by the sense of a gulf and that this feeling moved with him wherever he went."

Her mind, he gathered, was still back in those old days at Llanfairfechan. She began to talk again, and he was aware of the glee with which the child and her father watched the autumn come and the visitors go, and felt the wind rising, so that the tin buckets and wooden spades clattered more gaily than ever and the sand blew in little gritty whirls into the shop. And then the blue waggon would come with the wood. Every year for five years it was the same waggon, painted a delicious blue, and it would be laden with logs cut to a size handy for burning in a small grate. "Oh, I loved the blue waggon and the logs with their rough bark on them and the grey moss on the bark. It was all our winter joy being delivered at the door. I used to imagine how they had come creaking down the mountain where they had been growing for fifty years just to make winter fires for us."

And there the two were, when the snow was lying on the mountains behind them, and before them the sea was no longer slate-blue but iron grey, and the buckets and spades, the kites, tin ships and peg-tops were all packed away and the shutters up. "That was the time."

She said: "In the winter we lived in the upper room," and she made this sound significant. The upper room! They must have been a shade off the ground, a trifle off the common earth, Laurie thought, with the curtains drawn and the logs burning and the candles lit, and this old man, denied all other outlet, instilling an ancient language, an ancient spirit, into the child.

"Don't think," said Hesba, "we read nothing but Hebrew. Indeed, no! My father was a German, you know. He was born in Hanover – he and his brother. I don't know why he came to England, except that they were very poor, and the poor move about, looking for this and that. His brother stayed where he was and made a little money somehow, and with this he became a money-lender – oh, quite a financier, I believe, very rich. But Father never wrote to him. I don't think they liked one another."

"So you learned German, too?" asked Laurie.

Yes, she said, she learned German, and they read the novels of Dickens; and always at nine o'clock she would go down to the kitchen behind the shop and make supper. They always ate this as they sat by their fire, and the old man permitted himself one pipe, which was all the doctor thought he should have, and then they talked. "Oh, yes. Sometimes till eleven, sometimes till midnight. He would tell me about his family life in Germany, and sometimes he would sing old German or Yiddish songs, and I would tell him tales that I had made up."

An extraordinary upbringing, Laurie thought. "But what about this Baudelaire?" he asked. "What about this sense of a gulf?"

"There was an old Church of England parson living not far from us," said Hesba, seeming to ignore the question. "He hadn't a church. He was retired. He had had a church for many years in Manchester. He was more of a scholar than most parsons are, deeply interested in the Hebrew scriptures. In Manchester he had known my father's friend the rabbi. They had talked over points of scholarship together, and when he came to live in North Wales he would write often to the rabbi about things that puzzled him. 'But why write to me when you've got Israel Lewissohn, as good a Hebrew scholar as I am myself, living on your doorstep?' Something like that, I suppose, the rabbi said to him."

Whatever the rabbi had said, there was, as a consequence, that astounding interview, as it appeared to Laurie, though, as Hesba Lewison related it, there seemed nothing remarkable about it to her. It was a breezy summer day when all the ramshackle stock-in-trade would be at its chattering rattle about the wide-open door, and through this door came the tall thin grey parson, standing there for a moment smiling amid the Lilliputian tornado of gay painted tuppenny gimcracks. He said his name was Vereker, and then seemed to forget his name altogether as a hot freckled child, with a coin stuck to his palm, came to transact one of the momentous business deals that went forward in that shop. It was a matter of a humming-top, a bulbous tin affair girdled – "Rather like your cricket-cap," Hesba teased Laurie – with saturn-rings of blue and yellow, red and white. There was this very English child staring with wide blue eyes in his sun-burned face while the sallow dark-eyed lumpy girl no older than himself wound up the string, then deftly pulled it, and all those bands of colour flew madly round, merging in a daze that was every colour and no colour at all, but a great intoxicated tin bee, droning like a whole hive, a satisfying and dangerous hum. Then it staggered from its assured and upright stance, its roar diminished, and it collapsed into the mere tin bauble it was. "Bravo!" cried Mr Vereker. "A shilling," said Hesba, and the child, voiceless, shook the coin from his palm, seized his quiescent planet, and ran godlike into the blaze of the sunshine to set it whirling. Of such gay ingredients, Laurie gathered, the Lewissohn commerce was compounded.

11

When Mr Vereker asked if he might see her father, the little Hephzibah explained that Israel was out, taking the gentle morning exercise in the sunshine that his condition demanded. "But if there is anything I can do for you," she said, "I shall be only too glad."

She was nine years old at this time, a stage advanced from the black-scowling young person of the saharan photograph; but, even so, hardly one with whom Mr Vereker felt he could discuss the precise translation of a Hebrew phrase. However, there was already enough "to" her to draw from him an explanation of his errand, though he could hardly have expected any enlightenment on its purpose. She said simply: "Let me get the book," and ran out of the shop.

Laurie had put the punt under the green droop of some willows, and in that cool-smelling vegetable cave he sat down to rest for a while. The slow, sweet bell of Little Riddings church dropped the twelve notes of noon.

"Grace is right," Hesba Lewison said with her brief harsh laugh. "I must have been a little monster. I can remember the poor man's surprise when I laid the book on the counter, sweeping aside the trays of marbles and the monkeys-up-the-sticks, and said: 'Well now, exactly what is your difficulty?' "

Mr Vereker indeed felt at that moment that he could have been knocked down with a feather, but when everything is said and done, there wasn't so much in the situation as all that. A well-educated Englishman may easily be enlightened in French by a French child of nine, and for four years now Hebrew had been to Hesba a matter of daily custom. Mr Vereker's knowledge of Hebrew turned out to be, after all, elementary, and she was not so surprised as he was that she was able to tell him what he wanted to know.

Mr Vereker, who was a bachelor and lonely in his retirement, now became a familiar of this little family. Especially after the shop had been closed down in the autumn he sought the quiet and serenity of that strange home. He was deeply attracted to the Jewish child who was capable of such stillness, squatted upon a footstool with her knees to her chin, listening with dark-eyed concentration to the arguments tossing to and fro above her head. But never, it seemed to him, above her mind.

"He went away," Hesba said, "in the next June. We had known him just a year. And then, in the autumn after that, my father died."

Laurie was hardly shaped to realise all that might lie behind such simple words: that they knocked the bottom out of a life that had been wrapped up in love, that here was the gulf abrupt and terrible.

17

Mr Vereker was not the man to bear retirement easily. Indeed, he found that he could not bear it at all. Once a priest always a priest. He had enjoyed for years a large and influential benefice, with a canon's stall in the cathedral. Now he went humbly to end his days as a curate among Cornish fishermen. This was while "the season," as Hesba called it with a mischievous reminiscent twinkle of the eye, was still in full swing at Llanfairfechan, and the small jingling traffic of the shop was there to keep the mind off this defection; but there was not so much as this when her father died. There was nothing.

It was the more terrible because it was at the beginning of the time to which the child had for long looked forward: that time when the shutters were up, and the blue waggon had groaned down from the mountains, and the winter, endless to the mind of childhood, stretched ahead with its enclosed domestic joys. And instead of this, there was the sudden spasm shaking the doomed body of her father, the red spout of his blood gushing before her horrified eyes on to the hearthrug in the upper room, and not long thereafter the knowledge that she was alone to make what she could of a world that was all there for the taking of a ten-year-old.

12

"There was a Miss Price living in the village," Hesba said, and then paused to ask: "Have you read *The Happy Go Luckies* so far?"

Laurie said, making his admission with a blush, that he hadn't, adding hastily that he never read serial stories because the better they were the more annoying it was to be left month after month hanging by a hair. She accepted this, and said: "Well, a tale for children should always have an ogre of some sort. Miss Price provided me with my ogre."

A child of ten is helpless in the hands of adults who all know what is good for it. And one or two excellent people of Llanfairfechan, in committee assembled, decided that this small terrified orphan should go to Miss Price, who would give her "a good home" in return for her services.

Miss Price's good home, whose goodness was so great that wages would be a superfluity, stood a little way out of the village, on the road to Penmaenmawr. It faced the house of Miss Price's sister, Miss Myfanwy Price, and in all the front windows of these two houses the blinds were permanently down. The Misses Price, who had quarrelled over ten pounds in their father's will, hated one another with the sour vinegarish hatred of spinsters who had nothing to do. Their hatred was so great that, though neither, should they chance to meet, would speak to or even look at the other, they were powerfully attracted to one another, and from chinks in the lowered blinds each for long times at a stretch would gaze venomously towards the house of the other, hoping to ferret out some small discreditable fact. Hesba, who knew nothing of all this, was nevertheless at once aware that she had passed out of a kingdom of love into a kingdom of hate. The house was black with it. She was put to sleep in an attic lighted only by a skylight, though there were four bedrooms to spare in the house. On the first morning of her awakening in that place, her heart numb with a sense of her recent loss, she went downstairs, ran up the blind in the front room, and opened the window. She was unaware that the blind had been down for longer than she had lived in this world, that she had committed a crime of monstrous proportions. It was not till after breakfast that Miss Price went into the room, lighting a candle that stood on the hallstand in expectation of the accustomed darkness. Her puny flame was extinguished by the blaze of daylight. She stood for a moment dumbfounded, the candlestick shaking in her hand, and then perceived the face of her sister. Miss Myfanwy Price was not merely looking into the room: she was in the room, to the extent of a head and shoulders thrust through the open window, and with a gaze triumphant and malignant she was taking stock of Miss Price's intimacies. Miss Price dropped the candle and rushed forward, slamming down the window with a vehemence that would gladly have guillotined her sister had she not been too quick. Miss Myfanwy had time to exclaim before she withdrew: "To have waited all these years to see nothing but that!"

Hesba knew nothing of this encounter, and Miss Price was just enough to blame herself for not having warned the girl that the front windows must not be touched. But she was unable to prevent herself in the days that followed from taking it out of the author of her misfortune. A misfortune of the first order it seemed to her: the only advance upon her territory that the enemy had achieved in twelve years. There was only one consoling feature in the whole matter: Myfanwy had spoken to her; and Myfanwy had vowed: "I won't speak mortal word to that bitch while there's life in my body."

Hesba became an underfed and over-worked little drudge, toiling from morning to night in the dark house with its front shuttered and the mountains rising at the back. The thought of the summer gaiety of the shop, the dear tranquil winter intimacy of the upper room, was far-off and paradisal, something which seemed with the passing of the days to belong to a life irrecoverably removed from the loveless gulf in which she found herself. It was not the hard and dirty work, not the lack of pay, that enclosed her in misery: it was the discovery of this unsuspected world, without love, without beauty, without the mental strife to which she had been prematurely awakened. There had been no warning, no preparation: she had dropped out of the sunshine over the cliff.

13

Of most of this she said nothing to Laurie; and she did not tell him of the day when she met Miss Myfanwy Price by chance in the village Street, and Miss Myfanwy, who was a smiling little woman with golden pince-nez, spoke of the silver hair-brushes. These brushes, she said, had belonged to her dear father, and Hesba would see his initials J.R.P. on the backs of them. She was a soft-spoken sweet little woman, round and red as a robin, and she gave Hesba a round red apple from her basket. This was the first friendliness Hesba had known all through that winter, and she listened wide-eyed to Miss Myfanwy's story of the hair-brushes. Though her father had intended them for her, they had got somehow to her sister's. She was very fond of her sister and wouldn't on any account take the brushes from her now. But here is Chrissmass coming on, issn't it? she asked with a soft Welsh hiss of her S', and wouldn't it be nice to give her sister a surprise? So let Hesba bring those brushes to her. She knew a man who could take those initials off the back and put her sister's there instead. Yess, indeed, he was very good at that sort of thing. And wouldn't that be a lovely Chrissmass present for her sister? But not a word. All quiet, eh? Wasn't her sister out every Thursday at four o'clock? Yess, indeed. Very well, then. Bring those hair-brushes across the road at four next Thursday. But not a word — not a word, mind, to anybody.

And there the child was on that day, unaware of the complicated world of hate she was moving in, bringing the brushes; and what should Miss Myfanwy be doing at that very hour but entertaining half a dozen friends to tea, one of them no less a person than Evan Morris Magistrate. In the narrow hall where she received the child she raised a great outcry that brought them all crowding. A thief it was – a little thief! Offering to sell stolen property from her own sister's house! Did you ever hear the like? But could you wonder? Miss Myfanwy demanded. Servants, indeed! Some people were so grand with their servants, and here they were – thieves! And could you wonder? she repeated. "Not a penny-piece, I bet, that child is getting, and little to eat but bread-an'-scrape. Do you wonder if she steals? But so brazen! Comin' to me with my own sister's stuff!"

Hesba was petrified. She could not speak. A universe of unsuspected infamy opened before her and stunned her mind. Miss Myfanwy watched her sister return home, slide through a crack of half-open door. "She'll find no servant waiting for her," she crowed. "Servant! Some people and their servants."

14

Israel Lewissohn was too unimportant a person for the news of his death to travel far. Mr Vereker did not hear of it. At Christmas he wrote to Hesba, but she did not receive the letter. Mr Evan Morris Magistrate, whose opinion was effective, had decided that so small a girl should not be prosecuted. She should go to another "good home" whose saving influence would wash her sins away. The last known Llanfairfechan address being at Miss Price's, the letter was delivered there. Miss Price read the inscription "Miss H. Lewissohn," snorted, and decided to throw the letter into the fire. She did so, having read it first; and she did this with letters from Mr Vereker the next Christmas and the Christmas after that. Then Mr Vereker wrote no more.

From the time she was nine till she was fourteen Hesba lived in her gulf. She forgot all she had ever known of love and the strife of the spirit. Because she had once been Miss Price's handmaid Miss Myfanwy Price hated her; and Miss Price hated her because she had (the woman thought) conspired against her with Miss Myfanwy. They were, both, born writers of anonymous letters, and unknown to one another they pursued the child by this foul and secret means. With allegations that became more and more monstrous they hounded her from place to place. Hesba had not the wit to leave the

21

neighbourhood. She was there, an easily traceable prey, branded thief and liar and corrupter of men's morals. These two women opened up the sewers of their minds and paddled gleefully in what they uncovered. When they had done with her, Hesba herself hardly knew whether this dour, dark, secret child, chivvied from the most menial tasks in one wretched house after another, was not the perverted criminal creature she was generally held to be.

All she said to Laurie about those days was: "Yes, indeed; they were pretty wretched years after Father died. An absolute quagmire. I was fourteen – just getting towards fifteen – when I climbed out of it. D'you know," she added, in the abrupt seemingly irrelevant way she had, "when you're a successful writer – even just moving on to a bit of success like me – all sorts of people write to you. I had a letter only this morning about *The Happy Go Luckies*. The writer says luck never influences human lives. Well, I can only say it influenced mine. Yes, indeed."

The luck came one summer day in the shape of a stout bearded man who climbed the mountainside, laid his painter's outfit on the heather, and then sat down, smoking his pipe and looking over the sea to the coast of Anglesey. Presently he was disturbed by the sound of a strangled sob, and he found this to come from a girl lying face-downward behind a boulder. She was dropping salt tears into the roots of the heather and he doubted whether this was good for the plants. He said so in a gently reproving voice, and went on to add that the human face was never at its best when the eyes were red and the nose wet. "However," he added in a fat comfortable voice, puffing smoke down towards her, "you are keeping your nose so carefully hidden that I doubt whether it's worth looking at anyway. It's probably a shapeless splodge."

Listening to this rumbling voice, Hesba felt her tension relax. Her tears ceased to flow, but she did not look up. "All right," he said, "keep your nose to yourself. I can have the best noses in the United Kingdom any time I want them. I've turned down dozens of them."

Then Hesba got to her knees to inspect this man who turned down noses. There she was, with her hands and knees on the ground, her tragic face staring at him through a tangle of black hair. "H'm," he said, looking at her nose critically. "I've seen better. But why crouch there like a dog about to bark? Come and sit here." He patted the ground alongside him, and she obeyed him. He looked like a large friendly dog himself with so much hair on his head and chin and such shaggy blue tweeds on his body. She, who had learned to distrust most people, had confidence in him. From his pocket he took a packet of sandwiches. He handed her one and she began to eat greedily.

"No breakfast?" he said. She shook her head.

"No supper?"

Another shake as she wolfed the meat.

"On the mountain all night?"

She nodded.

"Running away?"

She nodded again.

He handed her another sandwich and began to eat one himself. They finished the packet between them, and then he emptied a bottle of beer, drinking from the neck. He rinsed out the bottle in a stream, filled it, and brought it to her. As she drank he filled his pipe and leaned back on a boulder. With his eyes half-shut, his pipe clenched in his teeth, his fat hands folded contentedly on his fat stomach, he said nothing. It was noon. The brilliant sunlight poured down upon them, and before she knew where she was Hesba was soundly asleep in the comfortable shade of that hairy haystack of a man. Mr Cecil Bond, R.A., the most sought after portrait painter of his generation, who had indeed turned down many a nose in his time, saw no reason why he should not sleep, too. A bit of landscape painting as a change from noses was his idea of a holiday, but he was not in a hurry even to paint landscapes. He understood the art of relaxation. He finished his pipe, put it into his pocket, and was soon comfortably snoring.

He woke just before Hesba did; and when she woke, the very fact of his being still there, in the same position, impressed her. It gave her a sense of something rock-like and unchangeable, and that was what she needed after the insecurities of the last few years. With no prompting from him, and with no preamble, she plunged into her story.

"What you should have done," he said severely when she had finished, "was to write at once to this Mr Vereker," and when Hesba protested that she hadn't his address, he said: "Pish, child, pish! Care of the Archbishop of Canterbury. That would have done."

Hesba looked with wonder at a man who so casually cut through the knots of difficulty. She was suddenly overcome by the thought that so simple an action might have saved her years of sorrow.

"Well," said Mr Bond, surging to his feet. "Ham and eggs, and then we'll consult Crockford."

Hesba had no idea who Crockford was, but she was able to help Mr Bond with the ham and eggs that were his idea of an afternoon tea. He was a mighty eater. They fed in the kitchen of a farmhouse where he was staying, and after tea the farmer drove them in to Bangor. There Mr Bond was able to consult *Crockford's Clerical Directory*, and he exclaimed with triumph as his fat forefinger stopped on the name of the Rev. Hubert Vereker, M.A., B.D., who, it appeared, was curate of Newpenny in the South of Cornwall. "There's our man!" he shouted, and then and there he sat down and wrote to Mr Vereker.

Two days later a telegram asked Mr Bond: "Can you send her to me? Vereker," and a telegram to Mr Vereker said: "I can *bring* her to you. Bond."

All that Hesba said to Laurie was: "Years later I managed to get in touch with Mr Vereker again, and after that it was all right." She felt that she could never make him or any human being understand the amazing overthrow of her life in those days: as great an overthrow as had followed the death of her father. She could hardly grasp the idea that she was a free creature, that she could come and go as she pleased from the farmhouse where she was living on the fat of the land with Mr Bond. The woman from whose bondage she had run away found her there, appearing importantly with a policeman. These two came upon Hesba in a field near the farm, and the woman swooped upon her with a glad cry: "That's her!"

"Now, my gel, you better get back to your place with your missus!" the policeman said, and all the dark clouds of sorrow and frustration closed again upon the child's heart. It was then that Mr Bond came rolling heavily across the field, exclaiming with easy good temper: "Hi! Buzz off! Leave that girl alone."

"This gel belongs to me. She's run away from me," the woman cried hotly; and the policeman: "She ought to be getting back where she belongs."

"So ought you," said Mr Bond calmly. "What are you charging her with?"

Well, sir –"

"Well, sir, nothing. You've got no charge and you've got no warrant. So buzz off. You, too," he said to the woman. "I don't like your nose."

The policeman nudged the woman, and they went. Hesba was overwhelmed. She looked at Mr Bond as at a god who disposed of the most powerful mortals with a casual gesture.

She would never forget this, and she would never forget the journey down through Hereford and Bristol, jumping out on to the sunshine of the platforms to eat sandwiches and drink tea with Mr Bond; and the flat Somerset landscape, and the red cliffs of Devonshire that the sea had chewed into fantastic shapes, and the small fields and wooded valleys of Cornwall.

"You know, Miss Lewissohn," – so Mr Bond now quizzically called her – "the joke is that I was coming down to Newpenny anyway. Oh – I've never told you, have I? I earn my living by painting people's pictures; and I'm going down there to paint one now. A Mrs Armitage. Ever heard of Sarah Armitage?"

"No, sir."

"Well, don't tell *her* that, Miss Lewissohn. It is to be assumed that there is no one living who has not heard of Sarah Armitage. She writes novels, and she is very rich. Fortunately, she has a passable nose . . . Oh," he added presently, "you'll find this Newpenny a fearful place. Reeking with artists and with writers gathered round the shrine of Sarah Armitage."

All of which was true; but what Hesba said to Laurie was: "It was a lovely life after that. Mr Vereker got me a job with Sarah Armitage. Yes, *the* Sarah, whose serial in *Dunkerley's* must have cost your father a pretty penny. I was a girl-of-all-work for a time, but old Sarah took a fancy to me and I became her secretary-companion. It was an interesting life. I met all sorts of people and had plenty of time to study. I brushed up all my old stuff. My French and German soon came back, and Sarah found that most useful when we travelled. We gadded about the Continent for half of every year. I saved money like a miser, and when I was nineteen I left her to go to Girton. She was very sweet, but furious. If you knew Sarah you'd know what I mean."

"And what did you principally take at Girton?" Laurie asked.

"Greek and Latin."

She leapt out of the punt as soon as it touched the wharf at their journey's end, and ran. Laurie followed slowly. Hebrew, Greek and Latin! French and German! A whole epic of vivid life behind her at twenty-two! A coming woman!

Her rusty black switched out of his sight round the twist of a path. Well, glory be to God! he thought. Glory be to God! He had not known there were such women in the world. Sir Daniel certainly knew how to pick 'em!

CHAPTER TWO

SIR DANIEL DUNKERLEY was rarely seen alone. It was to be assumed that a man controlling such complicated and wide-flung affairs might at any moment – even when walking quietly in the street or in his garden – have a surge of business to the brain, and this required that someone should be at hand to leap, as it were, into the saddle and ride some lathered horse from Aix to Ghent.

James Carmichael, as touchy and jealous as an old spinster who was permitted to worship and minister to a famous actor, was Number One of this Entourage, and anybody might at this time or that be Number Two. When all was well between Sir Daniel and James Carmichael, James would be Mike; but if Sir Daniel wanted, as he often did, to punish or tease him, then Isambard Phyfe, the secretary's secretary, who was, as a rule, simply and coldly Phyfe, would be affectionately addressed as Izzy. This was interpreted to mean that Mr Phyfe was walking the dizzy tightrope between Number Two and Number One, but such an interpretation could easily be wrong. Sir Daniel might well call Isambard Phyfe Izzy simply to see James Carmichael wince and keep him in his place. And there was another thing about it. Sir Daniel, who knew everything about everybody he employed, knew that Isambard Phyfe had been plain Sam Fife to his mates in an East End street. He was amused by the determined emergence of this young Cockney who had furiously besieged institutes, settlements and polytechnics for all the free crumbs of learning that august and liberal-minded men were tossing to the sparrows of the day. Yes; it amused him mightily to reflect that Izzy Phyfe, hopping and pecking among the overflow from the nose-bags of the rich, had picked up a better outfit of knowledge than young Laurie had acquired from Beckwith and Oxford. They were of much

27

the same age. Laurie seemed to turn naturally to Phyfe when there was some point to be cleared up. Phyfe had never been known to turn to Laurie. If "coming men" and "coming women" in the grand sense were Sir Daniel's main pursuit, he could still find time to fit Phyfe into his autocratic and benevolent whims. What Phyfe wanted to have knocked off him was not the corners but certain spikes of stridency and aggressiveness. There was too much naphtha-flare and Saturday night market and bargain-basement about him. He must be taken round to see something of a subtler and more civilised world. James Carmichael was a Master of Arts of St Andrews University, and his big bald solemn head and spectacled eyes were those of a suet pudding, most reliably there on the plate to be consumed at will. But it seemed to Sir Daniel that to try and get one's fork into Isambard Phyfe would be like trying to fork up peas made of quicksilver. He was happier in Phyfe's company than in Carmichael's, though he knew that in Carmichael's he was safer.

2

After lunch on the day before that one when Laurie took Hesba Lewison out in the punt Sir Daniel said: "Izzy, we shall be driving in half-an-hour." Miss Jekyll was not due until teatime, and it was unthinkable that Sir Daniel Dunkerley should do nothing, should just sit there and await her.

The look of an owl that has received sudden news of the loss of a loved one spread upon Mr Carmichael's face. He retired at once to the wing which Sir Daniel had furnished for the use of those members of the Entourage who accompanied him to Dickons. It contained two bedrooms and a bathroom and a large comfortable sitting room that was called the office. So Mr Carmichael could have a bath, or go to bed, or sit down doing nothing, or get through the afternoon by doing all three. Sir Daniel didn't care what he did. He was going to see Theodore Chrystal, and Chrystal, who had been a curate in Manchester when Sir Daniel's first paper *Hard Facts* was founded there, reminded him of youth and struggle. (But even now, with so much behind him, Sir Daniel was but forty-two.) For this mood, Phyfe would be a better companion than Carmichael.

"Izzy," said Sir Daniel, as the carriage drew away from the house, "when I was young my father used to say to me: 'We can be what we want to be.'"

"Quite right, sir," Izzy eagerly assented.

"Quite wrong," Sir Daniel corrected him calmly. "We can be what it's in us to be. Most people don't become even that, which is, as a rule, a long sight short of what they want to be. All we can do is *strive* to be what we want to be, and in that way we become what it's in us to be."

The Entourage was accustomed to Sir Daniel's homilectic note. Mr Phyfe murmured his acceptance of the wisdom that had been uttered.

"We are going now," Sir Daniel pursued, "to see a man who has known better than most people what he wanted to be, and has striven more than most to become it. I mean Mr Chrystal, the headmaster of Beckwith. It is just ten years ago that *Hard Facts* was founded in Manchester. It chanced that on that very day I first met Mr Chrystal. He was a curate in Levenshulme. In the ten years since then, he has succeeded in marrying a titled lady whose brother was a bishop, burying her, inheriting her considerable fortune, and turning a seminary for puking young parsons into a notable public school. These are no common achievements."

The victoria was passing through the pleasant hamlet of Little Riddings. Before them, to the right, on a rise of land, the buildings of Beckwith could be seen blurred by the heat of the day against their background of noble beeches. Mr Phyfe, who was aware of the dialectical traps that Sir Daniel sometimes spread before the feet of the unwary, ventured to say: "I'm not sure, Sir Daniel, that marrying a woman for her money is a great achievement."

Sir Daniel answered: "I didn't say he married her for her money. He may have done: I don't know. But it's a free world, Izzy. You are as poor as Chrystal was then, and as unknown. If you think that in those circumstances it is not a great achievement, in its way, to marry a woman with a title and a fortune, I invite you to try it and find out for yourself. In other words, don't talk like a fool. To marry the sort of woman Adela Pinson was, you've got to have something. I know because I knew her. It was largely her money that founded the school, and I became a governor of the school soon enough to see a good deal of her. She was a fine woman."

The carriage turned between the great stone pillars on which the iron gates of the school were flung back. In an arch from pillar to pillar was a metal plaque on which the school's motto, punched through the metal, shone against the sky: *Possibile est si ardenter desideratus*. Sir Daniel called Mr Phyfe's attention to the motto, and was surprised when Mr Phyfe translated as the carriage ran beneath: *It's possible if you want it badly enough*. "But, Sir Daniel," he said, "that's just what—"

Sir Daniel interrupted with a grin: "Yes, it's my father's motto, as translated by Mr Chrystal. You see, Izzy, when the school was starting they wanted a lot of money, and I was able to give them some. I made the use of the motto my condition. I thought it would please my father."

"But you think it's not true, sir."

"It's near enough for the young," said Sir Daniel complacently. "Keeps 'em on their toes. Where did you learn your Latin, Izzy?"

"Oh, a young parson used to teach a few of us in a Shoreditch settlement. Dunno what good he thought it'd do us."

"Keep it up," said Sir Daniel. "Keep it up. I must tell Carmichael you're a Latin scholar. He'll be enchanted."

Sir Daniel stopped the carriage and said they would walk up to the school. The fact was, he wanted to watch the boys playing cricket. From the field to their left, as he and Isambard Phyfe loitered towards the school buildings, came the occasional sweet smack of the bat upon the ball and the cries of the young voices. The small white-clad figures scurrying between the wickets or chasing into the long-field, or weaving their quiet change of pattern upon the green grass at the end of an over; the wide spread of the field which absorbed this small activity into its immensity, the colour of a few blazers clothing squatters on the pavilion steps, the grey already-mature-looking buildings perched upon the hill: all this affected both Phyfe and Dunkerley with an identical emotion which made them feel near together. Each was thinking of his own boyhood, the one in the dreariness of Shoreditch, the other in the dreariness of Levenshulme. An awareness of something missed, and never now to be overtaken, planted into the heart of each of them not a feeling of envy but a nostalgic sense of the brevity of youth, wheresoever and howsoever it might be passed.

"Well," said Phyfe unexpectedly, "I don't envy 'em. They don't see much of their mothers."

Sir Daniel gave him a sharp look, and Phyfe blushed as though he had been surprised into saying too much. But rather defiantly he added: "Mine was one of the best. I wouldn't have done without her for this, an' chance all the fish-and-chips and pawnshops that got thrown in with the bargain."

3

Isambard Phyfe was commanded to absorb the atmosphere of Beckwith's gardens and open spaces. Sir Daniel went alone into the headmaster's house. Theodore Chrystal received him in his study, and Dunkerley said to himself, as he had said a hundred times, that he had never seen a handsomer man. As Chrystal got up from behind his desk, all the six foot of his superb physique, topped by the golden-curled Greek head, seemed designed to impress and intimidate the beholder. Dunkerley could remember that cold classic face when it was young and defenceless. That was but ten years ago. It seemed to him incredible that so short a time should bring so great a change. Chrystal looked as though his clay had been through a kiln and come out fixed and glazed in lines of severity. But Dunkerley knew that there were occasions when the eye which men thought so cold could melt to tenderness and the hard set of the face dissolve into romantic promise. This was when Chrystal was with a woman whom he liked or wished to impress. Many a mother, investigating Beckwith as a possible school for her son, had left with the impression that her child would be safe with an angel; and it was not in the tradition that sons should disillusion their mothers.

The two men shook hands across the width of the desk, then sank into leather chairs with that tidy expanse between them. Chrystal, who was already smoking, pushed a tobacco jar across to Dunkerley; and Sir Daniel, filling his pipe, said: "Well, Chrystal, my warmest congratulations."

For a second, Theo looked surprised, then took up a book from the desk. "Oh, this," he said. "Yes. It's finished at last. But really, you know, it doesn't come to much. Just a monument of perseverance."

Sir Daniel smiled, taking the book and looking at the title: *Some speculations concerning the authorship of the Epistle to the Hebrews.* "A rotten title," he said. "You should have called it *Who wrote Hebrews?* And if you think it a monument of perseverance, let me tell you that if I employed you, you'd have to persevere a bit quicker. You've been messing about with that for all of ten years. However, I didn't mean that. I meant the deanery."

Chrystal looked at him coldly. "I don't know what you have heard about that," he said. "Nothing has been made public, and I must beg you to keep your speculations to yourself."

"Speculations be hanged," said Sir Daniel heartily. "Don't worry, Chrystal. I know when to keep my mouth shut. But I know also that you've been offered the Deanery of King's Mandeville and have accepted it. I think you're wise. It's not much of a deanery. An old controversialist once spoke of the Bishopric of King's Mandeville as 'this piddling and preposterous prelacy . . . ' "

"You are well primed with information," Chrystal interrupted, without warmth.

"I was going on to say," Sir Daniel continued suavely, "that, however small it is, you are right to take it. I know that the Church is your career and prime ambition, and that this school-mastering, for whatever reason you took it up, has been a sideline. A wise one, I admit. A lot of bishops have been headmasters, and as a headmaster you've done a fine job. And it isn't often a man gets a deanery – even such a deanery as King's Mandeville – at thirty-four. So again, my congratulations, Chrystal, and, for what it's worth, my prediction that you'll be a bishop at forty."

Chrystal's face relaxed a little of its severity. "Thank you, Dunkerley," he said. "I know I can trust you to keep this to yourself."

"You can," said Sir Daniel. "And now to talk business. That's what I came for. When you were a boy I used to pay you two guineas a thousand for sermons in *Hard Facts*."

Chrystal's face again became an ascetic mask. "When one is a boy," he said, "one commits innumerable follies."

"I don't see any folly about it," said Dunkerley, "except that you let me rob you. Your stuff was good for its purpose and worth more than I gave you. I want you to write for me again – for *Dunkerley's*."

Chrystal shook his head. Undeterred by this, Sir Daniel went on: "This time you'll write under your own name. The youngest dean in the country will mean something. You'll have twenty guineas a thousand, and your articles will be about fifteen hundred words each. I believe the people of this country are profoundly interested in religious matters, and it's my business to give the people what they're interested in, whether it's religion or stilt-walking. And let me tell you this, Chrystal. It doesn't end with what I'm proposing now. Dunkerley Publications haven't yet started a paper devoted to nothing but religion. We may do it. We may have a number of religious publications. We shall want a general Religious Editor. This may yet turn into a very big thing," he said with all the warmth he imparted to an idea that had just visited him. "I beg you to bear it in mind, and to begin with, make yourself known to our public by doing what I ask for *Dunkerley's*. Make it as good as you like. Send up the sales. That'll be for your good as well as mine. Remember your shares in the company."

"If I do this at all," Chrystal said icily, "that will hardly enter into my motives."

"Then you'll do it?"

"I haven't said so. I'll consider the matter."

Sir Daniel rose, satisfied that he had his man. "Well, have a good time tomorrow," he said. "I'm sorry I shan't be present. I must be in town. But young Laurie will be coming over. I believe he'll be bringing his cousin Grace Satterfield. You knew her, didn't you, in Manchester?"

Chrystal got up and walked with Dunkerley out into the sunshine. "Yes," he said, "yes. She was a mere child, but I remember her. Yes, indeed."

And when Dunkerley had rounded up Isambard Phyfe and walked away with him towards the waiting carriage, Theodore paced for a time up and down, recalling the days in Manchester – so long ago they seemed! So raw and callow came back the memory of the curate he then was when he had known Grace Satterfield. The child of that preposterous and objectionable person George Satterfield, whose sister Dunkerley had married. But, so far as he could remember, Grace was a nice child. Her father, he recalled, had had the sense to send her away from his own influence. The last time he had seen her she had returned to Manchester on a visit from school. A fair child, he remembered, intelligent and self-possessed. It must be getting on for ten years ago. She would now be in her early twenties. Then, out of the blue, came the memory of a remark that George Satterfield had once made: "You remember my daughter Grace, Mr Chrystal? You met her, I believe, the first night you were in Manchester. She often asks after the gentleman with the beautiful face." Even after so long a passage of time, Chrystal found himself able to be pleased by that remark of the child Grace. It fixed her for him more than anything else could have done, and made vivid for a flashing second that night of damp and fog in Levenshulme when he had seen her for the first time as she clung in the doorway of a cheap little house to Agnes Dunkerley's skirts and the light of a street lamp fell upon his own face.

Dan and Agnes Dunkerley of Palmerston Street, Levenshulme . . . Sir Daniel and Lady Dunkerley of Dickons, Sussex, and Manchester Square, London. Great changes, great changes. What had this passage of time done, he wondered, as he strolled back to his study, what had it done to young Grace Satterfield, who, he now recalled, completing the picture of that long-forgotten moment, had been clutching a formless newspaper parcel, odorous and soggy with tripe!

4

Grace Satterfield knew that the headmaster of Beckwith had been, for a time, a curate in Manchester when she was a child there. She had heard her uncle, Sir Daniel, speak of him in a way which suggested that he and Theodore Chrystal had been intimate then, and only a few months ago Sir Daniel had unearthed an old photograph of those who had been present when the first issue of his first paper, *Hard Facts*, was published. Mr Chrystal was in that picture, and she also: a small, incredible tot, yet indubitably she, just as the scowling little creature photographed at Llanfairfechan was indubitably Hesba Lewison. Well, this Mr Chrystal in the photograph was certainly a handsome creature, but, strangely enough, she could not remember the man himself. Sir Daniel had told her that she had met him several times, but he was gone out of her mind. He was now no more than a creature of report, and the latest report was Laurie's who always spoke of him with respect and a slight aversion.

When Laurie and Hesba had gone off together in the punt, and Grace was sitting at the little desk in her bedroom writing letters, she could not help reflecting, as the beauty of the day distracted her from her task and at last made her give it up altogether: she could not help reflecting, as she got up and stood at her open window gazing into the warm daylight and wishing she had gone with Hesba and Laurie, that this sense of aversion seemed to creep into many people's feelings about Theodore Chrystal. There was Mr Dillworth, the editor of *Dunkerley's*, whom she liked so much because he had been enthusiastic about Hesba's story and had fought Sir Daniel tooth-and-nail over the price of it. She often smiled as she recalled that scene last March in the dining room of Sir Daniel's house in Manchester Square. Only she and Sir Daniel, Hesba and Alec Dillworth had been present. Alec had read the story and reported upon it with immense enthusiasm, and then Sir Daniel had invited him to meet the author at dinner. With the fire crackling cosily, and the table-lights charmingly aglow, all was going with the smooth decorum of a well-arranged social occasion, when Dillworth, who looked, with his thin, excited and exciting face, as though he were born to explode decorum, suddenly said: "What are you paying Miss Lewison, Dan?"

He was the only person she knew who addressed Sir Daniel as Dan, and Sir Daniel preferred this, because if Dillworth, when in a bad mood, called him Sir Daniel, there was an ironic, almost contemptuous inflexion to the word that made her uncle wince. He said now, leaning back and snipping the end of a cigar: "Does that question arise, Alec? Aren't our rates fixed?"

"For God's sake, Dan, have a bit of sense," Dillworth retorted: and at that a tide of angry red, with which Grace was well familiar, began to suffuse Sir Daniel's neck and rise towards his face. Grace rose at this danger signal and gave a beckoning look to Hesba; but Hesba said in her abrupt fashion: "No, no. I want to hear this. This is interesting." Grace sat down again. Alec Dillworth went on: "You've got here, Sir Daniel, something that's going to send up the sales of your magazine. I'm *telling* you that – understand? If I prove to be wrong, you can kick me out in your celebrated ruthless and Napoleonic fashion. All right then. This young woman, I imagine, can write more stories like the one she's given us now. Is that so, Miss Lewison?"

"Oh, yes – yes, indeed. I'm sure I can," said Hesba.

"Very well, then," Alec continued. "When our sales go up, our competitors will want the stuff that makes them go up. Am I being fairly logical for a poet, so far, Sir Daniel?"

Sir Daniel looked at him as if he would like to wring his neck. "In that case," Dillworth went on remorselessly, "what fixes our rates is the law of competition. I didn't make that law, and I don't like it, but you do. And you'll have to abide by it. If Miss Lewison gives us this story at the rates we've fixed, we must give her a contract guaranteeing a rise to be agreed on for each of the next three serial stories she lets us have."

Sir Daniel was silent for a moment, then he said: "Alternatively, we could refuse to publish this story unless Miss Lewison were prepared to sign a contract giving us her next three stories at the same rates."

Dillworth's face blanched with fury. "My God, Dan," he said, "there's only one man I daily want to murder, and that's your friend Theodore Chrystal. I shall have to add you to the list."

Dunkerley smiled and threw a cigar across the table to Alec. "And don't throw things at me as if I were a performing dog," Dillworth shouted. He picked up the cigar and hurled it into the fire.

"You see, Miss Lewison," Sir Daniel said calmly, "what a proprietor must put up with if he wishes to keep a talented editor. After this, you may believe me it's a small thing to part with a little money in order to keep a talented contributor. Alec, fix it up your own way." He smiled and handed his cigar case across the table. Alec took a cigar. "Learn to keep your hair on, Alec," Sir Daniel said, leaning across with a lighted match.

As Grace recalled the scene now, with the thought in her mind of this afternoon's visit to Beckwith, it was Alec's words about Chrystal that stood out. She had no idea what was behind them, but they had been curiously reinforced the afternoon before this when Isambard Phyfe had come back with Sir Daniel from the carriage drive. She liked Mr Phyfe. Herself having enjoyed all the advantages that wealth could bring, she was impressed by his resolute pursuit of those advantages with little beyond his own persistence to back him. She asked him if he had enjoyed his drive, and he replied that the drive had been excellent but the destination chilly. She gathered that when Mr Chrystal had come out of his house with Sir Daniel and been introduced to Isambard, there had been no excess of cordiality. "Cordiality," explained Isambard, who was never unwilling to display samples of his knowledge, like someone selling at the door, "is a word based on the Latin *cor*, which means the heart. Believe me, Miss

Satterfield, nothing flowed from Mr Chrystal's heart in my mean
direction."

Altogether, thought Grace, the headmaster of Beckwith, whom she
was so soon to meet, did not appear to be a person who excited a
universal enthusiasm in the human breast.

5

For these reasons, when she found herself walking with Theodore
Chrystal on the lawn in front of the headmaster's house – that house
which had once been the home of Adela Pinson, Chrystal's wife – she
was surprised by the limpidity of his blue eyes which she had
understood to be cold, by the caressing quality of his voice which
report had called stern, and by the lingering warmth of his handclasp.
These three impressions all flowed into one moment as Chrystal held
her hand for just a second or two longer than custom demanded,
looking at the same time closely into her face and saying: "After so
many years, Miss Satterfield! Of course, you do not remember, but I
remember you very well."

The disturbing thing to Grace was that she *did* remember. Now
that the man was before her, it was as though time had switched her
back to that far-off night of cold and fog in Manchester, as though she
were seeing Chrystal now as she saw him then; and she saw him then,
with the light of a gas lamp falling through the murk upon the
perfection of his young untroubled face, as something superlative,
something beautiful and unattainable beyond the narrow world she
knew.

A tremor shook her heart. The warm June sunlight was flooding
the lawn, falling upon people walking here and there or seated at
small tea tables, from which their chatter and the tinkle of china rose
in brittle sounds into the air, fell upon the round pond near which she
and Theodore Chrystal were standing: a pond whose red fish moved
sluggishly, stirring the white gold-hearted cups of the lilies: fell upon
Laurie and Hesba who were now moving away to find a table for
themselves; and Grace was aware of all this only as something in a
dream. She could tell herself that this was no longer the young
untroubled face that rose upon her sight in Levenshulme, but a face on
which experience was beginning to grave its patterns and designs, that
she, too, was now outside the narrow world of those old days, was not

a child but a woman, was not trammelled by poverty and ignorance, but had wealth and more knowledge than came to most women of her time: in a word, she could tell herself that the gulf which then gaped between her and Theodore Chrystal was there no longer, that she could meet him now as an equal, indeed as one on whose side the balance might well seem to be weighed down.

But in that moment of hypnosis she did not do this, because there was no question of sides or balance: there was nothing but the blacking-out of this moment that stirred so brightly and busily around her and an awareness of a long-past moment so intense that she might be said to be literally living the moment again.

Chrystal could not but feel that something had deeply moved her. He said: "Shall we sit down? I've not yet had tea. Will you join me?"

The words recalled Grace to the present. She saw a great green dragonfly poised on metalled wings above the pond, heard the plop of a startled fish breaking the surface. This world which had been wavering like curtains of mist in the background of her mood steadied, became here and now. "Yes," she said. "Let us have some tea."

She and Chrystal walked across the lawn, threading in and out of tables, he exchanging a word here and there with a boy and his people, receiving, she could not help being aware, adoring glances from many a young woman whom many a young man would like to have for an adorer. He was pleasant, almost gay, with them all: he seemed everything that his reputation had not led her to expect. He was hatless, and the sun shone on his curled golden head and seemed to flash back from the blue deeps of his eyes.

At the farther end of the lawn a great cedar drooped its black-green wings along the turf, and in the shade of this majestic tree a small table was unoccupied. Grace and Chrystal sat themselves down, she in the wispy black whose cobweb texture permitted the white gleam of her arms to shine through, he in the uncomfortable and uncompromising black of his parson's habit.

Some of the schoolboys were acting as waiters, and one, seeing the headmaster come at last to anchorage, hastened forward with a tray. "Thank you, Barnby. Thank you," Chrystal said. His smile was charity's self. "You boys must not wear yourselves out. I think nearly everybody's had tea now, so off you go. Look after yourselves now. Tell the others."

"Yes, sir." And young Barnby sped away to give the glad news, to relieve apprehensive hearts which had contemplated behind anguished smiles the diminishing supplies of ice cream and French pastry.

Grace poured out the tea. Chrystal stretched his long legs and said: "I'm glad to sit down. I'm tired. Young Laurie is a wise boy."

Grace laughed. She was actually able to laugh. The weight of strangeness and gravity was lifted from her heart. She was here, now, in this beautiful garden, with the sun shining, with tea before her, and with a sense of gaiety flooding her. "Yes," she said. "He told us at lunch how wise he was, Mr Chrystal. He seemed well content to leave you to the business of addressing parents, and getting through lunch, and all the rest of it. His sense of duty to you and the school was just strong enough to bring him over to tea. No more."

"They soon forget us," Chrystal said. "I think a schoolmaster's life is the most terrible in the world. While growing old himself he is presented with the spectacle of youth ever renewed. The hungry generations tread us down." He added with a twinkle: "And how hungry they are! Look at young Barnby."

Young Barnby, furnished with a wastepaper basket, was raiding the tables whose occupants were now drifting towards the Boys v. Old Boys cricket match. With a deft shake of plate after plate, he assembled a monstrous load of cream, jam and puff-paste, his brown freckled face gleaming with young greed; then off he went to some rendezvous where, one might imagine, his fellow waiters attended him for the inauguration of a gigantic saturnalia.

Chrystal and Grace shared an intimate smile at this human glimpse. "I wonder," said Chrystal, "whether the instincts of my canons will be so frankly on the surface."

Grace looked at him, puzzled, and he said: "But, of course, you don't know. I'm leaving here. I have accepted a deanery. There's no reason why it shouldn't be known now. I announced my resignation when the governors met here this morning."

Grace's long white hand rested for a moment on his black sleeve, or, rather than resting, seemed to brush it lightly in a spontaneous gesture of goodwill. "I congratulate you, Mr Chrystal," she said, "for I'm sure you must be glad about this. Oh," she added, "don't look surprised if I seemed to know something about you. You're not utterly a stranger, you know. My uncle, Sir Daniel Dunkerley, often speaks of you, and he has always called Beckwith a stopgap. I've no doubt you know Sir Daniel's passion for coming men." They exchanged a frank smile, as though Dan Dunkerley's weakness made a bond between them, at which, slight as it might be, they eagerly grasped. "Well," Grace went on, "he always calls you one of the coming men of the Church. He prides himself that he knew this before you knew it yourself."

Laurie and Hesba got up from their table and, with a wave of the hand, walked away towards the cricket match. Chrystal asked permission to light his pipe, and then he and Grace got up and began to walk, too. But they did not follow the others. They paced to and fro in front of the house, Grace's left hand holding up the long trail of her black skirt, and in her right was the handle of a sunshade whose covering was diaphanous flounced black crêpe. Never did mourning more charmingly become its wearer.

"Sir Daniel," said Theodore, "appears to know things before they reach the public ear. He was here yesterday, you know –"

"With Mr Phyfe," Grace put in with gentle malice, remembering Isambard's pained account of his reception.

"With some young fellow or other. I forget," Theodore said airily. "Anyway, Sir Daniel knew then about this deanery. I had to ask him to keep it to himself. He wished to turn it to advantage."

"I should have expected that," Grace smiled. "A coming man is of no interest to my uncle unless he comes my uncle's way."

"Yes. Well, I used to write for him, anonymously, years ago. For *Hard Facts*."

Grace looked at him in real astonishment. "That is news to me," she said. "It rather surprises me. It's not – is it? – a . . . er – very good paper."

Theo said blandly: "One was young, and rather poor, and a clergyman can always find a good use for money. Of course, *Dunkerley's* is a different thing from *Hard Facts*."

"He has asked you to write for *Dunkerley's*?"

"Yes."

They had come again to the cedar, and there they paused, Grace laying a hand again on his sleeve, with a look on her face that expressed a gentle consternation. "You haven't said you will?" she asked seriously.

"I've said I'd consider it,"Theo answered. "What would your advice be, Miss Satterfield? Don't you think *Dunkerley's* is a worthy medium?"

She looked at him very straightly and frankly; and he was both enchanted and a little daunted by the quiet appraisal of her blue eyes. He was used to women who fluttered and blushed when he deigned to give them his company and consideration; but Grace Satterfield's glance was long and steady and unhurried like summer evening sunlight. At last she said, surprising him: "I don't want you to do it." Only then, she blushed a little, and her glance dropped.

Why am I saying this? What does it matter to me if he chooses to cheapen himself? Grace was asking in her heart; and again her heart, as when she had first met him, stirred and thumped. "I'm sorry," she said, and he was aware now that her voice was a little breathless and uncertain. "I had no right to say that to you, Mr Chrystal."

"But, my dear Miss Satterfield, we are old friends. I claim the privilege of hearing your frank opinion. Why don't you want me to write for Sir Daniel's paper?"

Now her mind was in genuine perplexity. "Please don't press me about this," she said. "I find it hard to say what I mean. But I know Sir Daniel so well, and though I like him – I really am immensely attached to him – everything he has to do with – even the flowers he loves – has to be profitable. Perhaps that's right. After all, if things weren't profitable, I suppose they wouldn't exist at all. And when all's said and done, I'm a rich woman out of all that. You see how confused and muddled I am." And then, with a burst of illumination, she added: "But, you see, I feel there are some things that ought to stand absolutely clear of buying and selling."

"And I'm one of them?"

"Your calling is one of them. *Dunkerley's* is better than anything Sir Daniel has ever done. But still it's catchpenny. That's all I was trying to say."

"What I wrote," he said with a smile, "might be the leaven that leavens the lump. And if Sir Daniel has the knack of assembling the multitude, who am I to refuse to speak my word to them?"

"I've no doubt," said Grace, "that you could give me ten thousand good reasons for doing this, and I could not give you one good reason for your not doing it. All the same, if you do it, I shall feel disappointed."

"It is time I showed myself at the cricket match," Theo said. "Let us go."

CHAPTER THREE

THE DEANERY, King's Mandeville.
December 1st, 1895

MY DEAR DUNKERLEY, I thank you for your letter of November 23rd and apologise for being so long in answering it. You will understand that at all times I have much to do here, and in these early days that much is multiplied to a truly grievous burden. But I have no doubt that the necessary strength for the discharge of my task will be granted now, as ever. At the moment it chances that I have a rare hour of leisure, and I shall give you some account of how I find myself circumstanced.

It is, of course, a great joy to me that I have been called to labour in this county of Somerset wherein I was born. I am blessed in other ways, for if King's Mandeville is, as you once took occasion to remind me, insignificant as a bishopric, it is abundant in beauty. The close surrounds a green circular lawn, and all the ecclesiastical houses are of honey-coloured stone, tiled with red. From my study window there is nothing to be seen but these charming houses, and the lawn, and some noble horse-chestnut trees. Perhaps you will say, my dear Dunkerley, a conventional beauty, but we can too easily despise the conventions – those good manners that have taken so long to build up. I, at least, do not fail to esteem them.

Among my blessings I count the discovery – the rediscovery – of a veritable Dorcas and Mary combined. You perhaps remember her – that good soul Mrs Hornabrook with whom I lodged when first I knew you in Manchester? I used in those days to think her an old woman, but the older we ourselves become

43

the more we modify our views as to what age is really "old." I am sure that when I am eighty, a man of seventy will seem to me a youngster, and a man of ninety to be just "getting on." Anyhow, Mrs Hornabrook, even today, has a youthful heart. My meeting with her was indeed an extraordinary chance. A dear friend of mine, holding a vicarage in Weston-super-Mare, had died, and at the widow's request I took the funeral service. Another funeral was in progress at the same time and when all was over the processions from the two graves came together. It was then that I recognised Mrs Hornabrook, in black and weeping bitterly. I learned that her daughter, of whom I saw little in those old days, had got into the clutches of a villain who had brought her to this remote place – as Mrs Hornabrook conceived it – and there abandoned her. The poor girl had died at her own hand.

To meet me in such a place and at such a time seemed to Mrs Hornabrook as if the finger of God had intervened in her affairs; and who shall say whether indeed that may not have been so? She was distraught, and I brought her here intending that she should do what I imagine she had never done before in her life – that is, take a holiday, waited on hand and foot. But before a week was out, she was waiting on me hand and foot. It seems her nature to do so, and each to his task. She has consented now to remain here permanently as my housekeeper, an arrangement greatly to my comfort, permitting me to go undistracted about my work.

I expect Miss Satterfield has already given you some account of the visit she and that strange girl Miss Lewison made here at the end of the autumn. They had been to stay with Sarah Armitage, the novelist, in Cornwall, in order, so far as I could gather, that Miss Lewison might crow over her, and they broke their journey in Somerset on the way back. I am never happy with people of what is called an artistic temperament, so often an excuse for mere moral slovenliness and disorder, and I found Miss Lewison no exception. I thought Miss Satterfield was developing into a grave and delightful woman.

By the way, since you first proposed to me in June that I should contribute regularly to your magazine, you have several times urged me to come to a decision. I have now done so. I do not see my way to do so as you wish.

I must be in London over Christmas, and I hope I may have the pleasure of seeing you. In the meantime, all my good wishes to you and Lady Dunkerley. Give them, too if you please, to Miss Satterfield.

Yours sincerely,

Theodore Chrystal.

Dunkerley at once telegraphed: "Use my house while in London"; and Chrystal replied: "With greatest pleasure."

2

At the top of the house in Manchester Square were a sitting room, bedroom and bathroom known to Laurie Dunkerley and his sister Dinah as "grandfather's apartment," and to Sir Daniel as "old Sim's den." As he grew older – and sixty-seven was "getting on" – old Sim cultivated consciously the manner of an old soldier. But not the mere non-commissioned soldier he had been in his Crimean days. Looking at himself now in the mirror on his simple dressing table that flanked the hard bed on which he slept beneath one blanket, he thought any one might take him for an old general. His frock-coat embraced him tightly. His grey trousers were strapped beneath the boots out of which rose his stork-like legs. He slapped on his tall silk hat, took up his malacca cane, and approved the orchid at his buttonhole, the defiant skewers of his moustache. His thin nose was webbed with blue veins. He descended the stairs holding himself straight. A hansom cab was waiting for him, as he had ordered. "Victoria," he said, settling back and sniffing the air that promised snow. The afternoon was drawing in, and already the lights were on in some windows.

This was a job he liked: going to meet Dinah. Dinah was eighteen and she was coming home for the Christmas holidays from Geneva, where she was at a finishing school. Extraordinary notions Dan and Agnes had about how to bring up children. Finishing school . . . Never heard of such a thing . . . But if Dan wanted it, that was all right. What Dan wanted was always all right to Sim. And certainly Dinah was all right, a merry girl. Ever since she had been away – a year now – he had insisted on doing this small duty of meeting her at Victoria at holiday time. He felt gallant. It was good, at sixty-seven, to be able to feel like that about meeting a merry girl.

Everything, taking it by and large, was good at the moment, old Sim reflected. It was good to be sitting here, in this sharp air spiced with winter, behind this well-moving grey animal, with the darkening expanses of the Park reaching away on his right and the Park Lane windows lighting up on his left. It would have pleased him to live in Park Lane, so that he could, whenever he chose, look out on the Park. He liked it as it was now, when the trees were bare and the street lamps turned their torches up into the traceries and patterns of the twigs and boughs. But Dan wouldn't have Park Lane. He saw something symbolic in Manchester Square. Manchester Square for Manchester men. Well, if Dan wanted it, that was all right too. He breathed on the silver head of his malacca cane, rubbed it up in the palm of his pigskin glove, and noted with satisfaction the procession of a dozen dreary scarecrows shuffling with sandwich-boards along the gutter: *Dunkerley's: Christmas Double Number*. For a flashing moment he wondered what sort of a Christmas *they* would have. Then he felt in his pocket to be certain that Dinah's present was there. He never met her without taking a present.

3

She was as delightful as he had expected. Suddenly all the stir and noise of the station – the coughing of engines, the shrill whine of escaping steam, the jostling crowds, the porters, the rumbling luggage barrows, the lights on the gay merchandise of the bookstalls – concentrated themselves into this one small vital figure, standing on tip-toe to kiss his cold leathery cheek. A fur muff was on the hand that reached up to go round his neck; her collar was of fur, and the little round hat on her head was fur too. Her merry brown eyes, between the hat that came down so low and the collar that was turned up so high, seemed to twinkle like a small confiding animal's, and the warmth of her kiss made his cheek tingle.

"Oh, Grandfather," she cried, "where's your overcoat? It's a perishing night."

"Overcoat? Overcoat?" he grunted, pleased to be fussed over. "You know I never wear the da – the stupid things. Where's your luggage – eh? Have you got a porter?"

"Oh, yes. I forgot. Mr Boys is looking after that."

"Mr Boys? Who's Mr Boys? I never heard of any Mr Boys."

"He's half-French," she said, "or rather, I should say, half-Swiss, because people living in Switzerland are Swiss, I suppose, though they talk French."

He held her at arm's length, drinking in the fascination of her youth and gaiety. "I don't know what you're talking about," he said. "French. Swiss. Mr Boys. You gabble on just as your mother used to when she was younger. I could never make head or tail of her chatter."

"Well, there he is," she cried, breaking from him. "Oh, Felix, here we are. This is grandfather."

Mr Boys was self-possessed. He looked about as old as Dinah. He was wearing a bowler hat, which he raised, held out his hand gravely, and said: "How do you do, sir. This is Miss Dunkerley's luggage. Six pieces."

4

Mr Felix Boys, thought Sim, might be half-French, or half-Dutch, or half-Japanese if he liked, but he looked wholly English with his fair freckled face and blue eyes. He had shaken hands, protested that he had not a minute to spare, that he must be off home at once; and then there he was, sitting with them at tea in the station tearoom, deferentially calling Dinah Miss Dunkerley every time she called him Felix.

Dinah poured out the tea, and Sim thought it was nice to be there enjoying the company of two such attractive young things, each so obviously interested in the other; but all the same he was wondering what Sir Daniel and Agnes would have to say about this. He remembered clearly a far-off frosty Sunday morning in Manchester when Dan could not have been much older than this boy was now, and he had walked across the street, accosted Miss Agnes Satterfield, and told Sim that here was the girl who was to be his wife. As casually as that Dan had set about his own affairs of the heart; but Sim doubted whether Sir Daniel Dunkerley would approve of his daughter being picked up in the same way. Perhaps he ought to have cut out this tea, though it was a treasured part of these homecoming meetings with Dinah. He ought to have put her into a cab and whisked her straight away to Manchester Square. But that, it seemed, would not have helped, for here was Dinah chattering again: "It's lucky Felix lives in Manchester Square, too. Now we can all drive home together."

"Manchester Square, eh?" said Sim. "Boys . . . Boys . . . Oh, yes, Mr Justice Boys . . ."

"Yes, sir – my father," said young Felix.

"It's all really quite simple," Dinah burst in. "You see, Felix's father married a Swiss lady named Colet, and that's what makes Felix half-Swiss. And Miss Colet's sister married a German-Swiss named Holst. But Felix's mother's been dead for years, and so has Mr Holst, and that's why Felix has lived in Switzerland. Madame Holst, who runs the school where I am, is his aunt, and he's lived with her for years. He takes some of the English classes, and they're terribly popular."

Yes, they would be, thought Sim, buttering a muffin and considering that fair ingenuous face. "And what now?" he asked. "Are you staying at home, Mr Boys?"

"I'm here just for the holidays, sir," said Felix. "Then I'm going to a crammer's. My father expects me to be ready for Oxford by next autumn."

"Ready, indeed!" Dinah cried indignantly. "You talk French and German like a native. My brother's at Oxford, and you should hear him! Why, he couldn't order himself a boiled egg in a French cook-shop."

"I'm all right with the living languages," Felix said with a smile. "It's the dead 'uns I've got to swot at."

"If Laurie pronounces his dead 'uns like his live 'uns," Dinah said, "Julius Caesar must turn in his grave."

Old Sim rose. "Well, we'd better be off."

"Oh, and Grandfather," said Dinah. "There's nothing *irregular* about all this. Mother and Madame Holst arranged that, as Felix was travelling at the same time as me, he should be my *escort*."

"Rather!" Felix said earnestly. "Otherwise . . . dash it all . . ."

Oh, well, that's all right, Sim thought with relief. "H'm. They might have told me," he said, with a sniff. "Well, my dear, take a look at this."

It was a lovely travelling watch in a red morocco case. She put her arms round his neck and kissed him again. "Oh, dear," she cried with comical dismay. "How everyone spoils me. I shall be utterly ruined!"

"Well . . ." young Felix began; then changed his mind about whatever he was going to say, blushed, and hurried out in search of a cab. As he was leaving them outside Sir Daniel's house, Dinah said: "You must join us at dinner on Christmas Eve. I'll arrange that."

Old Sim had hurried up the steps and rung the bell. He turned and looked down into the square. The darkness was fully come, with a sharpening cold. A street lamp shed its light on the huddled head-hanging horse, the cab, the two young people. Except for them, it was a morose spectacle. A little snow was falling, and the cabman was pulling trunks down from the top of the cab. Dinah and Felix seemed unaware of any of it: the worn-out old horse, the black inimical sky, the falling snow. The light of the lamp fell upon their faces, which were radiant, and showed the whiteness beginning to powder Dinah's fur hat and the boy's bowler. If I were not here, old Sim thought, they would kiss one another. They made a pretty picture but all the same they made him feel sad. He was aware suddenly of being old. It was so long since he, little older than they, had felt the snow – a heavier snow than this – falling out of the Crimean sky. The door opened, and there in the hall, behind the butler, was Lady Dunkerley. "Well, she's here, Agnes," he said, and plodded straight away to his room under the roof. A good fire was burning, and he let himself down into the chair before it. An hour's snooze before he need begin to think of preparing for dinner. It was nice to have a place of his own, so that no one need know of this weakness – this afternoon sleep that he found so necessary.

Dinah kissed her mother fondly. "Where's grandfather?" she asked. "He's disappeared very suddenly."

"Don't make a noise, darling," Agnes said. "I expect he's gone up for his afternoon sleep."

5

Of course, Agnes thought, I ought to count my blessings. Being Lady Dunkerley was something, after all. There was Lady This and Lady That, and when you heard their names announced at a drawing room or as you entered some great public gathering, you wondered who they were. You had never heard of them before, and ten to one you would never hear of them again. But when Sir Daniel and Lady Dunkerley were announced – well, that was another matter. You couldn't take up the papers without finding that Sir Daniel Dunkerley had presided at something, or opened something, or spoken in support of something or in condemnation of something. And he liked her to be with him. She had lost her terror of public occasions. She had only to keep her mouth shut and leave everything to Dan, and she was all right. He was on top of the world, and he liked her to stand there with him, holding his hand. He had a short way with anyone who did not give Lady Dunkerley her due. Sitting now in a billowy armchair by the fire whose gleaming flames made her bedroom look so charming, she remembered an occasion when Dan had come into the room where she was and had thrown a square of pasteboard on to the table under her eyes.

"Look at that!" he said. His face was flushed.

Somebody had requested the pleasure of Sir Daniel Dunkerley's company at some glittering occasion, and after the words "Sir Daniel" Dan had written in red ink, underlined, "and Lady."

Agnes looked at it with a puzzled wrinkling of the brows, and then turned a questioning face to Dan.

"Got to teach these beggars," he said angrily. "I'll send this back to 'em, amended."

"Teach them what?" Agnes innocently asked.

Alec Dillworth had happened to be present, grinning as usual at the comedy. "Why, Lady Dunkerley," he interposed, "teach 'em that everything Sir Daniel's light falls upon deserves the world's obeisance."

She had often seen Dan angry with Alec Dillworth, but that day she thought he would strike him.

"Who asked you to interfere?" he shouted. "This is nothing to do with me at all; I tell you I'm not thinking of myself. Do you suggest I can't see my wife as a person in her own right, with courtesies due to herself?"

Dillworth had made no answer. He had stood there, no longer smiling, but wearing the masked enigmatic look which made a guard Dan could never penetrate. And whenever, later, Agnes recalled that moment, it was this look of Alec's that remained in her mind, not Dan's final shouted protest: "They'll have us together or leave us both out."

Sitting there by the fire, waiting for Dan whom she could hear moving about in the dressing room next door, Agnes was content to have things as they were. Alec Dillworth had been right, of course.

She knew as well as he did – though she could not have expressed the thought – that Dan loved to take her about so that someone who knew what he had been should see now what he was. And what was wrong with that? If Dan wanted it she was prepared to give it to him, and more.

.The Christmas number of *Dunkerley's* lay on the table alongside her chair. The cover, which had been plain through eleven months of the year, was coloured for this once. Holly, mistletoe, the windows of a village church shining orange across snow. She turned the pages idly. An article signed simply "The Editor." That was Alec Dillworth. "With this number we end a year's work, and we end it with both thankfulness and satisfaction. Thankfulness to a band of readers who have grown in numbers with each issue, and whose support has been our assurance that we are fulfilling a task that needed to be done. Satisfaction because we have been able to give to these readers the best work of writers whether already known, like Miss Sarah Armitage, or making here the first steps in careers that are destined to be illustrious. Notable among these, Miss Hesba Lewison . . ."

Agnes smiled. Hesba Lewison . . . She always had to be cracked up. Those were Dan's orders. She was Dan's lucky find of the year. It was *The Happy Go Luckies* that had turned the corner for *Dunkerley's* and made it not just another monthly magazine but the magazine that everyone wanted. Well, good luck to her, Agnes thought. She was a nice little creature, if a bit of an ugly duckling.

She heard Dan's footsteps soft on the carpet behind her, and, raising her eyes to the mirror over the mantelpiece, rejoiced in the appearance of his image. For all the grey at his temples, he was still a young, handsome man. His evening clothes suited him well. He bent down, kissed the top of her head, leaned over her shoulder, and took up the magazine from her lap. He flipped the pages till he came to the instalment of *The Happy Go Luckies*. "The next thing," he said, coming round and standing between her and the fire, "is that this will have to be published as a book."

The next thing . . . How well she had got to know that phrase! From the time when *Hard Facts* was the next thing after the printer's shop on the Stockport Road in Manchester, there had always been another next thing beckoning Dan on.

"Ah, well," she said, "that won't be your business. At any rate you're not a publisher."

"Not at the moment." He stared at the wall, away beyond the top of her head, and she knew that now she was not there. "Look," he said after a while. "When we serialise a book by someone like Sarah Armitage, there's nothing we can do. She's an old stager. She already has her contracts with publishers so far as the book rights are concerned. But it's another matter with a youngster we're starting off. We could have it understood that publishing a story as a serial gave us the book rights, too. This *Happy Go Lucky* stuff is going to sell a hundred thousand copies. I'll bet my boots on that. Well – that's money."

"But do we need any more money, Dan?" she asked.

The question was so absurd that, almost literally, he did not hear it. "There'll be other people besides Hesba Lewison," he said. "And when the thing's really on its feet authors will come to us as they do to any other publisher, without reference to the magazine at all. It would be something for Laurie. I could put him in charge of that side of things."

"But, Dan, Laurie doesn't take the slightest interest in books. You know as well as I do that he doesn't read a book from one year's end to another."

She loved the frank boyish grin that broadened his face. "What's that got to do with it?" he asked. "A publisher's business isn't to read books. It's to sell 'em. He can get someone else to do the reading for him."

He looked down at her affectionately, admiring the flicker and scintillation of the flames in the shallow corrugations of blue silk falling from her knees to the floor. "You don't get a minute older, Ag," he said. "I find it hard to believe that you'll be a grandmother in a year or two."

"Well," she exclaimed, surprised, " I see no signs of that!"

"Don't you?" he teased her. "Do I have to be the watch-dog on the domestic side as well as where the shekels are minted? You mark my words, even if I didn't start a publishing house, the *Happy Go Lucky* money would stay in the family."

Her eyes went round with surprise. "But, Dan . . . !"

He laughed with frank enjoyment. "I'll say no more. Here! Give us your hand. No, the other one."

He slipped the ring on to her finger — a lovely square-cut emerald in gold claws.

"But, my dear, *tomorrow's* Christmas Day."

"Who's talking about Christmas Day? This is simply a present for a good granny."

"And I've got so much jewellery."

"Well, you should thank God you're not a Turk. I'd dangle rings from your nose if the custom allowed it. You're worth it, Ag. D'you know that?"

She couldn't answer him, and they went down together to the drawing room.

6

Grace Satterfield, Laurie and Hesba Lewison were already there, and it would have been strange indeed if Agnes' first glance had not fallen upon Laurie and Hesba. Hesba was all dusky red — even the shoe that peeped from beneath the hem of her red velvet dress was catching a ruby light from the fire. Laurie was standing beside her chair — very tall and fair in his evening clothes.

Hesba . . . Hesba Lewison . . . It was almost a stranger's name. It was the name of someone she had heard continuously discussed and whom she had met once or twice. She could not help turning it over on her mind's palate. Was it to become one of the flavours of all the days of her life?

She liked this drawing room. It was so different from so many drawing rooms that she had come to know. They were crowded, jumbled, embarrassed with a rich chaos of furniture and ornament. This was Dan's idea, of course. "Have you ever looked at Whistler's pictures?" Of course, she hadn't.

"You've never so much as heard his name," Dan accused her. "Space. That's the idea. Wall-space, floor-space. Wide spreads of simple colour. Down with the penny bazaar."

And this room was the result. You could walk in it. The carpet was almost white. The walls were cream picked out in gilt, and there was nothing on them but a few portraits. Dan had begun to accumulate the ancestral gallery of the Dunkerleys. Old Sim shone over the mantelpiece; she herself and Dan shared a wall. An electric chandelier, richly shaded, filled the room with a cheerful glow.

She looked now at the portraits. Two generations already. She looked at Hesba, and pictured her upon the wall. She saw for the first time what a vivid and forceful young thing she was: the eager eyes, lighting the sallow face, the wiry energy of the black, springing hair. The girl had risen as she came into the room. Her shortness seemed to emphasize her contained strength. "She's a regular little bomb," Agnes thought.

"Sit down, my dear," she said. She took Hesba by the hand and led her to a couch. They sat side by side. "Tell me what you think about this room."

"It's charming, and I think you're so wise not to have smothered it with Christmas decorations. I should hate it to look like the cover of *Dunkerley's* Christmas Number."

"Oh, my husband wouldn't have that! Oh dear no! No fear of that."

"Good. Then I suppose we shall not have to wear paper caps out of crackers after dinner. I couldn't bear that. To see old people making fools of themselves in that way is such a depressing sight."

"What do you mean – old?" Laurie asked, coming and standing before them. "You don't call yourself old, do you? I feel about five sometimes."

"All the same, I *don't like* paper caps," said Hesba with decision; and Agnes had a sudden feeling that this girl had, for some reason, a need to defend herself to give nothing away, to slip into no levity. She had not the easy gravity and self-possession of Grace Satterfield, who was now talking to Sir Daniel and seemed no more to think of defending herself from folly than a cool lily would do, existing in its own right; she had not, either, the expansive wayward caprice of Dinah, who now bustled into the room looking as if she could with impunity commit any folly, and asking with an ingenuous disappointment and lack of reserve: "Oh, isn't Felix here yet?" No, Agnes thought; everything that matters about this girl is packed down under the surface, like a kitchen fire after you've banked it up.

"Come here, Dinah," she said. "Let me have a look at you."

Dinah gave a perfunctory pirouette before the couch, displaying her flounced dress of sherry-yellow silk. "All right?" she lightly asked.

"Yes, you look very well. Now you may sit down. Mr Boys will be here in his own good time."

"You're lucky to get him at all," said Laurie. "A queer household, I should say, when the son and heir spends Christmas Eve at a stranger's, after not having seen his own people for heaven knows how long.".

Dinah gave him a mocking smile. "A lot you know about it," she said. "To begin with, there are no people, as you call them. Felix's father is just an old grump who doesn't give two straws—"

"Dinah, my dear," Agnes chided her. "Should you speak like that? — especially about someone whom you can't possibly know."

"I know enough," the girl answered lightly. "I can put two and two together. He went off to spend Christmas in Scotland, the very day after Felix got home, and there's no one at all in that dark old house except Miss Boys, the judge's sister, and a couple of maids. And Miss Boys is a real old gorgon with a moustache. A nice place to spend the Christmas holiday!"

"Well," said Laurie, "I'd rather spend it without the judge than with him. Isn't he known as 'the hanging judge?' Fancy having dinner with a chap who's just sentenced some poor devil to death! The hand that passes the potatoes dangles the noose! B-r-r! I'd hate the sight of him."

A sudden spasm of horror passed over Dinah's childish face. "What filthy things you say," she cried in disgust; and Lady Dunkerley intervened sharply; "Children! Children! Need you discuss such matters?"

Hesba had listened impassively to this exchange. Now she said surprisingly: "And yet it is necessary to remember that these things exist."

Dinah gave her a long cool glance. "Well," she said. "For a writer of fairy tales . . . !"

7

The electric plant in the cellar of Sir Daniel Dunkerley's house lived a capricious life. At times it dispensed light joyfully, but at others precariously, and occasionally most treacherously, plunging the whole house into sudden darkness. In the house opposite, in which Sir Horace Boys had known a brief ecstasy, ended when the birth of Felix meant the death of his mother, light was gloomily rationed out, once the day was done, with lamps and candles. There was not even gas, and Mr Justice Boys did not notice its absence. Now, after nearly twenty years of loneliness, he noticed little that had not to do with his work. His sister, who kept house for him, rarely saw him. He breakfasted alone, and after his day in the courts he would dine at his club. Then returning to Manchester Square, he would take his papers to his study where a trinity of three-branched candlesticks punctuated the length of his table. He would not be seen again till the morning.

It was of this room with the nine candles burning on the table, with the fire a dull smother of hardly glowing dust and ashes, the walls banked almost to the ceiling with brown-backed books, that Felix most often thought when he thought of home. It was to this room that he was summoned when his father wished to see him; he could hardly recall an occasion when they had casually met and exchanged careless casual words. A meeting was always in response to a call; it had the texture not of conversation but of examination; and though Felix always came well out of these encounters, for he was, despite his cherubic and ingenuous face, a serious youth, nevertheless it was never without a sense of apprehension and dismay that he presented himself to his father.

He was glad now that his father had gone to Scotland. It might not, otherwise, have been easy to accept the invitation to dine at Sir Daniel Dunkerley's. If Mr Justice Boys had none who could intimately be called friends, there were at any rate houses where he occasionally dined, and Felix knew that they were not houses like Sir Daniel's. There would have been a regular inquisition about Sir Daniel. Who was he? What did one know about him? Ought one to know about him? Felix could imagine the distaste with which his father would pick up a copy of *Hard Facts* or even of *Dunkerley's*.

All the same, he thought, awkwardly knotting his white tie before the mirror in his bedroom, I'm glad I'm going. Dinah had talked a lot about her house. The fascination of contrast was strong upon his young heart. Across the road, they had fires in the bedrooms and electric lighting. Think of that! He looked about his small lugubrious chamber, lighted only by two candles, where never to his knowledge a fire had burned, and pulled on his coat with resolution. Above all, he wanted youth. There were girls enough at his aunt's school – too many. He was sick and tired of them, glad he was not going back. They did not mean youth to him: they were just girls and the day's work. Broken off from the mass, shining in her own right, Dinah was something else: something apart from all that, apart from this dark house and his well-meaning aunt and the three ancient maids who looked like Fates. He thought of Dinah as existing appropriately in a place where the lights were at full blaze all the time, and the fires had eyes that were not sullen and withdrawn but dancing and merry. The square, when he stepped through the door, seemed no darker than the house he was leaving. He ran with a boyish eagerness round the small railed garden towards the cheerful windows opposite.

8

Sir Daniel's father, old Sim Dunkerley, had come down to the drawing room just as Felix arrived, and everybody, Sir Daniel noted, sipping a glass of sherry, was present now except the Dean.

Theodore Chrystal, whom the Dunkerleys had so intimately known ever since he was a fledgling curate in Manchester, was now always spoken of as "the Dean". Nothing which heightened Sir Daniel's own prestige was neglected. Theo had for a long time been the "Headmaster," so that anyone meeting him with Sir Daniel and knowing of his association with Beckwith should not think him a common schoolmaster. Now he was the Dean, for the benefit of those unable to read the significance of gaiters and other tiddly bits and pieces of attire.

It was characteristic of the Dean, Sir Daniel was thinking, that he should be the last to appear. He was staying here in Manchester Square as a guest, and ever since lunchtime he had been at work in his room. He hadn't even to change: a parson's rig was good for breakfast and dinner alike: but all the same he would want to make an entrance. He was not one of those people who came into a room: he made an entrance.

Effective enough, too, Dan thought, as Theo now appeared. He moved at once towards his hostess, took her hand as though he had not seen her for weeks, and held it in a warm pressure as he apologised for keeping everybody waiting. "Now I really am through," he exclaimed, leaving them all to imagine the mountains of work that he had assaulted and subdued while they had been engaged in the trivialities of changing their shirts and frocks. "I can promise you that tomorrow I am wholly yours."

He looked round the company, with an especial beam for young Felix Boys, the only one he had not till then met. Lady Dunkerley presented the youth, and Dinah, no more intimidated by gaiters and golden curls than she was by most things in life, at once cried: "Oh, Mr Chrystal, Felix is here to be prepared for Oxford. He's been living abroad for years, and now he's got to go to a crammer's, to be ready for next autumn. Couldn't you take him on? After all, you *have* been a schoolmaster, and I should think Felix would find it agreeable down there in the country with you. And I suppose now you're a Dean you have all sorts of canons and people to do the work, don't you? You could easily find the time. It would make me much easier in my mind. Didn't you say that old Mrs Hornabrook from Manchester was looking after you now? I suppose she'd feed Felix well. Manchester women have a reputation for that sort of thing."

Felix, uncomfortable enough already in his rarely-worn evening clothes, blushed and stammered: "Really, Miss Dunkerley . . . You must excuse her, sir."

"I don't see anything wrong with the notion," Dinah defended herself, aware of a general constraint, which, however, was not reflected in the Dean's features. He was smiling with easy amiability, and behind this unperturbed façade he was thinking: "How little money does, after all!" The girl was her mother all over again. He remembered how Agnes Dunkerley used to run on like a brook in spate, a deluge of inanity. Dinah had learned to put commas and full stops into her speech. That was all the difference. He looked at her over a glass of sherry that Sir Daniel had handed him, but addressed himself to Felix.

"So, Mr Boys, this impetuous young woman would sweep you off into the heart of the country, to fritter your time away with an ancient schoolmaster now turned into a dean eating his head off in idleness! We must save you from that fate. And I must protect my own reputation. You look an acute observer, and I should hesitate to expose to you the scandalous emptiness of my days."

He drank off his sherry and put down the glass with a decisiveness which said that that was that. A gong began to fill the hall and stairway with a mounting clangour. Suppressing the impetuous urge to turn at once to Grace Satterfield, Theo gave his arm to Lady Dunkerley and followed Sir Daniel and Grace through the door and downstairs to the dining room.

9

Hesba sat next to Laurie, and Agnes, plagued by the words that Daniel had let fall upstairs, could not keep her eyes off them. Of course, she told herself Daniel was always able to persuade himself that a thing must happen because he wanted it to happen, and he wanted this to happen, or he would never have mentioned it so complacently. But for the life of her she could not see a ray of response on Hesba's part to Laurie's obvious obsession. The trouble with the boy was that he was, still, so much of a boy, and Hesba, she suspected, young as she was, was mature. Her mind seemed to turn with more readiness and interest to old Sim, sitting on her other side, and full of reminiscent chatter, than to Laurie whose life had given him nothing much to talk about. And why, Agnes wondered, when they had returned to the drawing room, and the men were still downstairs, did such a change come over the girl when she suddenly announced: "Please don't think it too rude of me, Lady Dunkerley, but I must go soon." Now she no longer seemed to be holding down an excitement. She seemed to have given rein to it, as though she had made a decision which she had fought against, but which, once taken, pleased her.

Grace Satterfield joined her aunt in a little polite pressure upon Hesba to stay, but she was not to be moved, nor would she say why this decision, evidently sudden, had been taken. "I must be away by ten," she persisted, and relapsed into a moodiness that made her inaccessible.

She was thinking of the scene that had taken place yesterday in the handsome buildings of Dunkerley Publications on the Embankment. She had finished her new book *The Well-Bred Dragon* which it was hoped would begin to run in *Dunkerley's* as soon as *The Happy Go Luckies* was finished. But Alec Dillworth had to read it first and give his decision upon it. She had taken the manuscript along and found him in his room, high up over the Thames. He was standing at the window looking out into the closing winter day. Mists were rising upon the river. The barges were grey moving smudges on the lighter grey water, and here and there lights began to be lit. For a time she did not speak. He did not know that she was standing there, and as he was absorbed in the contemplation of the scene without, so she became absorbed in the contemplation of him. The small thin figure, lithe as a cat, no taller than herself, with the fair untidy hair and almost haggard face, had always interested her, given her the sense of a person rich in experience of suffering. Now, too, a sense of his loneliness rushed upon her, a sense that he was not so much looking at what lay beyond the window as seeing landscapes of the imagination – far-flung and desolate enough, she imagined.

Pascal avait son gouffre, avec lui se mouvant.

She recalled the words she had uttered to Laurie Dunkerley on a day of high summer; and something caused her to want to retreat, to leave Alec to his musings. She began to move quietly towards the door when her slight movement caught his ear and he swung round.

"I didn't want to disturb you," she said. "You seemed busy."

He laughed. "Busy? Why!" And then: "Oh, I see what you mean. You understand that, do you? But of course you would."

She wouldn't follow up his mood. "Look," she said. "Here's the new stuff. I'll leave it for you to read."

No light had yet been turned on in the room, and now that he stood with his back to the window, his head was an anonymous silhouette. But her face was to the window, and as she stood there, a tight and trim little figure, wearing a coat and hat of astrachan, with the bundle containing her manuscript tucked under one arm, she was aware of the closeness of his scrutiny, of his observing her with a frank sustained interest she had not known before. For an appreciable time they stood thus, saying nothing, but each aware of tension, of the invisible spark flashing from one to another. It was Hesba who ended that. She pulled herself out of that constraint, put her manuscript down on the table, and said: "Well, there it is. For better or worse."

And as she was sitting now in Sir Daniel Dunkerley's drawing room, seeming to Grace and Agnes so inaccessible and withdrawn, it was these words of her own that were back in her mind, divorced from their first intention and speaking with a significance that both dismayed and attracted her: "Well, there it is. For better or worse."

For, quite suddenly, not having given the matter much thought since yesterday, she had decided that she must see Alec Dillworth.

When she spoke and placed the manuscript on the table, he seemed unwilling to break the brief spell. He remained still for a moment, his figure blocked darkly against the *grisaille* of the window, then said in badly pronounced words: "*J'ai plus de souvenirs que si j'avais mille ans.*"

It seemed to Hesba an enchanted moment. She had been thinking of him in terms of a line of Baudelaire. Now he had answered her in words from the same poet; and, as though this had completed a circle, he immediately stepped forward, snapped on the light, and took up the small brown paper parcel. He weighed it in his hand for a moment, then opened a drawer and threw it in. "Why should I bother to read it?" he asked. "It will be all right."

"I'm lucky to have so complacent an editor," she answered lightly, glad to escape back into the banality of customary chat. Her hands were trembling a little, and she put them both into the pockets of her coat.

"Oh, well," he said, "I'm not so complacent as all that. I shall read it in due season, but I'm not worrying about it. I say it will be all right."

He sank into his chair before the desk, and, seated, his body seemed smaller. Though she was herself short, Hesba looked down on the top of his head. He threw his head back with a characteristic gesture, shaking the lank hair out of his eyes. "What do you call it?" he asked, without interest.

She told him; and he said: "Yes; that's all right." And then added, not to her surprise: "I was thinking what a bloody world this is."

"Yes," she said. "So I imagined."

"How do you manage to suggest – as you do – in writing mere fairy tales, that you, too, are aware what a bloody world it is?"

She laughed defensively. "What a carefully contrived sentence!"

She was pleased to see a smile come out like sunshine on a pale landscape. "It was, wasn't it? I shall become insufferable if I stay in this job much longer. At least we needn't stay in this room much longer. Come and have some tea."

He was aware of the hesitation that at once stiffened her attitude. "Oh, come, come!" he said. "You must learn the first principles of the world you live in. It is a world wherein ambitious writers leap at the chance of intimacy with editors and publishers, and editors themselves grovel on their knees before their proprietors. It's high time I composed an ode to Rare Dan Dunkerley."

He got into his overcoat as he spoke, took up his hat, and stood holding open the door of the room. She saw, beneath his banter, his need for comfort and reassurance. There was supplication in his eyes. "All right," she said in her short gruff way.

The evening had closed in when they got into the street, and there was a sharpness in the air. Alec pulled the collar of his coat up about his ears, and in silence they climbed the narrow way that led to Fleet Street. But they did not quite reach Fleet Street. Just before the two roads met, Alec turned into a teashop – a small cosy place, gratefully warm. "Of course," he said, with his rueful grin, "the best editors, when they seek to lure important contributors, take 'em to a slap-up restaurant and lash 'em up with oysters and champagne. But this'll have to do for us."

It was an old-fashioned place – nothing "slap-up" about it. The seats against the wall were of red plush. A coal fire was burning. "I like a *homely* place," Alec said; and she had a sense that this was a search for fulfilment, a desire to furnish what had been an empty room in his life.

"I wanted to talk to you," he said, when the tea and muffins were on the table, "about *The Happy Go Luckies*. It's high time you began to think about the book rights. Have you done anything about that yet?"

She said that she hadn't, and Alec went on with what seemed to her a comical air of adult wisdom: "You know, you young women want someone to look after you. I suppose if I hadn't taken the matter up you'd have let the rights go to the first rascal publisher who came along to steal them from you. Well, I've been looking after your interests."

"That's kind of you," she said. "But I don't think I should have been victimised anyhow. I was Sarah Armitage's secretary too long for that. What Sarah doesn't know about making publishers toe the line isn't worth knowing. I should have done something in time. I just hadn't bothered. You needn't worry about me."

"I was hoping I might. Worrying about you was just beginning to give me a new interest in life."

They were sitting side by side on the red plush seat. She was glad of that, because his words troubled her, and she need not look him in the face. She knew that when he said he was worrying about her, he

62

meant her and not her book. She asked: "Well, what have you been doing about the book?"

"I spoke to Carterson about it."

"That's Sarah's publisher."

"Yes. I don't think you could do better. He jumped at the chance and said he'd draw up a contract at once. He did, too; and what a contract!"

"Was it good?"

"Good! It was taking bread out of an orphan's mouth. I sent it back with a number of interesting amendments. Then we had an interview – by turns heated and chilly. Finally he agreed to all but one of my terms, and I've got the new contract in my pocket now. All you have to do is sign it. I don't think you're likely to get anything better."

He took the document from his inside pocket and laid it on the table between them. She, who observed everything, saw, as he opened it out, that the bones in the backs of his hands radiated from the wrists as visibly as the sticks of a fan. She read the contract expertly. Her experience had taught her what to expect, for Sarah Armitage was in the habit of writing her own contracts, and it had been Hesba's business to copy them. "Thank you," she said. "You've done excellently."

Alec called for pen and ink, and the contract was signed.

"I'll let Carterson have it in the morning," he said. "He thinks he can publish by April. I'll keep after him and see that he makes a decent-looking book of it."

She thanked him again and began to draw on her gloves. "Now I must be off."

She got up, but Alec said: "Look, here's something I'd like you to see. You can spare another minute?"

It was a copy of *The Yellow Book*. It fell open in his hands at a page that had evidently often been opened already. He laid it shyly on the table before her. At the head of the page she read: "*Confessional*, by Alec Dillworth,"

"Just a short story," he said with diffidence. And then, rather defiantly: "But it's something to have it in *The Yellow Book*. I saw Henry Harland. He congratulated me personally and wants more. It may lead to something. I'm not really a Dunkerley man, you know."

Hesba was deeply moved. Alec's blending of reserve, of pride, of dissatisfaction with his daily life, of hidden urgent aspiration, all came to the surface in this trivial moment. Her own life's experience allowed her to pierce to the heart of the conflict that was ravaging him. But she was now on shore. She was looking from a point of safety at the struggle in which he was engaged. A hard core of practicality in her warned her against plunging again into the waters from which she had escaped.

She congratulated him on appearing in *The Yellow Book*. "My own copy should be at home when I get there," she said. "I shall look forward to reading it this very night."

"You must let me know what you think of it," Alec said. "And you're the only person I've said that to. Let me know tomorrow. I'm taking my sister out to a little Christmas Eve dinner at the Café Royal. Could you join us? I'd like you to meet Elsie."

Again the warning bell sounded in Hesba's mind, and she was glad to have a reason for refusal. "I'm sorry," she said. "Sir Daniel's giving a dinner party at his house. I've promised to be there."

"Oh," he answered easily. "You don't need to stay long at a show like that. Clear out at ten o'clock, and join us. We shall have finished dinner, but we can have a drink together."

"I can't promise," she said. "You know how these things are. You can't rush away like that. No, you mustn't expect me."

Alec was putting on the overcoat that always seemed to engulf him. "We shall probably leave there at about eleven," he said. "Until then I shall not have given up hope. Goodbye for now. There's a thing or two I want to clear up at the office."

She watched the tiny lonely figure disappearing down the street towards the river; then turned into the bustle of the Strand. She was aware, as the bus took her towards her two rooms in the Bayswater Road, of the forces ranged in her mind: the attraction of all that was dangerous and adventurous, free and independent, in Alec Dillworth; and the urgency of the voice which reminded her that struggle was over and that the part of wisdom lay in consolidating what she had gained.

These two rooms, she reflected when she was home, which she had furnished in her own way out of the wages of her own hard battle, were dear and consoling. Here was the established point to be defended at all costs, the rampart against the gulf into which it was so easy to fall.

She stood for a moment at her sitting room window on the first floor looking down upon the lights of the hansom cabs that made a moving twinkling border to the sombre blanket of the park beyond. Then she dropped the curtain and sank into the chintz armchair by the fireside. She began to read *Confessional*, and found herself disturbed by the enchantment of a mind which seemed no more to belong to these streets and stones than a gull belongs to the garbage on which it feeds.

10

Young Laurie Dunkerley accompanied Hesba from the drawing room down to the front door. His father's parties did not much interest him: only the presence of the Coming Woman had made this one tolerable. He thought Theodore Chrystal a pompous bore, unable now even to intimidate him, for what Oxford undergraduate (since Tom Brown) has been intimidated by his old headmaster? Dinah he considered as interesting as a fluffy kitten, and as important, and this youngster Felix Boys that she had brought along was just a child that one couldn't talk to – even supposing Dinah had allowed anyone to get in a word edgeways with him. Grace Satterfield was all right: he was fond of his cousin Grace: but she made him feel rather small. She was so cool, unemotional (as he thought) and full of knowledge. To listen to her and old Chrystal talking of this and that was like being at the Convocation of Canterbury. He was right out of it; and the worst of it was that the Dean would keep turning to him with his damned glazed smile and saying: "What does Laurie think?" "Surely young Laurence can put us right on that?"

A rotten sort of evening, if you ask me, Laurie thought; and his mind turned wistfully to conversations he had had with his Oxford friends before they came down for the holidays. Hansom cabs, suppers at Romano's with broadminded women: these were the kind of ingredients they had promised themselves for their Christmas pudding. Laurie felt he would like to sample such joys; but for a child of the house of Dunkerley it was not easy. Dunkerleys did not squander: they invested: they Planned for the Future. Even on this which was supposed to be a festive evening, Sir Daniel had talked over his port, when the ladies were upstairs, of branching out into publishing. Something for Laurie. Keep it in mind, my boy. You could make a big thing of it. And you, Theo. This book of yours on the Hebrews is all very well, but do you think a thousand people will read it? And is that what a man's gifts are for – to tickle the interest of a thousand people, with luck? No, no. Surely – and how well by now Laurie had learned to expect the round generalisation that would follow when Sir Daniel threw *surely* with such confidence into the foreground of a sentence! – surely God expected us to use our gifts for the greatest good of the greatest number. "There can be no doubt, my dear Chrystal, that a great awakening to spiritual matters could be brought about by the right people writing the right thing in the right way. The popular way – the way to reach the masses: short books with spiritual punch. You should apply your mind to it, Chrystal. Handled as a publishing house of mine would handle it, we could reach thirty – fifty thousand people. We could put the Old Story across."

Laurie had not known him so enthusiastic since he launched his first gardening weekly. Well, the boy thought, stifling a yawn and shaking his head as Old Sim pushed the decanter towards him, thank God we can't dawdle here much longer, and Hesba Lewison is upstairs, and most exciting she looks with her dark eyes and that flame-coloured dress. He must get her alone and see if she would come out to dinner with him some night. Sir Daniel could hardly object to that. And they could talk about other things than profitably awakening the spiritual energies of the masses.

And then, as soon as they entered the drawing room, his mother had burst out: "Dan! What a time you've been! Miss Lewison is just off!"

Nothing would make her stay, nor did she so much as pretend to explain her going. She must go: that was all: and she seemed nervous and irritable when Dan, Agnes and Grace all in turn pressed her to stay.

"Let me get you a cab," Laurie said, as they stood in the piercing cold by the front door.

"Well – if there's one about," she answered ungraciously.

There was. It had dropped a passenger farther along the square and now came back towards the Dunkerley door. Hesba got in, and the apron slammed down. Laurie heard her harsh clear voice speaking to the cabby who leaned down towards the shutter in the roof. "The Café Royal. As quick as you can go."

Laurie shut the door quietly, and went upstairs perplexed. She had not even called good night. She had simply gone, as though with a sense of glad escape.

11

Hesba pulled closely about her the flowing cloak of black scarlet-lined velvet that she wore over her red dress. She was aware, as she sank back in the cab, of a feeling of relaxation, of extraordinary relief; as though, having for long struggled against a tide, she had given herself to it; or as though, after fighting for air, she could breathe again. She drew the sharp air of the night deep into her broad sturdy chest, and sighed with pleasure. On such a night, with fingers of frost lightly stroking the texture of the atmosphere, she could breathe as she used to do years ago when, a child, she wandered on a winter's day by the seaside at Lianfairfechan. Without consciously doing so, she was listening to the neat smart patter of the horse's hoofs and to the musical jingle of brass as he tossed his head – he, too, enjoying this lovely night – and these sounds were fused into her reminiscent emotion, so that she seemed to hear the pleasant clattering commotion of her childhood's merchandise, dancing and jingling in a wind off the sea. She was tired, and a little drowsy, and she would have liked this enchanting ride to go on for a long time, because when it ended she would have to consider why it had begun.

And now, looking out of the window, she saw the lovely columns of Nash's crescent, and the cab drew into the kerb opposite them. As she threw up the apron and stepped out, Alec Dillworth dashed across the pavement, paid the cabman, and cried: "Exactly ten o'clock! But I'd have waited till eleven. Come on in and meet Elsie."

He was hatless. His fair hair was tumbled, and his eyes shone with an excited glitter. Possibly, she thought, he has been drinking too much. He led the way into the room that was all red plush and gilt and mirrors and white littered tablecloths. The air was noisy with talk, blue with tobacco smoke. Before she reached them, she was aware of two pairs of eyes watching her with interest. One belonged to Isambard Phyfe, whom she knew as Sir Daniel Dunkerley's right-hand man now that old James Carmichael had been pensioned off; the other to a red-haired girl whose regard, unlike Phyfe's regard of open admiration, was secret, hidden and non-committal. So this, Hesba thought, is Elsie. This is his sister.

"Elsie," Alec said, "this is Hesba Lewison."

Phyfe had risen and shaken hands, but Elsie Dillworth remained seated and kept her hands out of sight. She merely inclined her head briefly as Alec said: "This is my sister Elsie."

Hesba sat down, and Alec removed the cloak from her shoulders and spread it behind her on the chair. She was aware, as he paid her this small conventional attention, of Elsie looking not at her but at him, as though, behind veiled green eyes, her mind was busy with calculation. There was something disturbing, Hesba thought, in that face: so beautiful but so unlit: the head a riot of red tendrils, the skin so white, the eyes so green. Izzy Phyfe made an awkward gesture and knocked a fork to the floor. Instinctively, Elsie raised a hand to catch it, and Hesba saw that the hand – the right one – was disfigured. A vivid blue scar in the middle of the palm seemed to pull the hand together towards that point, causing the two middle fingers to curve a little downwards and inwards. The small incident passed in a flash, and then Elsie's hands were lying again in her lap. But she saw now that Hesba had seen, and she said defiantly: "Pretty, isn't it?"

"Else, Else!" Alec chided her gently; but she was not to be comforted. She got up and said: "It's time we went home."

<h2 style="text-align:center">12</h2>

How long, Alec wondered, will it be like this? Will she never forget, never allow her mind to be reconciled to something that there's no changing? It had been difficult to persuade her to come. She loved to be out and about in this great city which had not ceased to fascinate her, but alone or with him. Especially she loved going to concerts and theatres. Many and many a night they wandered home from a concert arm-in-arm as though they were lovers, saying nothing. She would be exalted by the music which, since the dreadful day ten years ago when a dagger-thrust mangled her hand, she knew she would never herself make. Time had healed that wound of the mind, though it still itched, and occasionally a sense of almost insupportable frustration came upon her. But this other, this wound in the body, was always present. Listening to music, her mind could create its own interpretation; but for this physical hurt there was no balm. With those two incurving fingers, she *could not* shake hands with anybody; and so, more and more, she came to imagine a pity, a distaste, that caused her to shrink from new contacts. More than this, it intensified her sense of dependence on Alec, and caused her to resent, hardly knowing that she did so, any symptom of his affection finding fresh outlets.

They had rooms in Lincoln's Inn; and that morning as she was putting the breakfast on the table Alec stood at the window, looking out upon the plane trees whose blotched trunks and bare branches were petrified against the steel-grey air. He loved to be here where, in the very heart of the great city, trees could grow. He could never have abided a country or suburban life, but he loved the trees. To have these and the river almost at his door, with the throng and clamour of the town there at the same time, seemed to him an almost magical combination of desirable things. Now he was thinking of what he had said last night to Hesba Lewison: that he had asked Elsie to eat some supper with him at the Café Royal on Christmas Eve. He had done nothing of the sort. The idea of asking Hesba had come to him suddenly, and it had seemed to him that Hesba would think him too urgent if he asked her alone. He did not want her to read more into the invitation than in fact was in it; and how much was in it he did not precisely know. He only knew that he was at times excited, at times happy and comfortable, in Hesba's presence. He knew little about her, but intuition suggested to him, through both herself and her work, that in the profoundest things they ran on parallel lines. But while he would not ask her alone lest he should alarm her, neither would he ask her alone lest Elsie should sense a desertion. And so he had framed his invitation to cover the complicated case; and now, turning from the window towards the good smell of coffee, he said: "Else, this is Christmas Eve. It calls for some celebration. Let's go and eat our supper at the Café Royal."

There was a small gate-legged oak table drawn up near the crackling fire and covered by a red-and-white checked cloth. Elsie poured out the coffee and placed a cup before Alec who had now seated himself. "By ourselves?" she asked.

The cup was halfway to his mouth. He put it back in the saucer, reached his hand across the table and laid it on her disfigured hand that was resting on the cloth. "Look, Else," he said. "We can't go on for ever like that. I'm twenty-eight years old. You're twenty-seven. I hope

69

there are a good many years before both of us. We can't spend all of them doing nothing but holding one another's hands."

She looked hurt. "You mean you've asked someone else."

"Yes."

"Is it anyone I know?"

"Well, I've asked two people," Alec said, improvising quickly. "There's Izzy Phyfe. You know about him. And there's Hesba Lewison. You've been reading her story in *Dunkerley's*. I thought you'd like to meet her. She's just a youngster – much younger than either of us."

"I hate meeting new people."

"Else, if only you'd give up imagining things."

Her face flushed suddenly, and she thrust her hand towards him across the table. "Imagining?" she cried. "Look at that! Is that imagination?"

He took hold of her hand and held it caressed in both of his. A slight shudder shook him, as it always did when contact with that hand recalled that it was his own furious and infatuated blow that had wrought the mischief. He held the hand for a moment, then released it gently. "Else," he said, "you're rather hard on me."

At that, she broke down and cried. He came round the table, knelt on the floor and put an arm round her. "Else, we've gone through a lot together, you and I. There's not much that we haven't suffered one way and another. Don't let's deliberately create new suffering that isn't necessary. You mustn't misunderstand me when I say you're imagining things. I only mean this. When you look at your hand, the disaster of your life is staring you in the face. You can see the career that you were on the verge of enjoying and that you had richly earned. You hear all the music that you'll never play. You remember the dreadful events that brought the disaster about; and that it was I –"

"No!" she suddenly cried, leaping from the chair and tearing herself from his embrace. "No! I never think that. It was I – I alone – not you. Don't say that."

Alec got up and leaned his head on the chimneypiece, kicking absentmindedly at the coals that were beginning to emit hissing spouts of gas and yellow smoke. "I'm trying to tell you how I see it, Else. All these things, I suppose, are in your mind when you allow it to dwell on the matter. But you must realise that they cannot be in the minds of people who know nothing of the circumstances. All they see is an injured hand. All they think, probably" – and he turned towards her, calling up a smile – "is: what a pity such a lovely girl has that affliction. Really, you know, outside your own mind, there's no more in it than that."

"Isn't that enough?"

"Sometimes," he said sadly, "it's more than I can bear. It's all very well for you, Else, to say 'No, no,' when I remember what I did. But I can't forget it. And that's why I rejoice every time I see you pick up some new knack of using your hand without thinking. Every time you unconsciously lift a cup, or cut your meat, or wash a basin, I rejoice. And, you know, you *can* do so much now. I do admire the way you've conquered."

"Ah, well," she said, softening, "what else has there ever been left for the Dillworth kids to do? Sit down and get on with your breakfast. Your coffee must be cold."

Alec sat down with a happy grin on his face. "You know, Else," he said, "I sometimes understand what poor Charles Lamb had to put up with from his sister Mary."

But Elsie didn't take that in. She, too, had sat down, and she asked suddenly: "Why have you invited this Lewison girl?"

"Haven't you read her story?"

"Yes."

"Well, don't you think it would be fun for you to know people like that? She's a talented little creature. She's just finished a new book."

"But why her? – or why she? – or whatever it is I ought to say. Don't any talented men write for *Dunkerley's?*"

"No," Alec said frankly. "It's an appalling production. Can you read the short stories in it?"

"Yes, and enjoy 'em."

"Well, there you are. That's why it's so successful."

"Thank you," Elsie said happily.

"No, but really, Else, it's an abysmal production, but somehow it's what people want – happily for us. Hesba Lewison's story is the only thing so far that an industrious clerk couldn't have written."

"I shall fear to meet the prodigy. And so young."

"You *will* meet her?"

"I suppose so."

"She'll only be looking in for a drink after dinner. She's dining with Rare Dan Dunkerley."

Elsie looked surprised. "Oh! That's a funny idea, isn't it? Aren't we good enough for her?"

"You're good enough to meet anyone in London, Else."

"What about you? I shan't allow Hesba Lewison or any one else to treat you cheap."

"Don't worry about that," said Alec. "She'd got this engagement with Sir Dan before I asked her, that's all. It's a compliment to us that she'll leave his place early."

He had no doubt at all that she would do so.

13

On Christmas morning Hesba woke with a feeling of perplexity at the back of her mind, which presently cleared up and left her thinking of the strange events of the night before. Walking with Alec Dillworth through the crowded restaurant, threading in and out of the disordered tables, she was taking note of the girl they were approaching – his sister – and she was impressed by what she saw. That amazing crown of small red curls – small enough to be called tendrils – that pale face and full red sensuous mouth, those veiled greenish eyes: all this sprang at once to a regard ever alert for the beautiful and unaccustomed. It was difficult to believe that this regular and, she imagined, conscious beauty belonged to Alec's sister, for, though his face was one you would pick out in a crowd and not soon forget, that was because of a quality precisely the opposite of this: a quality ravaged by thought and suffering. However, there was no doubt that this was the girl she was to meet, for Isambard Phyfe was with her, and no one who had anything to do with Sir Daniel Dunkerley could be unaware of Mr Phyfe. Sir Daniel had taken lately, when in London, to riding early in the morning in the Row, and Mr Phyfe was to be seen, ungainly on a hack, rising and falling spectacularly at his side. Hesba smiled as she remembered the *bon mot* that was going the rounds. "There they were, pegging along like Napoleon and Marshal Ney," said someone who had witnessed this small cavalcade in the dewy hour before breakfast. "No, no," a wit amended. "You mean Marshal Yea."

It was with a smile unconsciously on her face as she recalled this witticism that Hesba advanced to the table with her hand held out to Elsie. But Elsie did not rise, and did not take the hand. She merely inclined her head – most regally, to be sure, but all the same to Hesba it was galling to feel a snub fall upon her gay expansive mood. A moment later, she glimpsed the flaw in this beautiful woman, and understood with a pang of pity why the hand had been withheld. All would then have been well but for Elsie's atrocious and self-pitying question: "Pretty, isn't it?"

Everything broke up at once. Elsie was on her feet announcing that she must go home; and Alec, after a placating moment, went white with annoyance. Saying nothing to either Phyfe or Hesba, he followed Elsie who was already making for the door, and as he went his clenched jaw drew all his face together in ticking, pulsing lines. When they were gone, the situation seemed beyond Phyfe to handle. He merely said "Well!" and then formally invited Hesba to have a drink. There was nothing to do but end the matter on that conventional note. She had her drink, bade Mr Phyfe good night, and walked home. She felt completely deflated. She had run away from Sir Daniel's in a sudden mood of adventure, of attraction, she admitted, to the qualities that she sensed in Alec Dillworth, and she had been brought up short against a situation that defeated her – a situation, she was wise enough to admit, that obviously contained far more than she was in a position to understand. There was more to it than Mr Phyfe's perfunctory "Well!"

Sitting at breakfast in her room overlooking the Park, where every tree was entranced in stillness and softened in shape by an opalescence of frozen sunshine, she could see no further into the matter. She put it from her mind, and, Christmas Day or no Christmas Day, settled down to her morning's work. The Happy Go Luckies was drawing to its end in Dunkerley's; The Well-bred Dragon was written; but all this was no reason to Hesba why she should not at once begin Barnaby and the Beautiful Beast. She was an industrious young woman and she had no intention of letting go now that she had taken hold.

She was not surprised, when she came in from her afternoon walk, to find Grace Satterfield and the Dean in her sitting room, for she and Grace visited one another almost daily. Nor was she surprised to see upon Theo Chrystal's face a look of mingled triumph and satisfaction, and upon Grace's one of supreme happiness. Grace, she knew, had been writing to Theo almost daily, and during the Deans' visit to town the two had been about together whenever Chrystal's business affairs made it possible. He had had, Hesba understood, a heavy financial interest in Beckwith, the school of which he had been headmaster, and that was not the only financial benefit that had come to him from his first wife. This visit to London had been concerned with selling his interest in the school, and Hesba had seen and understood enough of Theo Chrystal to be pretty sure that he had made a good bargain. Looking at him now, standing before the fire, with his imposing height and spectacular beauty dominating the room, with that triumphant look bent possessively upon Grace, who had risen from a couch as Hesba came in, it was this sense of possessiveness that Hesba was most clearly aware of. "He must be a very rich man," she thought. "And Grace, I suppose, is richer still."

"Well, Miss Lewison," he said, "I have just looked in to say goodbye. I must be off tomorrow on an early train. All my affairs are concluded – very satisfactorily – very satisfactorily indeed."

This with a smile in the direction of Grace, who could contain herself no longer but hurried forward and embraced her friend. "Oh, Hesba!" she said, as though that explained everything – as, indeed, to a person as quick-witted as Hesba, it did. She was not at home with caresses and embraces. She gently put Grace from her and said: "Well, I hope you'll be very happy, my dear. And you, too, Mr Chrystal. I'm sure you will – both of you. You were made for one another."

And this she knew to be true. She sensed in Chrystal a narrow-minded, ambitious and unimaginative man, but one not without the force and dignity that a stupendous and august institution could reflect into the right sort of mirror. And that was the sort of mirror that Theodore Chrystal was. He would contribute nothing to his church except the ability to receive and give back with interest all that the church as an institution could bestow. In her young wisdom, Hesba was aware that it was in alliance with such a life, regulated, punctilious and unenterprising, that Grace could be most happily herself. Her gifts and faculties were all of quietness and peace. A don or a dean. Hesba smiled quietly to herself. Yes. Almost inevitably, it had to be one or other of those.

"You must have some tea," she said.

The lilac dusk was thickening. She drew the curtains and lit the gas in the two round bowls on either side above the mantelpiece. When she rang the bell, her intelligent landlady, as she had hoped, at once came in with tea for three. The little trolley was rolled up to the fireplace and they grouped themselves comfortably in their chairs about it. Hesba poured out the tea. She switched her visitors violently away from their sweet preoccupation with themselves.

"Grace," she said, "when you lived in Manchester did you see much of Alec Dillworth?"

"No," Grace answered. "My Manchester memories are dim. I do most clearly remember the day when my uncle's first paper was published. That was *Hard Facts*, you know."

She considered for a moment, sipping her tea. "And yet, you know, when I take my mind back to it, it's the occasion itself, not any detail of it, that I remember. It's all very confused. I was there, and, what's more, you were there, too, Theo. What on earth you were doing there I can't for the life of me imagine."

"That's easy enough to explain," the Dean said. "I was a curate at the time, and your uncle up to that moment was simply a printer. I had gone round to his printing office to inquire about some church hand-bills, and I assure you it was the surprise of my life when I found myself involved in the ceremony of launching a paper."

"A photograph was taken," Grace said. "I was looking at it recently, framed in my uncle's office. You look impossibly beautiful in it."

This is all very well, Hesba thought, handing round the muffins. Here you are harping on one another again, but that's not what I'm asking about. "But Alec Dillworth," she said. "I'm asking about Alec Dillworth."

"I don't know much about him, my dear," Grace said.

"You know my romantic story – rags to riches in about five minutes. My father didn't leave me in Manchester. In no time at all I was away at school, and even during the holidays I didn't come back to Manchester. He used to join me in some seaside place. Then the university. No, Manchester's a dim place to me and becoming dimmer."

"But you, Mr Chrystal," Hesba persisted. "You were there on the spot."

She paused, her quick faculties arrested by a trivial fact. Theo was putting his cup down in the saucer, and there was an infinitesimal clatter as china met china. His hand was slightly trembling.

"I saw practically nothing of them," he said shortly.

Hesba pounced on the providential word. "Them?"

"I mean Dillworth and his sister," the Dean blurted. "He has a sister, you know – or had then."

"Yes; he still has," said Hesba. "She interests me as much as he does. I met them last night. She's one of the most beautiful women I've ever seen. But there's a terrible flaw. One of her hands is mangled."

She noticed the extreme deliberation with which Chrystal again placed his cup in the saucer. This time there was no clatter. But he rose rather abruptly. "I think we should be going, my dear," he said to Grace. "You must excuse me, Miss Lewison. A thousand things . . . packing . . . I expect I shall not see you for some time. In the meantime, if I may offer you somewhat uncharitable advice, it would be to see as little of the Dillworths as possible."

Hesba went down with them to the door. "All happiness," she said. "From the bottom of my heart, my dear, all happiness."

To Theo she said nothing.

She stood watching as the halo of a gas lamp caught them up and magnified them mistily; then passed them on, arm-in-arm, into the darkness.

CHAPTER FOUR

T HE DEAN was anxious to make some changes in the Deanery before his marriage, which was to take place in the spring, and, since these would concern Grace, she and Lady Dunkerley went early in the year to stay for a week at King's Mandeville. Sir Daniel went down to Dickons, taking Izzy Phyfe, Alec and Laurie with him. Dinah remained in Manchester Square to be old Sim's companion. She would have stayed in any case to see Felix Boys off at Paddington. He was due to leave in a few days for a parsonage in the Cotswolds, where his cramming would be taken in hand.

During the first day or two Sir Daniel simmered gently, doing no work at all and being, as Izzy put it to himself, as nice as pie. But this, Izzy knew, was nothing more than the lazy curl of smoke out of a volcano that might erupt at any moment.

There was to be a party one night at Dickons. It was fitting, as Sir Daniel saw it, that he, lord of the manor in a way of speaking, should shower largesse, and this he had resolved to do upon the heads of half a dozen village urchins. The vicar had been invited to select them and to forward them to Dickons in time for dinner. A teatime occasion would not do for Sir Dan: no mere bun-fight for him. These youngsters should come from the picturesque squalor of their cottages into the sumptuous light of Dickons at dinnertime. They would be given a memory to take away and treasure.

Alec Dillworth felt from the beginning that he was going to enjoy this occasion. So far, he hadn't got much fun out of Dickons. It was superb winter weather. Each day was blue and sunny from end to end; each night sparkled and crackled with frost. There was a pond in one of the meadows, and it was carrying four inches of ice. Laurie Dunkerley spent most of the daylight hours skating there when he wasn't out shooting with his father. But neither skating nor shooting meant anything to Alec. He did a little desultory walking, but most of his time was spent in reading in the comfortable suite that Dickons provided for Sir Daniel's entourage.

However, there was one encounter that pleased him. Sir Daniel and Laurie had not returned by teatime one day, and he and Isambard Phyfe having taken the meal together by the fireside in the hall, he had drowned himself in his large overcoat and gone out. It was dark, and the frost was hardening already under the sky's bright shiners. He strolled idly through the fields, collar up, hands thrust deep in pockets, appreciating the crackle and stiff resistance of the grass under the hedges where the sun had not reached and where from morning to night there was a tussocky tangle of grass and frost. He came out at last by the pond. It was a grey shimmer, like a dull tin tray put down there on the dark cloth of the field, and beyond it the elms lifted their intricate irregular mesh that had a fine haul of stars. Their twinkling gave them life: they slipped and shone in the net like fishes.

Being in the lee of a hedge, Alec was invisible, and he stayed still where he was when he saw a small figure moving cautiously out on to the ice. It was a boy, and he was dropping things here and there over the surface of the pond. Whatever it was that he was about, it did not take him long, and when he had finished he came up off the ice and walked so close to the hedge that Alec had but to reach out a hand to seize his arm. The boy squirmed and dodged, but Alec held him fast. "What are you up to?" he asked.

"Sowing death an' destruction," said the boy.

The answer was so unexpected that Alec crowed with laughter and let go his hold. The laugh had given back some assurance to the boy, who did not run. Instead he asked: "Who are you, mister?"

"Oh, just a chap taking a walk," said Alec easily. "And who are you?"

"The Tiger."

"Who says so?"

"All the fellers. I'm not afraid of God or man."

"And who says that?"

"Me mother."

"And what does your father say?"

"Ain't got none."

"What were you doing on the pond, Tiger?"

"I told yer. Sowing death an' destruction."

"Yes. But how?"

"Sticks an' stones. They'll freeze in by mornin'. Bring 'im a bloody flopper."

"Who?"

"The bloke that skates."

"You're looking for trouble, Tiger."

"I'm not afraid of God or man."

"But why d'you want to bring him a bloody flopper, Tiger?"

Tiger considered for a moment. "Well," he said, "there'd be a laugh in it for one thing. An' another thing: we used to slide there before 'e come."

"I'm sure he wouldn't mind your sliding. He's a nice feller. I know him. Why don't you ask him?"

"Would'n' demean meself."

"Well, that's your affair. Now you go and clean up the pond."

"Not on yer life."

Alec took his arm again, and at once the Tiger's resistance stiffened. "Lemme go," he said. "I'll bust yer snout. I'll drive yer teeth in. I've busted every snout in this village."

He wriggled free and retreated a few yards. Suddenly the promise of high lights in the future burst on Alec's enchanted mind. "Tiger," he said, "Sir Daniel Dunkerley has invited some boys to dinner the night after tomorrow. Are you one of them?"

"Yus," said the Tiger, and sped along the hedgeside like a March hare. Alec remained for a moment smiling to himself. The stay at Dickons, he thought, might not be so dull after all.

2

The six boys arrived in a horse-brake which Sir Daniel had ordered from the village. They were singing, with a musical accompaniment rendered by the Tiger on the mouth-organ. When they entered the hall of Dickons, where, waiting to receive his young guests, Sir Daniel stood warming his behind at the fire, the singing abruptly stopped. The boys were quelled by magnificence. They became sheepish and tongue-tied. All except the Tiger.

Sir Daniel did his best. He shook hands with each and hoped it was not too late to wish them a Happy New Year. Then he invited the Tiger to play his mouth-organ again and the others to sing. The Tiger was more than willing. He took the mouth-organ from his pocket, vigorously shook the spit out of it on to the carpet, and began to play "It's my Delight on a Shiny Night." It could not be denied that the Tiger was a master with the mouth-organ, but the singing was weak and quavering, though Sir Daniel added his voice to the chorus.

"No good," said the Tiger. "The little buggers are frightened, but I'm not afraid of God or man. I'll give you a solo. I'll do the bells."

He did so, producing a passable imitation of bells now ringing out clear, now fading away in a windy distance.

Leaning against a newel at the foot of the staircase, Alec watched the Tiger with fascination. He guessed he was the youngest of all these boys. He could not have been more than ten, and his figure was stunted even for that age. But his white face, crowned by a shock of black wiry hair, had an extraordinary animation, and as the mouth-organ slid to and fro across his lips, his onyx eyes were never still. They were searching and probing everywhere, with a fearless unashamed exploration. His short trousers revealed dirty bony knees; a grey woollen muffler was twisted several times round his neck.

The bells ended, and the Tiger knocked out the instrument into his hand, which he then wiped on the seat of his trousers. He wiped the mouth-organ there, too, put it in his pocket, and looked round with a grin. "Where's this dinner?" he demanded. "That's what we've come for."

Alec was thinking: There are three real people in this room – Dan Dunkerley, the Tiger and myself. And Dan is a bit nervous about the Tiger. I can see that already. Aloud, he said: "It must be gratifying, Sir Daniel, to feel that you have had a share in shaping this vigorous young intellect."

He laid one hand on the Tiger's shoulder, and with the other drew from the boy's pocket a folded paper. One glance at the sticking-out edge of it had shown him what it was. He flourished *British Youngster*, a horrible pennyworth with an enviable circulation.

"You and this young man," he addressed Sir Daniel, "ought to know one another better. You are in such close relation. You bestow upon him the means of culture; he bestows upon you – well, Dickons and such-like. No one has bothered with introductions, so allow me. Sir

Daniel Dunkerley, proprietor of *British Youngster* — Tiger, part donor of Dickons."

Sir Daniel maintained his suavity, but he gave Alec one glance which said: "I can't do it here, but we'll have this out later, Alec." To the Tiger he said: "So you're a reader of *British Youngster?*"

"Yus," the Tiger assented; and to Alec he said: "Gimme," and snatched the paper from his hand. "Listen," he commanded.

The Tiger undoubtedly was an extrovert. He was willing to oblige in any company, whether with a bust in the snout, a recital on the mouth-organ, or a reading from *British Youngster*. Standing with his back to the fire, his black spikes of hair not reaching to the height of the chimneypiece, while the other boys stood round enthralled, giving the worship that his being demanded, he read in a shrill voice:

Lying on the pyre, Saundersfoot worked away steadily at the thongs of oxhide that bound him hand and foot. Umzimvubu watched him with an evil smile playing upon his crafty features, while the ground shook from the stamping feet of the warriors. Saundersfoot could hear the rattle of their shields and the clatter of their assegais as they pounded out the death-dance. There was not much time. When the dance was done, one match to the pyre, and all would be over.

But now one hand was free, and turning his head warily, Saundersfoot computed that with it he could reach the knobkerry which Umzimvubu had allowed to fall to his feet. To crash in the skull of the ungainly savage and with one bound to melt into the forest, earning again his title of the One the Shadows Eat. Saundersfoot's mind was working like a high-powered engine, and his hands were never still. Now the second thong was giving a little, when suddenly a mighty booming sounded through the forest.

Six boys, and the Tiger among them, leapt with terror. It was the dinner-gong, choosing a fine dramatic moment to roll through the house, and it was Alec's hand that was wielding the stick. He had read that story long before it had come into the Tiger's hands, and now, working the gong up in a crescendo of alarming noise, he rocked with laughter to observe that even Sir Daniel, enthralled by his own vivid

81

wares, had given an alarmed start with all the others. He toned down the noise till it faded away as impressively as the Tiger's bells had done; and then said: "Well, Sir Daniel, I think the Tiger was right: what about this dinner?"

3

It was not to be a dinner of intricate and tricky courses. There was to be turkey, with all the trimmings, and after that there was to be plum pudding. There were to be no servants to alarm the boys. Everything was now on the sideboard. Sir Daniel would carve the turkey. Laurie, Izzy and Alec would dish up the vegetables and serve at the table. There was lemonade for the boys to drink and burgundy for the others.

The Tiger, whom Alec had taken care to place in a seat next his own, watched with a wolfish impatience while the preliminaries were going forward, filling in the time with an absent-minded representation of the "bones" performed with a fork and spoon dexterously held.

"You like turkey, Tiger?" Sir Daniel asked over his shoulder.

"Yus," said the Tiger, "but I prefer pheasant."

"Do you often have pheasant?"

"Often enough," said the Tiger briefly. It was evidently a matter not to be freely discussed, but one of the dumb little boys, anxious to give a hero his due, squeaked: "Tiger's very good at it, sir."

"You shut up, or else I'll bust yer snout. I'll knock yer teeth in," Tiger threatened.

All were now served, and Alec seated himself at the Tiger's side. He poured wine for himself, and accidentally – it may be – half-filled the Tiger's glass with wine, too. He topped it up with lemonade. "Come on, Tiger," he said. "Don't be nervous. Tell us how you get the pheasants."

But the blood of generations of poachers was in the Tiger's veins. He was not to be drawn. He merely kicked out viciously under the table, and drew a howl from the boy who had blabbed.

Soon six plates were being ferociously attacked, while four were more sedately cleared. The Tiger took a gulp from his glass, looked a little surprised, and gulped again. Dan isn't doing it so badly, Alec thought. He certainly has a way with kids. The turkey had been

82

brought from the sideboard and lay on the table before him. He kept on replenishing the plates. "A bit more, Tiger? Anyone else for a bit more?" till even the dumbest of the six thawed out into a timid cry: "Me, sir, please."

The Tiger looked at his empty plate, tossed back the dregs from his tumbler, and sat back smiling. He belched, and asked rather truculently: "Any presents?"

Five scared, admiring faces were watching the face of the leader. Presents clearly were expected, but no one save the Tiger would have dared to open the matter. "There's always presents after the Sunday school party," the Tiger announced firmly.

Sir Daniel was caught out. He had not thought of presents, and he turned meanly upon Alec. "What have you done about the presents, Alec?"

"That will be all right. The presents will be in the hall after the pudding," Alec promised. "You get on with it."

He waited till the eating had begun again, then ran into the drawing room. The Christmas tree had not yet been dismantled. It stood there shining with frozen filigree, hung all over with glittering baubles. Sir Daniel had spent his Christmas time in London, but he had not forgotten the servants who remained at Dickons. It was a fine tree, though the presents had now all been stripped from it. But that could be remedied. Alec ran into the kitchen and collected half a dozen boxes of dates and chocolates. He wrapped them in silver paper and hung them on the tree. He had it carried out into the hall. New candles were fitted into the holders, and when the party broke up and came out of the dining room the shining tree was filling the hall with light.

Sir Daniel appeared. "Splendid, Alec, splendid," he said, and Izzy looked as if he wished he had thought of this way of saving Sir Daniel's reputation as a host.

Five boys gazed at the tree with solemn wonder; the Tiger with a noticeable excitement. "If that fell over, you'd set the 'ouse on fire," he suddenly said.

"It's not going to fall over," Sir Daniel announced confidently. "Now come up one at a time and untie your presents. Then perhaps Tiger'll give us some more music."

Without waiting for prompting, Tiger exercised what he clearly regarded as his right and stepped forward first. He began to untie a small parcel and at the same time with the knuckles of one hand nudged a candle out of the straight. The flame came down under the dry shelf of a bough and a flicker ran up the tree.

"I told yer!" Tiger shouted, backing away. "I told yer! Fire! Fire! We'll put it out."

There was no need for excitement! The tree was not so dry as all that, and after the first alarming spurt of flame the fire went out. But the Tiger was not to be denied. He had rushed into the dining room and quickly returned bearing a full water-jug. Even as he appeared, he held it ready to throw. Sir Daniel interposed, but what now could stop the Tiger intent on heroism? The water flew through the air and Sir Daniel took it full in the stomach.

There was a moment's silence and consternation as Sir Daniel stood looking at his dripping trouser legs: silence broken by the Tiger's satisfied growl: "Got 'im!" Then Sir Daniel began to bellow. "Izzy, send these little devils home." He started up the stairs, shouting "Meaker, Meaker!" His valet came running. "Come to my bedroom," Dan commanded, and at the turn of the stairs he paused to add: "Alec, you too. Come on up."

Clearly the party was ended.

4

Alec waited for a few moments to enjoy the sight of Izzy Phyfe despatching five terrified devils and one triumphant devil into the cold dark. They would have to walk. The brake to take them home was not due for another hour. Anyway, they would have music to cheer them. Down the drive the sound of the Tiger's mouth-organ could be heard playing "God rest you merry, Gentlemen."

Laurie had disappeared. Alec grinned at Isambard. "Well," he said, "now to encounter mine host."

"I don't envy you," said Izzy briefly. "God! I feel gorged!"

Alec went slowly upstairs. A bright fire was burning in Sir Daniel's bedroom, and before it Sir Daniel was sitting in an easy chair. Meaker had just drawn off his trousers and long woollen pants; his legs were extended to the flames. Meaker came forward bearing new garments. Sir Daniel waved him away. "Get out," he said briefly.

84

He took a cigar-case from his pocket, lit a cigar carefully, and said: "Alec, I want you to give up the editorship of *Dunkerley's*."

Alec was flabbergasted. He had expected one of Dan's celebrated theatrical rages to burst out, linking him with the disasters of the evening. But evidently the evening was now far from Sir Daniel's mind. It had washed itself of all that and was on a new tack. Well, that, too, was part of the Dunkerley method and legend. Sir Daniel was looking with concentrated interest at the burning end of his cigar, his toes curling luxuriously in the warmth of the fire.

"It's time we spread out into something new," he said. "I've been thinking of going in for publishing books."

There was only one comfortable chair in the room and Dan was sitting in it. Alec slumped himself down on the white bearskin rug at his feet. He allowed himself the liberty of taking Sir Daniel's big toe between finger and thumb and squeezing it gently. Sir Daniel asked testily, drawing away his foot: "Aren't you attending to what I'm saying to you? What the devil do you think you're doing?"

Alec grinned up at him. "I shall now be able to contradict a rumour," he said. "It is generally reckoned that you have feet of clay."

Dan snorted. "Alec, try and be serious for once."

Very well. But I fail to see what your publishing has to do with me."

"It has everything to do with you. Don't get into a groove. You've got a comfortable corner as editor of *Dunkerley's* and you're just curling up in it like a snail into its shell. You should take an interest in all my enterprises."

Alec looked at him lazily. He felt warm and relaxed in front of the fire. The burgundy he had drunk at dinner was not calculated to make him take seriously the dawn of a Dunkerley tantrum.

"All right, Dan, all right," he said comfortably. "I do take an interest in your enterprises, in a way. Who would if not I? After all, I've known you ever since you had damned little shirt-tail to cover your backside in Manchester."

Sir Daniel sprang to his feet, deeply annoyed, but realised that he was no figure to make a show of dignity. He snatched a rug that was on the back of his chair, threw it over his knees, and sat down again.

"Listen to me, and don't interrupt," he said. "I am starting a publishing house, and when Laurie has finished at Oxford he will take control of it. In the meantime, it's got to be put on its feet. You will do it. You've got a certain amount of taste. You know a book when you read one. Well, then: that will be your side of the matter. So far as the business side is concerned, I trust I shall be able to pay a salary sufficient to detach someone from an established house. There's one thing I have in mind, and it's this: If we take on any new authors as serial-writers for *Dunkerley's* in future, it will be part of the contract that the book rights go automatically to us. We ought to have done that with Hesba Lewison. In any case, she'll be willing enough to give us *The Happy Go Luckies*. She owes something to *Dunkerley's*."

"Not so much as *Dunkerley's* owes to her," said Alec. "She set the thing rolling when it was stuck in the mud. And, anyway, she's sold the book rights of *The Happy Go Luckies* already."

"What! How do you know that?"

"Because I sold them for her."

Sir Daniel was silent for a time. Then he said: "This makes a new situation between us. I didn't know you had taken to plotting behind my back."

Alec sprang to his feet. "Don't talk damned nonsense," he said. "What did I know about your intentions? Do I have to come and ask your permission for every action, just in case some blessed scheme of yours will be interfered with? If that's what you want, you can go on wanting."

"Dillworth," said Sir Dan quietly, "I've put up with a lot from you in the last ten years. Nevertheless, I should be sorry if you forced me to end our association."

"Sir Daniel," Alec retorted, with the scornful twist that only he dared to give to the title, "I have no doubt our association will last just as long as you find it beneficial."

"Let me remind you, before you say anything irrevocable, that it's been of some benefit to you and your sister."

Alec's face tightened. "So," he said, "Elsie's one of your pensioners, too? Just get that right out of your head. Anything that's been done for Elsie, I've done. You've had value for your money out of me – damned good value for damned little money. You haven't been throwing charity about, to me or her."

Sir Daniel would have liked to get up and rave, but he realised the difficulty. Instead, he hurled his cigar into the fire and said: "Now we're at it, we'd better get things into the open, Mr Dillworth. After all, I am the proprietor of the magazine you edit, and I might tell you that the editor of any one of my magazines had better watch his step. My publications go into the homes of the decent-living people of this country, and I'll have no breath of scandal on the names of my editors."

"Go ahead," said Alec. "I don't know what you're talking about, but go ahead."

Sir Daniel got up, and holding the rug about his middle waddled towards his dressing table. He picked up *The Yellow Book* and waved it in Alec's face. "No editor of mine," he shouted, "is going to be associated with this unsavoury publication. It stinks of Oscar Wilde, and there's been quite enough stink about that gentleman recently."

Alec was livid with wrath. "You twopenny-ha'-penny hypocrite!" he shouted. "You don't even know what you're talking about. Never a line by Wilde has appeared in *The Yellow Book*."

"I know all about that, but the whole thing stinks of him, nevertheless. You can get on to the high horse as much as you like, but so long as you remain with me you'll have nothing to do with anything tainted by that set. Why, even when he was at Oxford the fellow was ducked in the river."

"Well," Alec retorted bitterly, "that's a fate unlikely to overtake your mediocre offspring. Anyway, it's a lie."

Now Sir Daniel was stung, and he leapt to his feet, allowing the rug to fall to the floor. His knees shook with his anger. "Throughout ten years," he said, "I have put up with a lot from you, Dillworth. I'm beginning to doubt whether I should have been so lenient. I believed you to have talents as a man of letters. Now I'm not so sure. To my face and behind my back you've laughed at the things I've given my life to. But let me tell you this — at any rate I've *done* them. What have *you* done? You've done nothing but set up a precious pretence of being superior to the way in which I've permitted you to earn your daily bread. You're too good to handle my manure. You're a writer — God, how often you've said it! You're a poet. So you tell us. And what is there to show for it in ten years? A couple of piddling verses in papers no one ever reads, and now, as the crown of your endeavours, an essay in this preposterous rag! I pity you! Get out! Go to your Wildes and Beardsleys and the rest of 'em. See if they'll keep you as I have done."

Alec's face was white, but he allowed the outburst to flow uninterrupted to its close. When Dan had slumped back into his chair, his legs stretched out absurdly to the fire, his toes twitching, Alec picked up the rug and threw it over his nakedness. "Now that you are clothed," he said quietly, "though hardly in your right mind, I shall ask your permission to give you as long a sermon as you have given me. You ask me to take over a publishing business – something I am completely unfitted to do. I decline, because I don't admit the right of you or anyone else to order me hither and thither as though my own wishes and inclinations were of no account. That's one thing. Here's another. I have managed to sell Hesba Lewison's book on good terms because I like the girl and wanted to do something for her. You say this is plotting behind your back. I answer that you're a liar and that you know it. You speak scornfully of my attempts to express myself in my own way. Well, I've got no complaint to make about that, because what you think of my work doesn't matter tuppence. So we pass that over. You command me to go to my Wildes and Beardsleys. I've never met either. I wish I had, but I'm not a big enough man by their company, and anyhow the decent-living people of this country, of whom you speak with such feeling, have put Wilde out of reach. You hope that these people will keep me, as you have done. They couldn't, if they wanted to. They're not rolling in money as you are. And they wouldn't want to, anyway. Rightly enough, they'd want me to keep myself. And I take leave to tell you that that's what I've done ever since I've been associated with you and your papers. Finally, you pity me. All right. I shan't try to rob you of what is necessary to prop up your self-esteem. Pity for what you don't understand and never will understand is part of it. So you may keep your pity. I think that covers everything."

He had spoken in a monotone, stoking down his fires. When he ceased, there was silence in the room for a moment. They could hear the exhausted coals contracting with a faint crepitation. Dan's head had sunk on to his chest. He brooded uneasily in the stillness. If Alec had played the wild-cat it would have been easier, but bluster was no answer to the quiet words he had listened to. Presently, he stirred in discomfort and said: "Well, Alec, perhaps I've misunderstood you –"

"No," said Alec in the same dispassionate tone, "there's no misunderstanding any longer. Not after what I've said. I don't think the situation could be made any clearer than I've made it." He held out his hand. "So, goodbye, Dan."

Then Sir Daniel leapt to his feet, tumbling the rug to the floor again. "Don't be a damned fool," he shouted. "You know the way I blow up and the way I cool down. If you're going to take offence at every paltry word I utter –"

Alec had nothing more to say. He was still holding out his hand, but Dan would not look at it. "Go to bed," he commanded. "I'll see you in the morning."

"Dan," Alec said. "You have a great capacity for fooling yourself. But please don't fool yourself over this. You will not see me in the morning. I'm saying goodbye. You'd better get someone into *Dunkerley's* pretty quick if the February number is to appear. I suppose you can sue me for breach of contract. You must please yourself about that."

Sir Daniel had strode gustily towards his dressing table. He turned sharply as he heard the door click. Alec was gone.

Well, let him go. There was no train to town, and anyway it was a bitter night that no one would go out in. A night's sleep, and Alec would see sense. Something could be devised to keep Izzy Phyfe out of the way at breakfast time, and over breakfast he and Alec would find some adjustment that satisfied them both. Dan sat down again, pleased to think that his diplomacy was usually successful. He had taken a piece of coal in the tongs and suddenly stiffened with it halfway to the fire. A hollow reverberation sounded through the house – the banging of the front door.

5

It had not taken Alec long to pack. It was not his habit to carry much with him. His few things were soon in a hand-bag, and he went quietly down the stairs, wrapped in his overcoat, eaved with his black wide-brimmed hat. He wondered what had happened to Izzy, and found his answer as he went past the billiards room. The door was ajar. He glimpsed Izzy contorted over the table, heard the clack of balls smartly struck, the soft swift roll on the baize, the muffled impact on the cushions. "Stunnin', Izzy, stunnin'," Laurie said. Alec left them to it, passed through the hall and confronted the cold pallor of the night. He took a deep breath of the frozen air and pulled the door behind him. The sound of it, so sharp, definitive, gave him a moment almost of ecstasy. He was surprised to feel no anger: there had been so much anger in his life: but now what he felt was the exaltation of a great decision. He had been offered a choice; he had made it; and he was satisfied with what he had chosen.

Ten years and more of Dan Dunkerley had taught Alec all that was to be known about him. He knew exactly what would happen in the morning, if he were there when Dan came down to breakfast. Dan would be as nice as pie. Perhaps what had happened this night would not be spoken of at all: it would be assumed that things should go forward as though true words had never been spoken. Or, perhaps, half with banter, half with friendly flattery, Dan would try to jockey him into doing what he wished. And, weak fool that I am, Alec thought, ten to one I'd fall for it. That was why he had packed and left at once: he distrusted his own power to maintain the stand he had taken.

There was no clear idea in his mind as to where he should spend the night. It was now ten o'clock; the moon, almost at full, was shining, and the air was bitter with frost. At all events, he decided, he must keep moving. He was in good shape for walking. It was the only exercise he ever took, and he took it mechanically, automatically, walking for hours through the streets, his thoughts racing with his small taut racing body. And so, he thought, there would be no difficulty about walking all night and getting a London train from whatever station he found himself at in the morning. There wouldn't be much light before seven, and that meant nine hours to go. Still . . . He felt as fit as a prize whippet. A fox slunk across the moon-washed road twenty paces ahead of him. He had never before in his life seen a live fox. It lifted up his heart. A sense of kinship with wild living things possessed him. A white owl drifted along a hedge like moving silence. He stopped still in his tracks, his heart pounding with excitement, as he watched it out of sight.

Ah! What things there were to see and know if one chose to go out into the darkness!

6

"And so, my dear," Grace wrote to Hesba, "we finally ran down the curtains we wanted at Bath. Theo is simply overwhelmed with work, but I insisted on his taking a day off, so that he could himself drive me and Lady Dunkerley over. The curtains were not new. We found them in an 'antiques' shop – a rich blue damask, sewn with stars of gold. Now that they are hung in what I *insist* on calling 'Hesba's room,' though everyone else calls it the visitors' room, the effect is delightful. The room is oak-panelled, with a basket-grate, and from the window seat you look on to our small but delightful close. Now, of course, it's winter-bleak, but, even so, most satisfying. This is the room I expect you to get to know, *well*. Last night I had a fire lit in it so that I could enjoy its full cosy effect. Believe me, my dear, it was most charming. The bed is a tiny copy of a four-poster. Alongside the fireplace is a writing desk. You can push your legs through the knee hole and toast your toes as you write. It's all yours, for working and sleeping. Lady Dunkerley and Theo came up and joined me in the room, and all agreed that it was charming. We spent a most agreeable hour there. I thought I should be able to send you some more information about the Dillworths. You remember you were asking about them the last time we met. I sounded Lady Dunkerley, and she and Theo gave one another what I can only call conspiratorial glances. She evidently didn't know what to say, and Theo said: 'I assure you, my dear, the Dillworths are not people who need concern you any longer.' So that was that, and I feel like a child who has been warned off a haunted room . . ."

For Hesba, the ghost was laid. The haunted room had been opened and she had seen all that it contained. It was on the night before this letter came that she had received Elsie's visit.

"Do you know where my brother is?" That was the abrupt uncompromising opening as soon as Elsie was in the room.

It was clear to Hesba that Elsie was under a great strain. She put her in an armchair by the fireside and herself sat down quietly. "Let us be still for a moment," she said. "My old father was one of the stillest men I've ever known. He died when I was only a child – a terribly fussy child, I'm afraid. He was always saying that to me when I got excited. 'Let us be still for a moment. No fuss.' We would sit down in a little room we had over a shop in North Wales, just saying nothing, but there was something in him, and it used to come out of him into me. It was just stillness. After a time, he'd say 'Well now . . . ' and as often as not there'd be nothing then that I wanted to say to him. I suppose I'd wanted some knot untied, and somehow he'd untied it without saying a word."

Hesba's voice, usually rather harsh and emphatic, seemed to recall the quiet in which her early life had been spent: the quiet of her father's life that had found so much because it had sought so little. To Elsie, listening to so unexpected an opening, there was something almost hypnotic in the other woman's dark eyes and sallow face. Hesba's mood transferred itself to her. She relaxed in her chair and said: "I know what you mean. Alec and I used to know a parson in Manchester – a Mr Burnside – who was like that. I should think no one ever knew more about other people's worries, but he was never worried himself." She smiled on a whimsical thought. "It's only just occurred to me – his name – Burnside. Being with him was just like that. You know. You can never be fussed if you lie down by the side of a stream and do nothing – just listen."

"Without even seeming to hear," Hesba put in, glad to see that the strain was going out of Elsie's face and that she was thinking sanely.

And then for some time they said nothing. Presently, Elsie said: "I'm afraid I was very rude to you when I met you at the Café Royal." She had raised her right hand from her lap and was looking dispassionately at her crooked fingers. "I must try to give up bothering about this. Whenever I meet anyone new, I'm all of a funk, wondering what they think. I was going to be a musician, you know, a violinist."

Poor child! Hesba thought in her grown-up way, though Elsie was older than she. That would explain everything. "Pretty, isn't it?" It would not be her hand she found you looking at: it would be the ruin of all her hopes.

"And now," Elsie went on, "all I can do about music is listen to it."

"No," said Hesba, "there's more in it than that. You can listen to it with love and understanding. I can guess how much that means, because it's denied to me. Beethoven doesn't sound much different to me from the latest tune at Daly's."

"There's something in that," Elsie agreed, "but not everything. It's because I understand and love that I know what I've lost for ever. And you see it was my one thing – the only thing I was ever any good at. If I'd been a writer, I could have learned to use my left hand, and even if I'd lost both hands I could have learned to dictate. But there's no way out of this."

It was a good thing, Hesba thought, that the child was talking about it so quietly. Probably she'd never talked about it before – kept it bottled up and seething. "How long ago was it?" she asked.

"Ten years."

That *was* a shock, and she saw Elsie as a child no longer. Ten years ago! Good gracious, she calculated, I should be, then, a mite of twelve or thirteen; and so long ago as that this girl could be thinking of music as work for a lifetime. And for all this time, no doubt, the frustration had been fermenting in her heart. She looked at Elsie with tenderness and pity.

"Were you very good?" she asked.

Elsie laughed outright. "What a question! You ought to know the answer to that, because you're an artist, too. Well, you know how it is. Sometimes you feel you're the finest thing under the sun, and at other times you want to take rat poison. Isn't it like that with you?"

"More or less," Hesba agreed with a smile.

"I suppose," said Elsie, "I should have known more about it when I got to Vienna."

"You were going to Vienna?"

"'Yes."

"Well, there you are! *Someone* must have thought you pretty good."

Elsie had nothing to say to that. She fell into a reverie before the glowing fire, and Hesba did not disturb her for a time. Then she said: "Well, this is the time for my afternoon walk. Would you like to come with me? Then you can come back and share my evening meal. And, if you like, you can stay here tonight. I can sleep on this couch and you can have my bed."

Elsie protested: "No, no. You'll want to be getting on with your work."

"No. My work's done for the day. I wouldn't let you interfere with *that*," she smiled. "No, indeed, I assure you. I am invisible in the mornings. My landlady has already learned to be a dragon. You certainly would not have been admitted if you had called before one o'clock. Not if you had been Sir Daniel Dunkerley himself. But after lunch I do as I please. So you'll stay?"

Elsie nodded. "Good," said Hesba. "I can fix you up with all you need. I shall be glad of your company. I'm feeling rather lonely now that my friend Grace Satterfield is gone away."

They walked along outside the park railings towards Hyde Park Corner. "It's strange," said Elsie, "how you know all the people I used to know when I was growing up. I don't think I ever saw Miss

Satterfield, but I knew old George Satterfield, her father. He took to drinking like a fish. Alec used to be most amusing about him."

Hesba smiled to herself in the darkness. She had never understood that Grace was grieving deeply about her father's death.

"Of course, it was before they all got rich that I knew them," Elsie prattled on. "Dan Dunkerley just had a printer's shop, and not much of a one at that. Alec was apprenticed there. I used to see Dan and his wife quite a lot in Levenshulme. Then, of course, once they started with that paper *Hard Facts* they were all up in the air and rolling in money. But I must say Dan and his wife treated me very well after that. They asked me several times to a big house they took in Didsbury. But I don't suppose you know anything about Manchester."

"Oh, indeed, I do. I assure you. I was born in Cheetham Hill."

"Well, I never!" said Elsie. "Well, of course, it was the young ones of the two families – the Dunkerleys and Satterfields – that we didn't see after that. They all vanished – away to school and what not. I did once, now I come to think of it, see Miss Satterfield."

They had reached the Marble Arch and turned into the Park. "She had come back from school to attend a big public lunch. It was when *Hard Facts* was a year old."

Suddenly she stopped speaking, stopped walking, just stood there, and Hesba was aware that she was trembling. She took Elsie's arm and led her to an empty seat. They sat down facing Park Lane, with the darkness of the Park behind them, and before them the winter – bare trees and the street lamps and the hansoms darting in and out of the buses drawn by ambling horses. Hesba put an arm round her trembling companion.

"I'm sorry," Elsie said. "Oh, what a fool you must think me!"

"No, no," Hesba assured her. "I'm certain you're nothing of the sort." She felt riven with pity for this girl whose life was evidently full of ghosts. What a pair they were – she and Alec – touchy as galled horses to a hand that tried to soothe them, yet so clearly in need of healing.

"It came over me all of a sudden," Elsie said. "I walked right into it without thinking. That day I saw Miss Satterfield – it was the day this happened." She held up her mutilated hand, then allowed it to fall back into her lap. "Miss Satterfield was only a child then. I can see her now. She was very beautifully dressed. Of course, she was already rich."

"Yes," said Hesba gently. "I can imagine it." She was remembering that she and Grace were of the same age. And there Grace was, beautifully dressed, already rich. It would be about the time Father died, she was thinking, and Mr Vereker had gone away, and I was living in Miss Price's attic. It was the time when all the years of her own gulf were before her – the long dark passage that seemed as though it had no end. She was overwhelmed anew by the sense of the gulf into which a human life might drop. She took Elsie's right hand into both of hers and held it in her lap. She said nothing, nor for a long time did Elsie. Presently Elsie said: "I was engaged to be married at that time. No one knew about it – well, except Mr Burnside, that Manchester parson I was telling you about. The young man was his curate. Even Alec didn't know. Well, Alec was half-tight that night. He got into a fight with this young man. He had a dagger in his hand, and I tried to separate them – and – and – this happened."

"But – but that was the time when Mr Chrystal was with Mr Burnside? I've heard Grace speak of that."

Elsie did not at once answer this. In the night, which had the strange quality of a city night that it was none the less quiet for all the noise that filled it, the immensity of darkness and remote stars lulling the immediate turmoil to a thread of undisturbing sound, she sat quivering under the memory of that old hurt, remembering the pain, and that she had sat, as now, under the sky in darkness, with a comforting woman at her side. "Don't imagine," she said presently, "that I ever think of *him* now." She got up, and Hesba rose, too. They began to walk on. "It's not even a question of forgiveness," Elsie said. "It's as though he'd never existed. If it came to forgiveness, there'd be need for plenty on both sides." There was a smile on her face again as she added: "No. You mustn't think of me as a Wronged Woman."

Nothing more was said about Alec till they had returned and eaten their supper. The fire was bright; the curtains were drawn; Elsie, Hesba thought, with her red tendrils glinting in the gaslight, was a most beautiful woman, and now, too, she was serene, delivered for a moment from the Dillworth intensity of spirit. She could speak quietly of what had brought her there. "I become so agitated about Alec," she said, "as though he were a child I had to look after. I know that's foolish, because he's really well able to look after himself. Do you know where he is?"

"No. I was at *Dunkerley's* office yesterday. Before he went to Dickons, Alec arranged for me to be there then to meet the man who is to illustrate my new book. Well, when I turned up the artist was there, but Alec wasn't. There was a man I'd never met before who said Sir Daniel had told him to carry on with *Dunkerley's* till Mr Dillworth returned. I asked him when that would be, and he said he didn't know; he understood from Sir Daniel that Mr Dillworth was taking a long holiday. There seemed to me to be something queer and unexpected about the whole business."

Elsie gave an uneasy laugh. "Well," she said, "someone's got to pay the rent of the place we're living in, and that certainly can't be me."

7

For a long time Alec walked on, fascinated by the night. The trees were trees to him. Even had they been clothed, he would hardly have known oak from elm or beech, and now that they were no more than charcoal silhouettes drawn on the white page of the night they had a complete and lovely anonymity. The writhen limbs of the oaks, the drooping branches of the beech, the abundant lacy skeletons of the elms, all pleased him alike, as it pleased him to walk in the streets and look at the faces of men – tortured or serene, vacuous or seamed with care – without having to enquire their names or circumstances.

And so for a long time his walk was filled with the uplifting sense of an experience altogether new and satisfying. The icy emptiness of the sky, pouring down its cold upon the earth so that it rang faintly beneath Alec's boots as he walked, exalted him and set his feet racing. But in time this mood gave place to another. Fascination can be near to terror, and at last the immense indifference of the silence began to oppress him. It was now that the road, which at first had climbed and had then run level, began to drop towards a wooded valley. Looking down into it, Alec saw it like a pit of darkness dug out of the pale luminosity of the still, enchanted earth. He was aware of a sharp reluctance to go down into that darkness, but thither the way led, and he went on. Once he had admitted into his mind the thought that this cold splendour had a quality of death, and that silence which could soothe could also menace, his imagination began to supply him with evils, both lying in wait and following after. For the first time he looked behind him, and was aware of fright in the glance. But there was nothing on the road that stretched back half-washed with bluish light, half-hid in the hairy shadow of the hedge.

Now he began the mile-long descent, and when he was halfway down he was in the darkness of the wood: not a darkness absolute as it had seemed when looked at from above, but a striped and chequered darkness, a darkness broken up by shafts and splinters of moonlight that suggested to his imagination the shapes of moving things. He looked up, and saw the ball of the moon fantastically floating upon the black scrawny fingers that seemed to be all that precariously upheld it from crashing into the pit.

Now he was walking with a conscious intention of making no noise. His delight in the ring of boots on iron earth was gone. It was not difficult here to go quietly, for the leaves had piled in long drifts at the roadsides, and not much frost had penetrated through the branchy and interlacing roof. There was but the faintest rustle beneath his feet. In this silence he heard the sound of water and soon came to a bridge which carried the road over the stream at the bottom of the dip.

Something of the fear slid off his mind as he leaned on the worn stone parapet and looked down at the glint and movement over the rocks. This was life at last. Amid the frozen air and the petrified trees and the very leaves which seemed, lying on the ground, to be thin arrowheads of copper nailed immobile by the cold, here was a chuckle of content, the quiet purposeful sliding of life. It calmed and soothed him. He did not want to go on, but, though the hold of the frost was not here so severe as on the uplands, he found it cold enough and turned to address himself to the steep uphill pull.

It was at this moment that a high thin scream brought him to a standstill, trembling. He knew at once what it was. A townsman to the marrow, he could nevertheless imagine the small creature, and the springing steel jaw, and the crunch of bone. Then the wood and all the night was full for him of the terrors that assailed defenceless things. He plodded up the hill with his nerves at a ragged edge as he pictured the trapped creature straining and tugging, escaping maybe at the cost of a leg left in the trap, agonising the night through as the blood flowed, and the pain throbbed, and the indifferent cold deepened.

And once he was off on this track, his imagination supplied him with an unending dance of life and death, life using death itself for its own preservation as the stoat's jaws sank in the rabbit's neck, or the shot left the wounded duck floundering inaccessibly in the morass, or the pole-axe thudded upon the ox's skull.

He had not till now been aware of his own overwrought condition. He had prided himself on conducting his quarrel with Dan Dunkerley quietly and reasonably, but below this thin ice of decorum the stream of his touchy sensibility had been raging. It was disturbing him the more now for having been kept in check. If he had flamed, he would have blown out his accumulated grievances like a volcano, as he had often done before, and Dan would have flamed, too; and by now they would have been ready to take breakfast amicably in the morning. As it was, his repressed rage had thrust him out of the house and was still bubbling and seething in him, complicated by the thoughts of life and death that had visited him in the wood. He began to see himself as a doomed and helpless victim, caught in the trap of Dunkerley Publications. But hadn't he just escaped? Hadn't he forced open the jaws and walked out into freedom?

He plodded slowly up the hill and knew the answer. He came out from the shadows of the trees into the cold unimpassioned light of the moon. Here the hedges were gone. He was upon a small heath and on either side could see a long way. He stood still, looking upon the lunar landscape, and he was never to forget this moment when he was utterly alone, face to face with himself in the silence that almost crackled with cold. He knew that he would accept the ignominy of crawling back. No doubt he would go with a brave defiant face, but it would be ignominious none the less. He had made a fool of himself with a dramatic gesture that could not be sustained. He saw himself with a clarity that he could never forget or forgive, for what he was: a man cursed with aspirations that were little more than bubble-chasing when he tried to bring them down to earth. "After all, I *am* a writer." For ten years it had been his defiance, flung into Dan Dunkerley's teeth, into Theo Chrystal's, into the teeth of anyone who would listen. He recalled an occasion years ago when he and Chrystal had stood upon a hill in Derbyshire, and he had cast this old challenge at Chrystal's face. "Well," Theo said, "plenty of writers have had to earn their living uncongenially while waiting for success. There's nothing to stop you from writing, is there?"

He could hear now, standing there on the bleached road, the young parson's cold reasonable accents and his own heated reply. And, by God, he admitted in a burst of heart-breaking candour, Chrystal was right. Names floated into his mind — so many that the road seemed to be haunted with a cloud of witnesses — of those who against every circumstance of poverty and disease and encumbering work had not only said, as he had done, but had triumphantly vindicated, as he had not: After all, I am a writer.

Alec was almost sick with the intensity of realisation that came to him. He was not free because he had not freed himself and he had not freed himself because it was not in him to do so. He could loathe and abominate the second-rate and the second-hand; he could worship what he felt to be authentic and creative; but that was not all that he had wanted. He had wanted himself to create the worshipful; and in place of the forests that his young imagination had pictured he had produced a twig or two; instead of setting rivers flowing, he had spilled a few cups of water upon the parched ground. And he knew now that this was all he was capable of doing. He had crowed like a cock, but no dawn had reddened: nothing had lightened but a few flickering candles.

He walked on, chilled to the marrow and frozen in spirit. He would think always of that little heath as his Gethsemane. His one thought now was to find warmth and rest. Presently he came to a cottage separated from the road by a strip of garden. In a corner of the garden was a shed; he tip-toed towards it and cautiously tried the door. This was unlatched and he went inside, shutting it behind him. He struck a match and saw that the place was full of gins and traps, and that in one corner was a pile of sacks. He was now shivering; uncontrollable tremors rippled down him from head to foot, engendered both by the cold and the emotional turmoil through which he had passed. He spread out the sacks, lay upon some of them, and pulled the others over him. He had a half-awake resolve to be up and away at first light. His head began to throb and swim, and he lost consciousness, not so much falling asleep as floating in a cushioned vacuum, in which he was nonsensically sensible of being surrounded by gins and snares.

8

In the cottage Mrs Rigby lay late abed. Downstairs there was a fire to be lit and breakfast to be prepared. But the blankets were warm with the night's sleeping of her plump body and she was reluctant to step out into the cold of the morning. Through the small frosted pane of the window she could see the sun's red plaque, all show and no warmth. It was a good thing that her husband was away, and a better thing still, she thought, that he would be away till the weekend. He was gone to his father's funeral in Cockermouth, which, thank God, was a long way off. She wished he had ten fathers in Lapland and that they would die one after another at nicely-spaced intervals. She snuggled down deeper into the blankets.

If only that dog would give over, she thought, a woman could have a bit of peace. But the dog did not give over. It had been whining and scratching at the shed door for half an hour. Effie Rigby got grudgingly out of bed, pulled on a dressing gown, shuffled into slippers, and opened the window. The astringent air made her wince. "Jess! Jess! Give over! What's come into thee!" she shouted. And then, to her surprise, the shed door was flung back, a skinny little man tottered out, staggered for a few yards, and fell flat to the ground. Jess began frantically licking his face. "Well, I never did!" said Effie. She pulled an old green coat over her dressing gown and ran downstairs. Before she married Rigby she had been a Queen Victoria nurse. Her blood was up.

She bent over Alec, clicking her tongue. She put her arms round him and picked him up. Well, well! Did you ever see such a slip of a thing! Light as a feather! She carried him upstairs, stripped him down to his shirt, and pushed him into the bed that was radiant with the warmth of her own body. He did not speak a word – not one that she could understand, anyway, though from time to time he muttered deliriously. He made such a small pitiful hump under the bedclothes, she thought, standing back and contemplating him with her hands on her hips.

She did not dress, but now that she was up she went down, lit the kitchen fire, and made herself some breakfast. It was a good one too. The fact is, Effie was in a holiday mood. It wasn't every day that Joe's father died, and she was going to make the most of it. Good feeding had always been included in Effie's notion of making the most of things. So she fried two eggs and a large thick rasher of ham, toasted plenty of bread, and put all this on the table with a pot of tea and a jar of marmalade. She pulled the table up close to the fire and sat down to a leisurely meal. She decided against taking anything to the chap upstairs. Whoever he was, poor little shrimp, and however it had come about, it was evident that he was clemmed to the bone. What he wanted at the moment was warmth, not food. Otherwise, she'd soon have a case of pneumonia on her hands, and that would mean going five miles for a doctor. Effie didn't want to go for a doctor; she didn't want to go for anyone. At the back of her simple and unsubtle mind she knew that well enough. She wanted this chap to herself. As soon as Joe had gone she had promised herself a holiday, and, by heck, she laughed to herself, it looked as though she was going to have one.

Her strong white teeth bit into the crackling buttered toast. Effie *would* put butter on toast to eat with eggs and ham. She rejoiced in the full feel of all her senses, and the sense of taste came high in her regard. She pulled the green overcoat up to her knees, spread open the dressing gown, and, dandling one knee over the other, warmed her robust calf at the blaze.

She savoured to the full her feeling of snugness and security. Looking through the window, she saw that the red sun had disappeared. Clouds were banking up. After a week of open weather, with a strengthless sun all day and bitter frost at night, a change was on the way. And it wasn't a change, she thought, for better weather. The cold was keen. She could feel an icy breath stealing under the crack of the door that opened straight into the yard. She got up, heaped an old rug in front of the door, and decided to put another egg into the frying-pan. This was going to be snow, if she knew anything.

She mopped the last smear of fat from her plate with a piece of toast, refilled her tea-cup, and fell-to on the marmalade. It was heaven, she thought, to be here like this, with Joe hundreds of miles away. Never before, in their three years of marriage, had she had a day – and, indeed, the prospect of three or four days – all alone. She had a fairly just understanding of herself and was constantly surprised that she was, after three years of Joe, a cheerful sensuous woman. She was twenty-five. He was ten years older. She had been on a holiday from her native Accrington, staying on a farm near Cockermouth, when she first met Joe who was visiting his father. One day she had packed her lunch in a bag and gone off walking. She had come out on a lonely

101

stretch of beach and there she had eaten her food with the sun pouring down. Then she lay in a corrugation of the dune, soaking in the warmth, flat on her back, her plump fingers crisping upon the sand that flowed through them like warm water. She fell asleep, and when she awoke and sat up she saw that a man was standing as naked as Adam twenty yards away. He was towelling a wet body and his back was to her. He had come up from bathing, and she, in the deep cleft of the dune, had been invisible. Effie gazed with frank interest at the wide shoulders, the well-shaped legs planted sturdily apart. The muscles of the back rippled under the sunlight. Her job as a nurse had shown her a good deal of male nudity, but male nudity in Accrington had lacked this rippling sun-browned intensity. She saw that the man's clothes lay on the sand behind him, and knew therefore that he would have to turn round in order to dress. She remained sitting up, watching him with interest.

That, characteristically enough, was how Effie met her husband. He was a grand figure of a man, but he was also a braggart and a liar. The "job on a Sussex estate," which was as near as she got to learning of his occupation, sounded good to her. She was, for one thing, an orphan, and, for another, more than ready for marriage. She had hardly known what sort of home to expect: a small manor would hardly have surprised her. This stark cottage of two rooms up and two down, on the edge of a heath, with the nearest neighbour a mile away, was something of a shock, and so was the discovery that Joe's job on a Sussex estate was no more than that of an under-keeper. But, Effie being what she was, all this would have been not only tolerable but enjoyable had it not been for something more serious. For all his thews and sinews, Joe was as impotent as a gelding.

Effie piled the breakfast things into the tin bowl in the kitchen sink. They could wait. She fed Jess, and then, in a riot of self-indulgence, raked the now-glowing fire into a shovel and in two or three journeys transferred it to the grate in the bedroom. Finally, she carried up the scuttle.

She stood for a moment looking down at the man in the bed. One arm, pitifully thin, was flung out over the coverlet. Fair hair fell in disorder upon his brow. She put her hand upon it and felt that it was burning. A few muttered incoherencies fell from the lips. Effie dropped her old green coat and dressing gown to the floor, kicked off her slippers, and climbed into bed. It was luxuriously warm. She put an arm round Alec and pulled him towards her. He came like a child, snuggled himself into the curves of her body, and sighed with content. Soon they were both soundly asleep. So was Jess in the kitchen, and there was no other living thing for a mile in any direction. The fire glowed and the snow began to fall.

9

It was noon when Effie woke. She found herself lying on her back, with her right arm under Alec's body. Her fingers could feel the shallows between his ribs. She turned her head and looked at his face. It was not so flushed. He was sleeping quietly, breathing easily. Warmth and rest: that's what he'd wanted, Effie reflected with satisfaction. Astonishing what they could do – warmth and rest. They had been her favourite prescription in her nursing days. Of course, you had to pretend to do what the doctor ordered, but there were no pills and medicines to beat this.

She looked up at the ceiling. The pallor of the snow was thrown up on to it. A little drift had piled on the window ledge. Through the glass she could faintly see the big flakes falling. Gently she drew her arm from under Alec's body, got out of bed, and mended the fire. She put on the dressing gown and coat again and went down to the kitchen. Time to be preparing her dinner. She was not one of those women who get along on a bun and a cup of tea if left to themselves. She lit the fire, peeled potatoes and carrots, and put them to boil. On an oil stove she put an iron saucepan containing a rich meat stew. She made a custard, put it on top of a half-eaten rice pudding, and popped this into the oven. She reckoned that if she followed this with some bread and cheese and a pot of tea she wouldn't hurt.

When these important matters were under way, Effie swept out the kitchen, rubbed up the dresser with bees-wax, polished two brass dogs that lived one on either end of the chimney-piece, and rolled up the rag mat which she had made during her first winter of marriage. How things looked mattered as much to her as how things felt and tasted. She liked her kitchen to shine.

It needed some resolution to open the kitchen door, for it gave directly upon the snowy yard. She buttoned the old coat tight about her and nerved herself to the job. She couldn't abide a mat that hadn't been shaken every day. A ledge of snow that had formed outside the door fell in a crisp white crumble upon the kitchen flags. She looked out into the grey whirl of the weather that hid all but the nearest objects and hastily shook the mat into its face, as though at all odds she must fly the banner of her irreproachable housewifery. Then, throwing the mat behind her into the kitchen, she was about to shut the door when a blur formed itself into a shape and the shape became indubitably the postman, coming along the path with his head down and a casque of snow romantically transforming his official cap.

Effie stood with the letter in her hand till the man was obliterated by the storm; then she shut the door, threw the bolts at top and bottom, spread the mat, and sat in her chair by the fire, assured now that there would be no other intrusion as long as that day lasted.

She turned the letter idly in her hand. The writing was her husband's; the postmark said Cockermouth. She felt no desire to read what Joe had to say. He would have the old man buried and be back soon enough. She tried the potatoes with a fork; they could do with another wobble, she decided; and while waiting for them she opened the letter. Joe was a writer who had no use for *finesse*. He went straight to the point:

DEAR EFFIE – The old man had more money than I expected. A sollicitor had a talk with me about how things are yesterday afternoon and they are better than I expected – viz five thousand or thereabouts to say nothing of the farm which is left if I want to work it to me, and I don't see why not seeing the years I've worked for others which will make it a considable pleasure to be my own boss. It is therefore not my intension to come back there at all but I shall write to the estate agent telling him not to expect me and if theres any question of legal notis he can soo me if he likes but I don't intend to work for other people any longer now that I have this oppertunity to be my own boss and I feel I have enough knowledge to handle the farm having been brought up here and not being exactly a fool. So you can make arrangements to sell up there unless theres any pieces you have a sentimentle value for in which case forward them by rail though this is not necessary this place as you know being amply furnished. So you won't see me down there any

more my heart being always in these parts and the south
something I've put up with not enjoyed.

Yours

JOE.

P.S. We bury him tomorrow. Bring Jess with you.

Effie put the letter back in its envelope and tucked it behind the
starboard brass dog. The potatoes were done, but for a moment even
that knowledge and the savoury smell of the stew did not stir her to
action. With her arm still stretched up to the brass dog, she looked for
a moment into the friendly fire. Then she gave a sigh of utter content,
stretched her arms to the ceiling, and yawned.

10

The honeymoon lasted a week. It was late in the evening of the day
when Effie received her letter that Alec came fully to his senses. He
lay still in the bed, taking in his surroundings. He was in a room filled
with mild radiance. The curtain was drawn. It was a dusky red curtain,
and its warmth, lying against the clean white-washed wall, pleased
him. This wall was tremulous with wings of light pulsing upon it, and
this, he saw, was the consequence of a fire burning in a grate on his
right. The ceiling was wearing a halo, flung up from a paraffin lamp
that stood, crimson-shaded, on a table. By the fire, in a cushioned
wicker chair, was a woman whose back was to him. She was wearing
a cheap-looking dressing gown which had none the less a pleasing
depth of dark-blue colour that the firelight caused to shimmer. The
lamp was behind her. He could not see her face, but the lamp
irradiated her black hair. The dressing gown had fallen back from her
crossed legs. He could see one of them, rosy in the light of lamp and
fire, gently jigging up and down as she read.

Alec did not speak. His mind was groping round the circumstances
which had brought him here, wherever here might be. Slowly he
assembled the facts: the quarrel with Dan Dunkerley, the long walk in
the cold brilliant night, the agony of the moment when he had stood
on the heath, face to face with himself. There his mind paused, reliving
all the emotions of that moment, reaffirming them. He felt as weak as
a rabbit, but cool and well. The burning of body and mind that had
afflicted him on the heath were gone. Now he was in his senses, and

105

in his senses he knew that the revelations of that moment must stand. He was Alec Dillworth, no one in particular.

It was with no perturbation or bitterness that he now accepted this fact. Long, long ago there had been dreams: dreams of the wonderful Dillworth kids: Elsie the musician, Alec the man of letters. Now they were gone like other dreams at cock-crow. In the cold light of dawn he saw a different situation: Alec Dillworth who had thrown up a job but who nevertheless had a sister to keep.

Then, his ruminations went on, there had been a gate, and a shed, and a bed of sacks. That was the end of the story as far as he could reconstruct it. He must have been ill; someone must have found him and carried him off to hospital. No; that was no good, he decided. There was never a hospital ward like this, never a hospital ward where the nurse sat reading by the fire, jigging a stout naked leg.

Wherever he was, it was all most pleasant. He had a confused recollection of having spent a long time half-waking, half-sleeping, his body dry and scaly-feeling, his head burning. Now his body and head were all right, and it was good to lie here in this peace and silence. Not quite silence. From beyond the curtained windows there was not a sound. Though Alec did not know that it had been snowing all day and was snowing still, the sense of the dumb white world without was somehow present in the very room. But within, there were gentle sounds: the flutter of the fire, the crisp turn of a page as Effie read, the occasional creak of a board or joist as the old cottage bowed its shoulders beneath the snow deepening upon the roof.

Alec felt that he would like to lie there forever, wrapped in this warmth and quietude. Of course, it was the woman. It was not for a long time that this thought formed in his mind. Never before in all his life had he lain in bed with a woman in the room – not, anyway, since he and Elsie were children, and Elsie was not a woman in the sense in which the word smote him now. It was the woman, sitting so tranquilly in the chair, so unaware, apparently, of his existence, who was the centre of this room, of its warmth and power to comfort. Not the fire, not the lamp, but the woman. The silence without and the tranquillity within seemed to flow out of the woman. He was overcome by a desire to see her face, and he said: "Where am I?"

He wondered if his voice would startle her, but it did not. She got up, and he could hear the wicker chair easing itself from her weight.

She composedly put a book-marker into the place where she had been reading and laid the book down on the table under the lamp. "She's like Hesba." That was the first thought that visited him as she came towards the bed. And she was, in so far as being short and dark and dumpy made a resemblance.

She stood looking down at him, and placed a hand on his forehead. Then she felt his pulse. "You're getting over it, lad," she said. "It was a near go for pneumonia."

That word "lad" and the broad pronunciation of the "go" made Alec smile. "Am I in Lancashire?" he asked.

"Near enough," she said briefly. "I'm a bit of Accrington."

"I'm Manchester," he said.

"You are, are you?" said Effie. "Well, you don't look like it. You look more like a skinned rabbit."

She turned to the fire and took up a small iron saucepan that was standing inside the fender. "Ah've been keeping this hot against time tha' waked," she said; and he sensed now that she was rediscovering and emphasising an accent long lost, in order to please him.

"Thanks, lass," he said.

She lifted him up in the bed, put the pillow into the small of his back, and spread a shawl over his shoulders. Sitting up, he realised that he was still anything but strong. Effie poured the broth into a basin and gave it to him on a tray. "A nice time to start eating," she said, glancing at the tin clock on the mantelpiece. Alec saw that it was ten o'clock.

"Where am I?" he asked again. "And how long have I been here?"

"Get that down thee, an' never mind questions," Effie answered. "Tha'll know soon enough."

The broth was delicious, and when it was finished Effie said: "Now come an' sit in this chair, an' Ah'll mak t'bed."

She helped him out, and he felt his knees weak and trembling. Effie stripped down the bed with the ease of long practice and made it up smoothly. "Now hop in, lad," she said. "Tha should sleep better for that, an' sleep's what tha still needs."

Alec crawled back into the bed and rejoiced in the feel of the smooth sheets. Effie moved about quietly, putting the room to rights. She made up the fire and put a guard in front of it; then blew out the lamp. For a moment the darkness seemed complete; but soon the fireglow spread in a warm silence through the small white-washed room. Alec could see Effie standing between him and the fire. He saw her drop her dressing gown to the floor, and the light made her thin nightdress transparent. He saw her sturdy legs planted apart, and then felt her climbing over him to the other side of the bed. She slipped in beside him, and he went into her arms as instinctively as a tired child. She held him close, and whispered: "Now go to sleep, lad. Tha still wants a lot o' sleep." He was asleep almost as she spoke, but Effie lay awake for a long time, not moving, smiling to herself and thinking of the snow. She could almost hear it settling upon heath and yard and roof.

<h2 style="text-align:center">11</h2>

When Alec awoke he experienced again the bewilderment of last night, but now he remembered more quickly. He was alone in the bed. There was no lamp-light, and through the window from which the curtain was drawn back he could see the dumb white light of the morning. The snow was no longer falling, but there was a sense of its impending, of this being an intermission, not an end. The fire had been newly made up. Alec felt well and hungry. A dog's bark under the window filled the silence with happy vital noise, and through the floor he could hear the clatter of pans and crockery, and the woman's voice singing. How lovely these simple homely sounds were! They were like life itself coming back after it had retreated for a long way.

He got out of bed and found that he was stronger on his feet. His clothes were folded on a chair and he put them on. He saw the small suitcase in which he had carried his few things lying on the floor, and he took out his toothbrush and shaving gear. A kettle was simmering near the fire. This woman, whoever she was, thought of everything. He poured the water into the basin on the washstand, added some cold from the great jug painted with pink roses, and washed and shaved. He felt fine. Well, he thought, I had better be getting downstairs. But now a strong disinclination to do anything of the kind came over him. He was too shy to face the woman. He remembered how she had climbed into the bed last night and how, gratefully, he had accepted the warmth and healing comfort of her body. No doubt, while knowing nothing about it, he had done the same thing the night before. They had brought young warm women and put them into bed with King David, he recalled, when the king was old and ill. It had done him no good; David was too far gone. But I wasn't, thought Alec. It did me all the good in the world. Perhaps it saved my life. I ought to go down and thank the woman. But it was a long time before he could do so.

When she heard his footsteps on the uncarpeted wooden stairs, Effie looked up from the frying-pan full of sizzling eggs and spluttering bacon. The cloth was on the table; places were laid for two. A golden-crusted loaf, a dish of pale yellow butter, and a green porcelain leaf containing marmalade all added to the colour and gaiety that Effie had set out to achieve. It wasn't every day she used the green porcelain leaf, a wedding present from one of her patients. The tablecloth was another rarely-used present: it was of primrose linen.

Alec paused for a moment in the doorway, looking at these bits of colour, at the glow rising to the woman's face from the kitchen range, all of it made more vital by the corpse-light that leaned flat upon the window. Effie looked round laughing and pushing back from her face a hank of falling hair. Her features were vitalised by more than the firelight. In this lull of the storm she had run out to feed the hens and bring in the eggs. The sting of the weather brightened her eyes. Her Wellington boots, with a scab or two of snow still on them, stood inside the door. She ladled fat from the bacon upon the eggs and then stepped to the window. She pulled the thin muslin curtain across. "We don't have many visitors," she said, "and in this weather they're as likely as a man in the moon. But you never know."

Her action and her words brought Alec up against the dubiety of the situation. He blushed beneath her frank appraising look. "I must say, lad, you look a lot better. A shave and a hair-brush make a difference. You're not bad-looking in a half-starved fashion. Sit thee dahn."

He ate like a wolf. Colour began to come back to his face, and with the return of a sense of physical well-being his courage grew. He began to thank the woman for what she had done, but she cut him short. "Ah done nowt but please myself," she said. "Ah've enjoyed having a Lancashire lad about t'place. What's thy name, Manchester?"

"Alec."

"Tha's keepin' back half, eh? Well, Ah'll do t'same. My name's Effie."

"You'd better tell me, Effie, just where I am and how far it is to a station. I shall have to be going."

"You're going to no station in this weather," she said firmly. "You'll stay where you are for a day or two."

Now her obstinacy began to irritate him. "But, my good woman—"

"Eh, none of that!" she said sharply. "Ah'm a nurse, an' tha'll do as Ah bid thee. For one thing, tha can get on wi' t'washing up while Ah mak t'bed."

She filled a tin bowl in the back-kitchen sink and left him to it. It was a job he was used to, but Effie watched him critically for a moment. "Be careful wi' that green leaf," she said. "That's valuable." And even as she was walking up the stairs, already unbuttoning her blouse, she was thinking that that curled green porcelain leaf was one thing she must take with her to Cockermouth. It was a nice thing, was that. A moment later she was calling down the stairs: "Alec, come an' help me with this bed."

12

At intervals throughout that day the snow continued to fall, but the sun shone brightly the next morning. By then, Alec was in no hurry to resume his journey. In the afternoon, alone in the cottage, he stood at the window looking out on the sun-dazzled snow. From the front door to the gate giving upon the heath he could see Effie's sturdy tracks and the light weaving pattern of Jess' ecstatic prancing round her. How magnificent she had looked, he thought, as she went forth: the Wellington boots on her legs, the red scarf wound about her head, the green coat, the huge basket on her arm. It was three miles to town, she said. She had set off at eleven. There was shopping to do, and she must make some inquiries about having her furniture sold and shifting a few things to Cockermouth. And she must send a telegram to Joe. Alec was well acquainted now with all these details of her life. Once she had begun to talk, she had talked volubly and frankly, and she had made him do the same. They knew all about one another.

He had been touched by Effie's mood almost of contrition, and of something like awe, when she found herself to be his first woman. But she was getting over that. She was beginning to feel a pride in having liberated him. "You've been living in fairy-land, lad," she said. "I've made you a human being." And there was something in that, Alec thought. He recalled the midnight clarity of that moment on the heath when he realised that all sorts of phantoms were too elusive for his embrace; and into the void that that moment had left Effie had burst with the revelation of a humanity that he had been inclined to overlook. Manna might be lacking, but life, it seemed, had a good deal of worthwhile palatable bread.

He was enchanted with Effie's commonsense. He had wanted to go with her to town. "Don't be daft, lad," she had answered. "What would milkman think if he saw two pairs of boots makin' tracks from t'door? They can put two an' two together in t'country as quick as in t'town, an' sometimes a good deal quicker. Stay where you are, and keep away from t'winder."

She had a good deal to do in town and she would have her lunch there. She said she would be back at four and that he'd better have tea ready. Not *about four*, but *at* four. He had already learned that she was precise and practical and did what she had made up her mind to do. "Not that it always turns out well. I made up my mind to marry Joe, an' look at that! But if you put your foot into something an' don't like it, well, you've got to lump it, that's all."

In this way she accepted Joe and never for a moment seemed to think of leaving him. "No man who deserved a worse wife ever had a better one," she said complacently.

Alec's feeling about Effie was compounded of gratitude and child-like dependence. She was older, though not, in years, much older than he was; but in the sort of experience which he was now entering upon all the guidance had to come from her. He was puzzled that she should go with such full enjoyment into this adventure, yet leave him in no doubt that it was fugitive. Her place, she said, was with Joe, and she must join him as soon as possible. Alec was always to remember with amusement how the ecstasies of the honeymoon had run side by side with practical arrangements for the life that was immediately to follow it. He had awakened out of a doze in the fire-warmed bedroom to find that Effie had not been asleep. She was lying with her arm under him, gazing up at the ceiling. When she realised that he was awake, she said: "Ah've been wonderin' about these sheets, Alec. They're good stuff. Should Ah tak 'em with me?"

The bed shook with his laughter, and she said: "What's funny? It's a practical point, isn't it? It's got to be settled."

111

She had quickly killed his first inclination to take the matter like a Quixote. He had suggested that she should not go to Cockermouth, that she should come with him to London, even that they might eventually marry. It was a sense of duty arising out of a sense of sin that caused him to propose this. Now it was Effie's turn to laugh; and that robust laughter put the matter on the footing where she was determined that it should stay. "Nay, lad," she said, "Ah've not wakened thee out of one folly to have thee fall into another." She handed him the brass dogs from the mantelpiece. "Rub these up, luv," she said. "Ah'm takkin' 'em."

"It seems to me," said Alec, mocking her accent, "tha's takkin' everything."

"Ay," she answered firmly, "everything but thee."

CHAPTER FIVE

I T WAS a London morning of miserable gloom, but Alec had never felt better. In the station refreshment room, though it was eleven o'clock, the gas was lighted, and as the door swung open now and then Alec could see spectral figures without, wrapped in the fog that oozed from the streets. He drank his coffee, picked up his suitcase, and went out to find a hansom. One pulled up under the canopy and discharged a passenger; Alec climbed in. To Dunkerley House. He looked with pleasure at the faint orange light of the lamps falling on the horse's flanks as it moved away slowly through the fog; smelled with pleasure the sulphurous air; heard with pleasure the muffled rumour of the town reaching him out of the morning's darkness. This was the place! It was good to be back. You can keep the country, he thought. Give me the city!

A young spectacled man sat at Alec's desk in the office of *Dunkerley's*. Alec threw down his suitcase and advanced to the fire, rubbing his hands. "Good morning, Titmouse," he said. "Everything in order?"

"Yes — I hope so," said Mr Titmuss, who was well used to this small play upon his name. "Anyway, if there's something not clear, I shall be about."

He gathered up a few papers and rose. Alec sat down with content in his chair. "Thank you, Titmouse," he said. "I don't expect I shall need to bother you."

"Miss Lewison will be calling at noon."

"Thank you."

A few minutes later Sir Daniel Dunkerley pushed open the door. "Oh, Titmuss—"

"Good morning, Dan."

For a second Sir Daniel hesitated. Then he came in and held out his hand. "Good morning, Alec."

They stood with hands clasped looking steadily at one another with ten years of knowledge and understanding in their eyes. Nothing, Sir Daniel decided, need be said. "I was going to tell Titmuss," he remarked, "that if Miss Lewison was free I'd take her out to lunch. She'll be here at noon. But I'm very busy. If you could do it for me, Alec –?"

"I shall be glad to."

"Thank you. I've written to congratulate her on finding such a good publisher for her book." There was just a flicker of the eyelids as he said it.

"That was good of you, Dan."

"Are you all right? I must say you're looking splendid."

"Never better. I've had a most refreshing holiday."

"That's all right then. By the way – did I tell you? – I'm starting a publishing house. Do you think Titmuss could handle that sort of thing?"

"I should think he'd do it excellently."

"Good. I must put it to him. That's all, I think. Oh – Laurie. If he looks in, just keep him busy. Find him something to do."

2

Lady Dunkerley was still in Somerset with Grace Satterfield. In her absence, Sir Daniel did not find the Manchester Square house congenial. In Dunkerley House he had his own suite of rooms: a sitting room, bedroom and bathroom. There was a kitchen where his meals could be prepared. He liked using this suite because it gave him a sense of importance. There was no reason why he should sleep on the premises, but to do so made him feel that Dunkerley House could hardly go on unless he was there like a ship's captain who stays on the bridge without taking off his clothes from one end of a difficult voyage to the other.

Sir Daniel did not carry the idea so far as to sleep in his clothes. He was very snug indeed, with his man Meaker to fetch and carry, and there was no case on record of his having been disturbed once he had retired to rest. The truth was that he was a good deal more quiet and comfortable at Dunkerley House than he was in Manchester Square.

To sit in the morning with the breakfast table drawn up close to the window and the good smell of coffee in his nostrils as he looked down on the bridges and the river: this was more satisfying than taking breakfast in the Manchester Square dining room, with nothing to see beyond the window but a few plane trees shivering in the winter murk.

Young Laurie had to put up with this unexhilarating prospect as he sat that morning at his solitary breakfast. Of course, he admitted, it need not have been solitary. Old Sim, his grandfather, had a spartan habit of rising at seven, breakfasting at a quarter to eight, and being at Dunkerley House at nine. Dinah never failed to keep the old man company, but this was beyond the reach of Laurie's resolution. It was now a quarter-past nine as he sat staring gloomily at the backbone of a kipper and the dregs in his coffee cup. Dinah peeped round the door, looking annoyingly bright and buoyant.

"Hullo," she said. "You look as though the sea had given up its dead."

"So it has," he answered, holding up the kipper by the tail without enthusiasm. " Isn't there a cook in this house?"

"There's a jolly good cook. And there are people who appreciate her cooking. And so they eat everything before you're out of bed. Old Sim eats like a horse."

"Talking of horses, why can't I ride in the Park with Father in the mornings instead of that odious fool Isambard Phyfe?"

"Because you're never up in time."

"Oh, chuck it. It's nothing to do with that. What's there to get up early *for*? Why do I have to spend my holidays here at all?"

"To give your family the pleasure of your company."

"All the men I know at Merton go away – to France or Switzerland or somewhere."

"Catch Father letting you go to France all on your own."

"Why, what does he take me for – a child?"

"No. I expect the fact of the matter is he thinks it's time you were a man."

"You mean all this business about learning What Dunkerley's Stands For?"

"Well, it's only commonsense, isn't it?" Dinah asked, coming into the room and looking at him in her practical way.

"Dear, dear!" said Laurie. "So the infant of the family has joined the Salutary Advice Committee. Are you panting to give me a Word in Season?"

"No. Not particularly. But if there were a pair of shoes I expected to step into, I'd learn to walk in them."

"I don't know that I want to step into any shoes."

"Oh, yes you do. What else will you do? It's not as though you were mad keen about doing anything else. Now if you were to offer Felix all Dunkerley Publications, he'd say: 'No, the law's my thing. I'm going to do that and nothing else.' And it's not because his father's a judge. It's because it's his own thing. He's mad keen."

"Oh, Felix! A wonderful child! I suppose that's why you're up at seven. Must be on the spot to catch the letters as they drop through the box. I'm surprised Father allows you two children to write to one another."

"Father knows nothing about it."

"Don't kid yourself. Father knows more than you think about everything. One of these days he'll Take Action in the approved Dunkerley fashion."

"Then I should run away."

"You'd be safe in school in Switzerland, my child, surrounded by guardian dragons."

"I'd run away from anywhere – Switzerland or anywhere else."

Laurie got up and yawned. "Well, I might be worse off than in London, I suppose," he said. "Did I tell you the latest? He wanted me to go to Manchester this holiday to learn to be a comp. Manchester!"

"What's a comp.?"

"There you are," said Laurie. "Talk about me! You live on Dunkerleys and you don't know the first thing about where the money comes from. A comp., my dear child, is a compositor: one of those men who pick up all the little letters and make 'em up into words in what they call a stick. That's a thing you hold in your left hand, and you flick the letters into it with your right. Then you put the type out of the stick into a long frame called a galley, and when your galley's full you have one column. And when you have as many galleys set up as there are columns in your page, you lock 'em in what's called a forme, and there you are, in a manner of speaking. You see, I know the theory perfectly, but His Nibs thought I ought to spend this holiday with my sleeves rolled up doing it all for myself. When I asked why, he said: 'Because I used to do it.' Now there's a reason for you!"

"But why go to Manchester to do that?"

"Because up there we do the whole bag of tricks. We produce our *Hard Facts* and *British Youngster* and lord knows how many other cheap pennyworths. We set it and print it and shove it all over the country. Down here we're more refined. Here we produce only our 'class' publications. Nothing but editorial work is done in Dunkerley House. The printing is sent out to various firms who go in for that sort of thing."

"Thank you. It's all news to me."

"It would be, you parasite. Anyhow, that's how you're kept on the fat of the land with nothing to do but indulge in schoolgirl flirtations."

"You don't do so badly, either."

"Except that I am looked on as the torch-bearer. Well, I'd better be getting along to Dunkerley House. Now that Manchester is off, the general idea is that I should pick up a few crumbs of knowledge from Mr Dillworth. Goodbye, you parasite. When you're married and have a son of twenty, remember that he'll just love to spend his holiday reading your husband's law-books."

"But, good gracious," said Dinah seriously, "how do we know what will happen in twenty years? Why, if I were to have a son right away now, he wouldn't be twenty till 1916. We'd be in a wonderful new century, and who knows how a boy would want to spend his holidays in 1916?"

Laurie laughed, and pulled her ear. "Why," he said, "since meeting our coming Lord Chancellor you're quite a serious woman. Don't overdo it. If you're writing to your little boy today, give him my love."

3

Dinah sat in the chair Laurie had left and spread out her letter.

DEAR MISS DINAH DUNKERLEY – The weather here remains cold. There is fully an inch of snow on the ground this morning, and last night it was necessary to spread my overcoat on the top of my blankets for warmth's sake. I have now settled into a useful routine. My tutor reads *The Times* newspaper aloud at breakfast, which is at 8 a.m., and then we have a discussion upon any matter of outstanding interest. He says that when I am dealing with my tutor at Oxford, I must not only have knowledge but also the ability to use it in debate, and so we have these morning talks which I find agreeable enough. At ten o'clock we begin our readings, one morning from the Latin and the next from the Greek. This continues until dinnertime at one o'clock. From two to four I walk, whatever may be the state of the weather. We take tea at four, and thereafter for an hour my tutor grounds me in the fundamentals of religion. The rest of the day, with a break for supper at seven thirty, is mine to do as I please with. Usually, I read English literature for an hour and spend the rest of the time on my Greek and Latin. It is a pleasant enough existence. My tutor is a reasonable person and I get on well with him. The house is comfortable and the surrounding countryside attractive.

"There is no news to send you, but I feel I must write to you nevertheless to inquire after your health and to assure you that I am well. My father remains in Scotland and has sent a few brace of grouse to my tutor. I trust I shall have the pleasure of seeing you again before I go up to Oxford in the autumn. Believe me to be,

Yours very truly,

FELIX BOYS.

Dinah replaced the letter in its envelope and took it up to her bedroom. There she put it with two others, equally passionate, into a sandalwood box which she hid beneath her clothing at the bottom of a drawer. She felt incredibly happy. To run away – from England, from Switzerland, from any place where she might happen to be – to dash on horseback to Gretna Green or to crawl on hands and knees through the icy loophole of an igloo: there was no end, she felt, to the things she could do to please the writer of this wonderful letter. Through the bedroom window she saw the fog's brown oily convolutions squirming round cowl and chimney-pot, and she was happy and uplifted as though there lay before her the turquoise and gold and green of sea and shore and field.

4

Laurie was in no hurry to reach the office of *Dunkerley's*. He strolled into Oxford Street and thence turned into Bond Street where, though it was mid-morning, the lights were up in the shop windows, radiant upon jewels and precious metals, glowing pictures, porcelain, leather, flowers, fruit and vegetables that looked too regal ever to have been grown in common mud. Likewise, the women's shoes and dresses were serene and apart, divorced forever from the tap of cobbler's hammer and the painful stitch, stitch, stitch, of sore fingers in garrets and back rooms. There was a window containing nothing but hams, some sliced down to the pink interior, some clothed in black leather and some in grey, but none with hint or souvenir of a pig's hindquarters thrusting the snorting, grunting snout into the ground or the garbage of the swill-tub. This was the street where the first whisper of thought was in guineas and the final shout might announce a king's ransom.

But none of this was in Laurie's mind. Bond Street was a pleasant place to saunter in, especially on a morning like this when the dun air without made each lighted shop glow and glitter, wink and twinkle, with the entrancing invitation of Aladdin's cave.

Here now was a shop dedicated to the huntsman. Such gleaming boots! Such dandy crops! Such hats and stocks, with fox-headed golden pins! Such gloves! Why doesn't father allow me to ride more? There are fellows at Merton hunting three days a week.

A light touch fell upon his arm. He saw a large comfortable-looking beaver glove resting upon the sleeve of his overcoat. "Good morning, Mr Dunkerley. Are you feeling blood-thirsty for foxes?"

"Oh, good morning, Miss Lewison. No. I'm just sauntering. Just getting through the morning."

Her short coat, like her gloves, was of beaver. Her eyes looked out, as bright as polished pewter from under her close-fitting beaver hat. Laurie was aware of a pleasant uplifting of the heart as he looked at her, so taut and assured, so much in possession of herself. They moved on side by side towards Piccadilly.

"Can you saunter in the mornings without a sense of sin?" she asked.

119

"Oh, yes," said Laurie buoyantly; and her chuckle, harsh but pleasing, made him feel, as so often, that he amused her, that she thought him very young.

"I can't," she said. "I suppose I have an Old Testament imagination. The morning is my working time, and if I don't work I suffer agonies of remorse. But sometimes I rebel. I prefer the remorse to the sense that I can't please myself now and again."

"It must be very pleasant," Laurie answered, "to be able to please yourself now and again. I imagine, anyway, that you always please yourself. Surely you please yourself when you sit down to write?"

"Oh, yes. Yes, indeed. I assure you that in that sense there's a great deal of pleasure in my job. But there's discipline, too. There are very few mornings when I couldn't find a charming excuse for not being at my desk."

There it is again, thought Laurie. Discipline – the word, the idea, that Sir Daniel was always handing him. A little discipline, my boy . . . A little concentration on some definite scheme or programme. Just try it. It works wonders.

A wistful sense of personal inadequacy must have clouded his ingenuously good-looking face, for Hesba asked: "You, too, have every opportunity to please yourself?"

"Well," he said, "it depends on what you call pleasing. I don't often have much reason for self-congratulation. I don't seem to satisfy other people, and when you're constantly aware of that, you don't satisfy yourself."

Hesba, whose own life was so assured and competent, felt a sudden pity for the unhappiness he so artlessly exposed. Not that it could be anything deep or serious at the moment. Say what you would, she thought, there were compensations in being Sir Daniel Dunkerley's only son. Nevertheless, Laurie was evidently in a state of mind that could become serious. She judged him to be a young man of no great force, but good-hearted, daunted and over-shadowed by his remarkable and ruthless parent. Well – yes – she said to herself – that could become very serious indeed. Her friend Grace Satterfield had not often spoken of this young cousin, but when she did, it was always with the air of a wise adult discussing a charming child. "Oh, Laurie! Yes, a nice boy."

"Let's go in here," she said.

Laurie was delighted to feel the glove laid again on his arm, and his arm squeezed as she directed him towards the door of a tea room. They had it to themselves. Even in this cosy interior there was a smudge of fog, but it was warm and intimate.

"How are you enjoying yourself at Merton?" Hesba asked. "I suppose you're looking forward to going back?"

Laurie considered this carefully, stirring the sugar into his coffee. "Yes and no," he said at last, evidently trying hard to get down to the root of his situation. "I shall be glad to be away from Manchester Square. That goes without saying. But I don't get much fun out of Oxford. I'm between two stools there. Some of the chaps are mad on sport. Well, that'd suit me in a way. Not that I'm as keen on sport as all that; but it'd be something to do, wouldn't it?"

"But Sir Daniel doesn't feel that that's what Oxford is for."

"That's exactly it. He doesn't allow me enough money to go in with that set; and as for the other set – well, I don't want to go in with them."

"Why not?"

"Well, it's not exactly that I don't want to. I can't. That's the long and short of it. I haven't got the brains. I admire those fellers. That young feller Felix Boys you met the other night at my father's – he's that sort. You'll see. When he gets to Oxford he'll just walk away with everything as easily as eating his breakfast. But the thing my father wants me to do at Oxford I can't do, and what I could do he doesn't want me to do. So there it is."

"I suppose," said Hesba, "that sooner or later he'll want you to go into Dunkerley Publications?"

"Oh, yes. But all that seems such a long way off. I shall be fooling about for another three years. That's why I can't take this holiday business seriously. He'd like me to potter round the office picking up this and that. But I can't take to that any more than to the reading my tutor gives me for the vacation. A holiday's a holiday, I say."

But it's not being a very jolly holiday, Hesba thought, looking at his puzzled puckered forehead. "Have you talked the whole thing over with your father?" she asked.

"Good lord, no! A fat lot of use that'd be! He'd shoot right up in the air."

"The higher he shoots the harder he'll bump when he comes down," she said. "Let me give you a bit of advice, Laurie. You won't think me intrusive?"

"Good heavens, of course not," he answered, delighted to hear her use his name. "I'm only too pleased to discuss the whole thing openly like this. I feel all the better for it."

"That's what's been the matter with you. You ought to have discussed it long ago. Don't bottle things up, and don't fuss about them. Now for the advice. Just tell your father that Oxford is wasting your time and his money. Tell him that you are anxious to begin at once in Dunkerley's, on a proper footing, with a salary. If he blows up, let him. He's no fool, and he'll see in time that you're talking commonsense. I think he'll be proud of you, though I'm prepared to bet that he won't say so. But above all things, be certain that this is what you want to do, and that when you begin it you'll go on with it."

She gave him a little smile. "All right?"

"Absolutely," he said with enthusiasm. "Hesba, it's wonderful to talk to you. You know, you—"

"Well now," she cut him short, "I really took this morning off to come along here and find a wedding present for Grace. Would you like to help me?"

"I'm due at Dunkerley House," he said.

"So am I. We'll see what's in the shops and then go on."

They chose the present together, and that gave them an agreeable sense of conspiracy. The present was conventional but beautiful: a cut-glass rose-bowl whose facets, under the lighted chandelier in the shop, seemed to drip opalescent fire. And then it occurred to Laurie, who was most reluctant to end these intimate moments, that he would have to buy a present, too. And thus an hour and more went agreeably by, as they dived in and out from the foggy morning to the warm glittering carpeted shops. It was half-past twelve when they came out into Piccadilly.

"Good lord, Hesba!" Laurie cried. "This is a fine way to show my change of heart! We shall have to make a dash for it."

He held up his walking-stick and a hansom pulled into the kerb. As they rattled through Piccadilly Circus he was not thinking any more of those lucky fellows who were spending the holiday in Switzerland or France. London was good enough for him. London was gorgeous

– a place where you set out in the morning feeling like nothing on earth and in a couple of hours found yourself on top of the world.

5

Alec Dillworth was aware of a growing impatience. Titmuss had kept things in good order. There was not much for Alec to do, and when that little was done his mind began to wander. On his table was a small clock in a leather case: a present from Elsie when he had first installed himself here in this pleasant eyrie over the river. Alongside the clock was a leather photograph frame containing a photograph of Elsie. Alec had put it there at the same time as the clock. Looking now at these two souvenirs of his sister, the woman whose life had been not only intimately but dramatically associated with his own, he felt an impatience with what he knew to be his duty. His long and unexplained absence would have worried and disturbed Elsie. He should have gone to her before coming here, but having come here, he should at any rate go at once to Elsie when his morning's work was done. But he did not want to do this. He admitted it to himself with shame but with candour. He would have gone but for Dan Dunkerley's suggestion that he should take Hesba Lewison out to lunch. He realised how well the suggestion chimed with his own inclination. The chance-met woman on the heath had subverted his Puritan and virginal conception of life. Women might still be worshipful, but now there was more than one way of worshipping. He recalled an occasion long ago when he and young Theodore Chrystal, a Manchester curate then, had been spending a few days together in a Derbyshire village. Chrystal, with an unaccustomed drink or two inside him, had thumped out tunes on the piano in a bar parlour. The place was full of hearty boozers, and for the only time, so far as Alec knew, Chrystal had let himself go, had been one of a community of rough-and-ready people. Alec remembered how, himself a little dizzy with drink, he had slapped the young parson on the back and congratulated him on being at last in touch with Jesus Christ's clientele. And there was, he now thought, something profound and important in sharing the common life of common people on the plane of their physical being. He had himself, in his writing and his living, been guilty of Chrystal's sins. He had absented himself fastidiously from earthly and earthy things. He did not know whether he would try to write any more; but he felt that, if he did, it would not be such writing as he had done in the past.

All this was by no means clear and codified in his mind: it was the impromptu and half-apprehended background of vague wandering meditation as he looked at Elsie's clock and Elsie's photograph. He thought with no enthusiasm of Dan's hint that young Laurie might be looking in. He had no wish to teach young pups their tricks, especially pups as reluctant as Laurie had shown himself to be. Well, he hadn't come yet, and that was something; but neither had Hesba Lewison, and now it was half-past twelve.

Isambard Phyfe came into the room, without knocking. "Well, well!" he exclaimed. "Sir Daniel has just broken the glad news to me that our wanderer has returned."

Phyfe was, for some reason or other, in a genial mood. His fair, thin and rather foxy face, with the eyes a little too close together above the pinched nose, was one grin. His appearance at that moment annoyed Alec, who said spitefully: "I've been intending to ask you for a long time, Phyfe. Where did you get your absurd name from?"

"It's a romantic story," said Izzy, by no means put out. He perched himself on the edge of Alec's table, took up the photograph of Elsie, and gave it a long scrutiny. He put it down and said, mocking the tones of a teller of fairy-tales to children: "Once upon a time there was a poor little boy born in the East End of London. His name was Sam Fife – not even Samuel – just Sam. Picking up crumbs of knowledge even as the sparrows picked their sustenance from the dung that surrounded his humble home, he became filled with ambition absurd in a person of his class. All that could be learned for nothing, or from books bought for tuppence apiece, young Sam learned. He was an industrious child, but a deep sorrow rankled in his heart. He hated his name. Sam – remember, it was not even Samuel – Sam was bad enough. Fife was worse, for it suggested the Boys' Brigade band with little round caps perched of a Sunday morning on hair pulled back with a wet comb. Like others of his class, young Sam did this and that for a living, and at the age of twenty found himself a night-porter in a hotel, wearing a dove-grey uniform with red piping. Instead of blessing the hand that bestowed upon him these gorgeous habiliments, Sam hated them even more than he hated his name, which was not even Samuel. In the quiet of a winter night, when all the bedrooms of the hotel were full of the peaceful sleeping of the just and the lecherous waking of the unjust, young Sam, in the night-porter's cubby-hole, read a celebrated journal called *Hard Facts*. Therein the munificent prize of one guinea was offered for the best essay in one thousand words on the theme 'Society Owes Me A Living.' Before the dawn broke as dove-grey as Sam's uniform over the roof of London, and the just were waking to a new day and the unjust falling into the sleep of exhaustion, young Sam had composed one thousand clarion words, and these, when released from his duties, he took down to the Embankment. Sitting on a public bench, he pondered them, with a mother's love for her first-born. All was perfect save one thing – the superscription at the head of the page – 'By Sam Fife.' Not even Samuel. Then, in one inspired moment, Fife saw written on the page as in letters of fire the word Phyfe, and quickly he wrote it in letters of lead pencil of a hideous indelible purple hue. In a second inspired moment, lifting his eyes he saw the rugged bronze trousers of a man standing upon a plinth and beneath this the information that the owner of the trousers was Isambard K. Brunel. Who Isambard K. Brunel was young Sam neither knew nor cared, save that he held the ringing name to mate with Phyfe. And so in due season–"

"For God's sake shut it off," said Alec. "How much longer could you keep up that stuff?"

Izzy – not even Isambard – hopped off the table. "You know the rest, dear children," he said. "How Isambard's essay was successful and how King Dunkerley summoned him to his castle, loved him at sight, and gave him those opportunities which a youth of his talents could not fail to make golden."

"An appealing narrative," said Alec sourly. "And now, what is it? I'm busy."

"I merely wanted to confirm with my own eyes that you had returned. I am taking your sister out to lunch and shall be able to give her the good news."

Alec was startled. "Oh, you are, are you?" he said cautiously.

At the tone, Phyfe dropped his badinage. "Well, what the hell!" he exclaimed. "You were the best part of a week down at Dickons with Sir Daniel, and another week God knows where. And in all that time she hasn't had so much as a postcard from you."

"I've never sent her a line in my life, nor she one to me," Alec said defensively.

"Anyway, she's been properly on edge. She doesn't seem to have a friend in this damned town—"

"She doesn't need any."

"—nor anything to do, and you expect her to sit twiddling her fingers awaiting word from Lord and Master Alec."

"I don't see what it's got to do with you, anyway."

"Don't you! Well, if I know anything about it, you'll damn soon find out," said Phyfe, desperately serious now. "Why should a woman like that hang on the whims of a bloody mountebank?" And with that he went; banging the door behind him.

6

"A woman like that." So, to some men, Elsie could be not just Elsie. She could be something special, "a woman like that". She had been "a woman like that" to young Chrystal ten years ago. Alec got up and paced the room, his thoughts racing as he recalled that old disaster. In one blow that his own hand had delivered, all the current of Elsie's life had been turned awry. She was then little more than a child, if a child prematurely steeped in bitter knowledge and experience. Now she was a woman, and he had forgotten that she was still a young woman and of great beauty. The searing years that had ended when Chrystal left her had been, for all their hardship and exaction, her years of perfect joy, for they had been also the years when her gift of music had blossomed miraculously. It was a different Elsie he had lived with since then – a woman recoiled upon herself, consciously withdrawing from a world to which she could no longer offer what it had been in her to give, from which she could no longer hope to receive what her endowments had entitled her to expect. Sometimes, thinking of their sedate life together in Lincoln's Inn, Alec brought to mind Charles and Mary Lamb, and saw no reason why their quiet and unadventurous days should not be indefinitely prolonged.

This morning, striding restlessly about his room, examining the fact that Isambard Phyfe had flung under his notice, he knew that this could not be so. Charles and Mary Lamb, indeed! They had had endless affinities. They had toiled together on common tasks and enjoyed the chatter of common friends. As for Elsie, she was not interested in anything he did except in so far as it was he who did it. Books meant nothing to her, and they had no friends in common. She had been a woman of one talent, and he had killed the possibility of its being used. A line of Milton was chiming in his head: "That one talent which 'tis death to hide." Well, Elsie's one talent wasn't hidden. It was gone forever, as far beyond recall as Herod's butchered innocents. He had always recognised but never spoken of his own guilt in the matter. It had laid upon him obligations towards Elsie that he had accepted without question. But now he saw that these obligations could be not a burden but a bubble, that his sense of Elsie's dependence on him could be a mere self-glorification. He had been thinking of a mummified butterfly, pinned forever by his wicked blow to an immobility that it must be his own crucifixion perpetually to observe and lament. Now, through Phyfe's eyes, he saw the stirring of the wings and realised that there were other talents than those he had been considering. It was surely something of a talent to be "a woman like that?"

The sound of footsteps in the corridor swung him round from the window. Hesba and Laurie came in together. They were laughing and in high spirits. Although physically it was not so, he felt as if they had entered hand in hand.

7

It was always pleasant, here in Dunkerley House, to feel that one was at the heart of things, and nothing stimulated this feeling more than that one told the time from Big Ben. Now, as Laurie and Hesba gaily invaded the room, one sonorous stroke vibrated through the fog.

"Lunchtime," Laurie exclaimed, and, seizing Hesba's arm, he swung her about, and, still laughing, they began to retreat towards the door.

Though Alec called Sir Daniel "Dan" more often than not, he had never advanced beyond a cold formality with Laurie. Now he said: "I have been waiting here all the morning, Mr Dunkerley, thinking you were coming to have a look at things." He felt annoyed and perplexed by the rather exalted attitude of his two visitors.

At the door Hesba disengaged her arm and came back into the room. "I don't think Laurie expected to find you here," she said, "and neither did I. We were both expecting Mr Titmuss." She held out her hand, looking at him keenly. "I'm glad to see you back. Elsie will be, too."

Alec took her hand with a feeling that too much had happened while he had been away. Phyfe's attitude, to begin with, had knocked him endways, and the familiarity of Hesba and Laurie was something new. It was new, also, to find Hesba speaking of his sister by her Christian name. So far as he knew, they had met but once – on that unfortunate occasion at the Café Royal. He had hoped to carry off his return with assurance; but his voice faltered as he asked: "How is Elsie?"

The answer unexpectedly came from Laurie. "Blooming," he said. "There's only one word for it – blooming. We just passed her on the stairs, going out with Phyfe." He grinned with an impudence that made Alec feel he could gladly choke him. "Blooming and radiant," he added. "The air seemed alight where she walked."

"She's naturally pleased," said Hesba more prosaically, "not to be alone. There are women who don't mind being alone. I'm one of them myself. But Elsie isn't."

"Well," Laurie ventured, "I hope you don't want to lunch alone. I'm afraid it's too late for my morning lecture, and the Cheshire Cheese is not inconveniently remote."

"This young man is waking up," Alec thought with fury: and aloud he said rather stiffly: "Sir Daniel asked me to take you to lunch, Miss Lewison. There are one or two small matters we ought to discuss . . ."

"I don't think," said Laurie, stumbling a little over his words, "that my father is in a position to tell Miss Lewison where she shall lunch, or with whom." His ingenuous face had suddenly flushed, and Alec's had darkened. Alec was being tortured by the phrase, so unexpectedly poetic, that Laurie had uttered. *The air seemed alight where she walked.* He was remembering another occasion – a disastrous occasion – when it would have been true to say that.

Hesba looked from one young man to the other, keenly sensitive to the tension which had flashed into the room. She drew her long beaver gloves slowly through her fingers. She was about to speak, and Alec and Laurie were poised like characters in a play awaiting words that the situation demanded should be pregnant and definitive when the door opened noisily, as though a hurricane had pushed it, and Sir Daniel burst in, radiating an energy strangely in contrast with the still, expectant mood. He could not fail to be aware that he had plunged into an atmosphere of tension. He stayed his rush, and stood there, heavily overcoated, with a white silk muffler round his neck, his silk hat in his hand, looking from one face to another. He decided to break up whatever it was that held the air so still.

"Ah, Miss Lewison," he exclaimed heartily. "I am lucky. I had hoped to take you out to lunch today, but a most boring business lunch cropped up. Thank God, it's fallen through. I was afraid you'd be already gone." He held the door open for her. "Come now. Let's be off." Then he became fully conscious of Laurie, standing there looking boyish and crestfallen. He was a good boy. Dan had no doubt of that. Life had been too soft for him, but life itself had a way of curing things like that. Laurie would be all right in time. Dan's heart warmed towards him. "You, too, Laurie," he said. "Would you care to join us?"

"Oh, rather, sir! Thank you," Laurie hastened to say, his heart uplifted by the thought that this was the first time his father had ever invited him out in this informal fashion, man to man.

The three of them had drawn together near the door. Standing with his back to the fire, Alec felt remote and overlooked, not a member of whatever community there was between those three. Even now, he thought, she can say *No*. She can say: *I'm lunching with Mr Dillworth*. She can show in some way or another that she's not that damned man's slave. She's one of the people who make him, one of the hearts and brains he lives on.

Hesba and Laurie went out side by side, Dan courteously holding the door open. When the door was shut, Alec reflected that she hadn't even looked round.

8

It would have been hard to define Izzy Phyfe's position in Dunkerley Publications. He was a Minister without Portfolio, but beyond question a minister. He was the man underlings took care to stand well with if they wished – and who didn't? – to stand well with Sir Daniel. He was known to have Sir Daniel's ear, and the timorous at all events believed him to speak with Sir Daniel's voice. He himself knew that the prime condition on which he held his job was that he must not call his soul his own. Happily, he didn't want to. There were only two things he wanted: he wanted to be safe, and he wanted to be powerful. He knew that in his present situation his power could not be absolute. All he thought and said and did was subject to the veto of a vigorous, capricious employer; but the very fact that this employer needed such a man as Izzy about him, a mentally pliant buffer of a man to intervene at need between him and reality: this gave Izzy as much power as was necessary to make him happy.

He was liable at any moment to be ordered to pack up and go to Dickons, to dine in Manchester Square, to dash off to settle a point in Manchester, or to sleep in Dunkerley House. When the day's contacts were over, Sir Daniel liked to have someone to talk to. In his sitting room he would talk and talk, almost unaware of Izzy's occasional word of agreement. Then he would say: "Excuse me a moment" and go into his bedroom. Izzy was used to this routine. He knew that in five minutes' time Meaker would appear and say: "Sir Daniel would like to see you in his room, sir. I'm going to bed now. Good night, sir."

And in the bedroom there would be Sir Daniel, propped up on his pillows, regally clad in a night-shirt of fine linen with a frogged bed-jacket over it. "Sit down, Izzy. Well, as I was saying—" And he would go on talking. It was often four o'clock when Phyfe dropped exhausted on to the pallet in his own office, with the knowledge that Sir Daniel would expect him, at breakfast at half-past eight, to have read all the morning papers and to be prepared to impart what should be known of their contents.

It was an exhausting life physically, but mentally Phyfe flourished on it. In the course of those interminable monologues he learned many things, about the business and about people. He could always tell you – if he had chosen to do so, which he never did – exactly what situation of warmth or disfavour any person occupied in Sir Daniel's regard. To be Keeper of the King's Conscience enthralled him, and he was of the utmost discretion. He himself did not know how often in the course of those seemingly aimless discourses Sir Daniel had laid traps for his feet. But he never walked into them, and Sir Daniel had learned that, so far as Izzy was concerned, he could, had he wished, have talked treason and *lèse majesté* without fear of betrayal.

Perhaps the craving for safety, even more than the wish for power, made Isambard Phyfe what he was. He had never known his father, who had been a labourer in the London docks. His mother had brought him up on a regime of affection diluted with virtue. The affection expressed itself in the stoic self-sufficiency of the poor, in her willingness to accept any labour, to wear herself to the bone, in order to keep a roof over the boy's head. The virtue flowed into clouts on the ear if young Sam consorted with the wilder, more lawless youngsters among whom he grew up. He had learned that his place was indoors, not in the streets, unless his mother were in the streets with him. Thus he became something of a solitary, and in self-defence against boredom he took to reading.

Izzy could always remember a day when he was fourteen years old. He was then employed in Smithfield Market, and one of his jobs was to sweep up blood and bone and fragments of meat. Out they went through a doorway into the gutter, and it was a glad moment, because his work was then ended. He would shut and lock that door, go in, put on his overcoat and hat, thinking with gladness of the two rooms which he and his mother shared in Whitechapel. One was a sitting room which was also kitchen and dining room and Izzy's bedroom; the other, a tiny chamber, was Mrs Fife's bedroom.

This night, which he would so often recall, was a bitter night of winter. With the closing-down of daylight a couple of hours ago, the frost which had been in the air all day had sharpened. Even inside the market the cold was intense. The boy was thinking happily of the evening before him. His mother would be there, and there would be a fire and a lighted lamp and a book that he was anxious to read. There were now no clouts on the ear. He and his mother had come to terms. They were happy and easy together. His constant thought was of the day when he would do all the earning, when his mother could stay at home – perhaps in a little house to themselves. Such miracles did happen. Tonight, on the way home he would buy some contribution to their supper: some faggots or chips or fried fish. Ready to go, he put his hand into his trousers pocket to be sure the money was there, and found that his shilling was gone: there was nothing in the pocket but a hole.

The shilling was nowhere to be found, and so he did what he had never done before: he unlocked the door through which he had swept the off-scourings of the market, hoping he might find the money on the pavement without. He was shocked by the sight that met his eyes. On the bitter-cold flagstones of that back-lane, under the light of a gas-lamp, barefooted children wearing rags, old life – battered crones hideously crowned with grey, dirty hair, old men, holding their tatters together with one hand as they foraged with the other, were turning over the sawdust, picking out scraps of bone and meat, filling pockets, baskets, bags, with the despised sweepings and scrapings of the market's opulence.

The knowledge suddenly smote young Fife that this poverty, beyond the reach of anything that even he had imagined when he thought of the poor, was always there; that night after night these vultures were waiting in obscure holes and corners, watching for him to close and lock the door before they pressed in to their obscene scavenging. One old woman, with a chuckle of sly indomitable humour, said: "Hey, mister, give us a cut orf the joint."

Mister! No one before this had called Sam Mister. There were deeps in which one could be so abysmally nothing that even Sam became something.

That was one thing that subconsciously lay at the roots of Mr Isambard Phyfe's being. He was like an animal that had smelled the blood, glimpsed the pole-axe, and miraculously escaped. And he knew that he had escaped because of his own will which told him that never must he be as these outcasts were.

That night his mother handed to him a dozen worn and battered books. She had spent her day scrubbing out an empty house. On one of the shelves, abandoned by their owner, were these books. After supper Sam settled himself with the modest pile on the table under the lamp. They were all paper-backed editions of classic works. He picked up one – a very small book with the attractive title "On Murder Considered as One of the Fine Arts." As he turned the pages, his eye alighted on the words: " 'The earthquake,' to quote a fragment from a striking passage in Wordsworth, 'the earthquake is not satisfied at once.' "

The name Wordsworth touched something in his mind. Yes there it was: one other of the books was called "Selections from Wordsworth." This seemed a strange and interesting fact to young Sam Fife. He pondered it for a moment, then said: "Look, Ma. When you start reading, you can go on from one thing to another. It all links up." He would have been surprised, then, to know that with this phrase he had stumbled on the golden key to all intellectual life and progress.

In the years that followed the night when Sam observed the street-vultures clawing over the broken meats of the market he himself, so far as his intellectual life was concerned, did the same thing. There were scrag-ends of knowledge, he found, to be gathered in all sorts of odd and unexpected places. Remembering that winter night when his young nerve had been touched on the raw, he built up for himself a fantasy of Oxford and Cambridge as the thriving market wherein at great cost the prime cuts and rich joints were sold, and behind these, in many a dark street and alley, the despised sweepings were to be garnered for nothing but the labour of picking them up in night-classes and in the books on tuppenny barrows. His discovery that "you can go on from one thing to another" held good, and an insatiable curiosity kept his nose on the trail. He had only to read that Wordsworth belonged to the Lake School of poets to have a burning wish to know what the Lake School was; and to his joy he found that this question was easy to answer. He found that most questions of fact were easy to answer; and he was happily unaware that when questions are not of fact they are not answered: they are only guessed at, under whatever high-sounding title of system, religion, or philosophy the guess is made. So far as philosophy went, Isambard had none, unless you could describe as philosophy the general working rule "Get On or Get Out." Although he did not know it, this was the dominant rule of life, both for men and nations, in his time and in all times.

Now, when he was Sir Daniel Dunkerley's Number One, he had as much knowledge as most university graduates get, though he had failed to systematise it, and had not managed to pack it away in the polished envelope that the universities provide. He had a fair knowledge of Latin; he could read with ease and write badly and with difficulty in French, but he could not speak it at all. In German he could read but neither write nor speak. He had read widely in English literature and history, and had taught himself the useful craft of Pitman's shorthand. There were few people in the country who knew more intimately the novels of Dickens or the plays of Shakespeare, but this was a point on which he was unaware of his own excellence. Of science he knew nothing, being in this a fair match for the customary university graduate of his time.

Thus, then, was the man of thirty who walked down the stairs of Dunkerley House that foggy winter's day, more aware than Laurie had been that Elsie Dillworth, at his side, seemed to set the day alight. It need only be added concerning Isambard that, though the structure of his speech was correct, it retained a faint Cockney intonation, like a dye that had not quite come out after repeated washings. A day to him, though never emphatically a dye, was nevertheless not a hundred per cent rhyme with hay. His figure was spare and inclined to be tall, and this was emphasised by the tight-waisted overcoat with flowing skirts which he loved to wear and which somehow gave him a horsey appearance. Out of doors, he was never to be seen without a rattan cane and a broad-brimmed bowler hat.

9

Elsie Dillworth came to this appointment in an exalted mood. She remembered a time when she was very poor and very happy. But for a long time now, no longer poor, she had not been happy: she had enjoyed, at best, an equable content, at worst a sense of frustration and futility. For weeks on end her tranquil life with Alec would satisfy her; even a visit to a concert would not be too deeply disturbing; but from time to time the effect of listening to the violin supremely played would be too make her feel like a hamstrung tigress watching a deer browsing a yard away. There was no consolation in it at all: only a violent and consuming desire that had nothing to feed on.

Alec's absence at first left her with no more than a sense of loneliness. She and Alec had few friends. Their upbringing had made them sensitive and a little awkward in social contacts. They shrank from going out to establish new ones, and those which could not be avoided they treated as casually as possible. They never entertained, and any one who entertained them found them curiously unresponsive.

Thus it was that, being alone, Elsie had no one to whom she might turn. She resolved, a few nights after Alec should have been back but was not, to go by herself to a concert; and this was one of the nights when the devil came upon her. Never before had he come so violently. The piece of the evening was Beethoven's Concerto No.4 in G Major, and she did not get beyond hearing the second movement. When it ended she rushed out of the building, and in the cold moonlit street she leaned against a wall, feeling sick, sucked empty, overwhelmed by a sense of irreparable loss. The grave discourse of the instruments flowed through her, and, as limbless men on a battlefield are said to feel use in the leg that has been severed, so Elsie found her fingers, stiff and impotent, contributing to the music that engulfed her. But, unlike them, she was conscious of the fraud, blindingly aware that only her mind was making its grave violin answer to the pleading piano, and that at the end of her arm there hung a bunch of atrophied twigs.

Though she had not till now felt any sense of loss from Alec's absence, she was aware that she must have companionship or perish. She hastened to Lincoln's Inn, thinking that surely by now he would be back, and the cold emptiness of the flat struck her like a blow. She gave it one look, then ran out, banging the door behind her. It was ten o'clock when she came out on to the Embankment. Under the stark arms of the winter plane trees, she leaned on the cold granite of the parapet and watched a faint wind breaking up the bars of moonlight into girdles of sequins upon the river. Long, low barges, like black coffins, were floating silently along the glory of the water, and in a dim, instinctive fashion they seemed to Elsie to be mortality fugitive upon the breast of timelessness. They had the pathos of mortal things, like the pleading voice of the piano that she had heard answered by the immortal finality of the violins.

She wept, hardly knowing why her tears fell: quietly at first, with the large drops squeezing out of her hot eyes, then with a complete abandonment that shook her shoulders and rained the tears upon the cold stones. It was not her loneliness that overwhelmed her. That was only an ingredient in her sense of everybody's loneliness, of the brevity and pain of life; and to this was added an upsurge of the feeling she had tried for so long to subdue: the feeling of her own loss when the knife drove through her hand, snipping the frail thread that tied her to the one great purpose of her life. Unconsciously, the fingers of her right hand crisped into a bunch, and she beat her fist upon the unresponsive stone.

It was thus that Isambard Phyfe found her. Sir Daniel was sleeping at Dunkerley House, but for once had told his henchman to go home. Izzy decided to take a turn by the river before doing so, and there, clearly visible by moonlight and lamplight, was this woman hanging in an attitude of pathetic abandonment over the parapet. He could not see her face. A large flowery hat concealed it, and a cape concealed her figure. He had no means of knowing whether it was a child or a crone, but he saw that, whoever it was, she was deeply distressed. He saw the fist beating on the stone.

Phyfe knew enough of the miseries of life to be moved by this spectacle, though, there, it was one by no means unaccustomed. He knew also that the Embankment was no place in which a wise man sought the company of strange women, however distressed. But there was something about that figure bowed over the stone that held him; pacing twenty yards beyond her and then back again, in a dilemma of indecision. He was always to be ashamed, when he thought of the incident later, that he left it to the policeman to make the first move. His own hovering attitude, to and fro on the pavement behind the woman's back, must have made him suspect in the policeman's eye, for as the blue, unhurried, majestic figure passed him, he cast a keen glance at Izzy, and then, approaching the woman, touched her lightly on the arm.

"You bein' annoyed, Miss?" he asked.

The woman swung round with a start, as though the sound of those firm approaching feet had not penetrated her wall of misery, and it was then that Phyfe saw her face and realised that it was Dillworth's sister. He had seen her only once: for an hour or two at the Café Royal, when her conduct had been very queer indeed.

She had not heard what the policeman said, and gazed at him with a face so dazed by unhappiness that Izzy's heart was rent.

"Are you all right, Miss?" the policeman asked.

She nodded dumbly, and the man said kindly: "You get off home now. It's always better in the morning."

Then Izzy stepped forward, emboldened by the recognition. "I know this lady, officer," he said. "Miss Dillworth, you remember me? Phyfe."

The policeman continued to look at Izzy with doubt. "Is that all right, Miss?" he asked. "You know this man?"

Again Elsie could only nod, but at last brought out: "Yes. Yes – it's all right."

"You'd better come home with me and have a cup of tea," Izzy said.

Without much spirit, her shoulders still occasionally shaking as the storm ebbed, Elsie fell in at his side and the policeman doubtfully watched them walk away.

Phyfe had enough sense to know that this was a moment for saying nothing. The night was extraordinary tranquil. The shadows of the planes were laid flat and unshaking upon the pavement; not a murmur of wind was heard in the cold air. Izzy decided not to go home at once — just to walk here for a while. It would do her good. In his mind he was saying: That bloody fool Dillworth.

Elsie's trouble was by no means ended. She was surprised to find that the emotion that had shaken her mind had been severe enough to weaken her body. Her legs felt uncertain. The ebbing tide of her tears was full of flurries that sent shivers through her. Presently she said: "Let me rest a moment." Phyfe stood still; she put a hand upon his arm to steady herself, then leaned against him. The presence and support of a human being — any human being — was grateful and comforting.

To Izzy, unaware of the nature of this moment, thinking only that she was worried by the absence of Alec, the situation was becoming rather more than he could handle. Elsie was trembling with a last expiring gust of sobs; her head had fallen upon his shoulder. He could not see her face. Only the top of her hat was visible. He felt there was nothing he could do, and so, wisely, he did nothing.

Then she was standing away from him again, and seemed more in possession of herself. She straightened her hat, wiped her eyes with a handkerchief, and for the first time looked him squarely in the face. "I'm sorry," she said. "It was the music."

Now Izzy was more puzzled than ever. "I thought it was your brother," he said. "I thought you were lonely."

"Yes, I was," she answered. "But it was the music that upset me. I went to a concert all alone."

They began to walk again, and Phyfe had no more to say. What a crack-pot pair the Dillworths are! he thought. Alec disappearing like that, without a word, from Dickons; and now this girl crying her eyes out on the Embankment about a concert! Well, one of these days Sir Daniel would have enough of it: Master Alec would go. For myself, Phyfe thought, if I were Sir Daniel he'd have gone long ago. An unreliable sort of tyke. Brilliant — oh, yes; but what was the good of brilliance that switched on and off like Alec's? And yet — there was something, he knew, that made it unlikely that Sir Daniel would ever throw Dillworth out. From those long talks in the night, Phyfe knew that, for some reason or other, Dillworth was the only man in Dunkerley House for whom Sir Daniel had affection. There were plenty whom he esteemed, whose gifts he valued; but with Dillworth there was more in it than that.

And this sister of Dillworth's, too. He began now to recall things that Sir Daniel had told him. She had been training to be a violinist in those old Manchester days when *Hard Facts* was starting. And then there'd been an accident – he never got to the rights of that – that smashed up her hand and stopped the whole thing.

Poor kid! he thought. So that was it. That was why this concert she talked about had upset her. After all these years she could still grieve for what she had lost. Now Izzy was really getting on to the track of the thing, though it would have been beyond him to understand that Elsie was crying for more than she had lost: she was crying for what could never be found.

There was not much traffic about at that moment, and in the silence he could hear the *tap, tap* of her heels on the pavement, a little quicker than the fall of his own deliberate step. It sounded to him very feminine, like the running of a doe, and rather pathetic. He looked at her with a smile, intending to cheer and reassure her.

Life had not left many romantic notions in Isambard Phyfe's head, but he was always thereafter ready to maintain that a man could fall instantaneously in love. "Just like that," he would say, snapping his long dry fingers. For he knew that in that moment, looking down to give Elsie reassurance with a smile, he fell in love with her. It happened that they were just passing a lamp, and also that, striving for a feeling of relief and freedom after the stifling that emotion had put upon her, Elsie had pulled off her hat and held her face up to the cold free air. She was swinging the hat in her hand, and her face was lifted to the sky. Phyfe had not seen her before without a hat. She was wearing one when he had first met her at the Café Royal. What he now saw was a neck like a slender tower of alabaster supporting a head tangled with red tendrils, and a face that was still and white, with eyes that seemed washed over with the mystery of the tears they had shed. The lips were parted a little, and still trembling. Izzy caught his breath. This was not someone who needed his reassurance. However, for a moment, her human defences had been struck down, causing her to turn to him, she was, in all that mattered, beyond him, inaccessible and free. He thought that she could not fail to hear the huskiness in his voice as he said, rather embarrassed: "We'd better go and have that cup of tea now, Miss Dillworth."

Elsie gave a start. He saw that she had not been with him. Just as the policeman's words had brought her with a jerk out of a pit of misery, so now, he felt, he had tugged her back from the contemplation of glory. She had this gift of withdrawal, of letting her body drag along unapprehendingly at a remove from her mind.

Now she came back. They halted upon the pavement, and she looked about her as though to recollect where she was. They had reached Westminster Bridge. The face of Big Ben glowed in the tower and the pinnacles of the House of Commons wore a cold rime of moonlight. Elsie looked at Phyfe and smiled. "Isn't it beautiful?" she asked, and she seemed now as happy as a child who has emerged from a storm of sorrow.

To Phyfe, also, the scene was beautiful, the moment holy. He was not accustomed to seeing the beauty of things, to feeling his heart beat with an apprehension of life's honour and transience. But these feelings now, though unanalysed, were powerful in him. He didn't want to say anything: he didn't want to go on walking; he would have been content just to stand there for a long time, with the river flowing under the arches of the bridge, and the lights of traffic winking across it like fireflies, and the plane trees laying their flat patterns of shadow upon the silver pavement: just to stand there alongside this girl who had suddenly knocked him endways. She lifted her arms to replace her hat, and the movement seemed to him inexpressibly beautiful. Now her face was all shadow. Which was lovelier: its mystery under the hat, or its pathos in the moonlight? He wanted to know her face in all its moods and tenses.

She turned from him and walked a few paces to the parapet and looked down into the river. Just so she had stood when he first caught sight of her. But what ages seemed to divide that moment from this! He could hear the water chuckling quietly against the huge ashlar blocks that confined it, and tides that had to be contained were flowing in him, too. He could not bear to see her go from him – even those few paces to the parapet. He stepped up alongside her, and said quietly: "Shall we go now?"

"Go? Where?" Elsie asked.

"I thought you might like to come and drink a cup of tea with me, and my mother," Phyfe said, and he felt, as he said it like a man who wishes to blow a mighty trumpet but possesses only a penny whistle.

"No, no. It's very kind of you. Thank you very much. But I must get away home. Look at the time."

There was no need to look. The clock in the tower began to drop its sonorous notes into the silence. They said nothing while the eleven strokes fell one after another upon the air, nor until the vibrant hum of the last one had died upon the stillness. Then Isambard said: "Come now." And they set off together.

10

The little narrow streets that rush downhill from the Strand and Fleet Street to the river have echoed with the tread of centuries, and the centuries have left upon them diverse signs and superscriptions. None is more happy than the gatehouse to which Phyfe now led Elsie Dillworth. It was not for its romance that Phyfe had chosen it, but because in the first place it was conveniently near to Dunkerley House, and in the second place because, being in the heart of things, it pleased Mrs Fife. So, if she had been able to sign her name, she would have continued to sign it, for she had no sympathy with Izzy's nonsense. She could not sign her name; she continued to call her son Sam; and she would have died rather than live away from brick and stone, chimney-pots and roof-tiles, which had always, to her, made up the most satisfactory scenery in the world.

But chosen by Phyfe for these reasons of plain prose, the gatehouse lay across the bottom of the street like a line of romantic poetry. The street flowed under its small-paned glass windows, set in mullions of crumbling stone. It was a delicate aery bridge joining the upper storeys of two houses. But now one of its ends was bricked up. Phyfe rented the house at one end of the bridge, and from the first floor had access to the bridge itself. From the house windows you could see nothing but Mrs Fife's beloved bricks and mortar hear nothing but the cheeping and twittering of grimy sparrows and the noise of traffic. From the graceful glass gallery that was the bridge you could on the one hand look down to the river and on the other look up to the street lights of the Strand; and, if you had an ear for that sort of thing, you could hear the flow, the irresistible rhythm, of the centuries.

Phyfe was apt to tease Elsie with the remark that she had married him for the sake of what he called "this junior Burlington Arcade".

Certainly it was this which finally dispelled her unhappiness that night and caused her to clap her hands with joy.

For her, the occasion began to take on a romantic flavour from the moment they entered Phyfe's little house. The place was so small that you were apt to overlook it as you hurried down the worn stone steps that, from the bottom of the street, gave you the extra-special sharp spill to the Embankment level. On the topmost of these steps was Phyfe's front door with its shining olivine paint, glorified by a large circular knocker that glowed like a saint's golden halo. Fixed above it in a wall-bracket was a gas lamp to light unwary feet down the steps. This municipal foresight created one of those vignettes that photograph themselves for ever on the mind. Isambard and Elsie, coming from the direction of the Embankment, had nearly reached the steps when Isambard ran ahead, took them in two leaps, and pulled a key out of his pocket. Then he turned to watch her coming, and Elsie was never to forget how in that moment it struck her with an absolute certainty that her going into his house had a rich and deep significance for Isambard. It was quiet and very cold. Not a soul was to be seen in the narrow upward-tilted street. Nothing could distract her attention from the figure of Isambard, standing there before the door, with the key in his hand, and the light of the lamp showing upon his face an excited apprehension. His shadow was thrown down into a vague pool about his feet.

"So this is it?" she asked, standing alongside him.

"Yes," he said, prosaically, with his heart puttering. "It's handy for the office."

The door opened into a small square hall, panelled in dark oak. A gas-jet was burning in a round white opaque shade. They didn't say a word as Phyfe shut the door, hung his hat and coat on a hook, and put his rattan cane into an up-ended drain-pipe painted with blue irises. But Mrs Fife, whose life had been Sam and little else for thirty years, immediately shouted through a closed door: "Who's that with you there, Sam?"

Isambard looked at Elsie with a smile, and whispered: "She's sharp — very sharp. Take your hat off and come on in." He wanted his mother's first impression to be of that glorious head.

"No. I'll keep it on," Elsie said; and then she was aware that a part of the panelling, which was a door, had opened a crack and that a small wrinkled face was peering round at her. The eyes were bright and sharp. Isambard, as he always did when he entered the house, kissed the small wrinkled face. He did not bother to open the door any wider. He just kissed the face which was all that was to be seen, and then said: "This is Miss Dillworth, mother. You know Alec Dillworth. You've heard me speak of him, anyway – the editor of *Dunkerley's*. This is his sister."

"Oh, it is, is it?" said Mrs Fife. "And what's she doing walking the streets at midnight I'd like to know? She'd better come in out of this freezing passage."

She held open the door, and they entered the room whose window was alongside the door at the top of the steps. But now it was curtained, and there was a fire in a basket-grate, and this room, too, Elsie saw, was panelled like the hall. It all made up a cosy domestic scene. "Take your hat off," Mrs Fife commanded, and this time Elsie obeyed. Phyfe took the hat and held it as if it were a diadem. Mrs Fife took it from his hand and laid it on a sofa. "Well –" she said.

Elsie Dillworth, at twenty-eight, knew enough about the world to be aware of what Mrs Fife was thinking. On either side of the fireplace was a wicker chair, and she sat in one looking at the shrivelled bright-eyed woman sitting in the other. Mrs Phyfe, who must henceforth, for sweet charity's sake, be given the name her son had thrust upon the world, was wearing, and always wore, rustling black from head to foot, and she was so small that she looked as if a couple of yards, cleverly manipulated, would clothe her. The only relief to this darkness was a collar of charming lace fastened with a cameo brooch. Her scanty hair was pulled tight off her head and arranged in a hard knob on her neck. "She's sharp – very sharp," Izzy had said; and certainly the impression which the least observant must gather on first seeing Mrs Phyfe was a sharp little wild animal that had long lived only by having the wit to evade its hunters. And, more or less, that is what her life had been. Even now, when for some years the View Hallo had been sounding more and more distant in her ears, she could not completely believe that it would trouble her no longer, that the day would never again come when she would have to dodge and double, using her wit and agility to find the small cracks which led through harsh circumstance closing in.

And she's wondering, Elsie was thinking, with her profound knowledge of the life and ways of the poor, whether I'm the end of her comfortable life, whether I'm going to snatch away the prop that holds up the roof over her head.

Nothing was formalised or put into words in the mind of either woman; but these were the ideas behind the wariness with which they considered one another, as Isambard, who had put a kettle on to the fire, now clattered at the table, laying out cups and saucers and biscuits.

To Mrs Phyfe, Isambard was the finest flower in the long painful unfolding of human destiny. She was proud of him, and more than a little afraid of him. She had always hoped that he would "get on," and she had done what she could to push him on. But now that he had got on to the extent of reading foreign books, of giving her a house like this, and being the confidential man of someone called Sir Daniel, she was inclined to shake her head and to wonder if, finally, any good could come of a situation which appeared to her at times to be so dazzling as to be presumptuous. The one thing that she feared above all others was that her Sam's manifest pre-eminence among the sons of men would lead to some designing woman sinking her talons into him. But Sam had reached the age of thirty with a life uncomplicated on that side. He had been too intent on his own advancement to have time for women. And now, here he was, diffusing into the atmosphere of the little room an affirmation that Mrs Phyfe recognised for what it was.

He put a small table between the chairs on the hearth and served the simple meal. Elsie was happy and at ease. In this homely yet beautiful little room the reaction from her profound emotional stress was complete. She seemed to be buoyed up by a clairvoyance which left her aware of both Mrs Phyfe's and Isambard's feeling towards her. She was by no means certain what she wanted to do about those feelings, but she knew that she, now, was the person with decisions to make, that these two attended upon her, and after so long a time of nonentity this gave her a feeling of responsibility and importance. She forgot the shyness and shrinking that made even the slightest social contacts painful to her, and the wound in her hand was the last thing now in her mind.

Because this had destroyed the exercise of all that was loveliest and most treasured, she tended to think that the outward evidence of it must shriek aloud to the most careless observer. In truth, this was not so. To her, thinking of the old subtlety and cunning of her fingers, they now appeared, by comparison, shrunken and useless twigs; but the fact was that, though the scar where the knife had driven through her hand was large and livid, the fingers were no more than stiff and awkward. She was now using them without self-consciousness. She lifted her cup to her lips, and Isambard and Mrs Phyfe were at once aware of the disfigurement.

If the sight of Elsie's face in its beauty had been the beginning of Isambard's deep feeling for her, this was its completion. He wanted to take that hand, to kiss and fondle it, to place himself between Elsie and the possibility of such things happening to her ever again. Strangely, the flaw made her doubly beautiful, thrice desirable, in his eyes. What it had meant to her he could but dimly guess, not understand. There was no side of his own character so endowed as to allow him to know what was lost when such things as that were lost. Indeed, looking now at Elsie's hand holding the porcelain cup: not one of the cups usually put upon the table, but one of a lovely Crown Derby set that Izzy had bought when he came into this house and whose appearance now had a significance that Mrs Phyfe noted, though she said nothing: looking at that hand, Isambard began to see himself as destined to be the deliverer, the one who would gradually coax those reluctant fingers back to their old aptitudes. So now he said: "You know, mother, Miss Dillworth is a musician. She plays the violin."

Then Elsie's hand suddenly quivered as though it had been struck. A few drops of tea spilled on to the table, and she put down the cup carefully, but not with enough control to prevent its rattling into the saucer. "I must be going, Mrs Phyfe," she said. "It's terribly late to be disturbing you."

Even his sudden passion was not enough to show Isambard the dangerous ground he was on. He was convinced that all he had to do was to bring Elsie and a violin together, and time and use would do the rest. He was becoming something of a magpie. Not only the Crown Derby tea-set but all sorts of other things were being collected into this net that he had set up; and among them was what he believed

144

to be a Stradivarius violin. So it had been labelled and as such it had been sold to him; and though he was innocent of music and this violin was nothing to him but an attractive shape of lovely wood, it was proudly hanging on a wall of the bridge that made so unusual a feature of his home. Above all things, he felt now, Elsie must see the bridge and play the violin.

So when she rose, he said: "Please don't think you're keeping us up, Miss Dillworth. Mother and I sit up till the most godless hours. Now that you're here, have a look round our little place."

"Some other time – may I, Mr Phyfe?" said Elsie, up to her old trick of holding her right hand almost behind her back.

They were all standing now, and Mrs Phyfe, so small, looked upwards at the two faces. She wanted to say: "Yes – some other time – this year, next year, sometime, never"; but she was aware of a swift telegraphed message from Izzy's eyes, and she could not bear to see him disappointed. He was asking her to come in as an ally. Whatever she might herself want, how could she refuse him? "Sam'll never be happy till you see his old bridge," she said. "Better get it over. You're not keeping *me* up."

She lit a candle in a brass candlestick and moved towards the door, leading this strange and unexpected woman into the fastnesses of her house. It was the moment of her life's supreme heroism and self-abnegation, but no one would ever know this, not even Isambard. Especially not Isambard. Perhaps, later, Elsie would understand a little of it.

There was nothing for it, Elsie felt, but to follow as the little woman walked ahead, shading the candle with her hand. The light fell into the concave hollow of it, brown and wrinkled like a walnut-shell. There was certainly plenty of oak about when this place was built. The whole house seemed little else. They went up an oak staircase and through an oak bedroom, and a door in that opened upon the bridge. Izzy took the candlestick from his mother's hand. On each wall of the bridge were three sconces and in each sconce were three candles. Izzy lit them all, and as the wavering dusky flames steadied, straightened, and burned with a clear yellow light Elsie was glad she had come. She suddenly clapped her hands. An elaborate many-branched brass candelabrum, containing a score of candles, hung from the ceiling.

"Light them, too," she cried, excited as a child who wants to see all the lights go up on a Christmas tree.

Well content with the success of his little surprise, Isambard pulled forward a chair, climbed on to it, and obeyed. Then he began to pull the chintz curtains across the windows. "No, no!" Elsie cried. "Please don't. It's like being inside a lantern. See how the windows shine with light!"

And indeed the long narrow chamber, with no furniture save the carpet on the floor and a window seat here and there, was now nothing but an entrancing scintillation of light on crystal. Mrs Phyfe had sat down, with her gnarled hands folded in her lap. Elsie sat beside her. "It's beautiful," she said simply.

The old woman turned towards her, and for the first time that evening, smiled. "It pleases Sam," she said, as though that would explain and excuse anything.

"It's truly lovely," Elsie emphasised.

"So is this," said Isambard. "At least, I think so." He lifted down the violin from the wall. "Look at that wood. Like satin. A Strad."

He rubbed his fingers over the wood, then held out the instrument to Elsie. "Take hold of if. Get the feel of it," he said.

Ten years ago, in the moment of her supreme tragedy, Elsie had taken her violin and swung it against rock, shattering both it and a dream. In the years between, she had never handled a violin, and she did not want to handle this one. The situation had for her a quality of fantasy: this span of crystal thrown across the street, this warm irradiation of honey-coloured light, and the bell which had marked all the phases of this night's adventure. It had struck ten notes as she ran, heart-stricken, down to the Embankment, and eleven strokes as she stood side by side with Phyfe watching the mystery of the river sliding under Westminster Bridge, and twelve now as Phyfe stood holding out this shape of hollow wood from which she shrank as if he had been offering her a poisoned cup.

The notes of the bell brought her to her feet, as eager to be gone from here as Cinderella from the ball. "Good gracious! Twelve o'clock, Mrs Phyfe!" she said. "I must go."

"Give us just one little tune," the old woman said. "Sam'd like it."

"Yes, just a little something," Isambard urged, plucking a note or two with his fingers. "I'd love to hear how the old Strad sounds."

She felt besieged, and for her own deliverance took the fiddle from him. "Where is the bow?" she asked, and, as she asked it, she remembered something that had happened years before – soon after her disaster, soon after Chrystal had left her, and she and Alec were alone in Manchester. He had done all he could then to mitigate the tragedy that beset her. "Look, Else, music isn't everything."

"To me it is."

"Yes; but there are other things. Life's full of lovely things. There's poetry. You must get to know how beautiful poetry is."

Night after night, as she sat with her eyes shut, her head back in a chair, the mass of cumbruous bandages lying in her lap, he would read his beloved poets, and the words would mean little or nothing to her, and her mind would be divided between the fullness of pain in her hand and the emptiness of joy in her heart. Only now and then a phrase struck through her inattention, and one night, when Alec was reading from Blake, there came a phrase that smote her like a whip. *Bring me my bow of burning gold.*

Oh, God, yes, it had been that. More and more, as her genius unfolded like a flower, her bow had been like burning gold, setting fire to all she touched. And as she thought of this, and thought that never, now, would any one be able to bring back her bow of burning gold, the tears squeezed out of her eyes, and she sat there with them flowing unregarded down her face, while Alec, who had forgotten her and was living only in his own realm of gold, read on and on for his own soul's delight. Presently, her quietness reached through to his attention, and he looked up and saw the golden head, and the great white sausage bound in her lap, and the tears flowing out of her eyes. He threw the book across the room in his impulsive way, and was kneeling at her feet with his hand holding her unwounded hand and his tired worn face looking into hers.

"Why, Else –"

She could not speak, and his sympathy turned her tears to sobs that shook her grievously, and he could do nothing but speak incoherent endearments.

At last she said: "Don't read to me any more. Not now. Not ever. Sometimes there are things that hurt too much."

"But what could have hurt you?"

"Bring me my bow of burning gold," she quoted.

"But, Else, don't you see. That's nothing to do with fiddling. It's the bow you shoot with. It goes on 'Bring me my arrows of desire.' No; it's nothing to do with fiddling."

She looked at him out of a gulf of misery. "It's to do with whatever it says to my heart," she answered. "That is, and everything is."

And now, standing there half-persuaded, with the violin in her hand, she had no sooner said: "Where is the bow?" than that old unhappy scene flooded back into her mind, and her heart cried: "Where is my bow of burning gold?" and, without another word, she laid the violin upon one of the window seats and said: "I must go."

Mrs Phyfe was astonished, but Isambard had the sense to know that he was in the presence of something which he did not understand, but which must be respected.

"It's very late," he said. "I shall see you home."

She had nothing to say during the brief journey, and Phyfe did not mind this. It was enough for him to be walking at her side, pondering upon the strangeness of her, the exaltations and depressions he had witnessed in her behaviour during these brief few hours. He had no key to the enigma of her conduct, and was still persuaded that she was worrying about nothing but the absence of her brother. She ought to know more people, he told himself. She should not be so dependent on that shiftless swine Dillworth. Isambard had a great respect for the qualities of Hesba Lewison, and he had good reason to know that Hesba was "well in," as he would have said, with Sir Daniel Dunkerley. And so he suggested to Elsie, as they said good night, that she should call on Miss Lewison. Thus, while Alec was away, Elsie's life began to shift from its too close alliance with his own.

11

It did not last so long now, the pain that recollection could bring. Once, it had been acute and violent, like indigestible food: now, when it more rarely came, she could digest it, and it became part of her, and without her figuring it out or indeed knowing anything about it, it was doing the work which an accepted sorrow alone can do in the finest hearts and establishing something strong, indestructible, in her character. And so, as she began in a day or two to look back on that evening at Phyfe's, it was not of herself that she thought but of the amusing house, and the fantastic lovely bridge cargoed with candleshine, and above all of Phyfe and his mother. She understood so well the primal emotions of a little household like that! No one had told her anything about Phyfe and his upbringing, but she had known everything as she watched the candlelight filling the hollow of Mrs Phyfe's hand while the old lady led them up the stairs. There, to be clearly read by eyes like Elsie's, was the palimpsest of laborious years, notched and scored and ingrained in the small walnut-brown cave of a curved palm and fingers. It was a household, she knew, where present security was a tranquil candle burning against a background of enormous darkness and uncertainty; and there would be fear, too, that out of that darkness at any moment the not-forgotten cold wind might blow, putting out the light. This fear, Elsie was aware, would be sharpest in Mrs Phyfe's mind, for it was she who had lived longest in the darkness, and it was not she who had dispelled it. Phyfe had done that, and the qualities which had permitted him to do it would in themselves engender confidence and dissipate fear.

Thus, thinking about that brief refuge from one of her own worst moments, she felt a warm sympathy with the old woman whose knowledge and experience of life must have shown her, in Elsie, not an ally to be welcomed but a waif blowing in out of the inimical darkness of life and threatening to bring with her God alone knew what complications of uncertainty and insecurity. Thus, such was the temper of Elsie's mind, the very existence of a timid hostility which she had sensed in Mrs Phyfe made her feel friendlier – because more understanding – to the old woman than a garrulous and demonstrative welcome would have done.

As for Phyfe himself, he would never realise how kind fate had been to him in choosing his moment for his meeting with Elsie Dillworth. He had suggested that she should see Hesba Lewison, and she had done so and found the girl good, and Hesba had taken her about the town a little and introduced her to one or two people. Elsie began to feel that, though Alec was absent, there was no reason why she should spend all her time brooding in their rooms. It was as though a wheel which Alec's presence had kept tied was now released and had begun to spin. She was not instinctively a recluse and she had reached a point in her life when it needed but a small impetus to thrust her out from her backwater into the flow of the river. This was what Phyfe's cheerful, shallow and rather impudent personality had provided.

Isambard would not have summed himself up in those three words. He was not given to introspection, but if he had been, and if he had tried to look into himself and report on what he saw, he would have discovered a resolute, realistic and tenacious young man. He would have overlooked his own pliability, his self-satisfaction with half an achievement, his readiness to creep through devious and crooked channels. In short, he would never have known that he had a merely political mind. It was not often that his mind moved on the plane of idealism, but it did so that night after he had said goodbye to Elsie Dillworth. He walked down the echoing empty canyon of Chancery Lane and into Fleet Street, where a few perambulating journalists passing into and out of the light of the gas-lamps had for him the air of supernatural beings. He took it for granted that this should be so: he did not question a mood which imperatively established its own validity. It seemed right and proper to him that he should not at once return to his waiting mother. He turned to the left, walked as far as Blackfriars Street, and then went down to the Embankment.

The glory of the moonlight had diminished. The moon had slanted away behind the roofs to the west, and though the air was still full of its frail light the pavement ran on, past the lamps rising out of their twisted iron dolphins, past the bare plane trees and the cold benches, without any shadow but that cast by the lamps themselves. Here and there on the benches misery huddled, poverty slumbered uneasily in the bitter cold, and these, to Isambard, were like the howl of the wind to a man whom it reaches as he watches the fire mounting warmly on his hearth. He walked quickly, his mind recreating the things on which his eyes had lately rested: the lift of her arms as she put on her hat, the piled tendrils of her hair, the bleak and woebegone tears, lovelier than pearls, falling down her face. At Westminster Bridge he came to a stand, coat collar up, hands thrust deep into his pockets, his rattan cane crooked over his wrist. He looked back the way he had come: at the majestic and mysterious flow of the water; the lamps in their lovely recessive curve, the light of them disembodied from what contained it, each a jewel hanging in the air: and Isambard felt that all this was his by right of what had happened to him that night, and that, as long as he lived, here on this hard stone beneath his feet, where no one else would ever see it, would be the monument that he would know and understand.

A policeman passed him and said good night. "Bitterly cold, sir." He hadn't known it, but at the words he started into life and began the brief walk towards his house. Now, for the first time, he wondered what his mother would have to say about Elsie Dillworth, but when he reached home he found that the old woman had gone to bed. She had never done so before. So long as she knew he would not be sleeping at Dunkerley House she would wait up for him, however late he might be. But now she was gone to bed. The kettle was simmering on the hob, and she had put a cup and saucer and a tea-pot with the tea in it on the table. Isambard looked at these simple reminders of devotion and was deeply moved. But he didn't want any tea, and he didn't want to go to bed. He sat down and began to read, and was soon asleep in his chair.

The old woman was not asleep. She heard him come in, and then for a long time she listened for his footstep on the stair. When it did not come, she pulled an old robe about her and went down. She stood for some time watching him, then gently shook his shoulder. He started up, blinking, and was instantly wide awake.

"Why, mother! Why aren't you in bed?"

"And leave you down here catching your death when the fire goes out. Get along with you now."

They stood and looked at one another for a long moment, and then Izzy said: "Well?"

"It's your affair, my boy," she answered. "You needn't worry about me. I knew how to look after myself before you were born, and I could do it again."

"You won't have to. Don't you think I'm capable of looking after two women?"

"Depends on the women," she said. "Bringing cash into the house is only the beginning of it. You get to bed now."

12

When Alec Dillworth, on that first day of his return to Dunkerley House, had watched Sir Daniel and young Laurie and Hesba Lewison go out together, he walked to the window and looked down upon the Embankment where the passers-by were wraiths in the fog. But he was able for a fugitive moment to make out the figures of Phyfe and Elsie. They crossed the road, Phyfe steering Elsie through the traffic with one hand under her elbow, turned under the weeping plane trees in the direction of Westminster, and were swallowed up in the gloom.

The brief spectacle left in Alec's heart a sense of pain and depression. He felt deserted by the world. He had been looking forward to having lunch with Hesba and that had been snatched from him as though his feelings needed no consideration. And now there was Elsie walking away with Phyfe. No one, no one at all, he told himself with gloomy relish, cared whether or where he lunched, or indeed whether he lived or died. Even Sir Daniel's calm and casual acceptance of his return added to his sense of injury. It was as though Sir Daniel considered him to be a mere eccentric, a dog given to wandering from home but always to be relied on to come sneaking back, so that it wasn't even worth while to waste time on scolding or beating it. For ten minutes he allowed the wheels of self-pity to creak and groan in his head, then put on his hat and went out. Halfway down the stairs he encountered Elsie, flushed and breathless with the effort of running up them. Isambard Phyfe toiled behind her, looking surprised and vexed.

Alec and Elsie met on a half-landing, and they halted and looked at one another without words for a few moments. Then, still without words, Elsie suddenly threw her arms round his neck, hugged him and kissed him on the lips.

Alec was deeply stirred. Never before had Elsie kissed him. Their relationship had been of a warm but wary cameraderie, each conscious of the other's sharp individuality, each touchily conscious of his own. Alec held his sister for a moment, feeling the supple warmth of her body, inhaling a faint intoxicating scent that he had not known her use before. He thought he had never seen her look more beautiful, or perhaps he had got into the habit of not seeing how beautiful she was. Today, there was something about her not to be overlooked. "Why, Else!" he stammered with a shy smile. "What's come over you?" He was aware of her with all the vivid physical awareness that the chance-met Effie had awakened in him.

Phyfe had now come up. "He'd better lunch with us," he said reluctantly.

"Oh, no. That's the last thing I want," Elsie answered. "But I had to see him. I shall enjoy my lunch all the more now that he's back."

Isambard looked relieved. "We were well away towards Westminster," he explained, "when I happened to mention that you were here. She came tearing back without a word."

"You might have been gone," said Elsie.

Alec recovered himself and grinned. "That would have been terrible," he admitted.

Isambard unbuttoned his overcoat and pulled a watch out of his waistcoat pocket. "Time's getting on," he said. "We shall have to take a cab."

Then together he and Elsie ran down the stairs. She looked as radiant on leaving as she had been when coming. Alec stood still, listening to the clatter of their shoes on the hollow stone, to the *diminuendo* of their talk and laughter. He was puzzled. Elsie had left a bright enchantment behind her. She was illumined, and yet how gladly, it seemed, she had gone, as though he himself were nothing to do with her mood once she had expressed it in that fervent kiss. Phyfe, too, was puzzled. What neither he nor Alec had realised, for each of them was thinking egotistically, was that she found herself caught up in a flowering love of life.

13

Elsie could not have enlightened these two young men. She could no more have explained what had happened to her than a thrush could explain why its song is loveliest in April. There was that terrible moment when she had wept on the Embankment, followed so soon by that moment on the lovely bridge in Phyfe's house when, in the profundity of his ignorance about all that had concerned her and all that she was, he had brutally forced her to stare in the face the ghosts that had bedevilled her life. Whatever secret and furtive hopes had lurked in corners of her being that she had not cared or dared to explore, were at that moment finally driven out. She was purged of all longing for the unattainable. It was the end of the long winter, and she would always thereafter see the bridge as the place where she crossed over into an acceptance of life as it was.

Isambard's association with all this was incidental and accidental, but this was not apparent to her. Alec was away, and Isambard was there, and he was supercharged with a devotion which she could never return but which, none the less, was the ambience in which she moved throughout those days. She could not but be conscious of it and grateful for it. She had long been unaccustomed to the company of men, and the innumerable attentions with which Phyfe showered her in the few days which he guessed were all that he was to be permitted before Alec's return were as tender and delicate as they were persistent. Fresh flowers reached her rooms daily, and, to the delight of one who had always been a lazy housekeeper, her breakfast was carried in every morning from a neighbouring restaurant. This combination of the poetic and the practical – the costly January daffodils nodding their heads against the dark walls of the room, and the incense of devilled kidneys that rose on the lifting of a plated cover – was surprising even to Isambard himself, so thrifty, practical and self-centred his life had been. It was he who had bought in Bond Street, at a great price for an insignificant-looking phial, the scent that had subtly made itself known to Alec's senses. To Isambard's, also. She had not used it before that day, and it seemed to him to have the significance of an invitation. Late that night, when Sir Daniel Dunkerley paused in the course of a long monologue, Isambard said: "I hope you'll think it a matter for congratulation, Sir Daniel. I'm engaged to be married."

Sir Daniel was, as often, lying in bed, propped into a nest of pillows. "Whether or not it's a matter for congratulation, young man," he said, "is something which you will have to find out for yourself as the years roll by. Even a newly-engaged man, I imagine, need not be reminded that it depends on the woman. Do I know her?"

"Alec's sister – Elsie Dillworth."

Sir Daniel looked at him long and hard. "H'm," he said. "H'm. Tell Meaker to pack up. I'm going to sleep. Good night to you."

But when Izzy was gone, Dan did not go to sleep. He lay there for a long time staring into the darkness, and many things out of the past started up before his eyes.

CHAPTER SIX

YOUNG FELIX BOYS, who felt that all one needed to say could be said briefly and without heat, was nevertheless pleased with the rambling incoherence of Dinah's letter. Easter had meant no holiday for him. His father and his tutor had agreed that the whole spring and summer should be relentlessly given to preparing him for Oxford, and this pleased him well enough. When he got to Oxford, he reflected, his life, except that he would be living in a college instead of a parsonage, would be much the same as it was now. He had no intention of rushing about a river like a maniac in a boat, though reading in a punt pulled up under a willow would be pleasant enough; and certainly he would not be found sweating and steaming on a football field in winter or chasing a bit of red leather across the green summer grass. No: the sporting life all seemed very silly to the grave youth. Perhaps, he told himself he would find it necessary to become President of the Union, and if it were necessary, then of course he would do it. For the rest, it would be agreeable to show Miss Dunkerley round if she found it possible to come up now and then; and, at the end of his time, he would take a couple of firsts and then settle down to a bit of real work. He wouldn't, he decided, become a judge like his father. A successful Q.C. made far more money than a judge. Of course, there was the question of prestige. From that point of view, it was a terrific thing to be a judge – in England, anyway; and so perhaps, when he was sixty or thereabouts, he would revise the matter again in the light of circumstances. This was the only point in the streaming road of his career where he hadn't decided his direction. Still he said to himself gravely, from now to sixty was a moderately long stretch: he would be able to look about.

The Cotswold roofs were lovely under the mild spring sunshine, and here and there on the fringes of the wood the primrose clumps were like half-pounds of butter on a green cloth. He thought it might be a good idea to pick some and send them to Miss Dunkerley, but, on the whole, decided against it. A letter would say all that needed to be said. So when he got back to the house he sat down to write:

MY DEAR MISS DUNKERLEY – You will perhaps be surprised to hear from me again, as it is scarcely more than a month since I last wrote. I cannot, however, neglect to thank you for your long communication addressed to me from Somerset. You seem to have vastly enjoyed attending this wedding. Since Miss Satterfield is your cousin, her husband, the Dean, I suppose, is your cousin-in-law: a droll relationship. Well, the affair appears to have passed off satisfactorily: that is the main thing. I need hardly tell you that the primroses are blooming here, for surely you have sense enough to know that primroses bloom at Easter. My tutor has been suffering rather badly from lumbago of late, though this, happily, has in no way interfered with our studies. You will be glad to know that he seems not dissatisfied with the progress I am making; and, indeed, it would be mere affectation on my part if I were to pretend any doubt as to my being accepted for Oxford or as to the probability of my doing well there. You tell me that your brother will not be returning to Merton and that he seems pleased to have left his Oxford course uncompleted. I confess that I find this difficult to understand. Still, give him my regards, and believe me to be, with deep respect,

Yours sincerely,

Felix Boys.

P.S. – Did you read my father's summing-up in the case against Henry Manningham? I thought it showed some skill. You will find a full report in *The Times* newspaper of the day before yesterday. F.B.

He read Dinah's letter through again, so as to make certain that no point had been left unanswered, then tore it into small pieces and dropped them into the waste-paper basket. The letter read:

DEAR MR BOYS – We have all had a lovely time here in
Somerset. Now that the happily married pair have gone away,
things are quiet but what a rush it's all been! I've never felt so
excited in all my days! Of course, if everything had been done
according to the best examples, the wedding wouldn't have
taken place here at all because a wedding ought to be from the
bride's home not the bridegroom's, but Mr Crystal was very
keen to be married in the church he's Dean of and my cousin
Grace Satterfield would do any mortal thing to please him much
less a little thing like that. I must say he looks a bit too much like
a plaster saint for my liking, what with his blue eyes and Grecian
curls and all the rest of it but that's neither here nor there, he
being her choice, not mine. At least, he gave me a sweetly pretty
watch on a long chain to hang round my neck, and tuck the
watch into my belt, and Miss Hesba Lewison, who was the other
bridesmaid, got an identical copy which makes the only thing in
which I resemble that terrifying brainy young woman! My
father of course gave the bride away and my brother Laurie who
by the way is never going back to Oxford but straight into
Dunkerley House to learn the business from A to Z which has
made a new man of him, I must say, never so cheerful before –
well, he was the best man, and a pretty pair he and father looked
in new frock coats and top hats and lavender ties and gloves with
white carnation and maidenhair button-holes got from goodness
knows where at this time of year! Mother looked sweetly
motherly in quaker grey silk and I should say the whole thing
was a great success what with the cathedral bells pealing away
like mad and the organ thundering out the Wedding March and
the Voice that Breathed and everything as it ought to be, even the
weather which as you don't need me to tell you is always chancy
at this time of year on its best behaviour with rooks building
nests and all that sort of thing going on – most appropriate, I
thought, for a parson's wedding because the whole place
seemed black with them cawing and croaking hither and thither
though that's the last thing I'd dare say to Grace or her husband.
He can give you a very cold blue look I can tell you for all his
sugar voice, though this is hardly the moment to speak behind
his back. The bishop married them and a nice old thing I thought

157

him with an appropriate "few words" to all concerned which made me blush. The happy pair have gone off to Scotland of all places, pretty frigid I should think at this time of year and Grace had the loveliest going-away outfit as she can well afford to, being as rich as Midas so that looked at from that point of view Mr Chrystal hasn't got a bad catch, not that he's lacking himself in wordly goods. And now the Cathedral will have to look after itself as well as it can for a bit and father and Laurie have gone back to London full of importance and wondering why Dunkerley House didn't fall into the Thames in their absence though I shouldn't wonder if both the cathedral and Dunkerley House manage to survive the catastrophe. Miss Lewison has gone on to Cornwall to see some old writing woman or other and here are Mother and I with a few minutes to call our souls our own and this big deanery to live in. Father says, though not in the Dean's hearing, Give him Dickons where he can be sure of the drains and where he's having the electric light put in this year. We are going back to Town on Thursday and then this sweet little holiday which I've managed to steal will come to an end and back I go on Monday to Switzerland. Thank goodness, I shall be "finished" at the end of the summer, for once I'm finished I suppose I can begin. Well, that's enough about us and I can well imagine you saying more than enough and no blame to you if you do; and now what about you? I've never been to the Cotswolds and of course where you've never been is terribly romantic as I know because I thought how romantic it was going to be in Switzerland – all mountains and snow and edelweiss and people yodelling, but how dull trying to steal a place nearest to the porcelain stove and translating *Il y avait une fois un corbeau* and being scolded if you raised your voice in an unladylike way let alone yodelling. Still, I think the Cotswolds must be a most romantic place and I'm longing to see it all some day – the places where you go for your walks and the rectory and your old tutor who I am sure is not so forbidding as Mr Chrystal. And I'm sure you're being a great credit to him and that you won't be so silly as Laurie and find Oxford a bore but will learn everything that can be taught and be a great man some day. Well what a rambling letter I must bring it to a close. If you were to write to

Manchester Square I should get your letter before returning to Switzerland and that would be most agreeable because everybody there will want to know how you are getting on.

Yours very sincerely,

DINAH DUNKERLEY.

2

Dinah thought that her letter had covered everything, but she had not mentioned Isambard Phyfe. Isambard was not a wedding guest, and so he did not need a new frock coat or lavender gloves; altogether, he was so inconspicuously in the background that it is small wonder he was overlooked. However, even when attending his niece's wedding – and, what was just as important to him, the wedding of the biggest shareholder after himself in Dunkerley Publications – Sir Daniel did not feel that it would be safe for the world if he were separated from his *aide*, and so Phyfe was lodged at the Lion and Lamb, in a lane leading off the cathedral close. A benevolent bearded lion, reposing in a green English meadow contemplated with detachment the gambols of a new-born tottering lamb upon the signboard that swung beneath Isambard's window, and just within the window, on a trestle table covered with green baize, were set out envelopes and paper, ink and pen-tray, and a Blickensderfer typewriter which had a revolving cylinder embossed with the letters of the alphabet and looked the last word in modern office equipment.

But, in truth, this was nothing but façade, and Isambard knew it as well as anybody. He was taking life easily, in a mixed emotional mood, enjoying this lovely village and this lovely spring weather with an intensity he would not have known but for his devotion to Elsie Dillworth, yet at the same time restless and loose-ended because of her absence. He wandered about the lanes and fields, wearing a cap, a Norfolk jacket and knickerbockers as a tribute to rural life, and was elated, depressed, a dweller in the seventh heaven and a wanderer in the last circle of hell all within an hour. In a word, he was an ardent lover separated from his woman.

It would have surprised him to know that the woman was haunting Sir Daniel Dunkerley's mind as much as his own. This wedding of Theodore Chrystal and Grace Satterfield churned up Dan's memories, tore off ten years of his life, and put him back into

159

Manchester at the moment when all his enterprises, now floating like galleons on a deep sea, were no more than a frail and tentative boat pushed out from a printer's shop in Levenshulme. He saw again the small group of people who had gathered around him then. George Satterfield was gone, but not before affairs had taken the fantastic turn which permitted him to leave Grace one of the richest women in the country. She could have married a peer's heir, Dan reflected with satisfaction. He hoped she would be happy with Chrystal, the curate of ten years ago, who then had seemed socially so far above her. Well, give the man his due: there was something about him, and no doubt he would become a bishop.

So much for three of that small group. Then there were Alec Dillworth and his sister Elsie. At the thought of Elsie Dan's face twitched with anxiety. He had liked the girl. She had a gay courage, and, he believed, musical genius. But, by God! he said to himself how life had been weighted against her! Whether she had loved Chrystal, whether she loved Phyfe now, he could not say. He believed she was a rarer spirit than either, as Alec was a rarer spirit than he was himself.

In this mood of analysis and confession, Dan got up from his easy chair in the best of the Deanery's bedrooms and strolled to the open window. His wife Agnes had gone down to the drawing room. It was the first moment he had had alone since this wedding-journey began. The night was falling, but it had been a warm day and the window was open. He leaned out, inhaling the scent of lilac that filled the grey-walled enclosure beneath him.

Something must be done about Elsie Dillworth.

Dan turned from the window and walked slowly up and down the room. Why should he meddle in the business? What had it to do with him or he with it? He knew the answer. He had everything that money could buy, and would continue to have as long as his life lasted. Out of all his past, the Dillworths alone stood for what money could not buy. Alec was perpetually a thorn in his side, a pebble in his shoe, a pea in his downy bed. And he knew it would be a bad day for him when he said "Get out!" and Alec finally went, and nothing was left but Phyfe and all that Phyfe stood for. Elsie had not touched his daily life as Alec had done, but she was a part of Alec, he was always there, and he was not going to see her hurt a second time. The affair with Chrystal turned to disaster when Chrystal discovered what he thought to be the truth about her. It wasn't the truth: it was nothing but one or two facts, but Chrystal was a green pup then. Even now, Dan thought, it was an even bet that the Dean would always let the facts blind him to the truth. Phyfe had had a different upbringing. Perhaps he could bear the facts in all their misery and cling to the truth that rose triumphantly out of them.

But someone had to tell him the facts. The way to disaster would be to let him stumble on them at the wrong moment and in the wrong fashion, as Chrystal had done so long ago. Perhaps Elsie herself had already told him? Damn it all, she ought to do it, he reflected. It's her affair, not mine. Well, if she had, Phyfe would soon make that clear and no harm would be done. This time, anyway, the thing was not going to be left to chance. He turned to the mirror, gave his strong wiry hair a rub with the brushes, and went down. Chrystal was in the hall, just crossing over from his study to the drawing room. Even at this crisis of his life, Theo spent a lot of time in his study, whether writing sermons or making financial calculations. Dan couldn't be sure. He took the Dean by the arm. "Theo," he said, "will you do me a favour? Send someone over to the Lion and Lamb and tell Mr Phyfe to stay in. I must go over there and discuss a few things with him after dinner."

3

"Put on your overcoat, Izzy," Sir Daniel said; "we're going to have a walk, and it's rather cold."

They walked for a mile with no word said on either side, Isambard making a swipe now and then with his rattan cane at the shadowy herbage, wondering what all this was about, Dan turning over and over in his mind the opening words, damning himself for an interfering fool, wondering whether even now to let Isambard and Elsie find one another out in their own good time.

"What do you think of Miss Lewison?" he asked suddenly.

"A charming young lady, and most talented."

Dan smiled at the glib acquiescence. Still, it was true enough.

"You wouldn't think, to look at her now, and to know what she is now," he said, "that she'd had such an unhappy childhood."

"I don't know much about that," Izzy answered. "I've only read the article about her career in *Dunkerley's*."

"Well, there was more to it than needed to be said there. Believe me, Izzy, she didn't have a pretty childhood." And, after a moment's hesitation, he added: "For that matter, I don't imagine that you did, either."

"I think you know most of it," said Izzy.

"Well, I don't want to know any more. What concerns me about a person is not what he was but what he is. I like to judge a man by where he ends up, not by where he begins."

"I think, Sir Daniel, young Dillworth would put on one of his one-sided grins if he heard you talking about judging people, anyway."

He certainly would, Dan thought, and felt he was getting off the track that had looked fairly clear a moment ago.

"What I mean is simply this," he said. "There have probably been some queer patches in most people's lives. But, if they are people of any worth at all, we should be damned fools if we paid too much attention to what, after all, are only patches. I've seen a lot of trouble arise that way, Izzy. A man isn't a drunkard because now and then he gets tight or a libertine because the flesh is occasionally weak."

Oh, God! he thought. What have I let myself in for? I sound like something on a soap-box.

They came to a field gate and leaned upon it, looking into the west where a feather of moon was fluttering down after the sunken sun. The scent of Sir Daniel's cigar was heavy on the cold sharp air.

"There was a case I came on in Manchester," he said. "It was a mixed sort of district where we lived. There were people a shade above real poverty like ourselves, and people who were poor and just struggled along somehow, and people who were damned poor, right down under the line. I knew 'em – all sorts of 'em. I remember a girl – as handsome as they come, a real beauty, and what's more, a really good girl. She lived with her parents in a miserable slum street behind the main road. They were dreadful people. They drank every penny that came into the house, and the man was in and out of gaol all the time – housebreaking and that sort of thing. The kids had a terrible life. There were two of them – a boy as well as this girl I'm telling you about. They were thrashed and kicked and dragged up anyhow. You wouldn't think it possible for a spark to survive in them, but they were two of the finest kids I ever knew."

He paused for a moment and drew on his cigar. The smoke went out of him like a sigh. "They didn't have a spark, Izzy. They had a flame."

Dan found that he was himself deeply moved. It was a moment or two before he went on: "Well, never mind the boy. I want to tell you about this girl. She was forced on to the streets. I've often thought about that and tried to get my mind straight about it. I've wondered whether any woman can be *forced* to become a prostitute. There's no doubt at all that in this case the father forced the girl to begin that sort of thing; but could anybody make a woman continue against her will? Personally, I don't believe it. Knowing that girl as I did, I should say that she was physically very passionate, and that, in the beginning, the life gave her a certain satisfaction. It's only later, I imagine, that it would become boring, even nauseating, and the thing about this girl is that she never reached that point. In six months she had fled with her brother from their parents' home, and thereafter to this day – because I still know her, Izzy – nothing ill has touched her name.

"Well, there it was – an isolated incident which arose out of her home circumstances and out of her physical passion, which is something not every woman has, and, believe me, is one of the most fortunate things a woman can give the man she at last really loves.

"And this girl did fall in love. I can believe that the experience she had been through had a good deal to do with it, but at that time her beauty opened out into something that I can tell you was surprising. But she was developing in other ways, too, and that may have had something to do with it. She was a gifted woman who could have made her mark in the world. Well, whether she became engaged to be married I don't know, but at any rate there was an affair, some sort of understanding with a man who wasn't fit to cut her toe-nails, though nine people out of ten, I suppose, would have called him her superior. I think myself that she should have told him at once what her past had been. It was an incident in her life – a terrible and frightening incident, I admit, but an incident all the same. I don't believe he would have been big enough to overlook it, but the poor devil was not given the chance, and the affair dragged on to a dreadful end when he found out everything by accident."

Dan paused, put the cigar to his lips, and took a long draw. Then he threw it into the field before them. Izzy watched the bright arc drawn like a firefly on the air, and the thin blue smoke that arose in a wavering spiral for a moment before the heavy dew killed the burning. Dan put an affectionate hand on Izzy's shoulder, the first time he had ever made such a gesture to him. "Do you know what I'm talking about, Izzy?" he asked.

Izzy did not answer, and, looking closely in the all but darkness, Dan saw the tears coursing down his cheeks, and caught the assenting nod of his head. He felt his own throat constrict and his eyes sting, but he fought back his tears and asked: "Whom are you crying for, Izzy – yourself or her?"

Izzy took up the cane which he had crooked over the gate and walked a few blind paces up and down the road. Then he began to hack savagely at the tall green cow parsley, whose colour was blackness in the dark. "For life," he said in a choked voice. "For life. It's so damned unfair."

"I didn't want her to be hurt again," Dan said. "I thought you ought to know. I think she ought to have told you herself."

"So do I," Izzy said, and strode away, leaving Sir Daniel leaning over the gate.

4

Dan stayed where he was for ten minutes after Isambard was gone. Then he began to walk back to the Deanery. Well, Elsie Dillworth, he thought: there it is: either I've cooked your goose for good and all or I've done you the best turn you were ever done. He didn't know. It all depended on what sort of man Izzy was. He knew so little about Izzy. The man's surface was so smooth and acquiescent that you slid off him without penetrating. What, if anything, was beneath that surface Dan would have given much to know. Well, at any rate, Izzy had wept. Somehow, Dan was comforted by the thought of those tears. They were the first evidence he had ever had that Phyfe's hard crust could be dissolved.

The whole episode affected Dan deeply: it had taken his mind back so sharply to his beginnings: and Grace's wedding emphasised this mood. Who would have thought, ten or eleven years ago, that Grace would be what she now was? He remembered the night before the first copy of *Hard Facts* was published. It was a foul March night of fog and gloom. He and George Satterfield and Alec Dillworth were at it late in the printer's shop. There was no time to go home to supper, and Grace had come through the fog bringing them a dish of tripe. Dillworth was in his daftest mood: excited because all the preparations had now come to a head, ironical about the nature of the journal they were to publish, getting on the nerves of George Satterfield, who had not yet overcome his fear that the venture would mean nothing but bankruptcy for them all. It had been left to himself to go quietly and resolutely to work on all the things these two were neglecting, the one because he feared they would succeed, the other because he feared they would fail.

Into the shop with its air of energy and with the gaslights whining like mosquitos came little Grace, bringing a puff of fog and a heartening smell of hot cooked food. The woollen hood upon her head was dewy like a bush on a fine autumn morning. Dillworth swooped upon the child, lifted the lid from the dish, and gave a great shout of derision. "Tripe!" he yelled. "By all the gods of the fitting, seemly, and utterly appropriate – Tripe!" In mock homage he fell on one knee before the pretty self-possessed child. "Miss Grace Satterfield, I bow my head before your wisdom. Mr Daniel Dunkerley, Mr George Satterfield, note that out of the mouth of this babe and suckling has proceeded the word that christens our endeavours. Tripe!"

He seized a sheet of paper and swiftly folded it into a fool's cap. He swept the hood back off Grace's head, dampening his hand in the dew of her fair hair, and put the cap upon her. Then he lifted a chair on to a table, leapt upon the table himself, heaved the child up by the armpits, and dumped her into the chair. He placed the dish of tripe upon her lap, and jumped to the floor, shouting: "Behold and worship! The Queen of Tripe!"

Grace sat there in complete self-possession, smiling a little at Alec's excitement, and after a moment she removed the cap, not throwing it down violently as many children would have done, but carefully placing it on the floor by the chair's side. "Now will you please take the dish, Mr Dillworth?" she said, and when he had done it, her father lifted her down and said: "You'd better run along home, Grace," and she did so after wishing them all good night very pleasantly. George Satterfield had been none too pleased by the incident. "Whether this affair wins or loses, Dillworth," he said, "there's going to be no room in it for bloody buffoons." But Alec was not to be damped. "Fill up, fill up, brother," he said, dishing the tripe out on to plates, "that tomorrow we may discharge a wind upon the heath."

Dan's meditations caused his footsteps to wander. He did not go back the way he had come, but took a side-road, turning over in his mind all that had happened from that day to this. Well, Grace was the Queen of Tripe with a vengeance now – a queen with a well-filled treasury, and there were few who were not willing to pay her homage.

He turned into the main road again, his thoughts back now with Elsie Dillworth. He would give a lot, he was saying to himself, if he could ensure for Alec's sister some small part of the security that life had brought to Grace. It was at this moment that he heard steps coming towards him on the dark road. Phyfe, almost running into him, exclaimed excitedly, when he recognised Sir Daniel: "It's come! It was there all the time and those damn fools didn't send it up!"

A great lightness of heart came upon Sir Daniel, as though a prayer had been answered. He smiled in the darkness. Phyfe's voice was that of one delivered. Dan took his man by the arm. "What is it, Izzy?" he asked.

"The letter. It's come. The letter from Elsie."

"We'd better go inside and you can tell me all about it."

Phyfe had almost completely lost his self-possession.

When they had entered the Lion and Lamb he danced up the stairs before Sir Daniel and flung open the door of his room. Dan wanted to prolong this moment, and so he did not invite Isambard to explain himself but looked around appraisingly at the drawn red curtains, the fire burning in the grate, the oil lamp swinging from a rafter. "Everything all right here, Izzy? You look snug, I must say."

Phyfe was standing in front of the fire, a letter trembling in his hands. Sir Dan sank into a wicker chair and looked up with a smile of invitation. "Now tell me."

"It came with the afternoon post," Izzy burst out. "Those fools never sent it up. I found it when I got back ten minutes ago."

"From Miss Dillworth?"

"Of course."

"And what does she say? If I may ask?"

"I don't know. I haven't read it. I'm not going to read it. Nothing beyond the opening lines, anyway. She begins by saying that she was on the point of marriage some years ago and that everything crashed because the man discovered something about her past life. She says she won't tell me who this man was, and that, if I ever find it out, I'm not to hold it against him because the fault was hers. Well, then she says this mustn't happen again. She apologises for having allowed our engagement to come about without having told me first, and then she begins to write what I'm not going to read – not now, or ever."

Isambard tore the letter into fragments and put them into the fire. "It's terrible – terrible – to think of her having to write that. But she did. That's the point. She did. She trusted me."

He smiled down excitedly upon Sir Daniel, and Dan smiled serenely back. He was feeling very happy. "Yes," he said. "That's the point. She hasn't let us down – not either of us. We must remember she was very young that first time." He got up and gave his hand to Isambard. "Izzy, you're a lucky man. I've said that to a good many people who've got engaged to be married, and no one knows better than you do what a liar I am. I hope you also know when I'm speaking the truth."

Izzy was too moved to answer, and Dan went on: "Look, one of our public lies is that it's always necessary for you to be hanging on to my coat-tails. It isn't." He waved his hand towards the table under the window, the writing paper, pens, typewriter. "Pack all this up and go back to London by the first train in the morning. It'll probably be foggy or raining like hell, but you won't notice that. You ought to be with her. Give her my love."

5

Old Sarah Armitage was fond enough of Hesba Lewison, but she didn't think much of the girl's books. She didn't see how they could do any good in the world. Doing good was the standard by which Sarah judged everything. You always had to be a bit ahead of everyone, Sarah thought: a bit more Liberal than the Liberals, a bit more agnostic than the free-thinkers, a bit more humane than the humanitarians; and all these things should go into your books. She was a very famous woman: she had thrilled her generation with a succession of novels about young clergymen who had lost their faith and discovered the humanities by working in boys' clubs in the East End and founding creches for little bastards and hospitals for

unmarried mothers and night schools for errand boys; and about
young Conservative politicians who had seen the error of their ways
and turned their eyes and hearts upon Mr Gladstone; and about
hardened males who had been led to realise that the world would
never be right till females shared their privilege of crouching in a
polling-booth and scratching a cross upon a piece of paper. She not
only wrote novels about these things: she spoke about them wherever
there was a platform, and she founded the Sarah Armitage Settlement
in Bethnal Green, which reformers considered to be a model of what
a Settlement should be. No "reformer" from anywhere in Europe
visited London without including in his programme a call upon Sarah
Armitage at her house in Duke Street, for she shared Byron's
enthusiasm for Greece, approved Mazzini's patriotic fervour for Italy,
and bled in her heart with Kosciusco for Poland. And to all callers she
was able to impart her own enthusiastic belief that it was only a
matter of time before these countries, and all other countries, under
enlightened Liberal regimes, would march forward inevitably to a
condition which she summed up vaguely as "liberty".

By putting her head out through her bedroom window, Hesba could
see Sarah Armitage at breakfast on the terrace of her house in
Newpenny. Rather an old duck, Hesba thought, forgetting the days
when she had been the formidable Sarah's secretary-companion and
had found her exigent and a little frightening in her egotism. Sarah's
large amorphous body was spread upon a cane *chaise-longue*. Her
breakfast sent a heavenly aroma up to the bedroom window: bacon and
kidneys, new bread and coffee. An empty porridge plate had been
pushed aside. There was marmalade to follow. Sarah was a great
gormandiser. Here and there on the outer edge of the terrace were
burning bushes of forsythia; the daffodils were long over; but in the
garden falling away below the terrace hawthorn of red and white, lilac
and pink cherry, trained in cascades, filled with colour a foreground
that stood out against the blue of the huge bay wherein the sun
illuminated the fantastic splendours of St Michael's Mount. Sarah was
all in flowing black, save for a ruffle of lace at her rather goitrous
throat. Grey hair straggled back anyhow off her forehead, climbed over
her head, and was arranged in a thin "bun" on her neck. Her face was
broad and fleshy: only the black alert eyes gave it distinction. Hesba
watched the plump hands reaching eagerly for the food, heard the

smacking relish with which it was consumed. Better get down, she thought. She herself was all in white with a cherry sash round her waist. The watch that Theodore Chrystal had given her as a bridesmaid's present was tucked into the sash. Sarah grunted when she saw her and pushed a cane chair forward. "What a heavenly morning," Hesba said.

"Snail's on the thorn, God's in His Heaven, eh?" the old woman grinned. "Don't be deceived by appearances, child. Get some food into you."

"Just a cup of coffee and some bread and marmalade," Hesba said.

Sarah looked at her with contempt. "Food, I said. How d'you expect to live and work if you don't eat? You can't live on looking at that." She waved a heavy hand towards the glittering loveliness of the bay. "Fish come out of there. That's what that's for – to give us fish. And the meadows are to feed beef. 'Fat as a thousand beeves at pasture,'" she quoted with relish.

Hesba poured a cup of coffee, cut a slice of bread, and let her run on. Sarah was rather ashamed of her own gluttony: it was her pose to pretend to be proud of it, to relate everything to it. "I've been thinking of rooting out a lot of these flowers," she said. "Asparagus should do well here."

Hesba did not answer. She sat back with her hands behind her head, looking out over the tremendous prospect of sky and sea. "What are you thinking about?" Sarah barked. "Some tom-fool fairytale, I expect, with that castle full of princes and ogres, lovely damsels and what not. Don't be deceived by appearances, child. Reaction. That's all that a place like that stands for. Reaction."

Hesba smiled with sheer lazy happiness. "I expect it did a job of sorts in its time," she said.

"Pshaw! You're engrossed with the past. You should look to the future." She rang a little silver bell whose note chimed beautifully with the morning. "I'll have another rasher of bacon if there's one left," she said to the servant.

Hesba thought rebelliously: Damn the future. Now, now, now is the time. There's always someone telling you that the only time you've got, the only life you've got, doesn't matter compared with other lives lived by other people whom you'll never know. I don't believe it. Now is the acceptable time.

Sarah finished her bacon and shamelessly wiped the fat from her plate with a piece of bread. Hesba poured more coffee for her and passed her the marmalade. "You'd better get out today, and stay out," Sarah said. "I'm going to do some work and I don't want to be disturbed. I've told 'em to put up some food for you, and old Fison will be calling for you at ten o'clock."

Hesba thanked her, knowing that the gruff announcement meant that perfect arrangements had been made for a day she was likely to remember. "There won't be much wind," Sarah said. "You'll just flop about and probably get very sick. You'll be sorry you didn't eat any breakfast. When you're sick, it's best to have something to be sick on."

"I never get sick," Hesba answered briefly. She got up, yawned and stretched. The glory of the morning seemed to rush down into her being.

She passed from the terrace through the open french windows that led into Sarah's long book-filled work room. The vast mahogany writing table was piled with books, newspaper cuttings, pamphlets, files. A strange way to write novels, Hesba thought, calling up an image of her own desk that contained nothing but a pen, an ink bottle, and a pad of paper. But there it was: there was more than one way of going about the job; and with Sarah this way worked. That stout lolling body that she could see through the window housed something important enough to make Sarah one of the best-known women in the world.

How well, Hesba thought, Cecil Bond had caught her! The portrait was over the fireplace, and Sarah hadn't changed much from that day to this. He had painted her overflowing the chair on the terrace, and had relieved the black she always wore by throwing a gay rug in careless folds across her feet. Behind her rose the cream wall of the house and a green shutter and a flowering honeysuckle. It looked a moment in the life of a giant sloth till you saw the glint of the sybil's eye, in which all mental speculation seemed to be lurking.

On an impulse, Hesba ran out and kissed the old woman on the back of the neck. "Pah!" Sarah cried. "You still here? Be off with you!"

Hesba went then up to her own room, her mind full of recollection. She could never look at that picture without recalling the time when it was painted. Cecil Bond, that hairy haystack of a man, had snatched her from what seemed almost literally the jaws of death. They had travelled down here to Cornwall from North Wales,

170

and she had been a small, timid, even terrified creature, black, dumpy and ugly, with little to commend her to Sarah Armitage or any one else. And Sarah had taken her in and fed and clothed and coaxed her, till she was once more in her right mind.

Sitting on the chintz-covered window seat in her bedroom, with the dramatic beauty of the bay spread before her, she was sharply aware of those days of the gulf, and it was this more than anything else that made her cry in her heart: Now is the acceptable time! She knew, as old Sarah, a rich wine-merchant's daughter and heiress, could never know, the not imagined but actual and present pang of loneliness and destitution; and, far though she had by her own work pulled herself away from that, now she was offered an even securer – a most dazzling – seat among the favourites of worldly fortune. For Laurie Dunkerley wanted to marry her.

6

If Hesba had been permitted to read the gay and artless prattling letter that Dinah had written to Felix Boys, she would have given her harsh chuckle and thought: It's not all there. No, indeed, a lot happened, my dear child, that you didn't notice.

She hadn't even been able to take refuge in Grace's company, for the Dean liked things to be done properly and in order. The bride should not go to her wedding from the bridegroom's house, and so Grace had been staying a couple of miles away at the home of Lord Chess, one of Theo's friends and neighbours. It was thence that Sir Daniel had brought her, in Lord Chess' carriage, to the cathedral on the wedding morning.

During the few months that had passed since she met Laurie, vacillating and despondent, wandering through a foggy morning in Bond Street, they had developed quickly in friendship. Once she had instilled into him the resolution that dissipated the troubles that had been hanging over him, she found him a pleasant and amusing companion. His mind was not disposed to speculation, and Sir Daniel himself now saw this and acknowledged it and took the young man more fully into his confidence in practical affairs. This was the best possible condition of things for a man of Laurie's simple administrative quality, and he did not forget that it was Hesba's guidance that turned his life decisively in the way he wanted it to go.

His secret boyish fear of his overwhelmingly successful father was overcome: they were, in however, as yet, a small degree, friends and co-workers.

It is little wonder that this new and mentally blooming Laurie took every means that offered, and devised means for himself, of improving his standing with Hesba Lewison. He said nothing of this to his father, but he had a sense that his father would put nothing in the way. There was a trivial incident, indeed, that encouraged him to think that his father would approve of the turn his mind was taking. Laurie now had his own room in Dunkerley House, but he spent some time every day in his father's. Towards lunchtime one day his father said: "I must be off. I'm taking Spencer out to Simpson's. Remember that, my boy. Lunch with the contributors now and then. It makes 'em feel there's more than a mere business relationship. Spencer's a good man. There are plenty of magazines ready to snap him up, and I don't want to see him snapped. Are you lunching with any one? Is Hesba Lewison coming in today?"

"Not that I know of."

"Ah, well, then come along with me. It won't hurt you to know Spencer better – if there's nothing more interesting to do."

There was a twinkle in his eye as he said it. Laurie thought it an encouraging twinkle. That was all there was to the trifling incident, but it cheered him.

Hesba enjoyed her lunches with Laurie, and he had taken her now and then to a theatre, but there was a moment that had stamped itself into her memory. It was the moment of that day when she and Laurie had come in after shopping in Bond Street, and Alec Dillworth was unexpectedly there, returned after the mysterious absence that had never been explained. She and Laurie were in a high-spirited nonsensical mood, and on the stairs they had passed Elsie Dillworth and Isambard Phyfe, whose mood was clear for all to see. And then Sir Daniel had come into the room, unusually expansive, and had taken her and Laurie off to lunch. She had gone willingly enough, but she was aware, as the other two had not been, of Alec's forlorn unhappy look, standing there watching them go. It seemed a jubilee for everyone – Phyfe and Elsie, she and Laurie and Sir Daniel – for everyone but Alec. Again and again during that day and days that were to follow she recalled the troubled face and the tumbled hair, the thin,

lonely, riven man who stood and said nothing as they went, and she
was haunted by a sense of betrayal.

7

The old Bishop's palace at King's Mandeville was once a fortress. Now
it was a ruin. Its outer shell stood, unroofed, with fantastic sprouts of
ash and alder and sycamore making hairy lines upon the sky as they
climbed out of the rubble that topped the walls. On the surfaces of the
walls, wallflowers had taken root in every crack and split of stone, and
now, at Easter time, they bloomed in patches of warm velvet, yellow,
brown and honey-black. The air was heady with the scent of them, and
the ancient walls boomed with the spinning wings of bees.

The walls which once had divided this place into rooms were gone
save for a few rough stumps sticking out of the earth like the stumps
of rotting teeth. The stone of these walls was used in the early days of
the seventeenth century to build the deanery at the same time when
the new palace was built for the bishop. It was still, after nearly three
hundred years, called the New Palace, but, like the Deanery, it had
sunk its honey-coloured Somerset stone into so rich a harmony with
the land out of which it had been dug that it seemed to be sleeping on
its mother's breast. The Deanery itself was built on the fringes of the
ancient palace, and the space within the old ruined palace walls was
the Deanery garden. The walls were not now very high, but here and
there their pleasing undulation rose high enough to embrace an
ancient window frame, filled with the crumbling stone foliation that
once had bloomed with the colour of stained glass.

It was, to Hesba, the sort of enchanted place that strongly moved
her imagination. Theo Chrystal had told her that the old palace was
built in the twelfth century, and thus, as she walked in the garden in
the warm spring sunshine, the path beneath her feet, which was part
of the antique flooring, grey and grooved, set her mind wandering
along the channels that it loved to follow. And even after the old
building was gone and the place had become a garden, no one seemed
ever to have bothered to make it a garden in any sense of formal
pattern and design. It was mainly turf that for three hundred years had
been tended, with a few of these stone paths wandering through it,
and here and there the rough outcropping of a wall fragment,
corroded by weather but lovely with cushions of warm fragrant

173

thyme. Here and there against the old walls roses, forsythia, jasmine, wisteria and fruit trees climbed in friendly confusion, and where the walls receded into occasional bays and indentations stone seats were placed, where one could sit and listen to the bees ravaging the wallflowers and feel upon one's nerves the soft treading of time.

On that evening when Sir Daniel had left after dinner to call upon Isambard Phyfe at the Lion and Lamb, Lady Dunkerley had gone to her room with a headache, and Hesba, wrapping a cloak about her, had gone out into the garden. She walked to its farthest end, and then turned to look back upon the façade of the house where a few lights were blooming in the dusk. The night was scented and utterly still, and slowly there seeped into her the sense of detachment from immediate things which experience had taught her to value as what she called, thinking back upon it in her alert moods, her reception room. Anything might come to her then, provided she could be quiet and do nothing to stir thought.

She walked slowly to one of the embrasures in the wall. Here the darkness was deeper still, and in her black cloak she felt with a secret smile of happiness that she had put on invisibility. She sat there for some time, tranced by the quietness, and then, floating up out of nowhere came suddenly the image of Alec Dillworth's face as she had seen it when she turned her back upon it in Dunkerley House. She did not chase the image away, but gladly dwelt upon it. She had seen but little of Alec Dillworth-less, she was aware, than Alec himself would have liked. She had felt a series of sudden impulses towards him. She recalled the evening when she had dined at Sir Daniel's, and, almost without premeditation, she had cut the visit short and rushed to meet Alec at the Café Royal. But that small episode had ended in frustration, and so it was whenever she was driven to make one of her impulsive movements towards him. On his part, she sensed a wild shyness, and also a social awkwardness, which would make it difficult if not impossible for him to meet her halfway. And she knew now that she did want to be met. There were things about Alec that stirred and excited her, hints of a quality worth discovering, and experience worth exploring. He was the sort of man with whom every morning would be new, under whose stimulus the dry bones even of life's routine would live.

Yet she had shunned him, she said to herself. She had consciously chosen the company of Laurie Dunkerley, who amused and entertained her but never could do more; and this, she told herself in that confessional mood, was because of her gulf, her fear of once more finding herself forlorn and down-trodden. Even now, with success come to her in her own right, she could not dissipate the shadows that arose from the old years. And, realising this, she despised herself.

She got up, shaking herself with a shrug of disgust, and the small movement betrayed her. Laurie's voice came out of the darkness. "Is that you, Hesba?"

She did not answer, and heard him walking towards her on the paved path. "Where are you? The night's like pitch," he said.

Then she went forward quickly with the intention of returning at once to the house, but she collided with Laurie in the darkness and he put out a hand to steady her. The hand remained, holding her arm lightly just above the elbow. "How beautiful the night is out here," Laurie said. His voice was troubled, and his hand slipped from her arm and took her round the waist. "Don't go in," he pleaded. "Sit down, and let us be quiet together for a moment."

"I ought to go in," she said. "I have letters to write. Everything's got behindhand since I've been here." She gently disengaged his hand, but allowed herself to be persuaded back upon the seat.

Once they were there, Laurie tried again to embrace her, but she pulled her thick cloak around her and said: "Please; let me be." Irrelevantly she added: "You ought to have an overcoat on. You'll catch cold. These spring nights are very deceptive."

"Please, Hesba," Laurie said. "Don't let's talk about trifles. We'll have all our lives to do that if only you'll marry me."

Dear God! Yes, indeed we should, Hesba thought, half amused and half distressed; and laughingly she said: "Really, Laurie, you shouldn't say that! Surely we should have all the weighty affairs of Dunkerley Publications to discuss."

He cried almost angrily: "Please don't twist my words. I know I express myself clumsily. But, Hesba – my darling – you know what I mean. You know – you must know surely – that I love you. I'm asking you to marry me. Will you? I know I'm not fit to clean your boots. I'm a bit of a fool, and you're a famous woman . . . " He paused, fumbling for words, and at last said lamely: "That's what makes it so awkward to ask you. I feel I've got nothing to offer. Not of my own, that is. Riches, I know, but I didn't earn them, and what are they, anyhow?"

She reached out in the darkness and took his hand in hers as if he were a child. She fondled it comfortingly. "Riches are a great deal, Laurie, however you come by them," she said. "Don't be such a fool as to run them down. I know what I'm talking about, because I've been penniless and now, with luck, I shall not be in want again. So, you see, that permits me to talk to you like a grandmother. Indeed, yes. Any woman who loved you would love you none the less because you're rich. You can't buy love, Laurie, but riches can make many things run smoother, even between lovers."

"I'm asking you to marry me," he said miserably, "and you treat me to a philosophical discourse. You sounded almost like Theo Chrystal," he added bitterly.

Hesba sighed and resigned his hand. "Laurie," she said, knowing in her heart that never, never could she thus practically talk if even an ember of love were waiting in her to be blown on, "Laurie, we are both young, and we are excellent friends. Who knows what may come of that as time goes on? Let it go on, my dear. Give it a chance."

"You're a regular manual of plain commonsense."

"It's the best I can do," she said unhappily. And all her unhappiness was for him, for his youth and inexperience and humility and for the hurt she had to bring him.

"Well—" he said, and got up. She remained sitting there, and he stood before her as she took his hand again and pressed it affectionately. "Go in," she said, "and leave me here for a moment." As he did not stir, she added: "I ought to thank you, Laurie. I do thank you. For this, and for everything."

He withdrew his hand and said awkwardly: "Oh, that's all right," and then he was gone.

What a child he is! she thought. A perfect dear, gentle and good. But what a child! And she surprised herself with a swift imagination of what she would have done in his place, of the hot attack that would have had few words in it; and this, she knew, was what she wanted. This was how she was to be wooed and would be won. When at last she stood up, her limbs were still trembling.

8

Standing at her window in Sarah Armitage's house, Hesba could see Fison's quay punt sailing in towards the shore. Despite what Sarah had said, there was enough weather to stretch her canvas and to put a ruffle of lacy water under her foot. Through glasses, Hesba watched Fison run down the foresail, which was all he had on her at the moment, throw over the anchor, and climb into the dinghy. Then, as he began to row ashore, she ran downstairs, waved to Sarah, and passed through the garden to the path which led to the quay of piled grey stones overgrown with turf. The dinghy was already rocking at the foot of the granite steps when she got there, Fison holding on with one hand to a ringbolt. This tiny private quay seemed to Hesba to be Sarah's most desirable possession: a stepping off place to anywhere in the world. And as for Fison's quay punt, whose happy name was Sea Wave, that, too, for all practical purposes was Sarah's, for, whenever she was in her Cornish house, it was perpetually on hire for the use of herself and her visitors.

Fison was a huge, round, red-faced, clean-shaven man, whose voice sounded as though from his youth up he had had to shout against hurricanes to make himself heard. As Hesba appeared at the top of the steps, fifteen feet above him, he roared: "Good morning, Miss Lewison!"

"Good morning, Fison," Hesba said, stepping into the dinghy. "Let me row, will you?"

She seated herself in the bows, Fison let go the ringbolt, and she pushed herself out expertly enough with an oar pressed into the granite. This was the moment she loved! This first sense of being cradled in a new element, of being upborne upon a measureless deep. "You're a good little ole rower, m'dear," Fison said approvingly; and, indeed, she had never lost the knack learned long ago in Llanfairfechan and practised during the time she had lived here with Sarah. Fison was an old friend. She had known him then. It was he who had taught her the delightful art of sculling with one oar over the dinghy's stern. She knew, too, every strake and knee and floor-board in Sea Wave, and now looked at her over her shoulder with pleasant anticipation.

"Where shall we sail to?" she asked.

"Anywhere you like," Fison grinned. "Keep you out of the way for the day. Them's all my orders from Mrs Armitage."

Hesba brought the dingy alongside and climbed aboard. She looked with a child's eager pleasure at all the things she had known so long: the mahogany tiller, carved like a rope finished off with a turk's-head that time and use had smoothed and polished; the forecastle under the half-decking; the one tall mast with the burgee of red and yellow telling of a freshening off-shore breeze. The very cleats and rigging-screws, the sheets and halliards, seemed like old friends: she handled them lovingly. "It's all the same," she said contentedly.

Fison looked over his shoulder from tying the dinghy to a cleat astern. "Ay, we don't change much down here, m'dear," he said complacently. "But you're quite a famous woman now, they do say."

Hesba did not answer this. Oh, it's all so good, she was thinking, so good and so unchanging. The kindly friendliness of Fison, the buoyant lift of the little ship, the clack-clack of the burgee whickering in the wind, the noble bay flooded with gleaming blue and white and roofed by the blue dome of the sky.

"Well, up she goes," Fison said, and she joined him at the mainsail halliards and thrilled at the music of the wooden rings sliding up the mast and the heeling of the ship as the wind leaned against the tautening obstruction. "Take the tiller, m'dear," Fison said, cleating down the halliard. He handed her the main-sheet, and she sat in the stern with her fingers wrapped lovingly round the turk's head of the tiller as Fison jumped on to the half-deck and hauled in the anchor. She brought the ship into the wind, and they moved out briskly as Fison hoisted the foresail and jib. Each was a note in the harmony, and now they purred along with all sail set, and the full music of the morning burst upon Hesba's senses: the sun and the sea and the wind and the hiss of water along the side as they surged forward with the loveliest movement in the world.

"Just keep 'er where she is, m'dear," Fison said. "You're doin' lovely." He got out the fishing tackle and sent the lines streaming astern with the gleaming spinners revolving. "We might catch an ole mackerel for dinner," he said. "You want to eat a mackerel when he's fresh. Boil 'im in salt water while the sea's still in 'im. That's food, that is. A pretty ole lot of rubbish I expect you eat in them ole towns."

He tried a line with the fingers of his calloused hands, giving it short gentle tugs. The fingers, Hesba knew, were more sensitive than hers. She could rarely distinguish the tug of the water hauling on the streaming line from the tug of a fish, and more than once Fison had had a laugh as she reeled in after an hour's fruitless fishing to find that a fish had been hooked all the time.

"Here she comes!" Fison shouted, pulling the line in rapidly in loop upon loop, and, looking astern, Hesba could see the silver shining of the fish streaking the water at the end of the gut. It danced and spun as Fison lifted it over the gunwale, unhooked it with one deft twist, and threw it down on the floor boards. It gasped and leapt, with the hot sun shining upon its miraculous shimmer of blue and green, white and gold. It arched itself till it was like a small rainbow, a small doomed rainbow that was beating its own beauty to death upon the boards. In no time at all, it seemed, the splendour of it began to fade, the rich wet colours to dry and die. It lay still, its foolish mouth occasionally opening in a wide gasp. Finally, it contorted itself into an arc, shuddered with a supreme spasm, and then was still.

And now it's dead, Hesba thought. She was glad that it was dead. You had to live, and in order that you might live other things had to die. It wasn't death that mattered: it was the dying: she was glad when it was all over, and she would eat the mackerel with no qualms.

The breeze held steady off the shore, and they sailed due south before it till noon. The land by now was no more than a smudge, and Fison took the tiller, put the Sea Wave about and sailed north-west. At one o'clock they dropped anchor off a deserted golden beach. Fison hauled a box out of the forecastle and dumped it into the dinghy. It was a box that always thrilled Hesba. She had seen it often enough: a Pandora box that contained cups and saucers, a kettle and a billycan, plates, cutlery and food. Fison rowed it ashore while she was busy with sail-ties, with lashing the tiller, and all the small jobs she loved to do. Fison came back for her, the dinghy beached on the yellow sand, and she jumped ashore. Now they separated, wandering off in different directions in search of dry firewood. There was plenty of it, and Fison lit two fires. On one he placed the billycan full of salt water, with two mackerel in it, and on the other the kettle. Hesba laid out the plates and cups, the knives and forks, on flat stones. She explored

Fison's magic box, found a loaf and butter, pepper and salt, and a pie-dish nobly filled with golden crust.

"Oh, Fison! What is this?" she cried.

"That's a little ole cold gooseberry pie, m'dear," he roared. "An' there's Cornish cream to go with 'er. 'Er be nothing without 'e."

And sure enough there the Cornish cream was, in a glass jar with a screw-lid, the whole wrapped up for coolness in two wet cabbage leaves.

The water was bubbling in the billycan, and on the bubbles dark green leaves were dancing. "Bay-leaves, they be," Fison said. "I brought a few in case we caught an ole mackerel. Salt water boiling an' bay-leaves: that's the thing for an ole mackerel," he explained.

Hesba cut the bread-and-butter and made the tea, and Fison put the fish out on to the plates. "I call this a nice little ole life," he said. "I dunno why you want to go away to them ole towns, Miss Hesba."

He had pulled off his blue jersey to take the sun on his arms. A sleeveless singlet was tight on his chest, round and sound as a good oak barrel. His arms were heavily tattooed. His face shone like a red Dutch cheese. He sat with his legs thrust straight forward and the plate resting on his thighs. With a deft flick of the knife, he separated the mackerel's flesh from the backbone which he tossed into the fire. The sun poured down upon them. Hesba could feel the scorch of it through her dress, but she loved it. She was a salamander. So, it seemed, was Fison. They sat with the two fires smouldering to extinction away beyond their feet, and were well content. Yes, Hesba thought. It's a nice little old life. The sand, when she rested her palms upon it, was hot. There was no wind. The smoke of the fires went up in two straight blue cork-screws. Out on the water gulls were screaming and swooping upon mackerel bait. The Sea Wave rode without motion. It's a nice little old life, but I wish Alec were here.

She had come straight on to Sarah Armitage's after Grace's wedding, and now she had been here a month. Sarah didn't mind. So long as you kept out of the way when she was working, you could stay on and on. She liked to have you about to talk to when she felt like talking. But all the same, Hesba was thinking, I didn't intend to stay here like this. I intended to say how d'you do to the old dear and be off again in a week at the latest. And she knew that she was staying on because she had not the courage to go back. She wanted Laurie to have a chance to cool, and, such had been her rush of feeling towards Alec after Laurie had left her in the Dean's garden, she did not want to see Alec, either. It was all most mixed and illogical, she knew; but there it was. She had a feeling for her own complete independence, and it was hard to overcome. There was little doubt now that she would be not only independent but well-to-do. *The Happy Go Luckies* in book form was enjoying sales that surprised her, and she felt the vigorous flowering of the mind that comes from success. She knew that she could go on and on for a long time. She had been asked to rewrite *The Happy Go Luckies* as a play for children, and goodness knew what might come of that.

And so she wanted to guard herself not only from intrusions like Laurie's, but also from her own impulses; but more and more, she was now feeling, this guarding of herself came to nothing but a sense of incompleteness and frustration. All that had happened today, all this loveliness of wind and sea and air, had never more exalted her; but, too, never before had it left her like this, longing to share it and knowing well with whom it should be shared. Fison, with a grin of childish gluttony on his face, had plunged a knife into the gooseberry pie. The thin perfect crust subsided beneath an uprush of clear greenish syrup. He ladled the gooseberries and juice on to the plates, placed a slice of crust above each, and handed Hesba the cream jar. He was wordless: the moment was too perfect for speech. When they had finished he gathered everything into the box, lit his pipe and said: "I'll go aboard an' have a little ole sleep. I expect you'd like to wander round, m'dear. I'll look out for you in about an hour's time."

He's a good little old soul, she thought, with a smile, when he was gone, but I'm glad to be alone. The cove was about a quarter of a mile long, with arms of rock embracing it at either end. It was full of the wet salt smell of the sea and the hot smell of thyme that grew upon the cliffs. These rose steeply behind the cove, and at their feet, uncovered now, were great teeth of rock on which, when the tide came in, the water would beat and boil. Beyond them, a track climbed the face of the cliff, a track she had often followed, for years ago, when she had first come here to serve Sarah Armitage, this had been one of the favourite points of exploration. It was always so lonely. Summer and winter alike, you could come here and see not a soul. She didn't know whether the cove had so much as a name. For herself she had christened it Seal Cove, because once, at half tide, she had found a pair of the sleek lovely creatures basking on the rocks there.

She climbed now, grasping at the briar roots and the tufts of sea-pinks, and came to the top where the wind found her again, blowing firmly into her back as she faced round to look out to sea. It seemed like a hand urging her towards the gulf and she was glad that this was a customary spot and that her nerves were steady, for standing now fifty yards or so from where she had come up, she was upon overjutting land beneath which was the void with the rocky fangs spread upon the sand. Often enough she had stood there when the tide was tearing in with a wind from the sea behind it, and she had looked with awe at the white confusion of water hammering the rock till the cliff itself seemed to tremble and the air was full of thunder and flying spray. Now the sea was a far-off level blue, misty and tender, and the rocks were a dry black jumble of stone slumbering in the sun. Nevertheless, a shudder suddenly shook her as she felt the gentle persistent fingers of the wind in her back, and she moved away from the edge with a sense of discomfortable foreboding.

They lost the wind on the way home, so that old Sarah had her laugh after all. They slouched and slummocked along, with a puff now and then lazily shaking the sails. They came towards Sarah's little quay with Fison rowing in the dinghy and Sea Wave barging along at the end of the tow-rope with all her sails tucked up to their spars. The eastern side of the bay was filling with a plum-coloured dusk while the west was a smoulder of dying fires. Even Fison spoke more quietly than usual when he came aboard to let go the anchor. "I'll leave the little ole girl where she is for the night," he said. He rowed Hesba ashore and tied the dinghy up at the steps. Then he set off to walk home. Hesba went slowly up to the house and surprised Sarah Armitage by saying that she must return to London in the morning.

CHAPTER SEVEN

IN JUNE of that year, which was 1896, Elsie Dillworth and Isambard Phyfe were married, and in July Sir Daniel Dunkerley sent Isambard to Manchester on a mission which would keep him there for a week. Elsie travelled with him, and they stayed at an hotel overlooking Piccadilly, in the heart of the town. Neither of them had much country inclination, and they spent their evenings in theatres and music halls. During the daytime Isambard was busy and Elsie found the hours heavy in their passing. Isambard was a generous husband, and Sir Daniel Dunkerley had taken more than a sentimental interest in the match. His wedding present had been a substantial block of shares in Dunkerley Publications, and he had, too, raised Izzy's salary. And so Elsie had money to spend and could pass agreeable hours in the shops and tea rooms, but none the less there were stretches of the day when she was intolerably bored.

Isambard was still a happy bridegroom who liked to have his bride all to himself, and so they did not go down to breakfast during that week, but had it served in their bedroom. They were thus, one morning towards the middle of the stay, pleasantly conscious of their happiness, with the breakfast trays on the bed, and the smell of coffee in the air, and the *Manchester Guardian* spread out on the sheets, when Izzy said: "And what are you going to do this morning, my love?"

"I've been finding it hard to fill the time," Elsie answered. "So I'm going to be thoroughly sentimental. I'm going off in search of my youth."

"Youth!" Izzy cried. "Why – you're the youngest, loveliest thing alive."

"I'm twenty-eight," Elsie said.

"And getting younger every day."

"And more sentimental, I suppose. That's why I want to go and have a look at Levenshulme. I want to see it all once more: Dan Dunkerley's old printer's shop, if it's still there, and the house I used to live in, and a church where I knew the parson. I want to wander through those streets again, and then I shan't care if I never more set eyes on it in all my life. I wish you could come with me."

Isambard surprised her by the sharpness of his reply. "No!" he said. "I can't spare the time, and if I could, I wouldn't. It's all done with, my darling. It doesn't belong to you. It belongs to what was imposed on you. I don't want to see it, because you and I have killed it between us. Let it stay dead."

She kissed his unshaved cheek. "Dear Izzy!" she said. "Are you afraid ghosts will rise?"

"You never know," he answered. "I like to keep out of graveyards. You must please yourself darling. But I wish you could find something more agreeable to do."

"Oh, it'll be agreeable enough," Elsie promised him. "I shall be the conquering heroine revisiting the scenes of struggle. And if any ghosts intrude; you may trust me to have a short way with them."

It was eleven o'clock when she got into an old four-wheeler at the cab-rank outside the hotel. The city stones were sweltering and the cab stank. The decrepit horse that pulled it was a parody of *joie de vivre*, wearing a yellow straw hat with his ears sticking through and a decoration of red paper poppies. The driver was his match: an ancient with thin dripping nose and a silk hat, battered and unshapely.

They jogged along, and not a puff of air came through the lowered windows from out of the brazen sky. London Road . . . Downing Street . . . Ardwick Green . . . offices, warehouses, fly-blown shops, pubs, and then the long vista of little houses, more pubs, more fly-blown shops. God! she thought, her gloved hands wilting in her lap, how did I ever live here? How did I ever put up with it? How does any one? And yet, here she had known happiness. Though here she had felt the sharp pangs of misery and betrayal, here, too, she had known happiness, the flowering of her youth, the tumultuous aspirations of genius. In these grey and miserable defiles her blood had run red, and her heart had sung, and her spirit had heard the trumpets from the other side.

At the corner of Palmerston Street she told the driver to stop. She said she would rejoin him in half-an-hour or so, and as he had a distrusting look she paid him for his work thus far, with an added shilling for blessing. Then she walked along to where Dan Dunkerley's shop had been, the fertile soil of so wonderful a tree, and nothing was there to suggest to the passer-by that this was it, that hence that towering *fantasia* had sprung. The frontage was now divided between two shops. From one green-groceries overspilled on to the pavement: sagging and sapless cabbage, a few sacks of potatoes whose purpose in life the wandering dogs misinterpreted, and within the window kippers lodged alongside cheap green grapes packed in crumbled cork. In the window of the other shop a melancholy man sat with an upturned boot upon a "foot" between his knees. His mouth bristled with tacks. The sound of the hammering beat out lugubriously into the hot still air. No doubt, Elsie thought with a smile, if young Dan Dunkerley of a dozen years ago were here to look at these shops now, his lively imagination would be busy with a chain of green-grocery stores, owning their transport and market gardens, spreading from Manchester to Salford and the farthest confines of Lancashire; and with boot factories turning out boots for the million. And if Sir Daniel as he now was could turn up here, why then, she thought with a grin, he would be horrified at the obliteration of his roots and would buy up both shops and affix upon them plaques recording their association with his glory.

She turned from the depressing little shops, and the old cabman, who had brought his hack pacing slowly after her, misinterpreting her aimless loitering, asked: "Where is it you're looking for, Miss?"

"Oh, nowhere in particular," she said. "I'm just wandering round. You stay about here and wait for me."

She crossed the road, which was as hot as a ribbon of burning asphalt, and walked towards Stockport, towards the street junction where St Ninian's church raised its awkward pinnacles against the sky. Next door to the church was the house where Mr Burnside had lived, and her head was full of the thought of all that that good man had meant to her youth. She remembered how she had said of him to Hesba Lewison that his name sounded like running water, and he had been that to her when her childhood had blown about like a soiled petal in these gutters. As she turned the corner, there came to her from some littered attic of memory the words "He leadeth me beside still waters," and at the same instant the resolution formed in her

185

mind to see him. She had intended to do nothing but stand across the
street and look at the house and say goodbye in her heart, but now,
she thought, let me say to him what I am sure he will be glad to hear.

And then she saw that the church doors were open and that a small
crowd of poor people was gathered there on the pavement, and that
some were going into the church, carrying flowers in their hands. She
asked a shawled grey woman what was passing, and the woman said
gently: "Don't you know, luv? It's Mr Burnside's funeral."

Then the tears came unbidden to Elsie's eyes, and the heat of the
day seemed fiercer, and she joined those who were going into the
church and stood just within the folded back doors. She was unused
to churches and did not go forward, but stood there in the cool gloom
and looked at the radiance of candles surrounding a catafalque, and
under the purple cloth upon it she knew was Mr Burnside. Never
before had she entered his church, and if he had been able to rise and
stand at her side he would not have reproached her for coming now
too late. He would have smiled and said in his gentle way: "Well,
child, you've come at last."

She wept unashamedly, and, through the mist of her tears, watched
the radiance swimming and dissolving, and the poor people passing
before the catafalque, lingering there for a moment, some bending
their knees, all laying upon the cold stone their tributes of flowers.
"Oh, I must do it, too!" Elsie thought. "It's too late, and he'll never
know, but I must do it, too, for me and Alec."

She ran out then, and it was as though she had plunged into the heat
of an oven. She went back to the little greengrocer's shop where, she
remembered, she had seen flowers, and was saddened to find what
poor wilted things they were. But among them was mignonette, and
she bought that for its sweet scent, and ran back towards the church,
the old cabman looking at her vagaries with distrust.

But when she was back the picture she had left was dissolved. The
building was shuddering with the music of the organ, the coffin had
been lifted from the catafalque; and on the shoulders of strong bearers
it was advancing down the church towards the hearse which was now
at the door. Oh, God! Elsie thought, I laughed to Izzy that I was going
to say goodbye to my youth, and there it goes. Her hand, grasping the
poor little pepper-coloured blossoms, trembled as the majesty of the
uplifted coffin was borne towards her. She edged into a pew, knelt,

and bowed her head, and was fearfully aware as it went by her. She did not look up when the shuffling feet had gone, and the lighter untrammelled feet of those who followed. She stayed there for a long time, till everything was very quiet, and her senses told her that the church was empty. But her senses deceived her. There was one person besides herself in the church, a man wearing an ironic grin upon his face. He watched her for a while, and then said quietly: "Well, I thought so! It is our little Elsie!"

Her fingers contracted upon the flowers in a fearful spasm. She looked up and saw her father's face.

2

We do not know our moments of fate. They are with us as raindrops before becoming overwhelming torrents and waterfalls. Only once had Mr Burnside and this man Dillworth come face to face. Often enough Dillworth had been to prison for theft or housebreaking, and this time he had seized a weapon and struck at the policeman who came upon him. That made it a serious business, and Mr Burnside, who was interested in him only as the father of Elsie and Alec, went to talk with him in prison.

"You're not fit even to be a burglar," he chided him. "A burglar who's such a fool as to use a weapon is losing his grip on his job. If you go on like that, one of these days you'll strike a blow too many. And then, some morning between seven and eight o'clock, you'll be doing some serious thinking. It would be better if you started doing it now, don't you agree?"

For a time, but not for long, the words haunted Fred Dillworth. His imagination played with the thought of that moment when a cell door opened, and his footfall sounded on the stone, and he made the first step of a last short journey. But on that day of summer heat, grinning down at his daughter as she knelt on the floor of a pew with a bunch of poor flowers quaking in her hand, such thoughts were far from his mind. There was nothing – nothing at all – to tell him that this was it, this was the first step of the short journey, and that the executioner was waiting round the corner.

3

Elsie stood up. Grasping the wood of the pew, she kept her trembling limbs steady. Fear and hate were equal in her heart. It was so long since she had seen him that his image had faded in her mind. He looked worse than she had remembered, and he was worse. Ten years of sin and iniquity do not tread over a face and leave no footprints. The scrubby unshaven features were blotched and sodden with years of drunkenness; the eyes were small and bloodshot. An uneasy grin bared the broken dirty teeth. Her father. The very thought of it made her retch. She could not look at him from the point of view of that moment in which they thus stood confronted. Had she been able to do that, she could have brushed him aside with a sweep of her hand. He had shrunk. He was in a wretched physical state, and she, overtopping him by inches, was in the strength of her young womanhood. But what she was looking at was not this crumbling ruin of a man but the incarnation of all that had been sordid and sinful in her childhood, all the beatings and bellowings, the fears and frustrations. All had flowed out of this man, her father, who seemed now to be terribly interwoven into the very stuff of her marrow, and yet at the same time more alien than the imagination could grasp.

"Well, Elsie," he said. "You're looking fine. A man ought to be proud to have a daughter like you. I came to see the old parson carried out in his box. A nice pretty cloth all round it, but a box all the same. He tried a bit o' preaching on me once. *Me!*" The thought of it made him grin. "Well, well! He found his box before I found mine. That's how life is. You never know. The silly old bugger."

Elsie was horrified. Outside the church she could hear the crunch and jingle as the hearse moved away. Stung beyond control not only by his present villainy but even more by the thought of all that she had suffered at his hands, she slapped him across the face. "Hold your tongue," she said. "And let me get out of this."

All the evil in him glinted for a moment in his red eye, but he fought down the impulse to strike back and said sorrowfully: "You'd strike your father! Your poor old father!" He stayed where he was, blocking the way out of the pew.

"My father!" She laughed, and said venomously: "Father, indeed! I wish you were dead, and my mother, too. I'd pay a lot to see you going by in your hearses."

"I can't bear to hear you talk like that, Else," he said. "Say what you like about me. Hit me. I'm a poor defenceless old man. But your poor old mother – she's dead, Else. Dead this coupla years."

"The sooner you join her the better," Elsie said. "I'm not weeping for her. Now let me go."

She did not feel as easy as her high words suggested. Her heart was thumping; her hands felt clammy. She pulled off her gloves and began drawing them through her fingers. Dillworth's quick eye saw the wedding ring.

"So we're not Elsie Dillworth any more," he said. "No wonder we're anxious to get rid of our poor old father. I hope he's a good man, Else. I hope he's giving you a better life than your old Dad was able to do."

She was nauseated. "Oh, for God's sake," she cried, "stop your snivelling nonsense. I want to get away."

She tried to push past him. He took hold of her wrist – the wrist of her maimed right hand that was always sensitive – and he squeezed it till she winced, then gave it a sudden twist that sent a flame of agony through her. He dropped her hand.

"Stop my snivelling nonsense, eh?" he said. "All right, Elsie Phyfe, we'll stop it; we'll talk sense."

Now he was all evil, and she began to tremble again.

"That surprises yer – eh?" he said. "That surprises yer to know I've kept track of yer doin's? Well, you shouldn't be such a bloody fool as to advertise yer marriage in the papers. It gets round – see? Isambard Phyfe! Lovely name. Sounds rich. 'Ow's 'e off – eh? Could you get a few quid out of 'un for yer old father? – just to shut the old man's mouth – eh? Or shall the old man look up Mr Phyfe himself? I expect we could find 'im out with a name like that. Yes. There's ways an' means, Else. But p'raps you'd rather it didn't come to that. We could settle it private and friendly."

She gave him then such a look of loathing and contempt that his assurance for a moment vanished; but he was not a sensitive man and quickly rallied. "Well," he demanded truculently. "What about it, you sweet little whore? What about a quid or two to be going on with?"

She had lived too soon in the gutter, and for too long, to have wholly forgotten its ways. She spat in his face, gave him a sudden hoyden shove that sent him reeling into the aisle, and walked quickly out of the church. Whether or not he followed her she did not know. She trampled upon the many fallen petals that littered the pavement without seeing them. She saw nothing, felt nothing, except an uncleanness, a sense of violated integrity, saw not even the old cab crawling along the kerb till the cabman hailed her. "Hey, Miss. Here I am. You goin' back now?"

She got in. "You ain't arf been a time. Potterin' round waitin' for you in the 'eat. It'll cost you a bit."

"All right," she said wearily. "All right. Pay covers everything."

4

She told Izzy what had happened. She must now, she knew, tell him everything. Fear of the past, which never yet laid a ghost but multiplied the gibbering crew, had already claimed its penalties from her. There must be no more of it.

Izzy was all tenderness. He had no reproaches for her. That night at King's Mandeville when Sir Daniel Dunkerley had drawn the curtain and shown him the young Elsie growing up, Izzy's life had reached suddenly to a point of nobility. Elsie had become for him the more completely Elsie because she was not Elsie alone. He had seen, as he was not accustomed to see, the hard and bitter life of men as something for acceptance and compassion, and she, as the immediate victim who exemplified all that he had so unexpectedly apprehended, was at the burning heart of his compassion and irradiated by it. There are two things that may be done to errant human feet: you can nail them to a malefactor's cross or break a vase of spikenard upon them. That was the night when Izzy broke the vase and the fragrance was never to pass wholly out of his life. It was now in such terms that Izzy thought of Elsie. Indeed, nothing that could be called thought had passed in his mind upon this matter. He had intuitively accepted all that she had been and might be, and found his love for her deepened thereby.

"Don't let this worry you, Else," he now said. "It's obvious that he has blackmail in mind. But blackmail's no good when you've got nothing new to reveal. I'm sorry about your old parson. I should have liked to meet him and thank him for all he did for you."

That was all. They went out to a farce in the theatre that night, and the next morning they returned to London. They were living in the house with the bridge. The bridge had become Elsie's private room. From one side of it she could look up towards the roaring Strand, from the other upon the flow of the river. She was happy, and old Mrs Phyfe, to her own surprise, was happy too. There had been no disruption of her life, rather an increase of its interests. In the long hours when she was waiting for Izzy to be released from Sir Daniel's whims, Elsie would join her in the childish games of cards that she loved, or read to her from simple story-books. Books of false emotions and improbable happenings, far different from anything which her own experience had shown life to be, held her spellbound. Only occasionally would her native astuteness and scepticism protest. "Well, well!" she would cry; and add: "But there! It's only one of them old books. They'd put anything in them old books, my dear."

But when she could do so without offending the old woman, Elsie liked to be alone in her crystal room. Izzy had filled it with cyclamens of all colours, and she loved the beautiful fly-away flowers poised like butterflies at the ends of their stalks. They looked eager and expectant, as though at any moment some word would be spoken that would set them all free to fly at their will. And in her heart, too, was the same eagerness and expectation, a longing for she knew not what. Once, she had been struggling through her tunnel towards the star of daylight at the other end, but the rock had fallen and now there was not, there, a way out. But in her aery room, swinging as in a cage between earth and heaven, she was aware of longings unfulfilled, of something that she asked of life, not yet knowing what it was.

5

Alec Dillworth could still not believe that this was happening to him. They had taken a train, disembarked at a rustic station, walked a mile or two and come to a grey crumbling wall. It had been easy to climb over, and now they were in perfect privacy. Not that they were in much danger of being disturbed even if they had not climbed over the wall, for the path they had come by had left the main road long ago. It was a mere track. They had followed it at hazard, along a singing stream green with cresses, through a small wood, and out again into the noontide that silenced the birds and lay in a haze almost as tangible as thin silk upon the countryside. And there was the wall. They climbed over it and leaned back upon the other side. They took out sandwiches and cheese and apples and munched without speaking, looking away over the downward fall of the land to a saucer full of dark green trees and its upward climb beyond that to the flank of the downs and the three beech trees standing there on top of the world. And over it all, field and wood and sky, was the enchanting blue silk veil of summer heat.

And then they were lying upon the ground, pressed close together, and he was saying: "Hesba. My darling. My darling Hesba." And she was saying nothing. Her eyes were closed, and her half-parted lips, her smile, were saying everything.

He still could not believe that it was happening, though it had happened several times before. It was as old as the hills and as new-made as morning. He lay back, rested his head upon his hands, and gazed into the blue. Hesba knelt and looked down at him. He was wearing no tie, and she opened the top button of his shirt. She looked intently at the white of his neck. Suddenly she buried her face in it and said: "Oh, your neck! Your poor neck."

"What's the matter with my neck?" he mumbled happily.

"It's so white and thin."

"What do you want it to be – red and fat? You should find a Prussian officer. They're not allowed to be lieutenants till they carry a pound of sausages above the collar. A captain must have a pound and a half and a major two pounds."

"Oh, you fool."

"And they can't become colonels till the general can play noughts and crosses in and out of their duelling scars. That's what you want – a real beefy swine, all slashed to pieces latitudinally and longitudinally, not a pure spirit like me."

She sat up. "Pure spirit! You eat like Sarah Armitage."

"Why not? Did you finish your sandwiches?"

"No."

"Then let me have them. The point is, I turn my sandwiches into pure spirit, not into rolls of fat on the neck. I've got a very special sort of metabolism."

"When are you going to turn your spirit into some writing? Why haven't you written anything lately?"

"Because I'm no good. I discovered that on a very interesting occasion."

"You fool."

"All right. But there it is. I'm going to be a pure spirit who eats like a horse named Sarah Armitage – not a fussy creative spirit."

"No, seriously, darling –"

"There's only one thing I can be serious about at the moment," he said, and began kissing her again.

6

He remembered how he had put some proofs into an envelope, addressed them to her at Sarah Armitage's, looked up, and seen her standing there in his room. He had been living in a state of great distress. The news that Elsie was to marry Isambard Phyfe had shaken him more deeply than Phyfe would ever know. Since they had been children sleeping together in the same bed, they had shared one another's exaltations and despairs. There had been a time when it seemed to Alec that Elsie would shoot like a comet beyond any possibility of his following, and this he had accepted. It was a matter of Elsie's growth, and therefore could not be contested. But that was dead: he himself had killed it; and, ever since, he had felt the obligation of Elsie upon his shoulders as well as the joy of Elsie in his heart. All through their lives, it seemed to him, their bonds had been tightening, and now that they had been cut he was raw and bleeding.

He would have cut them himself: he knew that. But the opportunity had not come. Hesba Lewison, he told himself grimly, knew which side her bread was buttered on. All right. Let her discover the joys of living with a stick like Laurie Dunkerley. There was nothing he could do about it or would do about it.

The knowledge that he would have been ready to marry Hesba did not mitigate the sense of betrayal he felt because Elsie was to marry Phyfe. There was no logic in the turmoil of his own emotions. The two women he loved had passed him by, and he was desolate.

That day when he had returned from his escapade with the woman Effie, and Elsie had come running back, and Phyfe had more slowly followed, and she had kissed him, he did not go home till very late. He did not need to be told what had happened to Elsie. He was as morose and savage as a bereft bear. He wanted to insult somebody. He went to the West End and found a woman – a slip of a girl hung all over with an immense feathered hat and a feather-boa fluttering behind her and flounced skirts trailing the pavements. She took him to a sordid room that recalled his childhood and made him retch. When she had stripped herself and lay naked on the bed, he gazed at her with a cold venom that changed her trade smile of invitation to a most real look of fear. He took a few sovereigns out of his pocket and tossed them on to her belly as one might throw a copper on to a Salvation Army drum. "You dirty little slut," he said, and left her. When he got home, he went straight to bed.

He was morose and silent at breakfast, and Elsie knew why. She sat down and cried when he was gone, and in the days that followed she had need of many tears. When the affairs of the office made it necessary for him to see Phyfe, he was cold and to the point. Several times poor Isambard tried to break down a situation that was far beyond his understanding. "Look, Alec. Why can't—"

But Alec's look of cold contempt would freeze the words on his lips. He would shrug his shoulders uncomfortably and go out of the room.

Izzy did not know how much he owed to Alec. Savage and suffering as he was, Alec would now gladly have killed any one who stood in the way of this marriage. When Phyfe had gone with Sir Daniel to King's Mandeville, it was Alec who said to Elsie one night: "Have you told that fool Phyfe about your life in Manchester?"

The question came out of the blue. He had been sitting with a book in his hands, and he did not look up as he spoke. Elsie paled. "No," she said.

"Well," he said, "you had better do it. I'm suffering enough. You don't want to add another fiasco to my troubles." He threw down the book, put on his hat, and went out.

This mood persisted until the day when Hesba Lewison appeared so unexpectedly in his room. It was strong upon him that morning. Looking up and seeing her there, he gave her no friendly greeting, but said shortly: "Good morning, Miss Lewison. Are you looking for Mr Dunkerley?"

He looked bitter and shrunken and ill, and the silly question was so complete a betrayal of his mood that she could not answer. She closed the door behind her and felt as though her knees would melt with her love and pity. Presently she managed to say: "Why, Alec, you look ill. What have you been doing to yourself?"

"Me?" he said. "Me doing? Of course it would be me!" He was shouting; and then he suddenly sunk his head upon his arms on the desk and mumbled: "You're right. I'm doing it all to myself."

The confession lanced his poisoned wound and the venom gushed out. He saw where he was, but for all that, the pain was no less. In a world of folly, it is not an immediate consolation to know that you are the creative fool. He remained bowed over the table. She laid first her hand and then her lips upon his hair. He looked up, and the shy wonder upon his face, which could be so seamed and ageless, moved her deeply. "Hesba!" he said. "Why did you do that?"

"Oh," she said, striving hard for a gaiety she did not feel, "I've been reading too many cheap romances. Don't you know? – they always seal a bargain with a kiss."

That night, Phyfe and Elsie, Alec and Hesba, dined together. Joy was unashamedly with them all. It seemed from that moment as though the clouds had been lifted.

7

It was to Alec as though a score of knots had been cut in his heart and guts and brain. For the first time, life seemed to him to have a joyful simplicity. He had always wanted to live with intensity, but he had not before realised that there could be intensity in the release from tension. Everything seemed easy in this mood. It was easy to be gracious in his human relations; it was easy to live; it was even easy to write.

He would surprise Hesba. He had told her he was writing nothing, but he was writing something new. What had happened to him upon the heath in his moment of self-acceptance was still valid. He knew now that he would never write as he had striven to write till then. It was in the striving that his failure had lain. He had always wrestled with his angel and won little. In his new mood, it seemed to him that he must strive only to submit, only to bring a whole, clean heart to his job. He must kick his self-seeking pride out of the window. Only by first becoming a servant could he hope ever to be called a good and faithful servant and to enter into joy.

These were the preoccupations of his secret heart as that summer unfolded. Externally, he bloomed. He was a lover and his love overflowed upon Elsie and Izzy and old Mrs Phyfe whom he often

195

visited and joked with and amused by a thousand monkey-tricks. He was walking one night with Hesba towards the Café Royal when he saw, standing in a doorway, the pitiable Danaë upon whom he had showered sterile gold. He went suddenly hot with shame, and stopped, and spoke to the girl.

"Do you remember me?"

"Not 'arf! You're cracked. Git along and leave me alone."

"I kiss your feet," he said.

"You're cracked, I tell you. Take him away, miss."

"Now what will Hesba make of that?" he wondered, but she made nothing of it – nothing at any rate for speech, and that seemed to him wonderful. What Hesba did and what she did not alike seemed to glorify her. All the summer was mounting glory till it seemed to him that the world would be too small to contain it. Then, meeting Elsie on her return from Manchester, he heard her say: "I met our father. He tried to blackmail me." And to Alec the words were a roll of fateful drums, the swinging of life into a new theme. The clouds of glory dissolved. He was standing on a hard material pavement as he said to Elsie: "Tell me about it. Everything. Every damn thing that happened."

8

Elsie said: "He can do me no harm. I told Izzy I'd met him. There's no way now that he can hurt either of us."

She said this because Alec's face suddenly made her afraid. She had loved the joyful rediscovery of Alec during the last few weeks: the Alec she had known when they were boy and girl, and when the world, for all its cruelty, had seemed to contain no dragon that could not be killed. Now this was gone. Her words had wiped the bloom off him as completely as a hand might wipe the bloom off a plum. There was now a look of cold rage which made her seek to diminish the effect of her encounter with her father.

They were in her crystal room. Old Mrs Phyfe was out shopping, and Izzy was at Dunkerley House. Alec had carried a tea-tray up to the bridge. The day was hot, and all the windows were open. In each window Izzy had hung one of those contraptions made of strips of thin glass, and a breeze, moving idly in at one side of the room and out at the other, set all these stirring and filled the bridge with the clash of aery cymbals. These butterflies of sound, and the stir of the muslin curtains, and Alec's voice talking happy nonsense, would always remain in Elsie's mind as the ingredients of an exquisite anguish. When she had said what she had to say, there was silence save for the tinkling of the foolish glass bells. It lasted so long that she said beseechingly: "Don't make too much of it, my dear. I'm sorry I told you. He's nothing now but a poor harmless fool."

Alec did not answer that directly. He said: "The world was so glorious before this happened. I knew it was too good to be true."

She got up then and shook him by the shoulder. "It is true," she cried. "Do believe that. You must believe that. He can't alter a thing."

"I must go," Alec said. He got up, and her heart cried at the look of him, at once savage and defenceless.

"Where are you going to?"

"I don't know. I'll just have a walk round."

He went back to his rooms and wrote a letter.

MY DEAR FATHER – Elsie is back from a visit to Manchester, and she tells me that she met you there. It is so long since we had any news of you that I was not even aware whether you were dead or alive. You may think it makes little odds to me one way or the other, and indeed there was a time when that would have been true enough. But as one grows older one sees many things in a new light, and I assure you that it gives me no pleasure to think that the years have drifted us apart and that you may be in some difficulties which it would be no more than my duty to relieve. I am by no means a rich man, but at least life has not treated me as harshly as it has treated you. Will you allow me then to send you this five-pound note as a sign that blood is thicker than water and that I can think of my childhood and Elsie's with understanding and without bitterness?

Your son,

ALEC.

He sealed the letter and addressed it to the house he had known so well and hated so fiercely. Then he went out to post it. He passed three pillar-boxes, and stood before each with the letter in his hand and a horrible indecision tugging at his heart. He rushed swiftly at the fourth box and thrust the letter in. Even as he listened, in the hushed

197

hot city evening, to the impact no louder than would be made by the fall of a leaf, a postman bustled up with his bag on his shoulder and a bunch of keys rattling in his hand. From the opposite side of the street, Alec watched him open the door of the box and sweep the letters into the bag. There! It was done! He felt an inclination, even at that late moment, to rush across the street and reclaim his letter. But he stayed rooted to that spot, heard the fateful iron clang as the door was slammed shut, and wondered that a postman carrying a letter charged with death should go away down the street whistling like a blackbird in April.

9

Through the sultry evening a whisper of wind, as hot as the air itself stirred now and then, rubbing the edges of the plane-leaves together with a sound like the friction of tinfoil. This harsh noise irritated Alec's brain as he sat upon a seat on the Embankment, not so much thinking of what he was to do as surrendering his mind to a passion of chaotic feeling. "And when he falls, he falls like Lucifer." The words were going round and round in his mind till he thought they would drive him crazy. The glory had been too great. Everything this year had switched and changed with too much emphasis. The vision of his spiritual worthlessness had merged into the physical encounter with the woman Effie. The sudden loss, as he took it to be, of the two women he loved had been a phoenix-blaze that sent him up on wings of glory. Heaven and earth are full of thy glory. It had been like that – an experience, so was he made, charged with mystical meaning. He had never before felt so whole, because never before had he been so merged into oneness with others. And now across the serene sky there flashed this stroke of stark white lightning that penetrated his brain. There was nothing on earth that could have convinced him that the bestial figure stirring out of his past would not trail its marks upon Elsie's life and Hesba's. He knew that man! He could feel, as he sat there beneath the sultry crepitation of the leaves, the fall of a buckled belt upon his naked body; he could feel the shame of what this man had done to Elsie. His mind had not embodied his father. It was not preoccupied with that poor flesh so far gone already in dissolution: but with principalities and the powers of darkness. The physical image of the man was strangely weak and distorted: the sense of his power, so bitterly felt in the past, so sharply feared for the future, was immense, soul-filling and soul-darkening. And now he had invited it to an encounter. The slam of the iron pillar-box door denied all compromise.

10

"Why did you call it Seal Cove?" he asked Hesba.

"My darling, what's happening to your memory? I've told you again and again."

"But I love to hear it again and again. You were a child, and you saw some seals basking on the rocks, and so, because it had no other name, you called it Seal Cove."

"You see, you know it all."

"No. There are all sorts of details. What were the rocks like?"

"They'd tear you to pieces. Horrible rocks when the tide is fierce, but heavenly at low water on a summer day. Rock pools full of hermit crabs and sea anemones and all sorts of lovely things."

"It must be a lonely spot if it didn't have a name."

"Yes. That was why I loved it. I've never seen a soul there. I look upon it as my own."

"But you say there's a path leading up the cliff?"

"Oh, a sort of a way. You've got to be a regular goat to use it. Seeing that no one ever goes there now, I imagine it's an old smugglers' track. Plenty of queer things came ashore on that coast, I can tell you. Indeed, yes."

"I never think of them. I think only of you – a small Hesba who had been cruelly treated in Wales, lying on the top of the cliff, and the waves breaking on the rocks below and the seagulls soaring and crying. And she's thinking: 'This is better. This is how it ought to be. This is how life ought to treat a dear little Hesba.' There's only one thing to make the picture perfect. The people who were beastly to you ought to be on the brink of the cliff and someone ought to come and push them over."

She rolled over to face him where they lay under their wall. "You blood-thirsty brute," she said.

"Don't you ever thirst for blood?"

"Do I look a vampire?"

199

He did not answer. He looked up at the face suspended over his, filling the world, and the thought of all that had harmed her, all that might harm her yet, went in hot waves through him.

"Come," she said. "I am a vampire. I'm going to suck your blood like this."

She lowered her face upon his and began to tickle his tongue with the red point of her own.

11

There was no address on the letter that Alec sent to his father. It was marked "Poste Restante. The Post Office, Fleet Street." A week later Alec saw the shambling figure walking up and down the pavement outside the post office. A deep sigh burst from his breast – a sigh in which relief was mingled with a sense of doom.

He had not asked him to come. A way had been left open. But he had come. To Alec the moment seemed decisive. He took care not to be seen, moving swiftly towards Ludgate Hill. He hailed a cab and had himself driven in the direction of Wapping. There he dismissed the cab and walked briskly through the hot summer afternoon, up and down the streets, peering at windows, many of which bore the legend he was looking for: Lodgings to let. He halted at last by a house in a mean street. It looked tidier than its fellows: a geranium bloomed in the ground-floor window, the curtains were clean enough. Even at that desperate pass, a fastidiousness insisted on not too unbearable a squalor. He satisfied himself that there was a public house on the street corner, and then crossed the road and knocked at the door.

The pallid and careworn woman who opened to him smiled with a pathetic gladness when he said he was looking for rooms for himself and his father.

She was no older than Elsie, but life had stripped her down to the bone. Evidently, he was a more engaging person than she had expected to find looking for rooms in that neighbourhood, and she asked him into her small parlour with an obvious anxiety to please. She explained that her husband had been a dock labourer and was recently killed in an accident at his work. She had never let rooms before. They had been proud to have their small place to themselves. But now – what could she do? Clearly she was at her wit's end.

She took him up the stairs covered with linoleum held in place by brass rods that were as highly polished as the prominent knobs of her own cheek-bones. There were two small beds in the front bedroom, both new. Her capital had been completely expended on this small investment. The beds almost filled the room. This and the parlour downstairs, she explained, was what she had to offer.

Alec said he would take the rooms. He was not quite sure when he and his father would move in. His father was not yet in London but he was expecting him soon. His father would be here all the time, but he himself would be away every day, and some nights, too, perhaps. If his father proved a bit unruly, he hoped she would overlook it. "The old man has had a hard rough life. It's time someone took him in hand and settled him down. I don't think he'll give you much trouble."

The woman was delighted. It was touching to see her gratitude to life for having for a moment lifted a burden that had threatened to crush her. No doubt, it would soon be upon her again, and in the long run it would be too much for her, but a moment's respite was enough to lighten her face with thankful smiles. She insisted on making a cup of tea, and as they sat there in a few moments' intimacy Alec said: "There's one thing. Don't let my father know that I've only just taken this place. Let him think I've been here a long time. He might be sensitive about it. He might think I'd given up a better place to make my wages stretch over the two of us."

He paid for a fortnight in advance and then went back to his rooms in Lincoln's Inn, packed the things he would need for Wapping in a suitcase, and fell asleep in a chair. His morning's work had tired him. He took the suitcase to Wapping that night and slept for the first time in his new quarters. Now he was ready to meet his father.

12

"It'll just about run to a cab," Alec said with a grin.

Fred Dillworth grinned too. Life, which had been on the downgrade, had taken an upward line. You could have knocked him down with a feather, as he would have put it, when he received five pounds from Alec. Never in his life till then had one of those fascinating pieces of crinkly paper come honestly into his hands. A good many had come his way out of safes and strong-boxes, but he didn't like them. They were numbered, and getting rid of them was likely to lead to difficulties. More than once, a note of high denomination had been his undoing. He left the things alone whenever he was strong-minded enough to do so. He was not happy with this one that Alec had sent until it had been transformed into five golden pieces jingling in his pocket.

It was a long time since anything had jingled there so pleasantly. Fred Dillworth knew that he had reached a decisive landmark. He would never, now, be able to obtain what he called with a grin "honest work," and if, again, he were caught at the work to which he was accustomed, that was likely to be the last he would ever do. In his own line he was an expert. He could assess the mentality of judges and the probable outcome for prisoners. This taught him that his next appearance at Assizes would mean a long stretch, and the premonitions of his heart told him that this stretch was likely to finish him off.

The ins and outs of a nefarious life had taught him ways and means of keeping body and soul together, but it was a puffing, piddling and anxious life, without the excitement of scheme and risk, and often with weeks on end when there were not two pennies to rub together.

The announcement of Elsie's marriage, upon which he had casually come in a newspaper advertisement – Elsie Dillworth, formerly of Manchester – "That's her all right, the little bitch" – had caused a hope to flame in his heart. Blackmail! But the very word had terrified him. He was too learned in the comparative weight of crime to be attracted to an adventure so hazardous. He thought it over calmly. Twenty to one she wouldn't dare to call his bluff. What he could bring against her was terrific. But there was that one odd chance, and a sentence for blackmail was something for which Fred had no appetite. He put it out of his mind. The accidental meeting with Elsie in St Ninian's Church had caused him to try his feet on the quaking ground, and when she was gone he drew back decisively. If his obscene decrepitude had appalled her, her radiant young womanhood, her elegance, the sense of the all but immeasurable distance that life had put between them, appalled him no less. He told himself that it was "no go". Meddling with people like that was a mug's game. He had shambled away from the church with a rueful acceptance of the shoddy remnants that life had left him. He shook his head over a pint. "No bloody good, Freddie. Finish." He was sorry for himself.

Alec's letter, and the money it contained, rose upon his life like a summer sun. He was warm again. His crafty brain looked at the matter from all sides. Money from Alec – money from Heaven – was not to be snapped at as a fool of a fish would snap at a fly. He wondered where the hook was, and decided that he had been luckier than he had thought possible. They were afraid of him, after all! He knew too much! They were trying to buy him off. By God! but this was a scream! This could be blackmail without a word said or written. He had to do no more than be on the spot – just trail his ugly mug round where they lived, and he'd be on velvet. He'd lived on Elsie before and now it looked as though his poor old bones, not good for much any longer, could once more lie comfortably on her charity. It was worth trying, anyway. No crime in that. No one could get him, and what he could get there was no saying.

Sitting in his filthy room, Fred planned his strategy as carefully as he had planned other enterprises of his life. The temptation to run out and drink those five golden sovereigns was tremendous; but that would not do at all. He went to town and fitted himself out with good secondhand clothes. If you knew the ropes, five pounds would go a long way. Suit, shirt, boots, collar and tie – all were clean and respectable. He had a shave and a haircut, bought a cheap cardboard suitcase, and took the train to London. That cost him nothing. It could be done, if you knew how. And Fred Dillworth knew.

It was with an affectation of surprise that Alec met him mooching about Fleet Street. "Well, father!"

They did not shake hands. Fred grinned at his son uncomfortably; Alec looked at his father with what he hoped was a smile dragging at the mask of his face.

They went to an eating-house in a side-street, and Alec asked lightly: "Well, what's brought you up to town?"

"You have, my son. You've given me 'ope again," Fred answered. "Ah, Alec, you little know what your poor old father has been through. Your poor mother's dead, an' there's not much left in my life. But thanks to you, son, there may be something."

Alec said nothing, and felt sick, turning over the sodden food on his plate. Fred lowered his voice and leaned confidentially across the narrow table, so that his bloodshot eyes gazed closely into his son's.

203

Alec looked at them with fascination, remembering how often he had looked at them with terror.

"Alec," Fred said in a hoarse whisper, "there's no need for me to try any bluff with you. You know as well as I do that I've been a bad lot. You've got nothing to thank me for – nor Elsie either."

Alec's fingers crisped on the table as the name was uttered.

"Well," Fred went on, "now she's a happily married woman, and good luck to her. And p'raps you'll be married, too, some day. Now, listen. That money you sent me just about broke my 'eart, Alec. I didn't deserve it. I don't deserve nothing from either of you except to be kicked from here to yonder. It made me cry, Alec, to get that money. I said: 'I got a good son.' An' take it from me, Alec, I'm through with the sort of things that – you know what. I said to myself that I was going to be the sort of parent what, if you or Else met him, wasn't goin' to be a disgrace. I don't deserve you, Alec, but, by God, I'm goin' to try to. I could've drunk that five pounds. But I didn't. I said: 'This is Alec helpin' you, you worthless sod.' So I bought this suit and I said I'd find something to do to keep me respectable if I had to walk my feet down to the ankles and work my fingers to the bone. But Manchester's no good. I'm finished there. It's my fault, I know. I'm making no excuses. But London, I says. What about London, where God knows there must be work and where now and then I may be allowed to set eyes on my boy and girl? That's what I said, and here I am. Now you know the story, Alec."

Yes, thought Alec. That's the story. I know it all right. I could have written it for you.

"Well, it's nice to see you," he said. "And don't think it's necessary to apologise to me. I expect I was a bit of a handful when I was a kid."

"You don't take it 'ard then that I've come to London – that I'm round about where I may run into you now an' then?"

"London doesn't belong to me," Alec answered lightly. "They say it's a free city."

"Look, Alec. I'm not goin' to be a nuisance. Honest to God I'm not. Work – that's what I'm lookin' for. Honest work: that's what's brought me to London. If I run into you I run into you, an' that's that, with no harm meant. If I run into Elsie, or maybe even Elsie's husband, or maybe some of your swank friends – an' I expect you've got a few – well, that's as may be. That's an accident that p'raps can't be avoided. But I'm here to keep myself to myself. I know my tongue, Alec – too bloody well I do. If I'd had a drop too much there's no knowing what sort of silly bastard I might make of myself, sayin' things there's no call to say. But I'm doin' my best to lay off the drink. Honest work – that's what I'm looking for. Barrin' accidents, I'll be all right. But you can't always avoid accidents – can you now, Alec?"

Alec noted the challenge, the hardening of the red evil eye, and let it pass unanswered. "Where are you living?" he asked.

"Doss-'ouse," Fred said sorrowfully. "I could 'a' done better, but a doss-'ouse is cheap, an' while I'm lookin' round I got ter make that bit o' money you sent me spin out. I don't want ter come on you again, Alec."

There was so much sorrow in the tone, so much rectitude in the fat, grey, recently shaven face, that for a flashing second Alec forgot the sense that had been elating him of playing this poor fish till the moment came to gaff him. What if, after all, there was a grain – even a grain – of truth in the whine? Even a faint breeze of rectitude toying with the sails of this hulk of sin?

Then Fred, replete and belching, leaned back in his seat, slightly raised his waistcoat, tucked his thumbs into his belt, and spread his fingers contentedly about his stomach.

This gesture, which the child Alec had seen a thousand times, was now more than itself. It was a complete evocation of all the circumstances in which it had been witnessed. All the uncertainties and miseries and cruelties of his life and Elsie's seemed there to be resumed and emphasised before his fascinated gaze. Fred's thumbs were rubbing idly over the great brass buckle of the belt. It was not a belt that had any part in holding Fred's clothes together. It lay about him with inches to spare. It was a weapon; and Alec could see again the well-rehearsed speed with which it slipped from the body, hear again the whizz of it through the air, feel again the bitter smack of the buckle upon his shoulders and buttocks. He closed his eyes to shut the buckle out from his sight, and he saw instead a red wheel revolving upon blackness. When he opened his eyes, Fred had pulled the waistcoat down over the belt and was scavenging between his teeth with a sharpened matchstick. Anyone looking at the two then – the gross, deteriorated man, and the fine-drawn nervy youth whose cheeks were pulsing in and out with a *tic* – might well have thought of a stoat and a rabbit too full to run. Alec paid the bill, and when they were on the pavement outside, jostled by the crowds hurrying back to shop and office, Fred held out his hand, with that sorrowful repentant look still on his face.

"Well, s'long, Alec. There's a few people I oughter see. P'raps we'll meet again, an' then I 'ope I'll be a father you can be proud of – a man with honest work to do."

Alec laughed lightly, looking up at the man who towered a head above him for all his falling-in and ruinous air. "Oh, no," Alec said. "You don't think, now I've got hold of you, that I'm going to let you get away again? There's been too much between us for that."

"What d'yer mean, Alec?"

"You're not to go back to that doss-house. Why don't you share with me? I've got a comfortable place, and there are two beds in my room. I've often laughed about it."

"I bet you 'ave," Fred answered. "Two people in one bed, I say; not two beds in one room." He was in a high humour. Things really were turning out incredibly well.

"Else and I lived together for a long time," Alec explained, hating to use her name in this man's presence. "Then when she got married I went to a new place. I've never lived alone before. I find it lonelier than I like. Why not use the place while you're looking round? It'll be company for me. And I can keep an eye on you."

Fred pretended to ponder this deeply, while his heart was beating loud with joy. Let him once get in, and by God he'd take a bit of prising out!

"Well, I dunno, Alec. The last thing your old Dad wants is to impose on your kindness. An' there's people I oughter be seein' . . ."

"Let 'em wait," said Alec decisively. "Take a day off. You look as if you could do with a rest."

With reluctance, Fred allowed himself to be persuaded. "Well – if you think it's all right . . ."

Alec turned over the money in his pocket. "It'll just about run to a cab," he said.

Cabs were not things that Fred Dillworth was used to. Indeed, never before in his life had he ridden in one. This was a hansom, and Alec, leaning back, could watch the face of Fred leaning forward and looking with sharp interest at everything that flashed by the window.

Fred turned and put a fat massive hand on Alec's knee. "This is a new experience for me," he said.

"You're going to have a lot of new experiences," Alec answered.

When they got into the mean streets about the docks, Fred's face fell a little. "Not very stylish here, Alec."

"No," Alec conceded. "It's not at all what I'd like, or for that matter what I'm going to have some day. You mustn't expect too much. My job isn't worth all that, you know. But it'll be better. And I can give you solid comfort, anyway."

"What is your job, Alec? We've been out of touch so long. It's a devil when a man don't know what his own children are doin'."

"Oh, it doesn't come to much," Alec answered lightly. "I'm in a printing place. It's something to be going on with. It keeps body and soul together. I hope it's not going to mean too much loneliness for you, that's all. Because I may often be away at nights. You'll have the place to yourself."

"That won't worry me, Alec, an' it needn't worry you," Fred said virtuously. "I won't be there all that long. I'm not goin' to impose myself on my son – not at my time of life I'm not."

It was teatime when they came to the house. The woman served their tea in the little parlour with the geranium blooming in the window. The window was open, letting a puff of air into the stuffy room. Nothing was to be seen on the other side of the street but a long hoarding which cloaked some dockside yards and railway sidings. It was not at all what Fred had hoped for, but at the same time it was better than anything he had known before. The meal was plentiful and he ate greedily. Then Alec took him up to the bedroom.

"Well, there it is," he said, "and such as it is, it's yours, and welcome. Make yourself comfortable. I must go now, and I shan't be back tonight."

"Well, thanks, Alec. I think I'll take a bit of a rest." He had already begun to draw off his boots and soon had the pillows heaped under his head.

"There's a pub on the corner of the street," Alec said.

Fred's head rolled over on the pillow, so that he might look at the man who had made this extraordinary pronouncement. Alec was smiling down at him gravely.

"Well, well. You know your old father's weakness. But I'm gettin' over that. Not a penny of that five pounds have I drunk."

"I should think not. What with those new clothes. And the railway fare."

"Ay. That was a pretty penny."

Alec laid five shillings on the dressing table. "When you've had a rest, give yourself a drink. There's no need to make a martyr of yourself."

Fred lay staring at the ceiling. He heard the front door bang. "Christ, crumbs and crikey!" he said under his breath. He still could hardly believe it. Here he was. Here be would stay. The drowsiness of the afternoon overcame him. He listened for a while to railway wagons clanking behind the hoarding, but soon he was in a deep untroubled sleep.

13

Alec slept that night at his rooms in Lincoln's Inn. When first he found that Elsie would be leaving him, he decided to give up the rooms. He had no taste for being his own cook and housekeeper. Better to go into lodgings where some woman could look after him. But now he was keeping the place on for himself and Hesba. When the world was full of glory, he had found himself time after time, coming back with a start from reverie. He had been hearing Hesba's footsteps on the floor, seeing her sitting at her writing by this window that looked into the branches of a plane tree, catching whispers and intimations till the place seemed as though no hole or corner of it was without her. But now she was gone. Suddenly and completely, from the moment he began to think about his father, there was no room in the place for love. Even when he was in Hesba's presence, there were moments when a cloud came between him and her, and she would say: "Alec, Alec, where are you?"

"Where am I?"

"Yes. Where are you? You're miles away. I feel as if I were embracing a ghost."

Then he would struggle desperately out of his obsession, smile bleakly, and tell her that she was his love, his darling, but when he had left her she would still be haunted, as she was to be haunted through so many years, by the feeling of having held a ghost in her arms.

CHAPTER EIGHT

THE SHORT winter day was closing when Hesba finished writing. She got up and moved to the window and looked at the mist drifting slowly over the grass in the park, and the street lights coming on, and the people exercising their dogs before going home to tea and toast by the fireside. She marvelled at the normality of life's appearance. What was that man thinking who was now calling his dog to him, bending down to fasten the leash to the collar before crossing the road? And this demure girl, skirt held from the pavement in a gloved hand – what monstrous schemes were building up behind the façade of her virgin look? Never, Hesba felt, would she cease to be plagued by the appalling discrepancy between the face and the heart of man. She went back to her table and took up what she had written, folded the sheets and placed them in a long envelope. She sealed this heavily with red wax, and wrote upon it: "For Mrs Isambard Phyfe. To be read by her only after my death, should she outlive me. Otherwise, to be burned unread."

Then she rang for her tea, and as she ate and drank, sitting by the fire, she thought of those words "after my death". Death seemed a long way off, whether for her or Elsie. And that was another strange thing. You could be as hollow as a tree that would never have leaves again; you could see life stretching before you endlessly as a grey street, and yet feel a mere physical vitality that assured you that down that street you would walk and walk, to the very end, whether you wanted to or not. She and Elsie, no doubt, would live to be old women. But they would never forget Alec. That was one thing that would always be between them. Perhaps there was not another person in the world who would remember him when a few more months were passed. But she and Elsie – they would never forget him.

The next day she went to her bank, and what she had written was locked away with her papers.

2

MY DEAR ELSIE – You will see by the date that this is written a few months after Alec's death. Whether his death was accidental, as the coroner's jury decided, or whether it was suicide, I shall never know, but there were many things connected with it that did not appear at the public inquiry. Somehow, I feel that you are aware of this, that nothing concerning Alec is altogether hidden from you. That is one reason why I want to relate the whole matter, and to say how I was myself concerned in it. Another reason is that only when I have written it shall I be free of it.

I first became aware that things were seriously wrong with Alec during the height of last summer. It was obvious that something was distracting his mind to a point where the affairs of everyday became ghostly and only this thing, whatever it might be, was real. I challenged him about it more than once, but he evaded me until one night when my persistence led to the only quarrel we ever had. It was shocking, but I can imagine it was the sort of thing you yourself must have experienced with Alec. He had gone even thinner than usual during the summer, and this with his deathly white face and flashing eyes, made him terrifying. What was worst was that the quarrel broke out in the public street. We were walking towards my rooms, and, once he had started, everything he had to say was shouted at the top of his voice, so that passers-by stopped and stared at us. He accused me of being just another damned interfering woman. If his appearance and manner shocked me, I could go to the devil; and if I didn't want to do that I had better understand from the first that he was under no obligation to tell me all that he was either doing or thinking. If I looked like an absent-minded ghost – well, that was how he looked, and would I for Christ's sake stop plaguing the life out of him?

This outburst showed me more clearly than ever that he was deep in trouble, and when presently he stopped shouting and began to shake with sobs, I felt I could not bear to intrude on a privacy so terrible. I kissed him hastily and ran away. Only once

I looked back, and saw him, under the light of a street lamp, holding on with both hands to the park railings, crying. He looked so small and shrunken, like a bird trying to break out of a huge cage.

But I was more tranquil than I had been for a long time, because I knew that now he would have something to tell me. I was right. The next time we met, we went to a place that was a favourite of ours: out in the country where no one ever came. There was an old wall we used to climb over to lie in the sun the other side. It was there that he told me about your father. He held my hand like a child clinging to a grown-up in the dark, and I shall never forget how again and again, as he related some incident of brutality, his fingers trembled and his body shrank as though he were still feeling the blows. He told me how he had not known whether your father was dead or alive until you came back from Manchester in July, and how he was now eaten up by the fear that this brute would wreck your happiness and mine.

You know of this, and now I must tell you of things you did not know. Alec had written a letter to his father which was a test as to whether he intended to follow you to London. He came, and Alec met him. I did not, alas! at that time know the whole truth. Alec told me that afternoon that he had put his father into lodgings in the East End, that he was paying him to stay there, and that he thought this was the best thing to do. "So long as he's under my eye I know where I am," he said.

Now all this seemed to me to be mere folly, but I was wrong about this because there were two things I did not then understand. I did not know what Alec's real intentions were, and I was thinking only of the ageing decayed man he had described to me. In my blindness, I did not see this man as Alec saw him: this is, not as himself but as the incarnation of all that his life had striven to overcome. The heart of the tragedy is that this apparition came to him at the very moment when you and he were both about to step finally, as he hoped, out of your past. Alas! dear Elsie, none of us can do that; but there this horror was, rising out of the swamp from which Alec had emerged and reaching out a hand to pull him back. Not so much him, but you and me. It was for us that Alec died.

211

But most of this was hidden from me then. All I saw was a
horrid man, sponging for the last few weeks on Alec's charity,
not moving far from a public house on the corner of the street.
I tried to laugh Alec out of his fears. I told him to pack the man
back to Manchester, and to call in the police if there were any
trouble. As for me, I said, if his father thought that any bogies
out of the past could shake my feeling for Alec – well, I would
soon let Mr Fred Dillworth know that he had come to the
wrong shop. Nor, I told Alec, was Isambard Phyfe the sort of
man who would stand any nonsense.

Alec seemed comforted, glad to have unburdened his mind –
comforted but not cured. When he had finished talking, he lay
in the grass with his head in my lap and slept. Even in sleep, he
looked exhausted – utterly spent.

This was halfway through August. It was a very hot
afternoon, and I lay there in the sun afraid to move lest I should
wake him up. I felt that it was a long time since he had slept like
this. You will understand how my mind was going over and over
this situation, and how I was trying to find a way to heal Alec's
mind once for all. Because it was clear that his mind was
saturated with fear and hate, and that, although he had confided
to me the cause of his trouble, there were depths to it that I had
not begun to understand.

But hadn't I? Thinking about it in this way, I thought of my
own childhood and of the cruelty and neglect that had afflicted
me. I was flung into that straight out of a time that had been
heavenly – the years with my father in the little shop at
Llanfairfechan about which I have told you. If I had known that
that change was coming, that the bright sky was to darken for
me and love become hate, then it would have been even more
terrible to bear than it was when the change came as swiftly as
the turning of a page. And this, I felt, was what Alec was now
enduring. I am sure, my dear, that life had become very
wonderful for him that summer. He had always suffered from a
sense of not being wanted or understood (except by you), of not
being appreciated; and our love changed that. It is not a matter
I care now to dwell on, but when he was cast down it was from
a great height. He endured agonies of anticipation, and it did not

help that in my view they were groundless, that your father could have been pushed out of Alec's life with half a hand.

Sitting there with his head on my lap, I tried to think of a way out. I was almost persuaded to explain the whole situation to you and Isambard, so that you could help me to laugh away his fears. But this would not do. He would have been at once infuriated and humiliated, and I put that solution aside.

One thing I felt was that I must know where this East End house was in which he occasionally slept. I could think of a dozen reasons why I might want to go there, and I had no compunction at all about taking up the coat which Alec had thrown off because of the heat and going through the pockets. There was a diary, with a section for addresses, and among them was pencilled 14, Waterside Street, Wapping. I felt certain that this was it. Easy to remember.

It happened that that morning I had received a letter from Sarah Annitage. She is a woman who is always making sudden decisions to travel to unexpected places, and now she wrote telling me that she was going to Albania for September and October. I have her letter before me now. "You know," she wrote, "what a suspicious old fool I am, and how I hate shutting up my house. Do come down here, with a friend if you like, and look after the place at least during some of the time while I am away – all of the time if that would please you. But I'm taking my invaluable Jory with me. If you come, you'll have to fend for yourselves, unless you care to arrange for a woman to come in daily from the village."

When Alec woke up, I gave him this letter to read. He looked shocked, and said: "Don't go away. Don't leave me now, whatever you do."

"I certainly shall not leave you," I said. "You shall come with me."

"No," he said, with a passion that surprised me. "I will not go to that place."

"But Alec," I protested, "it's a glorious place. You'll love it. We'll be happy there."

"It's not a glorious place," he said. "It's a ghastly place, with rocks that grind men to pieces."

"You know nothing about it but what I've told you," I said rather warmly.

"Don't I?" he asked, and looked at me strangely. "I know more about it than you think."

"We could get married and spend our honeymoon there."

"No," he said again. "There are things I have to do before we are married."

This was the first time marriage had been mentioned between us, and though he thus emphatically put the idea by, I could see that it moved him. I felt now that this was his only salvation. We must marry at once; he must get right away from this obsessed life that he was living. I felt strong and confident. Give him to me, O God, I thought, give him to me for a few weeks far away from these shadows, and I will bring him back cleansed and sane. And there is no time to waste, I thought, remembering the face that had lain in my lap, the twitching lips, the muttered words, that had shown how, even in sleep, he was haunted and oppressed. No time to waste. I must wrap my strength about his fears, give him my own warmth in place of his pallid ghosts. He must be all mine from this very moment. Now is the acceptable time. He had been kneeling on the grass looking anxiously down into my face as I lay beneath him, and there was that in my eyes which he understood and assuaged.

You know, my dear Elsie, that we were married in the beginning of September, and that we went to Sarah Armitage's house for our honeymoon. I cannot bear to write of the bliss of that time. I was exalted both by Alec's love and by the sense of my own success. I *had* succeeded. He was whole. He was sweet and frank and lovely, his mind without fears, his heart rejoicing in the beauty of that place, his body strengthening in sea and sun. I remember a morning when I woke and found he was gone from the bed. I was wondering where he was when the door opened and he came in, carrying a tray. He was wearing nothing but trousers. His thin small body had already become brown with the sun, and his feet made a dark track across the light green carpet, for he had been out walking in the dew. He had brought a plate of Alpine strawberries, which grow plentifully there, and had laid them in a bed of their own leaves, shining with the morning's moisture. He put these and coffee and thin bread and butter upon my knees on a tray across which trailed a long spray of yellow roses. Then he went out without a word, and I saw that there was a twist of paper under the roses, and on it he had written: "I have been out in the morning and talked with Ceres and Flora, caught sight of naiads and dryads, and seen God Almighty opening a huge red eye above the rim of the sea. And I turned from them all and said: 'Now I shall go back and serve my love, who has redeemed me.'"

Oh, Elsie! Was there ever a man like him? Do you understand how I prayed to be permitted to keep all harm and evil from him, now and forever? Yet it was in the evening that followed this morning that your father came, and it was I who brought him.

It had seemed to me that at all costs that man must be gone by the time we returned to London, that never again must the fears of Alec's childhood be allowed to materialise. And so I wrote to your father, and thus I killed him, and Alec too. Almost as soon as we arrived at Sarah's house I wrote to that address in Wapping. I said that Alec would never come to the place any more, that any hopes of sponging upon him or you must be abandoned because all your friends knew of your past and would have no mercy on one whose cruelty had made it what it was. I told him in so many words to be gone and not to be seen again, because you and Alec were now associated with people not disposed to be as merciful as his children had been. And, in my folly, I posted this, headed with the address of the house where we were staying.

We spent that day upon the water. We did not want any company but our own, and I was well able to manage a little ship. I therefore did without the boatman who usually accompanied me, and hired his boat for the time of the holiday. Sarah Armitage's house is remote from the village. It is a mile away, along a mere track, from the nearest house, and the garden goes down to a small private quay which always has deep water fifty yards out. Moorings had been laid down there, and there we kept the ship, with a dinghy at the steps for coming to and fro.

We were in no hurry to get back that day. We had first of all sailed right out to sea, and every moment was lovely. I have at least that to remember. There was enough wind to make sailing a pleasure without making it strenuous, and Alec rejoiced in doing little jobs like cleating down sheets when we went about, and he even for a time took the tiller, with my hand on his till he got the feel of the ship. She is a lovely ship about thirty feet long, carrying a jib, foresail and mainsail. I must put down all these details: every smallest thing concerned with this day. Sometimes Alec was singing with delight; sometimes he was standing up on the forepeak, holding on to the stay of the mast, with the wind making his hair wild, shouting passages from Keats and Shelley. Then again he would just stand tranced, listening to the wind in the sails, and the water running along the side, and the gulls screaming over patches of mackerel bait in the water. It was the sight of them that made me suggest he should trail a line and try to catch some mackerel, but he said: "No. Not today. This is no day for death – not even the death of a mackerel."

I told him that I had caught hundreds of mackerel in my time with the fisherman Fison, and that I could never get used to seeing them die. "But I always tell myself that it's necessary that some things should die in order that others should live."

He looked grave at that, and said: "I know what you mean. I used to think so myself, but today I'm in a mood to pardon sinners. My enemy could stand in my path and I would kiss him."

So we sailed and talked, and there was nothing visible but the sea's sparkle and the blue sky and here and there a smudge of smoke on the horizon. Then we put back to land. We anchored off a spot which I had named Seal Cove, and rowed ashore in the dinghy. It was about half tide, with the water on the ebb. I thought the place had never looked more lovely, so wrapped up in peace it was, with sand golden under the sun, the cliff purple with heather, and the sea, too, full of those bands of heather-purple colour and cool delicious green that you get down there. It was Alec, standing with wonder in his eyes, who pointed out to me that as the gulls flew over the water the reflected light was thrown up on to their breasts, so that now they flashed purple, now green.

"So this is it!" he said. He looked at sand and rock and sea, and the path climbing the cliff, and said: "It's not what I expected. I expected something savage and forbidding."

"I've known it so," I answered.

"But not for us," Alec said. "For us, even granite smiles, and ship-wrecking waves purr like cats at the fireside."

We stayed there for hours, eating and drinking, bathing, lying in the sun, climbing the cliff and making love. "Of course, it's you," he said. "It's because of you that nothing can plague me. You have persuaded Merlin to cancel his enchantments."

When we were aboard again, he said: "Why should we go home? Why should this day ever end? Let us sail and sail." And he began to recite: "It may be we shall reach the Happy Isles, and see the great Achilles whom we knew."

I wanted to gratify him, and so I kept on sailing till the sun was set. But even when it was gone, there was a crepuscular light and phosphorescence slipped along the side of the ship. "A perfect day always hates to die," Alec said, "and this has been the loveliest day of my life." He came quietly beside me and kissed me while I was standing there with the tiller under my arm. The wind had almost died, and we were going in as if blown by ghosts, but we would make it all right. We were nearly there. The land was vague and shadowy before us.

"Well, that's the last day with this wretched tiller," I said. The tiller had been a grievance with me since this holiday started. As long as I had known this little ship, she had had a mahogany tiller, with the end carved into a turk's-head knot. This had been broken, and when I took the Sea Wave over for that holiday she had an iron tiller that I disliked. I had been worrying Fison about it for days, and he was making another – a duplicate of the one I liked. He had promised to bring it that day: he would leave it in the shed at the top of the landing-steps where we kept oars and ropes and all the odds and ends that belong to sailing.

So we drifted in, with scarcely a ripple under the bows, with not a sound reaching us from land or water, and the dusk thickening. Neither of us spoke, because there are moments when you do not speak. The rings slid down the mast with a little clatter as I let the mainsail halliards go, and Alec on the forepeak fished up the buoy. I ran to help him haul in, because the chain was heavy and I had noticed that the small task was hard on him. When she was fast, we did all the small jobs that are done before you leave a ship for the night: putting on her sail-covers, squaring up ropes, and so on. We still said nothing, doing the accustomed work mechanically in the holy quiet. Alec pulled the dinghy round and I got in, holding on to the side with one hand while Alec took a last look to make sure that all was in order. He shoved in the doors of a few lockers, shut the forepeak door, and pulled the iron tiller out of its socket. "We'll take this ashore," he said. "We'll use the new one tomorrow." Then he climbed down into the dinghy and I pushed off. The tide was now full, but quiet, and in the east the sky was brightening before the advance of a full moon. When we had tied up the boat and climbed the granite steps, Alec put his arm round me, and we turned, still reluctant to go in, to look at that mounting glory. You know how quickly the moon rises. One moment it is a light, with no pulsing in it like the light from the rising sun. Then it is a rim of gold, and soon there it completely is, serene. The sun explodes noisily into the sky; the moon merely appears, silently. We watched that happen, with the sea before us strewn with moving flakes of light, and behind us the shadows of the boat-shed. It was out of these shadows that a voice spoke, as quiet as everything else was that night. "Very pretty. Very pretty, I'm sure."

Even as we both instinctively swung round, I knew who had spoken. Not another word was uttered. A fury had suddenly filled me, arising out of a sense that the chuckling sardonic voice had put a slimy touch upon the wonder of the day, so that, in a little way, I understand how Alec felt when this same wickedness came again into the glory that his life had reached. He had been enduring it for weeks; I knew it but as a momentary flash that caused me to advance upon the man I now saw standing there and push him roughly aside. I am strong, and my thrust caused him to reel. He recovered quickly, gave a grunt of surprise and anger, and caught me by the shoulder. In a second he was dead. I think, if he had not touched me, even then it would not have happened. As it was, Alec had taken a grip with both hands on the iron tiller, swung it through the air, and crashed it upon his skull. All the prisoned emotions of weeks flamed out in that single blow.

I felt sick. Alec's voice pulled me together. "Go to the house," he said. "I will join you presently."

I would not do this. "Whatever you have to do," I said, "I will help you in doing."

Not a word was said about who this man was: it was there between us: we knew. Nor was anything said as to how he had come there.

Alec seemed now like someone who had thought for long about all that had to be done. He brought a sack out of the boat-shed and wrapped his father's head, so that blood should not flow into the ground. Not that there was much need to do this, for though from the sound of the blow I guessed that the bones were crushed in, there was hardly any blood. Then Alec took the tiller, walked down the steps, and washed the end of it in the sea. He was calm, but his face was ghastly in the moonlight.

"Supposing," he said, "I don't think it will happen, but supposing you were seen sailing the ship at night, would that be thought unusual?"

"Not on a night like this," I said. "Fison has often taken me for moonlight sails. He knows my love of them, and he knows that I've often been out by myself when the moon shines."

"Then we shall sail back to Seal Cove. I knew it was an evil place. I've seen it in my dreams, and I've seen myself doing murder there."

When I look back on all this now, I am surprised that even the word murder did not make me turn in revulsion from Alec. The sickness I had felt was at that sudden crumpling of a live man into death; it was not at anything that Alec had done. Only once did he directly speak of his father. "The fool!" he said. "To come here! I was beginning to feel I would not kill him after all. And he must come here!" Then I knew why Alec had brought his father to London. And I did not turn from him.

He looked out to sea. "The wind is dead," he said.

"No," I answered. "It's just breathing. If you want to go, I can get you out. We shall steal a puff or two once we're from under the land."

He took his father's body under the armpits and dragged it towards the steps. The iron caps on the heels of the boots made a little clang as they were pulled down step after step. He pushed the body into the dinghy, threw the tiller in after it, and I rowed back to the ship. I went aboard first, and it was I who pulled the body over the gunwale. Alec was not strong enough.

It took us some time to coax the Sea Wave out to where there was a little wind, and when we stood off Seal Cove it took us some time again to move in under the shadow of the land. Hardly a word was spoken except for the giving of necessary orders. We seemed to be sailing through a dream, and the shape lying amidships under a piece of sailcloth had the inevitability of dream things. Alec, I am certain, had dreamed this dream before.

We put down the anchor a hundred yards off the shore and I lowered the body into the dinghy. I was acting as automatically as though by mesmerism. Alec had wordlessly communicated to me what he intended to do. We carried the body to the spot where the path climbs upwards, and half pushed, half pulled it to the top. Alec had removed the sack from the head, tied it into a piece of ballast, and thrown it overboard.

When we reached the cliff-top we were both exhausted. We sat for a moment in the shadow of some sloe-bushes, looking landward, with the witchy branches clawing over our heads. I could hear Alec's breath coming in hard gasps. The moon was overhead, smaller but brighter, and it was so light that I could see the purple colour of the sloes. Then, for the first time, speaking with difficulty, Alec said: "We will throw him on to the rocks you have so often spoken about. I went through every pocket while we were sailing and there is nothing to identify him except this."

I had been so absorbed in the dream that I had not seen Alec doing this, and now, when he handed me the letter I had written to his father, I suddenly broke down and cried as though my heart would break. He put his thin arm around me and pulled me to him but did not speak for a time. Then he said: "Nothing can identify him. He will be just another tramp who made a wrong slip. The rocks will account for the smashed head. Now let us do it."

My knees were shaking when I stood up, and the sudden wild cry of a curlew made my heart leap with terror. I had to drop my end and wipe my forehead with my sleeve. Alec waited patiently.

We came to the overhang of the cliff, and there we dropped our burden for a moment. Alec said: "Kiss me now."

Our arms went round one another for the last time. He was white but dry-eyed. I was crying bitterly. Presently he put me gently from him and said: "Now stand back a little."

I did so, and he sat down just inland of the corpse which lay parallel with the edge of the cliff. He applied his feet to the shoulders and buttocks, with his own knees raised, straightened out with a heaving push and sent the body over the edge. I watched fascinated, and, Elsie, I shall never know whether the thrust carried him or whether his hands, pushing down into the turf, propelled him. All I know is that he had said: "Kiss me now," and my heart knew it was our last kiss.

I staggered towards the bush under which we had so lately lain, and there I swooned. It could not have been for long, for when I came to myself the moon seemed not to have moved. And now the thought came to me that he was not dead, but lying there battered and broken, crying my name. I went clawing wildly down the path, and at the bottom I found them caught in the sharp fangs of the rock, so fallen that a hand of each rested against the hand of the other as though in forgiveness.

There was but one thing to do then. Should they thus be discovered, there would be no explaining the matter. If I took Alec's body away, how could I account for his death? But if that other body disappeared for ever, then the midnight misfortune of lovers, too daring in their love of moonlight at that perilous spot, would make a plausible tale, and that, you know, is the tale that was told and accepted.

221

So it was that I left my lover there, and took that other body to the dinghy, and back to the ship, and as we rode at anchor I fastened great slugs of ballast from under the floorboards to his hands and feet with ropes. Then I sailed out to water deep beyond the disturbance of tides, and with no prayer, but in sheer horror, launched this murderer, who had murdered my love, into the sea.

The moon was gone, the East was lightening, and the land was coming again into life as the Sea Wave rode at last off our little quay. Over towards Marathon I could hear a cock lustily crowing. His voice mingled with the creak of the rowlocks as I rowed ashore to cry my bitter news.

MYLOR:
March, 1944 – April, 1946.

Howard Spring

All the Day Long

Maria Legassick was born in 1876, the youngest daughter of a Cornishman. She lives with her two sisters Louisa and Bella and her brother Roger in a large house close to the sea in Cornwall. *All the Day Long* is a powerful saga, set against the backdrop of the dramatic and often hostile Cornish scenery. Howard Spring sympathetically chronicles the lives and loves of his engaging characters, telling their compelling stories with freshness and a gripping honesty.

Fame Is the Spur

Born into poverty, Hamer Shawcross is arrogant and ambitious. Entering politics he becomes a cabinet minister, then Viscount Shawcross. Ann, his wife, loves her husband but will allow nothing to diminish her commitment to the Suffragette Movement. This passionate novel is set against social and political changes of the early 20th Century – the rise of the Labour Party, Suffragettes, the challenge to the power of the landed gentry and the aftermath of the 1914-18 war.

HOWARD SPRING

HARD FACTS

In 1885 the young curate, Theodore Chrystal is struggling to come to terms with life in a working-class district of Manchester – a shock after having lived amongst the dons and landed gentry of Cambridge. Dan Dunkerley is the ambitious young printer who establishes the penny journal, *Hard Facts*, to help create a new future for himself, his family and those around him. Here, amongst poverty, violence and prostitution Theodore must learn some 'hard facts' of his own.

I MET A LADY

In 1916 the impressionable fifteen-year-old George Ledra is sent from Manchester to Cornwall because of his ill-health. Here he meets Hector Chown, a professor of Greek. Hector is living in a derelict house with his actress niece, Sylvia Bascombe and her young daughter, Janet. The story of how their lives become entwined spans the years of uncertainty between the two world wars and ever present in the tale, the house becomes a symbol of the fragility of their world.

HOWARD SPRING

THERE IS NO ARMOUR

Edward and Blanche Pentecost have grown up in a modest but artistic home. Their security is suddenly shattered by the conversion of their father to harsh religious beliefs. Only gradually can they break away from his control. Edward becomes an artist while Blanche marries an unscrupulous financier whose schemes bring many to ruin. While Edward looks back on the previous fifty years, his son and Blanche's daughter must face the impending devastation of the Second World War.

TIME AND THE HOUR
(Third in the *Hard Facts* trilogy)

Time and the Hour opens in Bradford in 1912 with a group of young people who later move to London. In the mid 1930s they are confronted by the influx of persecuted Jews and the looming tragedy of the Second World War. This is a compelling saga of personal challenges, a tale where a child discovers the true identity of his mother and where romance is tempered by the terrifying reality of the growth of fascism in Europe.

OTHER TITLES BY HOWARD SPRING AVAILABLE DIRECT
FROM HOUSE OF STRATUS

Quantity		£	$(US)	$(CAN)	€
☐	All the Day Long	7.99	12.99	19.95	13.00
☐	Fame Is the Spur	8.99	14.99	22.50	15.00
☐	Hard Facts	6.99	11.50	15.99	11.50
☐	The Houses In Between	7.99	12.99	19.95	13.00
☐	I Met a Lady	7.99	12.99	19.95	13.00
☐	A Sunset Touch	6.99	11.50	15.99	11.50
☐	There Is No Armour	7.99	12.99	19.95	13.00
☐	Time and the Hour	7.99	12.99	19.95	13.00
☐	Winds of the Day	6.99	11.50	15.99	11.50

ALL HOUSE OF STRATUS BOOKS ARE AVAILABLE FROM GOOD BOOKSHOPS
OR DIRECT FROM THE PUBLISHER:

Internet: www.houseofstratus.com including author interviews, reviews, features.

Email: sales@houseofstratus.com please quote author, title, and credit card details.

Hotline: UK ONLY: 0800 169 1780, please quote author, title and credit card details.
INTERNATIONAL: +44 (0) 20 7494 6400, please quote author, title, and credit card details.

Send to: **House of Stratus Sales Department**
24c Old Burlington Street
London
W1X 1RL
UK

Please allow following carriage costs per ORDER
(For goods up to free carriage limits shown)

	£(Sterling)	$(US)	$(CAN)	€(Euros)
UK	1.95	3.20	4.29	3.00
Europe	2.95	4.99	6.49	5.00
North America	2.95	4.99	6.49	5.00
Rest of World	2.95	5.99	7.75	6.00
Free carriage for goods value over:	50	75	100	75

PLEASE SEND CHEQUE, POSTAL ORDER (STERLING ONLY), EUROCHEQUE, OR
INTERNATIONAL MONEY ORDER (PLEASE CIRCLE METHOD OF PAYMENT YOU WISH TO USE)
MAKE PAYABLE TO: STRATUS HOLDINGS plc

Order total including postage:_____Please tick currency you wish to use and
add total amount of order:

☐ £ (Sterling)   ☐ $ (US)   ☐ $ (CAN)   ☐ € (EUROS)

VISA, MASTERCARD, SWITCH, AMEX, SOLO, JCB:

☐☐☐☐☐☐☐☐☐☐☐☐☐☐☐☐☐☐☐☐☐☐☐☐

Issue number (Switch only):

☐☐☐

Start Date: **Expiry Date:**

☐☐/☐☐   ☐☐/☐☐

Signature: _____

NAME: _____

ADDRESS: _____

_____

POSTCODE: _____

Please allow 28 days for delivery.

Prices subject to change without notice.
Please tick box if you do not wish to receive any additional information. ☐

House of Stratus publishes many other titles in this genre; please
check our website (**www.houseofstratus.com**) for more details